Acknowledgements

My family—Mom, Dad, Kelly, Alex, Mackenzie—thank you for giving me the idea to be an author and write this book and supporting me through the complete process, for all the index cards and other supplies that you got me because you knew I needed them. I love you all!

Meghan Witt, thank you for reading all the long chapters that either kept you rolling from laughter or something you didn't expect me to put in the book, and making sure what I said made sense. For reading my crazy thoughts, giving me ideas I wasn't sure I was going to go with, but did, no matter how crazy they were. For dealing with the millions of messages I left you asking you your opinions or what-should-I-do's. "Keep smiling and get ready for the next book coming."

To all the D wing team members who gave me encouragement and butt-kicking by telling me to get back to writing and the moral support when I passed an idea by you, telling me *that would be so funny*, or *I really like that idea*.

Christine Waters, thank you for doing a fundraiser for me with Color Street. You have a very caring heart, and I am so glad we can go the extra mile and be stylists together.

Janelle Maynard, thanks for doing a fundraiser for me with Parklane and being there to show me the ropes of selling jewelry. Thank you also for being a good friend.

To everyone else who in one way or another was there for me, asking how everything was going, I appreciate it a lot. Thanks for all your support with the fundraising and my book. I look forward to everyone enjoying reading it as much as I did writing it.

Table of Contents

Prologue	ix
Chapter 1: CEO to the Rescue	1
Chapter 2: From Heaven's Ridge	7
Chapter 3: Final Preparations	13
Chapter 4: To Mystic Senior Camp	20
Chapter 5: BBQ Blitz	37
Chapter 6: Blowouts, Magazines, and Buzzes	52
Chapter 7: Breakfast of Champions	65
Chapter 8: First-Day Shenanigans	75
Chapter 9: Next Day Blues	114
Chapter 10: Mona's Fried Chicken and More	121
Chapter 11: Operation Haze Seniors	132
Chapter 12: Hook, Line, and Sinker	160
Chapter 13: Crazy Arrival at the Funhouse	189
Chapter 14: Funhouse Experience and Gasoline Alley	204
Chapter 15: Pudding Ridge Road	216
Chapter 16: Sisterly Love—NOT!	229
Chapter 17: Vera Bites the Dust	241
Chapter 18: Seniors are MIA	254

Chapter 19: Pillow Talk Road	283
Chapter 20: Little Smokey Lane	297
Chapter 21: Bloody Mary Lane	309
Chapter 22: Knockout	314
Chapter 23: Farfrompoopen Road	343
Chapter 24: Hanky-Panky Lane: The Truth Must Come Out	355
Chapter 25: Making Amends	367
Chapter 26: Stub-Toe-Lane	400
Chapter 27: DUH Drive	405
Chapter 28: Booger Branch Lane	411
Chapter 29: You Are on Candid Camera	416
Chapter 30: Surprise!!	420
Chapter 31: Chip and Tallulah's Reunion	430
Chapter 32: The Beach and BBQs	442
Chapter 33: Goodbye Mystic Senior Camp, Hello Heaven's Ridge	461
Chapter 34: One Year Later	471
About the Author	474

Prologue

My name is Tallulah. I am seventy-seven years old, and I know you would never believe me. I know because people tell me I look half my age with my brown hair—and no, I don't dye it. People sometimes call me Marilyn Monroe, because I look like a superstar, but really, it's because I just have good hair genes. I'm good at things—especially with my hands—and feel free to take that any way you want to. As you can see, I love to be a smartass, and I do it because it's fun, and makes people laugh. I know I get a kick out of it. I'm a beautiful woman who took a shot at being an actress when she was younger than I am now.

But all joking aside, I know so much about flowers, and loved working with them every chance I got. Even here, if there are flowers dropped off and no one claims them, I like to make beautiful arrangements. I bet you never would have thought that, after all these years, I'd still have the knack for making a great arrangement, and know what every flower I get my hands on is. I used to run my own business—for more than forty years. Then, my daughter told me that I was too old to do it anymore. She wanted to take the shop away from me. Naturally, I told her she wasn't my keeper—which I know I shouldn't say to my daughter. But I should be able to continue to do what I love.

My own daughter telling her mother what to do . . . *no*, sorry, not in my lifetime will that happen. Why would someone like my daughter, who works a million different jobs, tell me I'm too old to do something I've been doing most of my life? I don't see myself as old, but unique in ways—and yes, I will admit, a little crazy. Great, I said it. Yes, I made bad choices in my life after I lost the love of my life, and that's how I lost my son—I have not heard or seen him in a long time. People make mistakes, and in my lifetime, I especially regret not being there for my husband when he was around.

But I made my share of mistakes with my kids too, and I regret it especially with my son. Because I was a little crazy, he decided he didn't want me to be his mother. That is so heartbreaking. And I just let him go, at the young age of fourteen. I'm still waiting for the day I get to meet him before I die, but it's not looking so good. Trust me, I know more than people think I do, because I believe that kids can make their own choices. And he decided to leave our family, get emancipated, and start a new life without his mother and sister. I believe he will come find me here and come back to our family.

I know not to tell anyone my friends' secrets. Even if they're so juicy it's killing me, I keep them to myself. I will admit it's not easy to do, but I do it for my friends—and I would do it for my family if they trusted me, which is yet to be determined. If any of the staff or residents around here knew half the stuff I knew, it would knock their pants and socks off. What a nice vision in my mind, of pants falling—and it might be a fun thing to watch, especially if they're only wearing boxers. The woman losing her pants, not so fun. But very entertaining on both parts. We have more to show than the men—at least I do! Enough about me. It's time I wrap up, before I say more than I should. But I just wanted to say my three best friends are the best family I have right now, and will ever have. That won't change.

Before I tell you about my friends, I would like to tell you about Heaven's Ridge Retirement home. It's not hard to keep yourself occupied here, so I doubt anyone would say they're bored. I think of this place as a big mansion. But not like the Playboy mansion, with all the bunnies hopping around—not that I have ever been there, though I would have loved to of met Hugh Hefner. If I must be honest, no one really checks on us unless we ring our bell in our room. It would be quite easy to just slip out, because they won't know you're even here unless they go in your room to see. I personally stay near the bar, because I love my Long Island iced tea. Don't get me wrong, the staff are great . . . and not so great, at the same time . . . so it's about fifty-fifty. It all depends on two things: who's on that day or night and who's there to work, not fool around. There's a lot of fooling around going on, but I'll save that for another time. It can get kind of interesting, and I'd be off topic of what I was really supposed to talk about. Which was what now? See . . . it's extremely easy to get off topic—especially for me. I'm more interested in talking about the summer and my best girlfriends in the whole wide world.

This summer is going to be the greatest summer for me and my four best friends, Agnes, Mona, Edith, and Wanda. I'm sure everyone is wondering how we all met. It was at Heaven's Ridge about a year ago—maybe two, my memory is sometimes foggy. But I'd call them all my best friends forever, because we just clicked. Even though we won't be around forever, we can maybe leave a legacy of some sort. We are always attached at the hip.

I thought Mystic Senior camp was the perfect place for all of us to go. I found the brochure lying on one of the tables in the library. And no, I wasn't in there to get a book, but I won't tell you why. Let's just say I'm a crazy bad girl all the time—and that's not a lie. I do think it's funny, because I'm not afraid to admit it.

Anyways, I hoped that we were going to be able to go to this camp, because we needed to have fun. This place can get way to serious sometimes, and it's good to get away. It's been so long since we've been on a field trip. It's not often you find a summer camp for seniors like us. They're always for kids—never adults, and especially not seniors. I think of it this way: you just never know when it might be your time to go up to heaven, and there's nothing wrong with wanting to get away and be with friends. I am so glad to call these women my friends, and this trip is just so important to go on. To me, at this time in my life, I want to be with my friends. We're like sisters, and we enjoy each other's company. That's why we're always together at our meeting place by the window, all day long.

I was so excited about going, but I started having second thoughts. But that was until a wise old aide named Hilda—who you'll learn more about soon—convinced me we would enjoy ourselves and everything would be OK, and that the most important thing was just to have fun. I believed her. I mean, she's such a hoot to talk to—especially when you get her on the subject of men, which I love talking about all the time. Her, not so much. See what I mean? I'm just bad, and damn proud of it. I guess you can say I trust her with everything I share with her, even though I hear her talk to other aides about our conversations. I don't let it bother me, even though they're private conversations. I learned that nothing is private here. I learned if the aides tell you something, though, you must keep it secret. I'm not sure how that's fair, but they're lucky, because half the residents here can't remember what you told them five minutes ago.

So, now, let me introduce my friends and sisters from another misters. I heard that from Dudley—and you'll learn more about him, too, but not now. I will start by talking about Agnes.

I met Agnes about two years ago. At eighty years old, she has the body of a fifty-year-old. With her short grey hair and slim body, she looks genuinely nice and sweet. Until you get to know her. Boy, she is a spitfire—very opinionated about anything and everything, and not afraid to tell you how she feels. She likes to have things her way—and if she doesn't, the pouting begins. She thinks when she crosses her arms and puckers her lips, people will give in. Some do, some don't. I just sit there and laugh, which pisses her off even more. She then tries to tell me off, which doesn't work—but I guess depends on what she says. She can be hurtful at times, but then we are back to being the best of friends.

I'm not exactly sure how we happened to meet. She was in a whole different unit, but moved next door to me soon after. Now, we sit at the window by our rooms and talk about her late husband, how they were meant to be, and how they were not able to have kids because she had women issues. Makes me think of the love of my life, who I lost because he did something stupid. I still regret not being with him. Then, maybe things would have changed, and I'd be with him now and not here. Then again, I didn't have many friends when I was married, so I'll take what I can get here—that's for sure. It's hard to find Mr. Right when you know you already had him all along. It's hard to love, and it's not easy to get back on the horse and ride it. *Whoops*, there I go again. When I told Agnes about going to senior camp, she was far from excited, but I convinced her. I maybe fibbed a little, but one little fib isn't going to hurt anyone. Whatever I said, with the help of the sides and nurses, turn her answer into a yes.

Mona was the next for me to get to know. I simply adore her. She's the best cook in the universe, and I am glad the staff lets her cook for us here every now and then. Mona has short grey hair, and like the rest of us (or maybe just me), Mona loves her men—even though she hasn't been with one in an exceptionally long time, by choice (I know that feeling—but it hasn't been my choice. I just can't find a man). Mona enjoys life to the fullest, and you would never guess she's in her nineties. She is extraordinarily strong-willed, and I love that about her. I have learned so many things from our chats by the window.

Mona could have a few drinks at the bar, and you would never know how many she'd had. Except the one time she got on top of the bar and started dancing. She reminds me of me. I wasn't the best child or teenager growing up, but I did have fun as an only child. But I drove my parents crazy, and that was so much fun. Mona doesn't really talk much about her family life, but that's OK. It will come out when she wants to share. We are all guilty of trying to get what we want—especially when it comes to men. Well, at least we have that in common. Even though she said she loves her men, she's still is not ready to move on after her third husband passed away. I do see that little spark in her eyes that most of us get when we want comfort in a man. Who wouldn't want that? I'd be first in line. There are a bunch of men here who are, as the young aides call them, eye candy. I don't know what kind of candy they're talking about, but I don't see it—because if I did, I'd have a hold of them by now

We both enjoy the activities provided for us, and we have as much fun as we can—especially with bingo. Mona is the queen bingo winner most of the time. She just has the luck. Mona gets a little competitive, but it's just a game to me. I just go to be with friends and do something instead of staying in my room, doing nothing. When I told Mona about the senior camp, she was so excited, she wanted to go right away. In fact, she has had her bags packed since the day I told her we were going. That's so cute. She wants to go just as bad, and she gets why it's important for us to go together.

Wanda might seem shy at first, but she's not afraid to speak her mind and have a little fun every now and then. And in her mid-sixties, a plumply kind of lady has a lot to say. Her gray hair is so long and healthy, like Rapunzel's, without someone climbing up it. I just can't believe Wanda likes to shake her rump when she's walking. I guess "rump" is not the best word, so I'll change it to "ass." She waits to see if anyone notices. I think she does that to impress the guys, because that ass doesn't shake like that all the time.

She also stands up for what she wants and what she believes in. If someone needs to talk, she always has an ear or two to lend, and will sit with you until you're OK. If she could give you her shirt off her back, she would. No one else is willing to do that.

Her daughter sees her with her grandkids at least once a week. She lights up when she sees them. They are her whole life, and that's the way it should be. Her daughter and her are remarkably close. They practically grew up together, because she was young when Wanda had her. The baby daddy split when she told him she was pregnant, so she took care of her daughter all by herself. So, seeing her with Wanda's grandkids it brings back memories. that's what should happen when you're in a retirement home. We should all see our families, so we can all be happy and feel loved.

Wanda wasn't too thrilled, but when she knew we were all going, together, she was right on board with it. It was our time for some real fun, for us to shine like the sun. No idea where that came from, but it's true. Wanda was looking forward to a little fun in the sun, and just to enjoy herself with everyone else that was going.

Edith is the last one of the of us that was ready to go to camp and have a good time. She is a feisty and fearless lady who loves to lend a helping hand. Edith is a goodhearted soul who listens to everything we talk about. There just aren't enough words in the dictionary to describe a woman who enjoys life to the fullest and isn't shy about getting wild and doing things she's not supposed to do. Expect the unexpected, because you will never know what she is thinking, and it will catch you off guard when she does it. Edith always tells me how she's going to kick me in the ass because I talk about men so much, but I'm not sure she can lift her leg up that high. I'm sure she'll try, though, because she's one hell of a devil. That's why everyone loves her so much. I know her daughter does, because she often comes to see her. She's so happy Edith loves it here and has such good friends.

So, those are my best friends, and we're going to get ready for a fun time at Mystic Summer camp. The brochure said there are activities going on all the time—swimming, arts and crafts, music, sports, and entertainment. So, I'm all excited—and they will be to once they get on the bus. And I will make sure they get on this bus. At least I hope so, because it's just a wonderful way to spend a week of summer with them. It makes me question if we will have another fun summer together next year, or the year after that. Trust me, there are going to be plenty of ways for us to have fun—because we will all be together.

CHAPTER 1

CEO to the Rescue

Heaven's Ridge Retirement Home is for seniors to spend the rest of their days. It has a hundred independent room for everyone to enjoy their own privacy. Each room is equipped with high technology, such as Wi-Fi and a cordless phone of your own, a big-screen TV with a satellite, and a queen-size bed that can move up and down for your comfort. It also has a call bell if you need anything and are unable to get it and a large bathroom with a tub and bars on both sides of the toilet.

At Heaven's Ridge there is also a large dining room, and the food is prepared by a professional chef with many years of experience who cooks right in the large kitchen, along with dietary aides, who all have different jobs to do that make the food service good for all residents, who hardly complain about what they're eating, and always leave with full stomachs.

So that the residents are never bored and to make sure that they come out of their rooms for a little fun, there are activities, which include swimming in the indoor pool with a lifeguard watching over them, bingo, crafts, movies, games, and field trips. One of the most popular places is the Heaven's Ridge bar, where residents can come and have a drink with their friends or dance on the dancefloor to the music they offer. They also have a DJ who comes in once a week and plays music for all the residents to sing karaoke.

And by the way, I'm Aspen. I am the CEO and director of nursing, and I made this place a home for people who couldn't live on their own. I wanted them to call it home, even know it isn't to most of them. I want the best for everyone, whether staff or resident, because they all deserve it. I don't let the power of my position get to my head. We have three full-time aides, Willa, Hilda, Florence, two part-time aides, Clark and Dudley, a full-time nurse, Felicity, and a part-time nurse, Delia. This facility is also a learning facility, so each employee can learn more about their job and maybe take a step up from what they're doing. Delia and Felicity are the best nurses around, and I'm so glad they're here.

Let me tell you about my staff and start I think I will start with Delia. Delia comes from a family full of doctors from a Pediatric doctor to a General Medicine doctor, and an orthopedic surgeon her family knew medicine well. She followed her heart and put herself through medical school without any help from her family who would help if she reached out to them, and Heaven's Ridge was happy to make her an employee right on the spot. Delia is right on the ball, and takes her job seriously, but has a fun, goofy side that makes all the residents smile. This is a good thing, but there is time for being playful and a time to be serious. It must be the red hair she has that makes her so unique and fun for everyone to hang around. She's here for the residents and the staff, and always makes sure if they need something, they have her attention 100%. You can tell she loves her job. I hardly hear her complain when I have her do things.

Felicity struggled through life, and all she ever wanted to do was go to medical school. When she took her boards, she almost didn't pass, but did because she had told them she had dyslexia, but was enthusiastic and passionate about being a nurse. You could see that she wanted it so badly. It was all she had wanted to do since her mother had passed away at an early age when Felicity was a fourteen years old. Her father wasn't around too much after her mother's passing, and she was left with her grandmother a lot. I guess you can say her father just couldn't deal with taking care of his children, so he got up and left Felicity and her siblings. Felicity and her siblings moved in with her grandmother.

Now, ten years later, she's a single mom to three kids, because her husband wasn't happy with their marriage and picked up and left them without any word. When I heard someone needed help, I reached out to her college professor, who just happens to be one of my ex's best friends, Harlow. I have to admit I was shocked to hear from Harlow, since we aren't friends, but I'm glad she did think of me for help. I hired Felicity right on the spot, without even thinking about it, after just one conversation. I told her I would be willing to pay for the rest of her schooling so her dream could come true, and she could work for my team and be there for her kids at the same time.

The aides that I have here at Heaven's Ridge are unique in their own way, and that's not a bad at all. They each bring something to the table. Willa, Dudley, Hilda, Florence, and Clark are all very diligent workers—some more than others, but that's why they're good together. They're my super aides. Though they might need a little push, trust me, they really do knock your socks off. I just can't say it enough. But I am modest. I enjoy my team I have here, and wouldn't want it any other way.

Willa is a genuine kind of gal with a personality that will leave your mouth open because she's not afraid to speak her mind, very kindhearted, and loves to joke around with everyone. She gets her work done, and has time to be there for her residents when they need her—which seems like all the time. Willa has a sibling, but she doesn't talk about her very much, and she keeps her personal life out of work and never brings any drama. The way I see it, we all have skeletons in the closet. That doesn't mean they have to come out and haunt you at work.

Dudley is a very down-to-earth kind of guy with a quirky sense of humor that no one gets sometimes. He needs to be told to get work done a few times, but he does work hard when he's motivated. I must always remind him to get the lead out of his pants and get working, because he gets sidetracked fast and no one understands why. One minute, he's cleaning the bathroom in a resident's room, and the next, he's helping our residents hang their clothes in their closet. He has no sense of direction. Tell him to clean the floors in the hallway and you might find him wiping down the railings instead. Things seem to go in one ear and out the other. The residents would always complain, telling him he doesn't make the beds well—or never does at all, because he does the opposite of everything.

Dudley is constantly either texting or talking on his phone to whomever he might be with that week. I just don't get that either, because you shouldn't be on your phone if you're working. I'm way to old-fashioned for that. I guess you could say that, even though I'm not that old. Maybe he's calling one-eight-hundred numbers—if they still have those—or something else that isn't mine or any else's business (unless I must make it my business—then it will be). I do wonder sometime how he even got a job here, because I don't remember hiring him. But everyone deserves a chance—and maybe a second chance, depending on who and what the situation is. By now, Dudley has wrapped up a few chances already.

One good thing is that he treats the residents with respect they deserve, which is especially important. So it's easy to look away from whatever he does with his time. That's all that matters to me as his director. Tallulah, one of our most famous residents, loves playing tricks on him, and is constantly slapping him on the ass every chance she gets. She thinks she can't do anything wrong. She'll never learn to stop, no matter how much you tell her to, and Dudley will never learn he needs to tell her or any of the residents not to do something—especially when his pants do fall. As for Tallulah, he needs to run when she's around—or keep his ass to the wall. If you really think about it, maybe he enjoys it, and that's why he lets her keep doing it. He'll learn his lesson eventually, though, when she has him pinned down on her bed and he can't get up.

We always say there's that one special person that has that special talent to be something in their life. Hilda is that person, because she has a special gift with the residents, which is so unbelievable. She is a good-hearted person—more than anyone I know. There is something called the ghost whisperer—and Hilda is the aide whisperer. Hilda knows how to make them smile when they're crying because they miss their family or lost something in their room that's right in front of them, or cranky because they didn't sleep well or are in pain. She takes time to listen if something is bothering a resident—or even a coworker—and genuinely talks to them. She won't leave them until they feel better. Hilda works more than I did when I was an aide at Heaven's Ridge, picking up shifts so the residents would not be without an aide. Hilda is an exceptional aide—one of the best, of course—along with Delia, my faithful nurse. Not that I pick favorites. I am just simply making an observation.

Florence is quiet as a church mouse. I enjoy having her as an aide, relating to the residents, but sometimes you forget she's here because she's so quiet. Florence has a lot of work to do to get her life together because being from Brazil caused her a major culture shock. Florence was in an abusive relationship and had to get out of the situation before something happened to her and the family she had taken in. So, she thought she'd come to the United States to start over. She has family here willing to take her under their wing and help her and the family she brought with her. Her job as a home health aide was to take care of the family she had been working for, and she wasn't going to stop doing it because of the abuse she was getting. She came here to apply for a job, and I was happy to sit her down and get to know her. We talked for three hours, and didn't even notice. Since Florence got her citizenship and became a part of the team, it has been a quite an adjustment. Since she doesn't know anyone from here, which can be quite overwhelming for someone. She is very energetic, enjoys learning, and loves taking the aides class I set up for her and our other new aides. She wants to be able to do her job right, which is important to her. Florence has done a fantastic job so far, and in time, she'll get the hang of things. Stay away from the men who treat you badly. They don't need your attention. The residents do.

Clark is an interesting kind of guy—and all in a good way. Sometimes, Clark is very clumsy. His shirt is always half in his pants or hanging out of them, and it looks like he doesn't even shave, but he's a husband and a diligent father, and everyone here knows it. Clark is a great asset to the team, because he works hard to support his family, number one in his life. He picks up a lot of time just to be there for the residents—just like Hilda does. When he's not here, it's noticeable. But we know he's with his family, and that's how it should be. Clark is a team leader, and if he keeps doing his magnificent work, he could probably move up from an aide to maybe going to school for nursing, which I know has always been a secret dream for him. Clark just needs to keep things up and keep being a family-oriented person. Being here for the residents is the one goal he wanted to achieve.

I hired these people because they all have the heart to be great nurses and great aides in their own unique ways. As for me, I love what I do, and if I can take the extra step and help a bunch of people I don't know and give them a job because they need it, I'll figure out how, and get it done. Everyone has the potential to do the best job they can if they just apply themselves.

CHAPTER 2

From Heaven's Ridge

"I don't see why I need to go on this stupid trip," said Agnes as she threw things in a suitcase, mumbling to herself.

"Agnes, my darling, you will have the time of your life. And you were excited to go with Tallulah and all your friends," said Hilda—who works hard for her residents and cares about their well-being.

"How can we have fun when you and the other aides won't be there?" asked Agnes, still throwing things in her suitcase.

"There will be other staff there to keep you occupied, Agnes—maybe you will get in a little trouble while your there, and that's OK, too, because you need to have fun," said Hilda as she took Agnes's suitcase and tried to fold all her clothes into it.

"You mean the good kind of trouble, right, Hilda? Because I don't like to break the rules," said Agnes, winking at Hilda.

"Well, yes, of course, Agnes, that's the best time," said Hilda as she finally closed the suitcase and relaxed on the bed with Agnes. "We must hurry up. The bus is almost here to pick you up."

Hilda left to help the other residents get ready that were going to Mystic Senior Camp.

"I still think I should stay here," yelled Agnes.

"No, you shouldn't," yelled Hilda down the hall.

Everyone was so excited about going, they couldn't control their excitement. But there was a couple who could care less if they went—which included Agnes.

"OK, everyone, here are your nametags to wear when you arrive," said Aspen.

"Now, everyone is going to know who I am, and I am not going to be able to get a man," said Tallulah, who was starting to pout.

"So, what now? They will know exactly what kind of person you are," laughed Edith.

Everyone waited by the door until the bus drove up and they heard the horn beep.

"Who's ready to go to camp?" called Delia.

Everyone cheered.

"Wait a minute, Tallulah—don't get on the bus yet!" yelled Dudley, running to try and stop her from going out the door before anyone else.

"What's wrong, Dudley?" asked Tallulah.

"I'm just wondering what you could possibly have in all these bags of yours," said Dudley.

"Seriously, you stopped me because I have too much luggage?" asked Tallulah, who wasn't very amused. "How do you know these are my bags?"

"You wouldn't be carrying them otherwise—and plus, they have your name on them," said Dudley, reaching for her bags slowly.

"Well, OK, I guess you got that right," said Tallulah, starting to laugh.

"So, why do you have so many bags?" asked Dudley.

"It's basically everything I own," said Tallulah, laughing.

"It looks like you got everything but the kitchen sink with you," said Dudley, rubbing his head as he looked in her suitcases at everything Tallulah was bringing, amazed at everything she could fit in them.

"Oh, I couldn't fit the kitchen sink in any of my bags," said Tallulah.

"Tallulah, you're only going to camp for a week—not the rest of your life," said Dudley.

"Yes, I know Dudley, but you never know when I might meet a good-looking man."

Dudley decided to bring most of Tallulah's bags back to her room that she didn't need. Tallulah just looked at Dudley as he took them away, watching him trip over his own feet.

"If you have the essentials—and I see you do—you'll have a fun time," said Hilda.

"What about my hair dryer?" asked Tallulah, pouting like a baby "I need that, or my hair's not going to look good in the morning."

"Your hair will survive fine. You're going to go for the fun," said Hilda.

"If you say so. But I need all my bags," said Tallulah.

"We aren't going to a beauty pageant. We're going to summer camp—which was your idea," said Agnes, trying to make a point.

It was time to go, and Art came in to get the baggage before everyone boarded the bus.

"I guess this goodbye," said Tallulah as she hugged Willa and Hilda, not wanting to let them go.

"It's only for a week, Tallulah—and you'll have a great time with your besties and everyone else," said Delia.

"Tallulah, time to get on that bus, sweetie, and have an exciting time," said Willa as she gave Tallulah a hug and made sure she and the rest of the seniors got on the bus.

"Have a great time, Agnes, and don't worry—everything will be just fine. So go and have fun!" yelled Hilda as Agnes got on the bus with Tallulah in front of her. Tallulah got on the bus and took one look at Art, who was making sure everyone got in their seats safely.

"Well, hi there sailor! How are you doing today, cutie?" asked Tallulah, trying to flirt with the Art.

"My name is Art, not sweetie. I'll be your driving you to camp. Pick your seat, and we'll be leaving shortly."

Art got off the bus and finished putting the rest of the luggage in the storage in the bottom. Art was a very diligent worker who loved his job at the camp. I guess you could say he was a jack of all trades. He drove the bus, worked in maintenance, and was a counselor at Mystic Senior Camp.

"Oh, I'm just delighted I get to go to camp," said Mona as she got comfortable in her seat with Tallulah, who was trying to see Art bend over while he was putting the luggage away.

"Would you like the window seat, Tallulah?" asked Mona.

Felicity got on the bus to make sure that everyone was on it who was supposed to be, and that they all had their nametags.

"I just wanted you to know you are all going to have so much fun," said Felicity, who, deep down inside, was sad they would not be there all week—though glad they got the opportunity to go. Felicity gave them all one last wave before she got off the bus and told Art he was all set to go. "Drive safe because you got a lot of precious cargo going to camp."

Art closed the bus doors. "Alright, everyone, here we go!" Art drove away slowly, beeping the horn. Felicity stood by. Hilda, Willa, Dudley, and all the aides and nurses came out and waved to the fourteen residents, watching the bus pulled away slowly.

"Have fun!" yelled Clark.

They all gave them one last wave before the bus disappeared.

"It's going to be a quiet week without them here," said Hilda, starting to cry.

"It'll be OK, Hilda—at least we don't have to worry about anyone sneaking up on us, listening to our conversations, or doing anything inappropriate," said Felicity.

"Or having someone spank you for no reason," said Dudley as he rubbed his ass just thinking about it.

Everyone just looked at Dudley and laughed.

"Well, it's time to go back to work and be there for the rest of the residents," said Delia, who was happy that her shift was almost over.

"Let's get this party started!" yelled Wanda. She was shy at first, but warmed up quickly, and loved just to have the time of her life.

"Someone's excited about going to summer camp," said Tallulah.

"Who wouldn't want to go to camp, where there's food, swimming, food, and other things I'm just too excited to talk about?" asked Wanda.

"You said food twice," said Agnes, not very amused.

"Well, *la dee da*, I love my food," laughed Wanda.

Agnes just sat in her seat and shook her head.

Tallulah yelled to Art to turn up, the music, and started dancing in her seat, doing the Macarena.

"Now this is more like it," yelled Mona getting into the groove of the music.

"Hey, sonny, how fast can this bus go?" asked Tallulah as she leaned over Mona and puts her hands out the window, feeling the breeze.

"My name's not sonny, it's Art. And sorry, this is an old bus, so there isn't much speed, and if you were smart, you'd put your hands inside the bus before something happened to them," said Art, laughing at Tallulah.

"What could honestly happen?" As she said it, a bird shit on Tallulah's hand. "Eww! That's so gross!"

Mona laughed hysterically.

"What are you laughing about?" Tallulah stuck her shitty hand in Mona's face.

"He warned you not to stick your hands outside the window, and karma bit you in the ass," laughed Mona.

"Why is it so damn bumpy?" asked Wanda. "I feel like I'm losing weight just bouncing around!"

"It wouldn't hurt you to lose a few pounds," said Edith.

"I guess it's my fault—I should have checked the shocks before I picked you all up, but I was running late," said Art. "But I'm really excited you're all going to Mystic Summer Camp! We'll be there soon. I really hope that you enjoy yourselves, and what Belle, your camp director, and her sidekick, Harlow, your camp administrator, have planned for you. They've worked hard on everything for you."

Art turned onto the dirt road that led to the camp. Agnes read the sign that read "Mystic Senior Camp" and started to get excited. "So, who's ready for fun?!"

Everyone started screaming with excitement.

"Yes, we want fun—that's why we're all here," said Wanda. "Right, girls and men?"

"Love your energy, Miss Wanda," said Art with a grin on his face.

"Easy, sonny. I'm old enough to be your grandmother," said Wanda. "So no flirting with me!"

"I wasn't flirting with you!" said Art, laughing to himself. "But I get the message."

CHAPTER 3

Final Preparations

Belle and Harlow were busy with last-minute details before the seniors arrived.

"Harlow, is everything all set for today?" asked Belle.

Belle was nervous about everything happening that day, and wanted to make sure everything was perfect. She was very focused on what she needed to do, and could sometimes be all business. When she wasn't working, she enjoyed having fun. She had a profound sense of humor. She had never been an owner of a camp before, much less anything at all, so it was important everything turn out right. The camp meant so much to her, and when she found out from a broker friend of hers it was going up for sale, she wasted no time making a bid.

"Yes, Belle, everything's fine," said Harlow. "That hasn't changed since the five seconds ago when you asked, or the five seconds before that. Like I reassured you fifty times yesterday, and a hundred times this morning already, we're going to be fine."

"OK, I get it. Sorry, I'm just so nervous about today, and this week. It has to be perfect," said Belle.

Harlow knew how hard Belle had worked to get the camp up and running, and how important it was, but loved to joke around to get her going. It was something Harlow had been doing since they were kids. She definitely had the knack to make any situation better. Harlow had a good heart, and a witty sense of humor that could make anyone smile. But if you ticked her off, she would not hesitate to tell you what she thought of you.

Harlow had been happy to take the summer off from being a professor to help Belle out with the camp because it held memories for her, too.

"I still think we should have found good-looking guys to have fun with them before camp opened," said Harlow, laughing. It seemed lately that was all Harlow thought about. But that was one thing Belle enjoyed about her. She was not afraid to go out and grab what or even who she wanted. She had not changed since high school.

Belle, on the other hand, was more well-rounded, and pretty much had her future planned out. Harlow had been her ride-or-die since high school. It would always be that way with them. They were attached at the hip.

"I guess blond-haired people do have more fun," said Harlow.

"How would you know? You haven't had fun in long time," laughed Belle.

"Maybe you should try it Belle," said Harlow.

"I already shaved my head once, remember? And dying it blonde is not me," said Belle.

"Yes, I remember," said Harlow, "and that was for a worthy cause. I was so proud of you. And look at you now—your hair grew back!"

"That's one reason I wanted you here, to go on this journey with me—because we spent a lot of summers here. And I love planning things with you. And you have so many promising ideas for this place, like me," said Belle.

"Well, that's not the only reason. You know I have a great heart, and I'm not afraid to get my hands dirty," said Harlow.

"That is so true," said Belle.

"Can we go through the list one last time to make sure we have everything covered and I'll leave it alone?" asked Belle.

"I will if you promise to calm down and remember to enjoy yourself," said Harlow. "OK, I'm calm now. Can we do the lists?"

"Breathe, Belle, please!"

"I'm breathing, Harlow," said Belle, as she gave Harlow a shitty grin, crossing her arms and puckering her lips together.

"OK! Is an updated list of all the seniors who will be here done?" asked Belle.

"Yes. We did have one add-on, but it's all good. And it's been settled which cabin they're staying in," said Harlow.

"All blankets and pillows are on the cots in the cabins?" asked Belle as she paced, like she did when she got nervous.

"Yes, Bessie did that this morning," said Harlow.

"Wonderful. That's what I call teamwork," said Belle.

"Bessie and Serena made up the activity schedule and the days there will be night events," said Harlow.

"I'm glad they're on top of things," said Belle.

"Belle, all you need to do is relax and things will be OK," said Harlow, who was getting tired of watching her pace the floor.

"I just want them to have a wonderful experience here and enjoy it as much as we did when we were younger," said Belle.

"I still can't believe you bought the whole camp," said Harlow as they looked around at everything the camp had to offer.

"So many memories here." Belle was thinking about how it had been when she and Harlow had come to camp so many years ago.

"Yeah. I remember the time we didn't want to sleep in the cabin, so we decided to sleep in the hammock," said Harlow.

"It was so cold that night I thought we were going to freeze to death," said Belle. "Oh! I forgot one last thing!"

"Of course you did, right in the middle of us sharing memories. You know everything's all set!"

"I'm afraid to ask, but is everything all ready with Frankie?" asked Belle.

"I can give him a call and check if you like, but I'm sure he's got things under control," said Harlow.

"That is what I'm worried about. I'm just going to go make sure the food came and that he's not doing anything that he shouldn't be," said Belle.

"Are sure you don't want me to go?" asked Harlow. She knew the history between Belle ad Frankie.

"No, it's OK. I got it. I'm just going to make it quick and easy," said Belle.

"That's what I'm afraid of," said Harlow.

"I'll be fine, then. I'm going to go for a walk, I'll be back before the seniors get here."

"No, you're going to raid the cabins and see if everything has been correctly done," said Harlow, sticking her tongue out.

"OK, you know me too well. You're right, but I'm also checking on Frankie," said Belle, giggling as she walked off.

"Don't do anything I wouldn't." Harlow smirked.

Belle turned around and gave Harlow the finger.

Harlow laughed hysterically.

Belle walked to the into the dining hall, to the kitchen, and saw there was no Frankie in sight. *It's so hard to stay in one place, I guess.*

"Hey Frankie!!"

Where the hell could he be? I swear he's a man-child. He has to be watched all the time.

Suddenly, Belle heard the pots and pans rattling in the back where the storage room was. But she didn't see anyone near them when she started to go back there. She went further into the storage room, and still didn't see anything—not even Frankie.

"Frankie! Where are you?"

Frankie finally came out of storage room, humming to himself. Belle jumped when he appeared.

"I'm right here, Belle, relax." Frankie wiped his forehead.

"Why didn't you come when I called you before?"

"I did, and I'm here now with you," said Frankie as he moved closer to Belle.

"I've been here for ten minutes, and you weren't answering me."

"I was in the freezer and didn't hear you calling me," said Frankie.

"Hail King Casanova!" said Belle, rejecting Frankie as he got closer. "I'm here to make sure you're ready for tonight—and this week."

"Yeah, that's what I was doing in the food storage room and the freezer. It looks like we'll be OK—the truck came yesterday," said Frankie.

"I hope so, because all the food supplies you need should already have been here."

"You're right, as always, Belle. They did come yesterday, like I said a minute ago," said Frankie. "I'm just little nervous about cooking for everyone here."

"Why? You're a fantastic cook, and that's why I hired you," said Belle. "Are you sure it's not because I'm good-looking, and you want to get back with me?" Frankie smiled.

"Not at all! That has nothing to do with it," said Belle. "You are incredibly talented."

"Don't worry, Belle. I have everything planned for tonight and the week ahead, so there won't be one thing that goes wrong."

"I'm glad you have everything thing under control."

Belle began going out the kitchen door, then turned around and asked Frankie if he was OK.

"Yes, Belle, I'm fine. It's just a little warm in here." Frankie fanned himself with his hand.

"Yeah, you're right about that—it is hot in here!" Belle could feel the sweat dripping off her. "Should I bring in a couple of fans to cool it off in here?"

"No, I can deal with the heat," said Frankie, winking.

Belle shook her head. "If you think you'll be OK, then fine. I'm going to make sure everything's going OK with the rest of the employees, so

I'll see you when the seniors arrive—which should be soon, I'm guessing. I left my itinerary with Harlow."

"I'll be there with bells on. I'm looking forward to meeting the seniors when they come."

"That's OK. You can leave the bells out of it and show up without them," said Belle, going out the door.

Frankie went back to the storage room and told Tory it was safe to come out.

"Wow! That was a close one!" said Tory, fixing her blonde hair so no one noticed it was messy. Tory and Frankie continued to make out in the kitchen before Frankie pulled away.

"OK, we need to stop, or we'll never leave," said Frankie. "We need to be more careful where we make out."

Tory, could be a daredevil when she wanted to be. "We won't get busted, so don't worry."

"Frankie, we've been careful so far," said Tory. She wrapped her arms around Frankie's waist as they continued to kiss.

"You better go before I rip off your clothes right here and now," said Frankie as he tried to control himself. "The seniors are going to be here soon, plus I must get dinner going."

"OK, Frankie, if that's what you want," said Tory as she tried to tempt him into one last kiss.

"See you after the campfire tonight, and we can continue where we left off," said Frankie, getting all hot again.

"See you later, Frankie," said Tory as she left the dining hall.

Oh my god, what am I doing? Frankie thought himself. He couldn't believe what had just happened.

"Everything all set with Frankie and everyone else you went to check on?" asked Harlow with a mischievous grin.

"Yes, Harlow you were right. Everything exactly the way it should be," said Belle.

"Things went good with Frankie, too?" asked Harlow, knowing they had a little history together.

"Yes, he's just fine." Belle felt her face getting red. "Have the seniors from Heaven's Ridge Retirement Home arrived?"

"No, not yet. They should be pulling in anytime now."

"Art left a while ago to get them. I just hope he doesn't do anything clumsy."

"He has a good head on his shoulders. He's the best guy for the job to pick them up—and all the other things he's good at!"

"I can't believe we've known him since we were in high school!"

"Yeah, me neither," said Harlow. "And he's still sweet as he was twenty-something years ago."

"So excited about this! I still have the jitters, though," said Belle, looking around and feeling proud of what she had accomplished to get the camp up and running.

"Oh, you've been talking about this from the day you found out this camp was going up for sale!" said Harlow.

"I just can't help it! This is the first time we're hosting a camp for seniors, and like I said before, we have such memories of this place!"

"Well, Belle, it's your time to shine," said Harlow. "This will be the greatest week we'll ever have!"

CHAPTER 4

To Mystic Senior Camp

Beep, beep! Art beeped the horn as he got closer to camp.

"I hear the bus coming," said Frankie as he came running out the dining hall with a sandwich in hand (which is typical if you know Frankie).

"No, really? You heard something over your chewing?" asked Belle sarcastically as she walked past him. "That food is supposed to be for the seniors!"

Frankie shoved the sandwich down his throat.

"Really, Frankie?!"

"Hey, I was hungry! I've had a long day getting everything ready!"

"That's not all he was doing." Tory winked.

Everyone looked at Frankie as he wiped his mouth on his shirt.

"I honestly have no idea where he puts it, but that's why he's best suited to the kitchen," said Harlow.

"I can totally agree with you on that!" Belle laughed.

Frankie thought his blonde hair was going to make every girl swoon over him, which was far from the truth. He thought he was funny most of the time, and sometimes, he was. Frankie was the type to wear his heart on his sleeve and be a helpful hand when needed. So, he did have some good qualities to him, when he wasn't screwing up.

The bus pulled up in front of the dining hall. All the seniors were looking out the window, looking around.

"The seniors have finally arrived! Can everyone come over here and meet them?" asked Belle.

Everyone went to the bus.

"I know you guys already know this," said Harlow, "but I just ask one thing of you— treat the seniors with kindness and respect, and be on your best behavior."

"That means you too, Frankie," said Belle, with her arms folded. And he knew that she met business.

"Alright, ladies and gentlemen, we're at our final destination. I'd be more than happy to help you with your bags once you get off the bus."

Art opened the door, went down the stairs, and opened the side door to where all the luggage was stored. He opened the side door to get the bags.

"Sonny, I have a question for you," said Wanda.

"My name is Art. But yes—what is your question, Miss Wanda?" asked Art as he read her nametag.

"Why are your shorts not pulled up?" she asked, her sunglasses just over her nose, looking at him.

"Hey, I can see your underwear!" Tallulah yelled through the window.

Art felt his face get red as he looked up at Tallulah. He pulled his shorts up.

Art is helped the rest of the seniors get off the bus and grab their bags to take to their cabins.

"Art is such a harder worker!" said Harlow.

"You can stop drooling now," said Belle. "I agree he is. He'll fit in great as a counselor."

"This is extremely exciting! I can't wait to meet them," said Iggy as she got in line with the others. Her ginger hair was blowing in the breeze as she danced a little from excitement. Iggy was extremely easygoing, loved her job as an art therapist, and was an extremely talented painter.

If you saw her paintings, you would see just how talented she was—and will be, if she keeps working at it.

"Just remember to be professional and have fun with them," said Belle.

"Well, then, that'll be easy for most of us," said Chip, winking at Belle.

"Please try and behave, Chip," said Hazel, elbowing him in his side.

"That means keep your hands to yourself, Chip!" said Belle. "And I've told your sidekick, Frankie, the same thing."

"Yes, ma'am! I'll do that—just for you."

Chip had blonde hair and blue eyes, and thought he was God's gift to women. But he *was* caring—and knew how to do his job.

Chip gave Belle a smirk as she went to greet the seniors.

"This is going to be a long week, but a great one!" said Belle, watching the seniors come toward her on the basketball court, looking around.

Once everyone got off the bus, Belle prepared herself for her speech.

"Hello, and welcome to Mystic Senior Camp!" Belle looked at all the seniors' faces. "How was your bus trip here?"

"You call that a trip?!" asked Blanche.

"It was more like a rollercoaster ride," said Edith, putting gum in her mouth.

"Well, I'm sorry to hear that," said Belle. "But if you need anything at all while you're here, don't hesitate to ask me—or any of your counselors."

"OK, darling! What was your name again?" asked Edith.

"I'm getting to that right now," said Belle. "My name is Belle, and I am your camp director."

"Big title for such a small person," said Wanda, starting to wave her arms around as if though was at a rock concert. The rest of the seniors stared at her, not knowing what to think of her little dance.

"Oh, my aching back! Good thing I brought a heating pad," said Clara.

"Honestly, there should be warning signs on that bus about the hard seats!" said Agnes.

"*Bumpy when moving*," said Tallulah, laughing.

"Unfortunately, sweetie, you can't use your heating pad here," said Harlow.

"Who made that rule?" asked Clara.

"There aren't many outlets in your cabin to plug it in," said Harlow. "But don't worry—I'm sure once you relax, you'll feel so much better."

"Listen here, Virgin Mary!" said Clara angrily." If I want to use my damn heating pad, I will damn well use it, and you can't stop me! Is that clear?"

Harlow looked down at Clara's nametag before saying anything. "Well, Clara, first, let me introduce myself. My name is Harlow, and I'm your camp administrator. My name's not Mary, nor am I a virgin—not that you needed to know that." Harlow was right in Clara's face, speaking loudly to make sure Clara could hear her. "We will accommodate you the best we can."

Wanda came closer as Harlow was talking to Clara.

"Wanda, dear, things are OK," said Clara. "I can manage her."

"I just wanted to scare the Virgin Mary a little bit," said Wanda.

"Things are hunky dory, Wanda."

"Backup if you need it." Wanda gave Harlow the evil eye.

"We'll see what we can do to accommodate you, Clara—no problems here." Harlow backed away, giving Belle a look. Belle just shook her head. This was not how she wanted things to start off.

"Thank you. I appreciate it, Harlow," said Clara.

Oh my, this is going to be a nightmare, thought Belle, She couldn't believe what had just happened. "What kind of place doesn't have a place to plug in a heating pad?!" asked Clara. Clara would just not let it go the heating pad issue go.

"I don't understand it, either," said Agnes.

"It is almost like we are camping—we can't use any appliances!" said Wanda.

"If you think about it, we are camping!" said Agnes. "Just in cabins. At least, I hope it's cabins we're staying in and not tents!"

Belle got on top of the picnic table to make the second part of her speech. Her first had not gone so well.

"Before we get you all settled in your cabins and you meet your counselors and the rest of the staff, I just wanted to say welcome to Mystic Camp and introduce Harlow, our camp administrator."

"Hi, I'm Harlow. Welcome to Mystic Senior Camp. I'm here if you need anything at all—within reason." She looked at Clara.

"Did your mom show you how to dress, dear?" yelled Tallulah.

"No, I taught myself, thank you very much," said Harlow.

"Well, someone should have—because I can see your belly!" said Tallulah, giggling at Harlow. "Harlow looked at Belle with her eyes bugging out of her head and Harlow," whispered how brutal they are. "Just keep going it will be OK," said Belle. Belle just looked in horror maybe it was a bad idea to try to recreate the same feeling she had when she was here all those years ago. "Anyways, I hope you enjoy your experience here as much as I did when I was younger, said Harlow. Then she realized that they were seniors, and not young like she was. "It is not going so well so far, sweetie," said Wanda, kicking the dirt like a child. Why are you doing that Wanda, asked Tallulah. Wanda gave her a blank stare and said to Tallulah because she wanted to, and it was fun. Tallulah just shook her head and continue listening to what Belle was saying.

"Let's have Bessie, our camp activities coordinator, come on up and tell you about all the activities she has planned for you this week."

Bessie was a very energetic girl. Her long brown hair was blowing around. "Hello, seniors," said Bessie, perky and excited. "So nice to finally meet you."

Bessie was made for the job. She had a great head on her shoulders and could think quick under pressure.

"So, for this week, we have indoor and outdoor games," said Bessie, "which Serena, one of my activity staff, will be doing with me."

Serena was tough. She knew how to deal with anything that came her way, because she had been dealing with a rough life for most of her life. She was extraordinarily talented, and loved to take care of people.

"We will be playing things such as shuffleboard, cornhole, Pokeno, volleyball, basketball, board games, bingo, dominoes, noodle ball, and card games," yelled Serena, so excited to be there.

"Did she say butthole?" asked Edith.

"No, she said *cornhole*, you dingbat," laughed Agnes.

"I like playing butthole more," laughed Edith.

"There's no such game as butthole," laughed Agnes.

"We also have arts and crafts with Siena, who's also part of our team," said Bessie.

"Lastly, we have art therapy with Iggy," said Serena.

Iggy waved to everyone.

"We also have music therapy with Eden, who you'll hear sing later tonight, at the campfire," said Bessie. She started to sing a tune, but quickly stopped when the seniors booed her.

"Of course, we also have swimming with our lifeguards, Chip and Tory," said Serena.

"Well, *hubba, hubba!*" said Tallulah. "Where have you been all my life, sweetie pie?"

"Probably not born yet," laughed Chip.

"Last but certainly not least, we have Fay, who will be doing your morning exercises," said Bessie, trying to do some jumping jacks.

"I already do exercise! I call it eating breakfast, lunch, and dinner, and maybe a few snacks in between," chuckled Tallulah as she rubbed her stomach.

"I plan to whip you into shape, ladies and gentlemen," said Fay.

"Did she just say she'd *whip* us?" asked Miles, a smirk on his face.

"That *is* what she said," said Felix, getting a little turned on.

"This could get kinky," said Miles. "Which is right up my alley! I'm going to love it."

"Sounds good to me, too," said Felix, licking his lips as he stared at Wanda.

"Sounds fun to me!" yelled Tallulah as everyone turned around to look at her. "Sign me up."

Fay was very tough—and not afraid to show you exactly how she felt.

"I'd also like to introduce Nurse Juniper," said Belle, "who's here if someone needs anything like aspirin, their meds, and so on."

Juniper shook her head. She couldn't believe Belle had introduced her that way, but whatever—it was just how she could be sometimes.

"We have one last person, who does all the maintenance," said Belle. "His name is Casper."

Harlow couldn't stand to look at Casper because it was too painful. She was stuck getting over him leaving her.

"So, that's our camp team," said Belle. "We look forward to making this the best experience for all of you."

"Um, Belle . . . we forgot someone," said Harlow giving Belle a funny look.

"Who could we have possibly forgotten?" asked Belle.

"That would be me," said a voice from the crowd. Frankie popped up behind Agnes and came up to join them all on the picnic table

"Oh crap!" said Belle, feeling bad. "I have one more person to introduce, and his name is Frankie. He's your cook while you're all here."

"You are hot to trot!" said Tallulah, licking her lips, trying to act sexy.

"I'm looking forward to serving you tons of different dishes this week," said Frankie. "I hope that you enjoy the barbecue I have prepared for you tonight."

"I'm sure we will cutie," said Edith.

"Just about to get to the BBQ, Frankie, but thank you for sharing," said Belle, giving him a dirty look for not waiting for her. "There are so many things happening this week, I realize it will be hard to choose what to do first. But we have it all mapped out for you, so you'll all get to do everything this week."

"We also have a couple of things planned for nighttime," said Harlow.

"Also," said Bessie, "at the end of the week, we'll have our goodbye party—and I think you'll enjoy the theme!"

"What's it going to be?" yelled Tallulah.

"Well, thank you for asking, Tallulah," said Bessie. "The theme is going to be 'roaring twenties.'"

The seniors looked satisfied with that, which was a relief for Bessie, because she had worked hard getting everything for the party.

"Thank you, Bessie," said Belle. "It looks like we'll have a fun time with everything. I know I'm looking forward to it! . . . Next, I wanted to tell you about the mealtimes, because I know how important they're for everyone. Breakfast is at eight, lunch is at twelve, and dinner is at five."

"So, now we're on a food schedule," said Hank. Hank was a handsome man, but could be very grumpy at times.

"We're babies, with scheduled eating times," said Blanche.

"At least we're getting fed, Blanche," said Ethel. "I mean, think of the times the dietary people because didn't bring enough food for all of us."

"I guess you're right, Ethel," said Blanche looking embarrassed. "I didn't think of it that way."

"It's OK, Ethel," said Agnes, giving Ethel a wink, "don't you worry,"

"To start off our first night here, we're having a welcome BBQ. Then, after the BBQ, we will have a singalong by the campfire with Eden," said Belle.

"It is tradition to have a welcome campfire so we can all get acquainted with you," said Harlow.

"The BBQ will be at five, so that gives you time to meet and greet your counselors as well as them getting to know you," said Belle.

"Just remember to have fun and enjoy yourselves, and maybe make memories here, because special things have known to happen here when you least expect them," said Harlow.

"Naps are how we enjoy ourselves," chuckled Agnes as she looked around and laughed.

"Then, if that's what you want to do, that is fine," said Belle. "But you're here to have a fun experience, so why not enjoy it with your friends?"

"I agree with what you're you are saying, shorty. That's exactly why I'm here, and glad my three best friends are here, too," said Tallulah.

"It's Belle, but thank you for sharing that with us, Tallulah." Belle shook her head at what Tallulah had called her.

"We'll now let you know what cabins you're in and which counselors will be staying with you," said Harlow.

"Will I be rooming with you, sweetie pie?" asked Tallulah, trying to flirt with Chip.

"No, we won't be sharing a cabin," laughed Chip.

"Cabin one, when I call your name line up with your counselors."

"Are we going to jail?" asked Tallulah.

"No, I don't think so. Why you're asking?" asked Agnes with a curious look.

"She wants us to all stand in a line. That is why I was wondering," said Tallulah.

"We haven't don't anything in a while since we called 911 to get the cute cops to see us," said Tallulah, laughing.

"Yeah, it was fun and to see their faces when they saw two elderly women waiting for them at the door," laughed Agnes."

"Oh, that was a riot—with their guns out and everything!" laughed Tallulah. "That was a good time."

"When was the last time you were in a line?" asked Wanda.

"Probably last week at Denny's, when we all went to breakfast for a trip," said Agnes.

"That wasn't Denny's. That was our dining room," said Wanda.

"I wondered why the food wasn't that good," said Agnes.

"Agnes, Mona, Wanda, and Vera you're in cabin one," said Belle.

28   April Carter

"Oh boy, this will be interesting with Vera," said Mona, rolling her eyes.

"Now, we must be good, so we don't set Vera off," said Agnes.

"Your counselors are going to be Eloise, Fay, Penny, Tory, Tinsley, and Iggy," called out Belle.

"Is her name Tinsel?" asked Wanda.

"No, it's Tinsley. Now shut up," said Vera.

"Maybe you need tinsel to brighten you up, Vera," said Agnes.

"You are so rude, Vera. I wish I understood why you're the way you are," said Wanda.

"Bite me."

"Oh really, Vera—you really want to go there?" asked Tallulah.

Before anything else happened, Eloise stepped in and told the seniors it was time to go to the cabin. Vera was your typical problem adult. She acted like a child from time to time. She was very uptight, and could be mean, She was not afraid to tell you how she felt, and could be violent at times—never with any of the seniors but the staff, because they egged her on. But she could be a sweetheart occasionally—when she was sleeping.

"A little piece of advice: you should watch out if Vera gets mad. She likes to hit or bite," whispered Wanda, letting the counselors know.

"Oh, great. Just what we need—someone who gets violent and kicks everyone's ass," said Tinsley, playing with her hair.

"We will be fine. I wouldn't worry—because if she was that violent, they wouldn't let her come," said Fay.

"I hope you're right, Fay," said Penny.

"Cabin two will be Tallulah, Edith, Ethel, Blanche, and Clara."

"Oh boy, are we going to be in trouble now," said Tallulah.

"I honestly can't believe Ethel and Clara are in our cabin," said Blanche.

"Your counselors are Serena, Hazel, Eden, Siena, and Bessie."

"Nice to meet you all! I've been so excited to meet you," said Eden. Eden was very bubbly, and loved people. But you shouldn't let her smile and her red hair fool you—she was a party girl at heart when she wasn't working, and not afraid to put you in your spot if you started any trouble.

"What's wrong, gals?" asked Serena.

"Why do you look upset?" asked Hazel. "It is supposed to be a happy time here at Mystic Senior Camp!"

"Yippee!" said Eden as she put her arms up in the air and laughed. Everyone looked at her as she started dancing around.

"All we're going to say is watch out what you do or say to anyone in the cabin," said Blanche.

"Why do you say that?" asked Serena, puzzled.

"Ethel and Clara can be big trouble at times. Ethel's not afraid to squeal on you about anything—even if you look cross-eyed to her," said Edith as she looked around, making sure no one could hear her.

"Clara enjoys all the gossip she can get, so she can tell on you," said Tallulah.

"They can't be that bad," said Serena, thinking about what they had said.

"Just don't say we didn't warn you," said Blanche.

"Finally, for cabin three, we have Jasper, Hank, Felix, Miles, and Beau," said Harlow.

"Really? No women in our cabin?" asked Miles, looking disappointed.

"Sorry. No coed cabins," said Harlow.

"Well, this really sucks."

"Oh, calm down, Miles, it will be OK," said Beau, who was admiring Mona from a distance.

"Your counselors are Ace, Art, Frankie, Casper, and Chip."

"Wow—that Beau is hot," said Mona to herself, drool coming from her mouth. Beau was tall, skinny, and very polite. He knew to always enjoy life before it was gone—because you never knew when that would be.

Mona had a puzzled look on her face when Iggy went by her.

"Are you OK, Mona?" asked Iggy.

"Yes, I am. I just don't know how to get him to notice me. It's been so long since I've been with a man. I've forgotten what to do," said Mona, trying not to panic.

"Who do you want to notice you, if you don't mind me asking?" asked Iggy. He loved making love connections with people. "I'm not trying to pry."

"Beau is a very handsome man, and I saw him a lot at Heaven's Ridge, but never went up to him. He has done the same with me," said Mona, staring at him again.

"Yes, he's handsome, I do agree," said Iggy.

"Wishful thinking, I guess," said Mona.

"There is someone out there for everyone," said Iggy, a sucker for love. "And if Beau makes your mouth water, go for it. Make him notice you."

"How do I do that?" asked Mona. "It's been so long for me."

"If you don't mind me asking, with your last husband, how did you get him to notice you?" asked Iggy.

"Oh, that's easy! All I did was wear a dress, lift it up right, and show a little—or in my case, a lot—of leg, and he was all mine," laughed Mona.

"Wow! That's what got you two together?" asked Iggy, who thought it sounded a little too easy. "My legs don't look like that now, so it won't work—I'm damn sure of that."

"You are one of my counselors, right?" asked Jasper.

"Yes, I am Jasper. What can I help you with?" asked Ace. Jasper got closer to Ace, to tell him his hemorrhoids were out and he needs help getting them back in.

Ace couldn't tell if he was joking or serious.

"I think you need a nurse to do that for you, Jasper—and I'm not a nurse yet," said Ace. When Ace realized that he was serious, he started laughing to himself.

"Come on, Jasper," said Ace, "let's go and see the nurse." He turned to Jasper. "I'm going to be right back. I'm going to take Jasper to see Nurse Juniper."

"I thought you said you were going to be a nurse?" asked Jasper.

"I am studying to be a nurse, but we can't do things like that," said Ace, trying to keep a straight face, "yet I'm still learning."

"Sonny, don't laugh. This will happen to you one day, when you're my age," said Jasper.

"My name is not sonny," said Ace, "and I have got a long time before that happens, Jasper." Ace had been a counselor for a while at other camps and when he wasn't doing that, he was studying to be a nurse at a local college and hospital. He was a happy-go-lucky guy. "Are you ready to go to the nurse's station?"

"I guess so, since you're not up to the challenge," said Jasper, spitting and sputtering all the way there.

"It will be OK, Jasper," said Ace, patting him on the back.

Fart!!

Ace looked behind him when he heard the noise, but all he could hear was Jasper laughing.

They got to the nurse's station, and Nurse Juniper was putting all the medication away.

"Hey guys," said Nurses Juniper, her brown hair blowing from the fan.

"Hey Juniper, I was hoping you could check out Jasper. It seems he has a hemorrhoid issue that needs your attention," said Ace.

"Oh my God, this is so embarrassing," said Jasper, his face in his hands.

"It's OK, Jasper. I've done this a few times before. I'm an expert," said Nurse Juniper as she grabbed some gloves on the counter. "Let's go in this room right here, so that we can have some privacy."

She went to turn the light on.

"I'll just wait out here," said Ace.

"Come on, Sonny, you can join us," said Jasper, getting on the table while Nurse Juniper got ready.

"Plus, it's a good learning experience for you, since you're studying to be a nurse," said Nurse Juniper.

"Oh, sonny don't be a wuss, and get the hell in here now!" said Jasper, waiting for things to start.

"OK, I will if you don't mind teaching me, Nurse Juniper," asked Ace.

"I invited you, so of course she doesn't mind! Now get in here," yelled Jasper, who was getting irritated.

"The patient has spoken," said Nurse Juniper, grinning at Ace.

"Yes, OK, I am coming in to learn about hemorrhoids. So excited!" laughed Ace.

"See? That wasn't so hard to get your ass in here, was it?" asked Jasper.

"Alright, Jasper, it's time to get started," said Nurse Juniper as she closed the door.

All you could hear outside the door was a loud groaning sound. The hemorrhoid was history for the moment.

"Well, hello, sweetie. My name is Eloise. I will be one of your counselors, I will show you, our cabin," said Eloise.

Eloise was an on-the-go kind of gal. Her long red hair makes her seem sweet, but her devilish eyes can put you in your place if necessary. She is also very caring, always there for everyone to help if needed. But if she doesn't want to do something, she will stand her ground and not do it.

"How did you get your name, dear?" asked Agnes.

"It was my grandmother's name and my mother's middle name, so it's been in the family for a very long time," said Eloise.

"Oh, I see, dear. That is so nice it's a family name," said Agnes as she shook her head like she really didn't care.

"Yes, when my grandmother and mother were around, they were the best, and I learned a lot from them. There is not much I can't do," said Eloise.

"Well, that's not a terrible thing—to have more tricks of the trade," said Agnes. "More women should be doing more with their life than men, because we are just as capable as they are," said Eloise.

Agnes and Eloise headed to the cabin where they would be staying for the week. Each cabin contained four or five seniors accompanied by four or five counselors.

The cabins were very rustic, medium-sized, painted brown and on the inside and out. They had cots in a row, with blankets and pillows set up for each senior. There were no windows or doors, exactly—only screened-in windows and a green tarp for the door. There was also a firepit and a picnic table outside for everyone to sit at.

"What kind of dump is this?" asked Agnes.

"Oh, this place is so cozy and rustic! My two favorite things. And you can breathe in that fresh air," said Eloise as she took a deep breath to show Agnes how wonderful the air was.

"I can smell gas," said Agnes, plugging her nose.

"Hmm. I don't smell anything, Agnes," said Eloise as she breathed the air in again. "Maybe it's a skunk. We do have them around here quite a bit."

"Like I said before," said Agnes, "you will smell it soon. Just keep breathing that air." Agnes squeezed her ass cheeks together, moving her hands so the smell would go toward Eloise.

Toot! Eloise started gagging and coughing up a storm. Agnes kept going, like the Energizer bunny.

"I need a little air, Agnes. I will be right back. I'm just going to move to this side of the firepit," said Eloise. *Oh my god what did she eat before she came here?!*

"I told you, Eloise," said Agnes, laughing hysterically.

"It's only for a week," Eloise whispered to herself.

Harlow was walking by when she saw Eloise and Agnes, and decided to stop to see if everything was OK.

"Eloise is everything going OK?" asked Harlow.

"Fine and dandy here. I'm just breathing in the lovely fresh air we are lucky to have," said Eloise as she breathed in and out. Harlow looked at Eloise kind of funny, but went on her way.

"That was close," said Eloise, taking another deep breath before going into the cabin.

"Alrighty, Agnes, let's go see where you'll be sleeping," said Eloise. Agnes looked around, not knowing what to think of the cabin.

"Here is your bed. I hope that you will be nice and comfortable. If you need extra blankets, let me know."

Agnes sat on the bed, bouncing, looking around.

"So, what do you think, Agnes?" asked Eloise.

"It's too lumpy. I won't be able to sleep on that," said Agnes, rolling around on the bed.

"Well, sorry Agnes it's the only bed we have for you," said Eloise.

"Why can't I have that bed over there?" asked Agnes as she pointed to one of the counselor's beds, higher up and a little bit bigger.

"No those are our beds. These are your beds," said Eloise, folding her arms. There was no way she was giving up her bed.

"Fine, so be it. But be prepared—my tooting can get louder and smellier," laughed Agnes. Eloise shook her head and went back up to see if any other seniors were ready to come down to the cabin—and to see if there was anything else she could help with.

"I'll be right back, Agnes. I'm just going to see who else is ready to come down here," said Eloise.

"They really expect me to stay in here for a week? Seriously? What the hell were they thinking?" said Agnes to herself as she started to unpack her things.

She thought about it, then decided to pack everything up again—she was out of here. Penny came in the cabin with Vera, wondering what Agnes was up too.

"What are you doing?"

"Not staying here! I need a comfier bed and something that has windows."

"Agnes, you're going to be fine," said Penny. "And you will have a lot of fun!"

"We'll see about that," said Agnes as she put her suitcase under the bed, waiting to see if that was going to be true.

"Well, here you go Miles I will just put your stuff on this bed and let you settle in," said Casper.

Miles was a handsome, clean-cut guy with a mustache, who was the life of the party.

"Are you the man who drove us here?" asked Miles.

"No, that was my buddy—your counselor, Art," said Casper.

"Oh, OK. Sorry about that, sonny. You just looked like him," said Miles.

"But he will be in the same cabin as us, and like I said before, he will be one of your counselors."

"Well, then this should be a fun week for all of us," said Miles.

"I hope everyone has a fun time this week. I know that I am looking forward to it," said Casper.

"Where are we going to be sleeping?" asked Miles.

"Your bed is right here, and I made it up especially for you," said Casper.

"You did an excellent job, but I was looking for something a little comfier," said Miles, trying to get Casper to give up one of the beds in every corner.

"Sorry, dude, but this is how things are here at Mystic. And trust me, the beds are not that bad to sleep on," said Casper as he went outside to see what else he could do for the others.

Miles looked around to see if anyone was watching. *I am just going to move my bags over to this nice high bed.* He laid down on it, next to his bags. *Now this is more like* it, he thought as he drifted off to sleep.

CHAPTER 5

BBQ Blitz

"Good evening, seniors, I just wanted to let you know we have ten minutes until the BBQ. So please, come to the basketball court!"

The loudspeaker got everyone's attention.

"Don't forget to bring your appetites! The cook has made some special BBQ for your first night here. So come on up and enjoy!"

Frankie came up to Belle and tapped her on the shoulder. Belle turned around and saw he looked like he was up to something. She didn't like what she saw.

"I've seen that face before. I am guessing something happened," said Belle.

"Well, you can kind of sort of say something happened," said Frankie.

"What's wrong, Frankie?" asked Belle.

"First you need to promise me you won't get mad at me," said Frankie, taking a step back from Belle.

"I'm guessing, since you're stepping back, that it's truly not good that you have to tell me? asked Belle, trying not get mad. Belle was worried.

"Well, the BBQ I planned isn't quite going to happen," said Frankie, looking really scared. Belle was trying not to get angry, but Frankie could see in her eyes that she was.

"Why isn't it, Frankie?" asked Belle, clutching her teeth together, holding in her anger.

"I will tell you if you promise to breathe and not look like you're going to kill me," said Frankie, hoping that Belle would calm down once he told her everything.

"Please just tell me what happened," said Belle.

"I dropped the tray of hot dogs, hamburgers, and chicken on the floor on the way from the refrigerator," said Frankie, who knew he was going to hear it now.

"*WHAT?!*"

"I was getting ready to pull it out of the refrigerator to bring it to the grill, and I hit my hand on the door and lost my grip, and it went all over the floor," said Frankie, ducking because he thought Belle was going to hit him.

"Were you on your phone again?" asked Belle.

"Well, that could have been what happened," said Frankie.

That unfortunately wasn't the truth. Frankie just didn't want to tell Belle it was because he was making out with Tory and didn't see the tray when it fell off the counter.

"I keep telling you to stay off your phone while you're cooking," said Belle, ready to wring Frankie's neck.

"Yes, I know I was stupid, and I am so sorry, Belle," said Frankie, who felt really bad for what had happened with the food, though not what happened with him and Tory.

"*Sorry* is not going to make this situation better," said Belle.

"I checked if we had any more, and we didn't. It seems the company we went through shorted us," said Frankie.

"I checked all the paperwork, and everything matched," said Belle.

"Well, something got overlooked, because the sheet didn't match what they gave us," said Frankie.

"Why is this happening to me now?!" asked Belle.

"Hey! You two need to stop for a second and take a breather," said Harlow, coming in after having heard them.

"Not now, Harlow. We have an unpleasant situation happening," said Belle.

"OK, that's fine. But can I just do one thing before you tear each other's eyes out?" asked Harlow.

"What could be so important you have do it right now?"

"Well, for one thing I need to turn off the loudspeaker you left on for everyone to hear," said Harlow, reaching between Frankie and Belle to turn it off.

Belle couldn't believe what Harlow had said. She was ready to cry.

"Now, you may go on with your little rant," said Harlow, going out the door quickly.

Oh my God, I am so stupid, thought Belle.

Belle just could not believe this was happening. It was like a bad dream.

"What are we going to do now?!" cried Belle.

"Well, we still have all the salads I made, and the desserts! And the good news is I ordered pizzas for everyone, so no one will go, hungry," said Frankie.

"I wish you would have run it by me before doing that, but I am glad you were trying to fix things," said Belle.

"You're not going to like what I am going to say next, but I don't have the money to pay for it and it will be here in about ten minutes," said Frankie, taking off through the door before Belle could say anything to him.

"I'm going to kill him," Belle said angrily. "Tonight has been a disaster so far!"

Belle started crying.

"Aww, what's wrong, honey?" asked Harlow, who came over to give Belle a big hug and reassure her things would be OK.

"Can I fire Frankie?" asked Belle, who was stressed. She didn't know what to do.

"No, you can't fire him we don't have another cook to replace him," said Harlow.

"Then I don't know what we are going to do," said Belle, panicking.

"It will be OK, Belle, we will get through this together. And you've got to remember, it's only the first night," said Harlow, always trying to be the peacemaker.

"I really hope you're right, Harlow." Belle wiped the tears from her eyes.

"I am here, so it must get better," laughed Harlow.

"You're so full of yourself," said Belle, trying not to laugh at Harlow.

"See, I made it better for you already! And pizza really doesn't sound that bad right now. Plus we still have other things to eat," said Harlow.

"Can I at least blame Frankie for all this mess he put on us?"

"That you can do," laughed Harlow.

Belle laughed for the first time since the whole situation had started.

"Thank you for being here with me the million times I've said that to you."

She gave Harlow a hug.

"I know this was a crazy idea when you talked to me about it, but you did it, and I am still so proud of you," said Harlow.

"You know how my brain works. All I wanted to do was make things perfect! But I was dreaming," said Belle.

"That is true, but I also know that you care and are very enthusiastic about things and when you have a vision, you go for it. I have learned to just let you go with it," said Harlow.

"You're sweet, Harlow, but I think you're buttering me up!"

"Wow, I give you a compliment and you think I am up to something!" said Harlow with a mischievous grin on her face.

"Well, are you?"

"Who, me?" Harlow pointed at herself and laughing.

"Yes, you!" Belle shook her head.

"No, I am not up to anything." Harlow winked.

"Harlow, I've known you a long time. I know when you're up to something."

"Belle can't I just be happy to be here with you?"

"OK. I'll believe you this time. But you're up to something! And I will find out eventually," said Belle.

"Belle, please just relax," said Harlow. "Oh, look! The pizza guy is here."

Harlow ran toward the pizza guy.

"I have fourteen large pizzas, and the bill comes to thirty dollars and forty-five cents," said the pizza guy as he stares at Harlow. Belle just shakes her head as she sees Harlow take off towards the pizza guy.

"Thank you so much for bringing the pizza in such a hurry," said Harlow, handing him the money.

"No, thank you! By the way, you're gorgeous," said the pizza guy.

Harlow started blushing and giggling. "Well, thank you, sweetie, for the pizzas—and for saying that!" She grabbed the pizzas. "You aren't bad yourself, sugar." She winked at him and took off with the pizza.

Casper grabbed Harlow's arm and told the pizza guy she was his.

"I am *not* yours!" yelled Harlow. "Leave me alone! I was getting somewhere with him,"

The pizza delivery guy got back in his vehicle and took off like a big bird.

Edith and Wanda overheard the yelling and turned to watch the action, their drinks in hand. Casper was very respectful man, but when it came to Harlow, his mood would change. He thought he had always to protect her.

"You are going to get yourself in a whole mess of trouble," he said.

"You should know I love trouble! That's why you left me!" said Harlow, rubbing her hand on the side of Casper's face, trying to get him all hot and bothered.

"This is better than a soap opera," said Wanda.

"Knock it off, Harlow," said Casper as he pushed her hand away.

"Knock what off? You used to love it when I would do that to you!"

"What's going on?" asked Tallulah as she sat down next to Edith.

"It looks like a lovers' quarrel," said Edith.

"Wow. I only get to see those on television!" said Tallulah, taking Edith's drink out of her hand to drink it herself, watching everything going on.

"I can't do this drama now, Harlow. I have to get the campfire ready for tonight," said Casper, walking away from her.

"Sure! Turn away like you always do when we fight!" said Harlow.

"Wow, that was very exciting!" said Wanda, standing up to clap.

"Damn fool! I'm sure you will be sad that you missed a chance to be with me again," said Harlow to herself, watching him walk away.

Casper looked back, but continued walking away.

Harlow couldn't believe he'd reacted like he had. And she couldn't believe how hot he still was.

She and Casper had a past. It had been so good. Then, with a snap of a finger, it was gone, just like that. Harlow was heartbroken, and was never the same again. She even refused to date anyone for a while. Harlow and Casper had an on-again, off-again relationship. It had been like that since high school. They couldn't seem to let go of one another and move on with other people.

"I guess the show is over, girls. And the way my sniffer's working, I'm guessing that it's time to eat," said Tallulah.

"That bummer that has been the most exciting thing I've seen in the four hours we've been here," said Edith.

"I agree," said Wanda, looking around.

"That woman, I swear, is going to drive me to drink one of these damn days!" said Casper, kicking a rock on the pavement on the way to the firepit.

"Whoa, easy, bud," said Chip, getting out of the way. "What seems to be lighting your fire? And I don't mean in a good way."

"Harlow—she's an immature bitch sometimes. I just had to take her out of a tough situation involving a pizza guy," said Casper, pacing around the firepit.

"Relax, man. It's going to be OK—even if I don't know exactly everything that's going on," said Chip.

"Harlow just goes for any guy who walks and talks, not watching what she's doing. It's so frustrating sometimes," said Casper.

"Well, I hate to say it, man, but that's a woman for you," laughed Chip, trying to joke around.

"I can't think about her right now. I need to get the campfire going for tonight." And off Casper went to get more logs for the fire.

"If you need to talk, man, I am here," said Chip.

"Thanks, man!" yelled Casper, waving at Chip.

"Men are so stupid sometimes," Harlow said, heading back to the dining hall, trying to hold back her tears—and how angry she was about little scene Casper had put on.

"I totally agree with you, darling. That's why I stopped getting married after my first husband died," said Tallulah, sitting on the picnic table by herself.

"Oh, sorry to hear that, Tallulah. That must have been so hard for you," said Harlow

"Our marriage would not have lasted to long anyway, even when we were happy in love," said Tallulah.

"How long were you married? If you don't mind my asking," said Harlow.

"Thirteen exceptional years, said Tallulah.

"That is a long time," said Harlow.

"So, why wouldn't it have lasted if he were still alive?" asked Harlow.

"He snored quite a bit. Drove me fucking crazy. But I did love him, and we both had our flaws," said Tallulah.

"Sorry about all the questions. You don't need to answer them if you don't want too," said Harlow.

"Even though I wanted to put a pillow over his face every night, I didn't," said Tallulah.

"Sure, you did. I can tell!" said Harlow sadly. "If you don't mind, me asking what happened to him?"

"Are you sure you really want to know?"

"If it's too painful, you don't need to tell me. It's up to you, Tallulah," said Harlow.

"He died from too much sex. His heart couldn't take it, because he had a heart condition I never knew about," said Tallulah.

"I can't believe he never told you about his heart," said Harlow, who was sad after hearing that.

"I wasn't aware of it either, until one night, we were going at it like two pigs fighting under the blankets, and the next morning, he was gone," said Tallulah.

"Oh no, Tallulah, I am so sorry," said Harlow. But deep down, she wanted to burst out laughing, because she was thinking about two pigs in a blanket.

"I tried to wake him for work, and he was colder than an icicle," said Tallulah.

"Again, I am so sorry, Tallulah, you had to go through all of that." Harlow put her arms around Tallulah.

"I guess it got a little too rough, and he couldn't handle it," said Tallulah.

"Enough of this mushy stuff! Let's go get a slice of pizza before everyone eats it all," said Harlow.

"I know Wanda can eat a lot of pizza, because I have seen her eat, and sometimes it's not pretty," said Tallulah.

"Oh, boy. Then we better hurry up and get it before she does," laughed Harlow, grabbing Tallulah's hand.

"I'll wrestle you a piece of pizza out of Wanda's hand," said Tallulah.

"Sounds good," said Harlow as they went to the dining hall, laughing.

Belle knew she needed to make an announcement to let the seniors know what had happened with the BBQ, but she was still too upset with Frankie. Harlow sneaked in behind her, grabbed the microphone, and told everyone what was going on.

"Sorry, everyone, for the mix-up. We had a little mishap in the kitchen, so we will not have the BBQ, but we will sometime this week."

Belle looked at Frankie as she was listening to Harlow.

"As you see, we have pizza instead," announced Harlow. "I hope you all get a piece, have some of the amazing salads and desserts, and have a great time. Thank you for your cooperation and patience, and let's have a good night!"

"I'd rather have pizza anyways!" yelled Edith.

"Of course you would. Because you like the simple things," said Agnes.

"Nothing wrong with that, Agnes!" said Edith. "Maybe you should try it sometime. Then you wouldn't be a grumpy pants."

"Maybe I will. You will have to wait and see," said Agnes.

"So far this has been Camp Not-So-Fun, "said Wanda.

"Why would you say that after what we witnessed earlier?" asked Edith.

"Yeah, it was good! But there was no real action. It's not like they were slapping the crap out of each other," said Edith.

"You watch too much damn wrestling," said Agnes.

"Hey, you guys," said Fay, sitting at the table, listening to what they were saying, "don't worry. It will get better here. There are always kinks with things—especially on the first night, but then it turns out good."

"Hey, Tallulah, is that your real hair color?" asked Wanda.

"Yes, of course it is!" said Tallulah.

"It just looks like you got in a fight with a wild animal," laughed Wanda.

"There is nothing wrong with my hair," said Tallulah, starting to get really ticked off.

"OK, if you say so," said Wanda as she left to go bug someone else.

Wanda went to sit next to a girl with blonde hair with a pink stripe going through it.

"Hi, my name is Tinsley. You're Wanda, right?"

Wanda giggled. "Yes, I am."

"I'm one of your counselors. I am so glad to meet you." Tinsley was acting bubbly and cheery.

"Why is your hair pink?" asked Wanda, getting up to move to another table.

"I just love being colorful, like a rainbow," said Tinsley.

"Then why is there a big glob of gum in your hair?" asked Agnes as she turned around to keep talking to Tinsley.

"There's no gum in my hair! You can't fool me," said Tinsley, getting up from the table to leave. Tinsley was sensitive and shy, but could hold her own if she needed too.

"Maybe she can't take the truth," said Agnes as she turned back around.

Wanda went outside to the picnic table to get a little air. She took the bottle of wine she had smuggled in out of the sweatshirt that she was wearing. She takes a couple of sips when she heard somebody talking to her.

"Excuse me where did you get that bottle of wine from?" asked Ace.

"Why? Who wants to know? The wine police or something?" asked Wanda.

"My name is Ace, and I am one of the counselors here," said Ace.

"Oh, really? You are? That's nice," said Wanda, who didn't really care.

"I know they don't serving any alcoholic beverages here," said Ace, taking the bottle away from Wanda.

"They aren't? Really?" asked Wanda. "Thanks for letting me know. Give me back my bottle!"

"No, I can't do that," said Ace, snorting.

"Are you on drugs or something?" asked Wanda.

"No, I am just high on life," said Ace.

"Listen, friend. No one touches my damn wine but me—and that's final," said Wanda

"Well, friend, I *have* your wine and there's nothing you can do about it," said Ace

Wanda managed to steal back the wine from Ace's hand, took one more drink, put the cork back in the wine, stuck it down her sweatshirt, and ran off to her cabin. As she did, she tripped and fell on her face. But she managed to get back up, still holding the bottle of wine in her sweatshirt.

"You will never get my wine!!"

"What was that all about?" asked Tinsley, coming out of the dining hall.

"Long story. I just feel bad for the poor counselors who have her in their cabin tonight," said Ace.

Tinsley looked at Ace with a *oh no* look, and Ace wasn't sure why.

"Are you OK Tinsley?" asked Ace.

"I guess it will be me taking care of her," said Tinsley.

"Oh, I am so sorry," said Ace."

"Yeah, right. Like I believe you," said Tinsley, walking away to go back inside.

"She's one crazy bitch," said Ace to himself. He went back to the dining hall.

"May I have your attention?" Belle shouted out to everyone. "Thank you for being patient with everything. I know it hasn't gone the way it's supposed to. I just wanted to let you know that everything will get better and by the end of the week, you will be having the time of your lives.

"I hope so! Because it's not happening so far," a voice from the crowd yells out.

"Now, if everyone could start heading down to the campfire, we'll be singing songs, roasting marshmallows, and getting to know each other," said Harlow.

"Well, that didn't go so well," said Belle.

"Don't worry, Belle. Everything will be fine, like you said before," said Harlow.

"Please don't tell me to relax," said Belle. "That isn't working."

"OK, I won't. I'll just eat my words on that," said Harlow.

Everyone left the dining hall and walked to the campfire with their flashlights. Belle looked up to the illuminated sky at all the stars that were out. Harlow came up to her, looking at the same view.

"What are you doing?" asked Harlow.

"Nothing. Just stargazing—something I enjoy doing from time to time," said Belle.

Harlow could see her discouraged face. She had the same face since the mishap with Frankie.

"Listen, Belle, you have had only one issue get in the way on the first day, and it's done and over with now, and everyone is enjoying themselves," said Harlow.

"How do you know, Harlow, that everything will get better after what Frankie did?"

"I know because I am your best friend, and because we planned every little detail from beginning to end. And as for Frankie, he made one mistake, that's all. And he tried to make things better by ordering food for our seniors," said Harlow.

"Yes, but still, I don't know why it happened tonight," said Belle.

"So what you had kinks along the way? They're going to happen no matter what. But it will get better. It's only the first night," said Harlow.

"Hope so. I just want everyone to have an enjoyable time," said Belle.

"They will have the best time," said Harlow as she smiled and gave Belle a hug.

"It is time for us to get marshmallows. Hopefully we don't burn the trees down," laughed Belle as they skipped down the path to the firepit.

They reached the campfire. Everyone was laughing and enjoying themselves, which was what Belle needed to see.

"I told you everyone was having fun," whispered Harlow.

"OK, I get it. You were right, as always, Harlow," said Belle, looking around at everyone's faces.

"Can I have your attention?" asked Belle loudly.

"Oh boy, here we go with another long speech," said Vera.

"Be quiet. I want to hear what she has to say," said Blanche to Vera.

"Oh, shut your piehole, Blanche," said Vera. "And of course you can't really hear what she's saying!"

"I can so, Vera—if you'd shut up," said Blanche.

"Blah blah blah," said Vera.

Blanche was not afraid to say what is on her mind—especially when it came to Vera.

"So glad you're all here. I can't wait to show you all what a fun time we will be having," said Belle.

I can show you what I have in store for you, too, sweetie," said Felix in a sexy voice. Belle looked at him strangely.

Chip sat next to Edith, and she got extremely hot—and they weren't by the fire.

"Well, hello, good-looking," said Edith.

"Hi, Edith, how are you?" asked Chip.

"Wow, you know my name!" Edith got so excited, winking at Chip.

"Well, of course I do—it's on your nametag!" said Chip.

"Oh, right. I forgot that was there," said Edith, who took her nametag and threw it in the firepit. Miles moved to the other side of Edith.

"Do you want my bottle of Viagra?" asked Miles.

"No, thank you, I don't have any problems in the romance department," said Chip.

"Then why don't you have a girlfriend?" asked Miles.

"Who said I don't have one?" asked Chip.

"Why don't you just take it?" asked Miles as he put the bottle in Chip's hand. "I'm not going to be using it anytime soon."

"I think you should hold on to them. You never know when you might get lucky with Wanda. I've noticed she has been eyeing you the whole time."

Wanda winked at Chip, and Miles thought she was winking at him.

"Maybe you're right. I have been trying to get her attention since I moved into Heaven's Ridge," said Miles.

"That guy is unbelievable," Chip whispered to Hazel.

"Let's get Eden up here so she can sing for us," said Belle.

"We are going to have so much F-U-N," said Eden.

"Does she think we don't know how to spell?" asked Felix, scratching his head.

"Not sure. Just like I am not sure it will be F-U-N, because it sorts of S-U-C-K-S," laughed Tallulah.

"So, it's my pleasure to introduce Eden," said Belle.

Everyone clapped and she began to sing, and they quieted down to listen to her extraordinary voice. Eden started singing "By the Light of the Moon."

"She sounds like an angel," said Felix.

"She's good, but a little pitchy," said Agnes.

Beau whispered in Mona's ear: "Would you like to dance with me?"

"Well, yes, sir, I would."

Beau took her hand and held her tight.

"Oh, that's so sweet—our first camp romance," said Belle.

"Thank God they're not coed cabins," said Harlow, laughing.

Beau kissed Mona on the cheek, and she blushed. The song was over, and they both went back to their seats, still looking in each other's eyes.

"What the hell was that all about, Miss Mona?" asked Tallulah.

"I haven't felt like this since I was with my first husband thirty years ago, when he was still alive," said Mona.

"Aww, sweetie, you have finally opened your heart—and its sweet," said Tallulah.

"You should just enjoy whatever feelings you're having," said Tallulah.

"Before Eden begins to sing again, did everyone get a marshmallow to roast?" asked Belle.

"Oh, Wanda, you didn't get one!" said Belle, who felt horrible.

"Do you want me to make you one?" asked Eloise.

"No, thank you. I am a diabetic. I shouldn't have them," said Wanda. "But thank you for offering."

"You're welcome," said Eloise.

"Wanda leaned over to Agnes and whispers in her ear that she must watch her girlish figure.

Agnes giggled. "Mine left years ago—and now I have junk in my trunk."

"My last song for tonight is 'Kumbaya,'" said Eden before she started singing.

Everyone joined her in singing, holding hands. Eden sang very loud, and everyone clapped at the fantastic job she did.

CHAPTER 6

Blowouts, Magazines, and Buzzes

The night was finally over, and everyone returned to their cabins unharmed, full of pizza and marshmallows, and very tired. The counselors felt the same way, and turned in early once the seniors were all in bed. It had been a long first day for everyone.

In the middle of the night, Edith awoke in pain and wasn't sure what was going on. She had never felt the pain before, so she was concerned. So she went to the bathhouse up on the hill, so that she wouldn't wake anyone up.

"Whoever thought of putting a bathhouse on a hill was crazy," said Wanda.

Nurse Juniper was coming back from the campfire when she heard noises coming from the bathhouse.

"Hello, who's in here?" She was worried with what she was going to find.

"It's me, Edith! I am in so much pain. It hurts so bad!" said Edith, holding her stomach.

"Are you OK?" asked Nurse Juniper, looking in the bathroom stalls for Edith.

"I must really have to shit really badly—or maybe it's my insides about to burst, I don't know," said Edith.

" OK, Edith, I am here to help you. So, can I come in the stall with you?"

"No, I am fine. I can try figure it out myself, so you can go," said Edith.

"Let me come in there with you, just to make sure you're OK. I can examine you so we can figure out what is going on," said Nurse Juniper.

"OK, fine you can come in," said Edith.

Nurse Juniper shut the door behind her in the stall so Edith and her could have privacy. Edith was grunting, grabbing her stomach.

"Are you OK, Edith?" she asked. "Let me ask you this—did you have to many marshmallows tonight?"

"No, I had only had a slice of pizza and a little pasta salad, and I was fine," said Edith.

Nurse Juniper saw the pain in Edith's face as she continued to examine her, listening to her grunt. She began leaning over in pain, and Nurse Juniper tried to hold her up so she didn't fall off the toilet.

"When was the last time you had a bowel movement?"

"I don't remember—maybe a few days!"

"So, I'm guessing the problem is you really need to have a bowel movement, since you can't remember the last time you went," said Nurse Juniper.

"Just can't get the shit out," cried Edith.

"I really need you to stay calm, and everything will be OK. I am going to help you. All I need you to do is to trust me," said Nurse Juniper.

"Can you just make me shit?!"

"Can I try to give you an enema?"

"No way, Jose! I am *not* doing that!!" said Edith, still pushing and grunting.

"I can give you Milk of Magnesia or MiraLAX," said Nurse Juniper.

"I don't care! Just give me something!" said Edith. "Do you have any prunes?"

"No, I am afraid not sweetie."

Camp Funhouse

"What the hell kind of place doesn't have prunes?!"

"A summer camp for seniors like yourself, that's what!" said Nurse Juniper. "OK, sweetie, I need you to stay here. I'll get you something that will make you go." She closes the bathroom stall door behind her. *Where does she think I'm going to go?*

Nurse Juniper ran to her office and made up a cup of MiraLAX, for Edith.

Belle was looking out the window when she saw her rushing around, and decided to make sure everything was OK.

"Nurse Juniper, is everything OK?"

"Yes. I just need to help one of the senior's shit—or poop—whatever you want to call it," said Nurse Juniper.

"Do you need any assistance?" asked Belle.

"Yes, I do—but I don't want to make the senior more embarrassed than she already is. But thanks for asking," said Nurse Juniper on her way to the bathhouse.

On her way back, Nurse Juniper could hear Edith screaming.

"Relax, Edith, I'm back now. Try to breathe for me," said Nurse Juniper. She handed Edith the cup of MiraLAX and told her to drink it all.

"What hell is going on here?" asked Tinsley.

"Why are you here Tinsley?" asked Nurse Juniper.

"I could hear her screaming all the way down the hill, in my cabin," said Tinsley.

"Edith will be fine. She's just having problems with constipation," said Nurse Juniper

"Oh my God, this is so embarrassing," said Edith.

"Don't worry—no one will know you're pooping on the potty," said Tinsley.

"What is this, kindergarten? No one said potty anymore!" Edith tried to shit again.

"We are going to help you," said Nurse Juniper. "You're going to help me right, Tinsley?"

"Yes, of course. I'm here for you," said Tinsley, grabbing Edith's hand.

"Oh my God, I am in trouble," said Edith.

"When I count to three, I want you to push as hard as you can," said Nurse Juniper.

"You make it sound like I am about to have a baby," said Edith.

"Well, that's not happening, obviously," laughed Tinsley.

"I don't want to do this! Get me off the damn toilet now!!" screamed Edith.

"Edith, trust me—it's the only way. Unless you want me to put Vaseline on my finger and put it up your ass to try to get it out," said Nurse Juniper.

"No, we can do it your way. You're not sticking your finger up my ass."

"That's what I thought," said Nurse Juniper. "Here we go, Edith. One, two, three, push!"

Edith grunted hard, and then there was a big plop in the toilet.

"Excellent job, Edith," said Nurse Juniper.

"Ewe, which was so gross," said Tinsley plugging her nose. Nurse Juniper gave Tinsley a dirty look after she make that comment. "Do you feel you have to go again?" asked Nurse Juniper

"Oh my God, no, I feel so much better," said Edith.

"Ugh! It stinks so bad," said Tinsley.

"I'm sure your shit doesn't smell like roses, either, Miss Gum-in-Her-Hair," said Edith

"What about gum in my hair?" asked Tinsley.

Edith ignored her as she kept talking to Nurse Juniper.

"Never had that problem before," said Edith.

"It can happen at any time Edith, and I think I am going to make a note and call Heaven's Ridge to let them know what happened, just so they're aware of it," said Nurse Juniper.

"Thank you so much for helping me. I don't mind you calling them and letting them know what happened," said Edith.

"You're welcome, Edith. I am here anytime if you need me."

"Tinsley would you mind cleaning her up for me?" asked Nurse Juniper.

"Sure, no problem. I would be more than happy to help."

"I am fine with it, too, but I do have one question," said Edith.

"Sure, ask me anything—I'm an open book," said Tinsley.

"What happened to your hair?" asked Edith.

"Why asking me about my hair again?"

"You do realize you've had gum in your hair all day?" asked Nurse Juniper.

"Are you fucking serious?" asked Tinsley as she checked her hair in the mirror.

"It's been there all day. Sorry—I thought you knew," said Nurse Juniper.

"Besides Edith and a few other seniors, I really didn't give it much thought, because I thought they were just going senile," said Tinsley.

"It grows out after a while, and it'll just be one big knot once the gum hardens," said Edith as Tinsley reached for a comb and trying to comb it the best she could.

"It's fine. You're just going to sleep on it anyways," said Edith, who couldn't stop laughing.

"OK, Edith, are you ready to go back to the cabin?" asked Tinsley.

"Yes, I am, I guess, since I am not full of shit anymore." Edith laughed. "What a mess we left!"

If you're feeling better, that's all that matters," said Tinsley.

"Who's going to unplug the toilet?"

"Don't worry, we got a maintenance guy," said Tinsley.

"Oh, yes—Mr. Cutie Pie," said Edith.

" I better call Casper and let him know," said Nurse Juniper. "We wouldn't want anyone to have any surprises tomorrow morning." She picked up her phone and dialed.

"You just happen to have his number in your phone?" asked Tinsley.

"I have all your numbers, just in case I need to get a hold of you for any reason."

"I don't remember giving you my number! But that's OK—I'll just go with what you're telling me," said Tinsley.

"Well, look at the time! It's time for me to go to bed," said Edith, taking off down the hill.

"I guess I'd better go after Edith before she gets lost or something," said Tinsley as she went down after Edith.

Nurse Juniper looked around to see if anyone else was around.

"Hey. Casper, it's Juniper. Sorry to wake you up," said Nurse Juniper, looking at the time on her watch.

"Don't worry, I was awake anyways. And I was just lying here thinking about you," said Casper. "I'm glad you called."

"I just wanted to let you know one of the toilets in bathroom is clogged up badly because someone had an accident," said Nurse Juniper. "When you get a chance, could you fix it?"

"Yes, sure I can check it out now so it's ready to go in the morning," said Casper.

"Thank you very much—and so sorry for waking you up," said Nurse Juniper, biting her lip.

"No problem. Like I said, I was already awake. Maybe next time, you could join me for a nightcap."

Nurse Juniper was very tempted by this offer, and could feel her face getting hot.

"Not sure that's a clever idea right now. But thank you for asking—and again for fixing the toilet." She hung up the phone before he could say any more.

"Who would have thought shitting could take so much out of you?" Edith giggled.

Tinsley laughed as they walked into Edith's cabin together. Serena just happened to be up when Tinsley and Edith came back in.

"So, I heard that you had a long night, Edith?" she asked.

"If you must know, it was a very shitty situation. And if I was you, I wouldn't go in the bathhouse until it's safe," laughed Edith.

"Well, OK, good talk—and thank you for the warning."

"You're welcome," said Edith. She said goodnight to Tinsley.

"Goodnight to you, too," said Tinsley.

"What are you doing up so late?" asked Serena.

"I was just reading," said Ethel, snippy. Ethel liked to get all the attention, and got upset when she didn't. Sometimes, she'd throw a fit. She could also be nosy at times.

"It's time to go to bed now. It's late," said Serena.

"OK, no problem. I'll go to bed."

Ethel quickly said goodnight. Serena saw Ethel putting a magazine under her pillow, which she thought was very suspicious. Serena also thought the way Ethel was acting was odd, but she was tired, so she decided to stop thinking about it until the next day. Serena walked away, but heard another noise from Ethel, so went back to see what she was up to.

"Now what are you doing?" asked Serena. Ethel was looking down at the floor and wasn't sure what to say. Serena looked down at the floor to see what she was looking at and couldn't believe her eyes. Serena bent over and picked the magazine off the floor. Ethel was getting antsy because she knew she had been busted.

"Is this yours?" asked Serena.

"Yes, it is. So what?" said Ethel, getting snotty with Serena.

"Why do you have a Playboy magazine in your bed?" asked Serena.

"It's my business. I don't have to tell you if I don't want to. It's a free world," said Ethel, putting the covers over her head.

"OK, fine. I'll just take it and show Belle tomorrow," said Serena as she walked away

"No, don't!! It's not mine—I just borrowed it," said Ethel.

"I have no choice. I have to bring it to Belle. You shouldn't have this kind of stuff at camp—and you said it wasn't yours," said Serena.

Ethel started to cry because she wasn't getting her way.

"I'm sorry, Ethel, these are the rules," said Serena, who almost felt bad that she took it away.

"It's not fair!" said Ethel.

"Don't worry, I'm sure you'll get it back after camp is over. Just relax," said Serena

"Yeah, sure, if you say so. But you don't know it's a free world when it comes to having magazines," said Ethel who wasn't going to give it up.

"You're right it's a free world. But you're not back at the retirement home—you're at camp, and here, we have certain rules we need to follow."

"I don't care. Do whatever you want!" Ethel pouted with the covers over her head.

Serena walked by Tallulah's bed.

"Hey Serena, it's OK. You're doing the right thing about Ethel," said Tallulah.

"Why is that?" asked Serena.

"Ethel is always in trouble. She never gets what she wants, so pouts and then, the next day, it's done and over with, and she is fine," said Tallulah.

"Well, thank you, Tallulah, for letting me know. That does help a little bit," said Serena. "Goodnight, Tallulah. I will see you in the morning."

"You're welcome. Goodnight, Serena," said Tallulah as she laughed about Ethel to herself.

Everyone in the cabins were fast asleep.

Except in Fay's cabin.

Wanda woke up when she heard a bizarre buzzing noise.

"What the hell is that noise?"

"I don't hear a damn thing, so shut up—I am trying to sleep," said Vera.

Wanda tried to go back to sleep, but couldn't, because she could still hear the annoying buzzing noise.

"I can't sleep," said Wanda as she sat up in bed, trying to figure out where it was coming from.

Fay gets out of bed and went to Wanda. "What's going on?"

"I keep hearing a buzzing noise, and it's not going away?" said Wanda.

Fay tried to figure out what the noise was. "Ha, I hear it!" She looked who had the suitcase, and of course it was Vera.

"Oh no, it's the cranky, evil one you don't want to mess with," said Wanda.

"Hey Vera," said Fay as she shook her a little to awake her, even know she already was awake. Vera opened her eyes to see who was bugging her.

"What the hell do you want?"

"Can you please open your suitcase?"

"I don't have to do nothing. It's my business not yours."

"Now what's your plan?" asked Wanda, who was still hiding behind Fay.

"Leave me the hell alone," said Vera, holding onto the suitcase so no one could get a hold of it.

"Come on, Vera, open the suitcase. Or I'll be happy to do it for you," said Fay.

"Oh no you will *not*," said Vera.

"Then please, open it, like a good girl," replied Fay.

"I'm not a child, so don't speak to me like that," said Vera.

"Come on, Vera, it's late, and everyone is tired of hearing the buzzing," said Fay.

"No, I am not going to," said Vera.

"I'm going to have to call Belle and see what she says, since she won't give it to me," said Fay.

"Hi, Belle, it's Fay. Sorry to call you so late, but we have a little situation here in the cabin. We have a suitcase that has a loud buzzing sound coming from it."

Fay hung up the phone.

"Do you think that she will be able to reason with Vera?" asked Wanda.

"You know her better than I do," said Fay, looking at Wanda "I honestly think your screwed, but we will wait and see."

"Belle is coming over to talk to you, Vera," said Fay.

"Pin a rose on your nose I am still not going to open it, no matter who is there," said Vera.

Wanda decided since she was awake, she would sit on the edge of the bed and wait to see what the mysterious buzzing was. She loved all this action and excitement. She wondered if she should wake up Agnes and Mona, so they didn't miss out.

There was a knock at the door.

Fay opened the tarp for Belle.

"Sorry again that I had to call you," said Fay.

"It's OK. I was awake anyways," said Belle.

"First-night jitters, I guess you could call them," said Fay.

"So, what seems to be the problem?" asked Belle.

"Vera has something buzzing in her suitcase and is refusing to open it," said Fay, rubbing her eyes because she was tired.

"That's right! No one's going to touch my stuff!" said Vera.

"How about we open it up, and I promise to not take anything out unless it's the cause of the buzzing? You can watch me to make sure your stuff is untouched," said Belle.

"Fine. But I will unzip it myself, because it's my suitcase," said Vera.

Belle and Fay stepped back and let Vera open her suitcase herself. She unzipped it and flipped open the top.

Belle lifted a folded T-shirt and could not believe what she saw underneath.

"Is that a vibrator?!" asked Fay, looking over Belle's shoulder.

"You are right," said Belle. She took it out of Vera's suitcase very discreetly so she would not get mad. Belle hit the off button and looked at her.

"Is there a reason you brought this with you?" asked Belle.

"Do I really have to explain that, or are you too dumb to figure it out yourself?" asked Vera.

"I know what it's for," said Belle feeling a little uncomfortable. "Is that why you brought it with you—because you were horny?" She didn't even want to know the answer.

"No, I brought it with me so no one would steal my stuff!" said Vera.

"OK, no problem. I get it," said Belle.

"I don't care what you do with it—that's personal, not my business. And also, something I don't want to have nightmares about," said Fay, trying not to laugh about the whole thing.

"You know what? Just take the damn vibrator!" said Vera. "I don't even use it anyways."

"You just said you didn't want anyone taking it," Belle said.

"I didn't use it. I found it at the retirement home in someone's room," said Vera.

"Wow! This happens in retirement homes?!" asked Fay.

"Will you stop?" asked Belle. "You're not making this better!"

"Sorry, Belle. I won't say anything more about it," said Fay as she went back to her bed.

"If you're sure, you don't need it. I'll take it with me."

"No, I don't. Just get out of here," said Vera. "Vera, you can have it back at the end of the week," said Belle.

"Throw it the hell out if you want, I don't care," said Vera.

"We won't do that I can assure that, Belle continued. "I will see you both tomorrows," said Belle on the way out of the door.

Have a good night, Belle and sorry again for calling you," said Fay.

"Fay, can you come out here for second?" asked Belle.

"Oh my God! So shocked that we found that," said Fay as she followed her outside.

"I can't believe she had that in her suitcase." Belle didn't know what else to say about it.

"That just blows my mind," said Fay, still chuckling about it.

62   April Carter

Belle couldn't hold it in any longer and burst out laughing, too. "Well, I guess everyone has special needs."

"What are you going to do with the vibrator? I'm just wondering," said Fay.

"Probably just stick it in a Ziploc bag with her name on it and leave it in a drawer like I told her. So when she leaves, I can return it to her," said Belle, still giggling.

"Goodnight, Fay," said Belle as she started walking away.

"Have a good night," said Fay. *What a night it has been!* Fay said to herself before going back inside.

Belle headed back to the main house, still laughing about the situation. She stopped and looked up at the sky one more time to see the stars. She went in the main house and found Harlow watching television, wrapped up in a blanket on the couch.

"So, what was the big emergency?" asked Harlow.

"It was a suspicious buzzing in a suitcase," said Belle.

"Oh, really? Did you figure out what it was?" asked Harlow.

"Well, I guess you can say we did," said Belle, who took the vibrator out and showed Harlow.

"Are you flipping kidding me, Belle?" asked Harlow, trying not to laugh.

"Yeah—and you'll never guess who had it," said Belle.

"Oh my God. You need to tell me who, Belle," said Harlow.

"It seems there is a senior who had one of these at the retirement home, and somehow Vera found it and brought it to camp with her," said Belle.

"Oh my! I am speechless," said Harlow.

"I find it incredibly hard to believe that *you're* speechless," chuckled Belle.

"I have to say, these seniors are remarkably interesting. I am glad we did this," said Harlow.

"Oh, really? I am amazed to hear that," said Belle sarcastically.

"You know I was never against it.. I just wasn't sure how it would come together, and it has come together so great, and I am so glad we are both here," said Harlow.

"You're super-impressive, and I'm glad we did this—even with the minor hiccup we had tonight," said Belle. "Tomorrow is coming quick, so I am going to bed."

"Goodnight, Belle," said Harlow.

"Same to you, Harlow."

Belle laid in bed, and she was so glad she made it through the first day. But for some reason, she couldn't sleep—and she had no idea what it was.

It has been a strange, wonderful, and stressful day all in one, but finding the vibrator take the cake.

In her mind, she had been waiting for this day to prove herself—and show she could do this job. Having the seniors here had always been something she has been wanting to do. Seniors are people too, and they needed a little fun in their lives.

And Belle new this was the place it should happen.

Well, tomorrow is another day.

CHAPTER 7

Breakfast of Champions

"Good morning, seniors it's 7 a.m. Time to wipe the sleep out your eyes and make it up to the dining hall for the fantastic breakfast buffet waiting for you, with three types of eggs, bacon, sausage, fresh fruit, and so much more," said Belle on the loudspeaker.

"It's probably pizza like last night. I am not complaining," said Mona.

"Do you think they're just saying that to get us up there for breakfast?" asked Agnes.

"It smells like bacon to me," said Wanda as she sped around Agnes and headed out of the cabin.

"Yes, I know you love food and will eat anything," laughed Agnes.

"I don't just *like food*. I *love* my bacon," said Wanda as she came back into the cabin to see if anyone else was coming.

"We know. We've seen you eat," laughed Mona.

"Where's the beef?" yelled Wanda as she charged up the hill.

"She's going to turn into a piece of bacon because of all the bacon she eats," said Mona

"How can you turn into a piece of bacon if you eat too much of it?" asked Agnes.

"I was trying to be polite and not call her a *pig*," said Mona.

"Knock, knock, knock! Is everyone up and ready for breakfast?" asked Belle. "Oh, good morning, Mona, how are you doing today?"

"I'm fine and dandy. It's a beautiful morning here at Mystic. So peaceful, I slept like rock," said Mona.

"That is great to hear, Mona. I hope your stay here this week will be like that every day," said Belle.

"It would be so nice if it was," said Mona.

"Hi Eloise, Fay, Penny, and Tinsley. Everything seems to be going good so far," said Belle.

"Yes, things are shipshape," said Fay perkily.

Belle looked at Tinsley and wondered to herself if she should ask what had happened to her hair. She decided not to say a word.

"I'm so glad to hear that, girls. I will be seeing you all at breakfast. It looks like a great buffet," said Belle as she went out the door.

"How is she so chipper this early in the morning?" asked Mona.

"Well, you're chipper yourself," said Agnes. "Should we go and meet the girls?"

They all agreed.

By the time they got to the dining hall, everyone was sitting down, enjoying each other's company laughing, and having a good morning. The buffet Frankie had made was wonderful, with a lot of variety of food—that he hadn't dropped this time.

"I'm guessing that he is trying to redeem himself for last night's fiasco?" asked Belle.

"I guess so. And he sure outdid it," said Harlow.

"So, how do you like it?" asked a voice behind them. Belle turned around and realized it was Frankie.

"You did a wonderful job Frankie," said Belle, "and everyone loves the food you made."

"Thank you, Belle. I am really glad everyone enjoyed it."

"I know I have told you this a million times, but I really think you should start your own catering business," said Belle.

"Then, I could make a million," laughed Frankie.

"You need to do some serious thinking about this, Frankie. You're good at it—when you're not distracted by something," said Belle.

"Thank you. I appreciate you saying that to me, Belle. I just don't make enough to make that dream come true at this moment," said Frankie.

"I do appreciate everything you do here, even if I don't always show it," said Belle.

"Do you want to show me how much I am appreciated?" asked Frankie.

"Whoa, cowboy, hold your horses there," said Belle as she put her hand against his chest to hold him back. "We are going to be adults about this, and not take it any further like we did back in high school—is that clear?"

"I don't agree," said Frankie, getting closer to Belle again.

"Well, I'm not going to be changing my mind anytime soon. Sorry, Frankie," said Belle as she walked away and winked. Frankie watched her walk away, and loved the way she walked.

"She still has a great ass," said Frankie.

Mona and Agnes finally got to the dining hall for breakfast, and they realized they weren't that late, like they had thought.

"Hey, Mona and Agnes, come sit with us," said Wanda as she waved her hand.

"Good morning girls how are all of you doing today?" asked Serena as she sat in the chair next to the seniors, trying to strike up a conversation to get to know them.

"I'm doing good. I slept well here. It was so quiet and peaceful," said Mona.

"The only noise I heard was Wanda snoring," said Agnes.

"How are you doing today, Vera?" asked Serena.

"I am fine, and you can go and mind you on damn business," said Vera.

"OK, so I am guessing she woke up on the wrong side of the bed this morning," said Serena, shaking her head.

Maybe Vera is just pissed off that her vibrator, was gone, Serena thought to herself, because Fay had told her all about it.

"No, that's normal for Vera," said Agnes.

"Where is the beef this morning?" asked Wanda again.

"It is coming Wanda just relax," said Mona.

"Wanda acts like we are going to have a bacon or beef shortage," laughed Agnes.

Everyone looked at Agnes after she said that.

"Yeah, the bacon is here," said Wanda.

"Oh, nice, now we don't have to keep hearing about it," said Agnes.

"The bacon is so crispy and greasy, I'm in heaven! So yummy," said Wanda, enjoying every little piece.

"OK, so I will get the bacon," said Mona as she chuckled.

"Yes, you should," said Wanda as she put another piece in her mouth.

"So, how did everyone sleep last night?" asked Agnes.

"I had to shit bad," said Edith with a serious face.

"Oh wow, sorry to hear that," said Agnes, trying and to hold down her food—and not to laugh.

"I hate when that happens. It can happen at any moment!" said Tallulah.

"Do you feel better now?" asked Mona.

"Yes, I do. So much better. That was so horrible," said Edith as she stuffed her mouth with scrambled eggs.

"Would you compare it to giving birth?" asked Wanda.

"How exactly do you mean?" asked Mona as they all look at Wanda, wondering where she was going with this topic.

"Well, when it's time to push, it can come quickly, and before you know it, you hear it go *plop* in the toilet," said Edith.

Everyone just stopped and looked at her.

"I hope when you give birth you would not just let your baby plop down anywhere, unless someone was there to catch it," said Tallulah.

"No, I was talking about shitting last night," said Edith.

"I was born in a barn," said Edith.

"I was, too. It was quite the traumatic experience for my mother, but she got two great kids," said Tallulah.

"That is great, Tallulah. I never could have kids. It was just me and my husband—and forty years of marriage, and him always working," said Agnes.

"Unfortunately, my son has decided to not be a part of my life anymore, because he thinks I am too crazy," said Tallulah sadly.

"Are you crazy?" asked Agnes.

"Where would he get that from?" asked Mona sarcastically.

"Not funny! I am not crazy," said Tallulah.

"What did you do to make him think that?" asked Agnes

"I accidently hit on one of his friends when he was young," said Tallulah, not proud.

"I'm sorry to hear that, Tallulah. Maybe things will change, and he will come around," said Wanda.

"It's been twenty years. If he were coming back, he would have by now. He probably has family and kids," said Tallulah.

"Yeah, you might have grandkids," said Wanda, still eating her bacon.

"I guess I will never see them," said Tallulah sadly.

Mona sat there with a confused look on her face.

"What is wrong with you?" asked Agnes.

"I'm so confused," said Mona.

"Why, Mona?" asked Tallulah.

"Well, one second, we are talking about Edith's shitting problem, and then we go on to the topic of giving birth," said Mona.

"Well, maybe you need to try and keep up," said Agnes.

"Well, aren't you sweet as pie this morning?" said Mona.

"OK, you two, cool it—we're trying to have a nice breakfast. We don't need both of you squawking," said Edith.

"You're right, Edith," said Mona.

"The cutie maintenance guy was unclogging the toilet this early morning," said Mona.

"Well, that sounds remarkably interesting, I am glad I didn't use that toilet," said Agnes.

"I'm glad that Tinsley was there with me. I mean, she doesn't look so bright with the way her hair is, but she was nice to me, and there for me," said Wanda.

"Well, isn't that sweet of her? Anyone else got something to share this morning?" asked Agnes, who thought it was time to get off that subject of shitting.

"Got my vibrator taken away from me last night," said Vera.

"Did she just say she has a *vibrator*?" asked Tallulah.

Wanda spit her milk all over Agnes. Serena started choking on her bacon.

"Are you OK, Serena, or do I need to do mouth-to-mouth?" asked Tallulah.

"No, no, I'm fine. It just went down the wrong pipe," said Serena.

"So, did I hear that right or not?" asked Tallulah.

"Yes, Tallulah, for the love of God! She said vibrator," yelled Agnes.

Everyone stared at her.

"I don't think my hearing aid is working right," said Wanda.

Agnes shook her head.

"Can you repeat that, Vera?" asked Wanda.

"Yes, I had a vibrator, and it got taken away. So now, shut up!" yelled Vera.

"That's what I thought I heard her say," said Wanda to Agnes. "And I can hear finally."

"Why did it get taken away?" asked Tallulah.

"None of your damn business," said Vera.

"You tell us you have a vibrator here, then you say it's not our business why you got it taken away?" asked Wanda.

"We are just trying to figure you out, Vera," said Mona.

"You are a very strange bird, Vera."

"You are a nosy person," said Vera snottily back to Wanda.

"Not nosy—you started the whole conversation!" said Wanda, shaking her head.

"Where did you get the vibrator?" asked Tallulah, suspicious.

"Never mind. She won't tell us," said Wanda.

"Why would someone need a vibrator anyways? I personally loved to do sixty-nine. That was always my husband's favorite number and position," said Tallulah.

"Wow, OK. It's time for me to go. I will see you girls later," said Serena as she got up quickly.

Serena saw Iggy and thought that was the best way to get out of the dining hall quickly. Serena yelled to Iggy to get her attention.

"Hey! You ready to go to that thing we said we were going to?" asked Serena.

"I don't remember what thing you're talking about," said Iggy, very confused.

"I'll go anywhere," said Eden, shouting to Serena and Iggy. Serena just shook her head and went out the door, yelling for them to come on.

"Wait, I'm coming, Serena!" said Iggy going after her.

"I'm coming too," yelled Eden, "and I don't know why!"

"Seriously, Tallulah, you don't know what a vibrator does?" asked Wanda.

Everyone stared at Tallulah.

"Yes, I do know what one is! I never said I didn't! But I loved to be more hands-on with my husband, if you know what I mean," said Tallulah, grinning and turning red.

"Are you OK, Blanche?" asked Agnes. "You look like you just saw a ghost!"

"I am fine. I am just trying to absorb all the information about Wanda shitting everywhere and Vera having a vibrator," laughed Blanche. Everything was finally clicking in her head.

"Can we drop this conversation now?" asked Agnes.

"No, we can't, because I still have one question," said Wanda.

"Fine. Wanda, ask your question, so we can move on," said Agnes.

Wanda started shouting at the top of her lungs: "How is Vera's vibrator more important than Edith shitting on the toilet?!"

Everyone in the dining room stared at the table. Agnes slid down in her chair so no one could see her.

"Great. Now everyone is staring at us," said Mona.

"Wonderful job, Tallulah," said Agnes.

"What did I do?" asked Tallulah.

"You're the one that started talking about it in the first place!" said Agnes.

"No! That wasn't me! That was all Vera and Edith," said Tallulah, who wasn't going to get blamed for something that she *hadn't* done for once.

"That was all Vera not Tallulah. So she isn't the one who needs to get off the damn vibrator," said Edith.

"Oh, why did you have to go there?" asked Agnes.

"I can't believe you just went there," said Vera.

"What did you expect us to say?" asked Tallulah.

"I don't know. Just leave me alone," said Vera.

"Vera is not the innocent one," said Agnes.

Vera finally got up from the table.

"I'm out of here, you bunch of jerks," said Vera as she stormed out of the dining room as fast as her legs would go. Everyone started to laugh as she left the breakfast table.

"She can't take a joke," said Tallulah.

"She doesn't have our sense of humor, I guess," said Mona.

"That is so true, Mona," said Wanda.

"Well, we cleared out the whole dining hall, so I guess it's our turn to leave," said Agnes.

"Yeah, I guess you're right, Agnes. Plus, I am sure it's time for whatever fun they might have in store for us," said Wanda.

"It's really exciting here so far!" said Tallulah. "And I just wanted to say I am so glad that we all came here together."

"I know I didn't want to come at first, but this place is honestly not that bad," said Agnes. "It's time to let Mystic Camp show us what it has in store for us."

"Maybe we can show *it* what *we* have in store," laughed Tallulah.

"Very true. They have no idea who we are and the chaos we can create," said Edith.

"Let the fun begin!"

They all went out of the dining hall together.

Belle went back to the dining hall to see if Frankie needed any help cleaning up breakfast.

"Do you need help, Frankie?" asked Belle as she went in the kitchen.

"If you want to help me, please, be my guest! Unless you're just here because you just can't resist me, and want a piece of me," laughed Frankie.

"I *can* resist you, so it will be no problem. And since it looks like you don't really need my help, I will go back to the office and get ready for the activities," said Belle, dropping a dish towel on the floor.

"Don't worry, sugar, you will be mine again. Whether you know it or not." Frankie started cleaning up what was left in the dining room. "One day that woman is going to figure out what she is missing and come crawling back to me."

"Who's going to be crawling back?" asked Tory, standing behind Frankie.

Frankie stood there, stunned, turning around slowly.

"Hey, babe. How are things with you this beautiful morning?" asked Frankie, giving Tory a little smooch on the cheek.

"I just thought I would come and say good morning, and tell you how much I missed you since last night," whispered Tory in Frankie's ear.

Frankie grabbed her in his arms and gave her a long, enthusiastic kiss, leaning her against the table.

Tallulah sneaked in to use the bathroom, because she didn't want to go into the bathhouse. She stood behind the bathroom door so no one could hear her, and watched Frankie and Tory make out. She was amazed at what she was seeing.

Tory wrapped her arms and legs around Frankie tight and looked into his eyes. "When do you think we can get together again?"

"Didn't you have fun last night after the campfire?" asked Frankie.

"Yes, I did—and that's why I want more of you right now."

Frankie lifted her head up and looked into her eyes. "How about later tonight, when everyone is sleeping?"

"Why don't we meet down by the beach and take a little skinny dip?" asked Tory, continuing to kiss Frankie.

"Sounds good." Tory kissed him again before going down to the pool.

"Bye, babe," said Frankie.

Tory waved and blew him a kiss as she went out the door.

Frankie decided it was time to go back to the kitchen and prep for lunch.

Tallulah peeked around the corner of the bathroom to make sure the coast was clear.

Wow, Frankie was making out with the lifeguard. She was in shock, wondering what she could do with what she just witnessed. *So, this is what they do when we aren't around. I think for now I will just keep it to myself and see what else comes to me.*

Tallulah went out the door, shutting it quietly so that Frankie wouldn't know she had been watching through the bathroom door.

To think, I wasn't going to come! Boy, I am so glad Hilda convinced me to do it. This week is going to be so much fun. She danced down the hill to her cabin.

CHAPTER 8

First-Day Shenanigans

Siena announced that arts and crafts was in ten minutes, going to each cabin to let everyone know.

"Wow! She is perky this morning," said Ethel.

"Maybe she took perky pills—like Miles and his bottle of Viagra," laughed Edith.

"They all seem to be very perky here at camp," said Blanche.

"Kids today. You never know what they might do," said Tallulah, thinking about what she had seen happen in the dining hall between Frankie and the little lifeguard.

"Well, we better go now, before we are greeted by the perky one again. We don't want that!" said Tallulah.

"Oh no, anything but that," laughed Ethel who didn't normally make jokes.

"What is taking you so long, Ethel?" asked Blanche, waiting for her.

"I'm coming! I'll be there soon. Go ahead without me. I'm right behind you."

"OK, Ethel, we'll see you there," said Edith.

Ethel looked around to see if anyone else was around, then she went to Serena's bed and found the magazine under it. She went back to her bed and put it in her suitcase so no one would know she had it.

OK, I am all good now. Off Ethel went to arts and crafts.

"Good morning, everyone. How are we doing today?" asked Siena. Everyone was talking in their low voices, not listening to what she was saying.

"OK, so today, I thought we would make a colorful sailboat, since it's summertime," said Siena, talking over everyone.

"Wow, really, it's summer? I didn't even know notice," said Vera sarcastically.

"Anyways . . . we have all this colorful construction paper, straws, paint . . ." said Siena, "so you can just pick what color you like, and we can go to the next step—shaping your straws into a sailboat."

Everyone picked the color that they wanted their sailboat to be but Vera.

"Do you want to do a sailboat with us, Vera?" asked Siena.

"No, I don't. Leave me the hell alone."

"OK, well, no problem. You can just sit there and watch everyone else make their sailboats."

Siena loved collaborating with seniors, and was so glad she got to be there that summer. She had had a rough year with the surprising passing of her mother, and the rest of her family in separate places, not as close as they used to be. She had been uncertain if she would be there that summer, because she thought that her father might need her around to help—but he up and left her too. Now that he had, she had only this job to fall back on.

After everyone was finish making their sailboats, Siena got out the paint.

Vera took one of the paintbrushes, dipped it, and flicked the paint so it would hit Agnes and Mona.

"Vera, what the hell are you doing?!" asked Agnes.

"Now my clothes have paint on all over them!" said Mona.

"Oh, so sad, too bad," said Vera, laughing like it was the funniest thing. Mona decided to give Vera a piece of her own medicine, and did the same thing back to her.

"Hey, you bitch! That's it! Paint fight!!!"

Everyone grabbed paint and threw it everywhere.

"Whoa, no!! We can't do this!!" yelled Siena, trying to stop it.

Then, behind her, she heard a voice yell *STOP!*

Everyone froze.

Siena looked to see who it was, and was surprised to see it was Bessie.

"What is going on here?!" she asked.

"Vera decided to throw paint at all of us!" said Wanda.

"Why would you do that, Vera?" Bessie kneeled to look at Vera.

"They are all a bunch of jerks, so I threw the paint at them."

"Well, that wasn't very nice."

"Oh, really? You don't think it's nice?"

Vera took more paint and rubbed it over Bessie's face.

Siena and everyone just stood there in shock.

"Vera, that wasn't nice," said Bessie, standing up.

"I think that it's time for the activity to be over now. And it's time for lunch soon," said Siena.

"Let's go back to your cabins and cleaned up," said Bessie.

All the seniors when back to their cabins.

Siena and Bessie couldn't believe what happened and decided to clean up the mess.

"I can't believe the seniors can make such a big mess just like that," said Bessie.

"I thought seniors were going to sweet and not bringing down the house," said Siena.

"They didn't really bring it down, but definitely painted one," said Bessie.

"What a mess we must pick up."

"I guess really the only way we can get rid of the paint is to maybe take a hose to the pavement and wash it out before it dries."

"I'll go see if the pool has a hose."

"I bet they do, since they have a pool," laughed Bessie, looking funny at Siena.

"Yes, you're right. I am so dumb sometimes," said Siena.

"You are not dumb! You're a great asset to the team here, and I am glad you're on my team."

"Thanks, Bessie, and sorry this got so out of hand so quickly."

"Not your fault at all, Siena. They're crazy seniors wanting to have fun. It's the best way to say it. It was exciting to see them have so much fun at our expense," said Bessie. "Why don't you see if Chip and Tory are at the pool, and get the hose so we can get the paint before it dries?"

"I will be right back."

Siena ran to the pool. She got there and saw Chip, and just stopped and stared at him for a second. *Wow, he's hot.* She went over to him.

"Hey Siena, how are you doing?"

"I'm good. No, I'm great," said Siena, stuttering.

Chip looked at her and shook his head. "Which one is it, Siena?"

"I'm good—definitive answer." Siena felt embarrassed.

"OK, good. What can I do for you?"

"Um, we need your hose," said Siena.

Chip chuckled.

"OK, let me start again. Bessie and I are trying to pick up a paint mess, and we could use your hose to get it off—I mean the paint."

"Oh, I see," said Chip, finding the conversation humorous. "Well, the hose it right over there, and it should reach to where you need it to go," said Chip.

"Thank you, Chip," said Siena as she went and grabbed the hose. "Nice going, Siena—now he thinks I'm an idiot," she said to herself.

"What did you say?" asked Chip, standing behind her.

"I just said I can't believe the seniors made such a mess with the paint," said Siena.

"Would you and Bessie like help with getting the paint off?" asked Chip.

"Sure, we would appreciate it," said Siena, tripping over the hose. "Today is just not my day." She shook her head.

"Are you OK, Siena?" asked Chip, helping her up.

"Yes, I am OK—but my pride is not."

"It's OK, Siena. It happens to everyone—and things with the seniors will get better!"

"You haven't had them yet, so don't get too excited," said Siena.

"Tory and I have them this afternoon for the pool. We'll see what happens."

"Hopefully it's better than what we went through," said Siena as she and Chip headed to the arts and crafts hut. "Good luck and be careful."

"They don't really scare me. Nothing to worry about."

"Look who I found to help us with the paint!" said Siena.

"Well, I volunteered," said Chip.

"That was sweet of you, Chip. I knew you always had a kind heart," said Bessie.

"I'm just that kind of guy," said Chip as Bessie and him looked at each other.

Siena watched them flirt with each other and wished she could flirt like Bessie could.

"Hey, Siena. Are you going to help, or just stare into space?" she asked.

"Help, of course," said Siena, grabbing a rag to clean up the tables.

All the tables were cleared off, and everything was nice and neat in the arts and crafts hut. Bessie took off so she could help get lunch set up, leaving Siena and Chip by themselves.

"Well, we're all set now. Thank you so much for helping us, Chip," said Siena.

"It was no problem. I just wanted to make sure you didn't hurt yourself bringing the hose over." Chip winked.

"Yeah, that was very embarrassing," said Siena, blushing.

"It was my pleasure helping such a pretty girl." He winked at Siena.

"Thank you."

"Keep up the good work, Siena. You're a good egg." Chip left her there, grabbed the hose, and went to the pool.

"I hope so," said Siena to herself, watching him walk away. *Now I am an egg—seriously? Could this day get any better?*

She went back to the cabin, and could hear a lot of noise coming from it. *Oh, boy, I wonder what's going on.* She opened the tarp.

"Siena, I am so happy to see you," said Hazel.

"What is going on here?" asked Siena. "They have been like this ever since they came back from arts and crafts."

"What happened there?" asked Hazel.

"Vera started throwing paint, and before I knew it, they were all throwing paint around," said Siena, showing Hazel every place she had paint on her.

"Yikes! That doesn't sound too fun."

"Bessie was also less then pleased that I let things get so out of control, but it really wasn't my fault," Siena rambled on.

"We need to calm them down or something, before one of them has a heart attack and dies on our watch," said Hazel.

"Well, I think you're being a *little* dramatic . . . but we can't have that happen, no."

"OK. Everyone needs to cut it out right now!!" yelled Hazel.

"I want to know what's going on with you gals!" said Siena.

"Wow—you still have a lot of paint on you," said Tallulah.

"Yes, I am aware of that."

"So, who's going to tell us what's going on?" asked Hazel.

"Nothing! We're just figuring out why we were a target with Vera," said Edith.

"I believe I told you to come back and get cleaned up and here. You're not doing it!" said Siena.

"I honestly don't think you *were* specifically targeted by Vera," said Hazel.

"Have you *met* Vera?" asked Tallulah.

"I don't think I have yet," said Hazel.

"I can give you a hint . . . I'm sure if I say it, you will know her," said Tallulah.

"OK, try me." Hazel sat down on her bed.

"Do you remember the person who mentioned the word *vibrator* at breakfast time?" asked Tallulah.

"Oh, she was the reason Serena needed to leave the dining room so quickly! She told me about that," said Hazel.

"So, we think she's mad because we thought it was funny she had one and wasn't laughing," said Tallulah.

"I don't think it was that—because it's not like you talked about it during the activity," said Siena.

"I guess so, but *something* set her off," said Tallulah.

"She honestly thought throwing paint was fun, and wanted to see if anyone would react. That's when you got involved," said Siena.

"I really wouldn't worry. Things will be fine. They will get better," said Hazel.

"OK, little miss goody two-shoes, you don't know Vera like we do. Once she's upset, she doesn't let things go," said Edith.

"OK, enough about Vera," said Siena. "All of you who have paint on you, please go wash up and get changed before lunch."

Everyone went to the bathhouse—or just changed their clothes in the cabin without moaning and groaning.

It was time for lunch, and none of the seniors really wanted to go, but new they had to.

Tallulah, Edith, Agnes, Mona, and Wanda sat at the same table together, but didn't say much. Agnes wondered why everyone was so quiet and what was going on with them. They had been more talkative at the cabin then they were being then.

"I'm just going to take a stab at this, but what's the reason everyone is quiet?"

"We just don't think it was fair Vera aimed at us," said Tallulah.

"Neither do we, but it was fun—and I can say I'd never been in a paint fight in my life," said Agnes.

"I enjoyed it, too," said Wanda, laughing. Tallulah started laughing, too, and agreed it was fun.

"We got upset for no reason. I guess if you really think about it, it's Vera, and she probably didn't even realize what she was doing it," said Agnes.

"In a way, I think she did know what she was doing, because as soon as she saw that paint she went right after it and started throwing it," said Tallulah.

"We just need to let it go and enjoy ourselves," said Tallulah.

"It's not bad here—at least so far today, since it's our official first day," said Wanda.

"Yes, I agree. Let's rock this place and have the best time," said Edith before they said cheers to being there.

"Let's not forget to have fun—that's the most important thing," said Tallulah.

She saw Chip come in the dining hall and got an idea.

"Does anyone want to play a prank?"

"Sure, I love pranks," said Wanda, all happy about it.

"What kind of prank do you have in mind?" asked Agnes.

"Have you ever heard the prank *hide the clothes*?" asked Tallulah.

"I think my sisters and I used to do that to my brothers, but that was a long time ago," said Agnes.

Everyone comes closer to hear Tallulah's plan.

"Do you honestly think that's going to work?" asked Agnes.

Yes, it's going to work perfectly," said Tallulah.

"What if we get in trouble?" asked Wanda.

"Why would they get mad at innocent seniors?"

"We aren't that innocent," said Agnes.

"True, but they don't know that," said Mona.

"Especially since we are all good-looking for our ages," said Edith.

"That's right, Edith," said Agnes.

"Hey, you all said you wanted fun, and here we are—our chance to have fun," said Tallulah.

"I say let's do it," said Wanda, putting her hand on the table.

"I'm in," said Tallulah, putting her hand on top of Wanda's.

"OK, I can have fun. I'm in, too," said Edith, putting her hand on Tallulah's.

"I'm in, too," said Mona, joining the other hands on the table.

"OK, Agnes. You're next—are you in or out?" asked Tallulah.

"I'm in." Agnes put her hand on top of the rest.

"OK, then let's do it. I already know who our target is going to be," said Tallulah.

"I think we should choose a man, because it would be a lot more fun," said Agnes.

"I know I'm in," said Mona.

"Don't worry. It will be a man," said Tallulah.

All five seniors sat outside the bathhouse and watched to see for their target going in. As they waited, they wondered if it was the right time for any of the employees take their showers.

"Maybe we should come back tonight, because people like taking showers at night," said Agnes.

"Maybe you're right, Agnes," said Tallulah.

"Can I have that written on paper—that I am right?" asked Agnes.

Then, as they were about to wrap up their plan, Tallulah saw Frankie go into the bathhouse with all his shower stuff.

"We found our target, ladies."

"Who?"

"The chef guy—oh what's his name? Frankie, I think?"

"Oh, this is going to be real fun," said Mona.

"Oh boy this is going to be great," said Edith.

"So, who's doing what?" asked Agnes.

"Well, who wants to go into the men's side of the bathhouse?" asked Tallulah.

"I will," said Mona.

"Who'll go with her?" asked Tallulah.

Edith, Wanda, and Agnes stayed quiet.

"Well, then I guess I will."

"Go for it, Tallulah," said Edith.

"Let's hurry, before he comes out, Mona," said Tallulah.

"I'm right behind you," said Mona.

Slowly, they crept into the men's side of the bathhouse.

"Wow. This bathroom is so much bigger than ours," whispered Mona.

"Have you ever been in a men's room before?" asked Tallulah.

"No, I haven't."

"Who's in here?" asked Frankie, looking out from the shower. Tallulah and Mona hid in a corner where he couldn't see them.

"He's going to bust us," whispered Mona.

"No, he won't—don't worry about it," said Tallulah. "There are his clothes."

"What 's that awful noise?" asked Mona.

They both stopped and heard Frankie singing in the shower.

"Oh, my ears hurt," said Tallulah, sticking her fingers in them.

"He must be tone deaf or something, to sing like that," said Mona.

"Let's just grab his clothes and go," said Tallulah.

"That sounds OK to me."

They grabbed his clothes and the towels he was going to use.

"Hurry, Mona—we must go now," said Tallulah.

"Coming," said Mona as she heard the shower stop.

"Oh, crap!" Tallulah said as she tried to free one of his towels that was stuck on a nail. As she pulled, the towel ripped. "Mona, we need to get out of here!"

Tallulah runs outside to the other three women waiting.

"Where's Mona?" asked Agnes.

"She was right behind me!"

All of a sudden, Mona came running out. "He's coming!"

Let's hide his clothes in various places so that he doesn't see us right away," said Tallulah. She passed out his clothes out.

Everyone agreed.

Frankie came out of the shower and tried reaching for a towel before realizing, after opening his eyes and getting all the soap out of them, that his was gone.

"Where the hell did my towel go?!" He began to look for something else to dry off with, and saw that his clothes were gone. "Who took my damn clothes?!"

Oh, crap now what am I going to do? Frankie was starting to panic. He rubbed his fingers through his wet hair as he waited to see if anyone would come. Then he yelled over to the women's side to see if anyone would answer, but no one did.

"Well, I guess the only way I'm going to get clothes is to go commando to my cabin," said Frankie to himself.

"Get ready—I can see him coming!" said Mona.

Frankie peeked around outside to see if anyone was there.

Tallulah put her hand over her mouth. It was funny to see Frankie buck-ass naked.

"Hey, sonny, did you lose something?" asked Wanda as she held up his shirt, waving it around like a flag.

"Give me my damn shirt!" said Frankie, coming after Wanda to get it.

"You've got to catch me first!" Wanda started to run down the hill, throwing Frankie shirt in a tree. "Oh, darn it! The wind took it and put it up the tree!" She laughed.

"Oh man, look what you did!" said Frankie, looking at his shirt in the tree. "I can't climb the tree like this!"

"Oh, Frankie catch me if you can," said Mona as she holds on to his boxers.

"Ew, gross," said Mona as she tossed the boxers.

Frankie decided to run after Mona, but realized his boxers were stuck on the tree limb.

"Give them to me!!" exclaimed Frankie.

"Oh, what's the matter, cupcake? Are you not having any fun?" asked Tallulah.

"No, I am not having fun!" said Frankie.

"What's wrong, Frankie? You can't catch us?" asked Wanda.

"Do you think this funny?" asked Frankie.

"Yes, we do, Frankie!" said Agnes.

"I really thought you were bigger than that," said Tallulah.

"*Yoo-hoo*, sexy, look what I got!!" said Wanda, throwing the rest of Frankie's clothes at Agnes. "Watch out, Agnes, he's coming your way!"

"Ugh!" Frankie shook his head. "This is a nightmare!!"

"Here go your socks!" said Agnes.

"Here go your pants!" said Edith.

"Are you all done now?!" asked Frankie, having watched them throw all his clothes in various places in the trees along with his towel. He decided the only way he was going to get them back was if he climbed the tree naked. The seniors watched him as he began.

"He climbs almost like Tarzan," said Mona.

"I'm thinking more like a monkey," said Agnes.

"So glad you think this is funny!!" yelled Frankie. He climbed up another limb and lost the towel that he had gotten off the one below and wrapped around him.

"*Woo-hoo!* Sexy baby!" said Tallulah.

Frankie could feel his face is getting red. He felt embarrassed.

Tory came up the hill, wondering what the five women were looking at. Then she heard a tree limb starting to break and looked up to see Frankie.

"Oh boy, do I love this view!" said Tory. "Frankie, what the hell are you doing up there?"

"Why don't you ask the fabulous five?! They started it!!" said Frankie.

Tory looked at the innocent faces the five of them were giving her.

"What did you do to Frankie to make him climb the tree?" asked Tory.

"I guess you can call it a senior prank," laughed Tallulah.

"If he falls out of that tree, it'll be your fault," said Tory.

"It's not our fault he's in the tree! He lost his clothes!"

"Did you lose something?" Tory asked Frankie.

"Yes, my mind—to want to climb a tree naked!" he said.

Even though Tory loved the view, she decided to hand Frankie the towel and his boxers.

"Thank you so much Tory," said Frankie as she gave him his shirt and pants.

"You're welcome," she said. "You don't need to explain things—they already told me."

"Sure they did," said Frankie.

He jumped out of the tree. All the seniors were acting like nothing had happened.

"Anything you might want to say to me?" he asked.

"Not that we can think of now—but when we do, we'll let you know," said Tallulah.

The five seniors went down the hill and started laughing.

"Who would have thought I be the lucky person to get their clothes taken by five mischievous seniors?" said Frankie.

"Yeah—and you even gave them a peepshow," laughed Tory. "Sorry, I know it's not funny. But once you've thought about it, you'll laugh, too."

"Thank God you came when you did," said Frankie, finally all dressed.

"I know. I am the greatest," said Tory doing a little dance.

"Yes, you are," said Frankie as they went down the hill together. "I still can't believe that five seniors outsmarted me!"

"Well, look who they were dealing with!" laughed Tory. "I'm just kidding, Frankie. You know I am. Plus, I have seen you naked before."

"Yeah, I know . . . maybe next time, they should take your clothes!" Frankie laughed.

"I don't freaking think so, Frankie," said Tory.

They both laughed on their way to both their cabins.

Frankie went to see how things were going in his.

"Hey, Frankie, what are you doing here?" asked Chip. "I thought you're cooking a masterpiece or something!"

"No, I have time before I need to get dinner all prepped and ready," said Frankie.

"Why are you so chipper?"

"No reason. I'm just a happy kind of guy!" said Frankie.

"You expect me to believe that, the way you're grinning?" asked Chip.

"Can you keep a secret?" asked Frankie.

"You know I can. I'm your buddy."

"I've been sneaking around camp, seeing someone," said Frankie.

Chip looked surprised, and looked at him kind of funny. "Oh, really? And who's the lucky girl?"

"I've been seeing Tory. And I'm also trying to get Belle under my spell," said Frankie, proud of himself.

"So, you're trying to juggle not one girl, but two?"

"Yes, that's right, my man," said Frankie, all happy about it.

"Oh, really? It seems to me that you're trying to turn into a man whore!" said Chip, laughing.

"Damn right I am! I love my women—what can I say?" Frankie laughed.

"Can you just do me a favor, Frankie?" asked Chip.

"Sure, man. What can I do for you?" Frankie smirked at Chip.

"Just save a few women for me!" Chip laughed.

"I'll try! But I can't help that I'm a ladies' man!"

"You are going to get busted somehow. I can just see it now," said Chip.

"There is no feasible way in hell," said Frankie.

"Sure, Romeo." Chip threw a pillow at Frankie.

"Let me ask you this, Chip—is there a girl you'd love to hook up with?"

"No. I guess I'll just let you have them all."

"Seriously—if you could date someone here, who would it be?"

"I honestly don't know. I don't have my eye on anyone right now," said Chip.

"Your lying, I can see right through you."

"Oh, really you can?"

"You have a little twinkle in your eye," said Frankie.

"You are going to have more than a twinkle in your eyes if you don't knock it off!"

"Whoa! Look who's getting testy now!" Frankie laughed at how he could get Chip going. "I'm going to keep teasing you until you tell me!" Frankie laughed, poking Chip.

"Knock it off, Frankie!" Chip was getting angry.

"OK, I will. But one of these days, it's going to come out, my friend."

"No, it won't, because I'm not interested in anyone," said Chip.

"OK, if you say so. I must get going and start prepping for dinner, so I'll catch you later," said Frankie, going out the door.

"I thought he would never stop!" said Chip to himself.

"You do know he's right, don't you?" asked Hank.

"What are you talking about, Hank?"

"I see the sparkle in your eyes, too, so I agree with that guy—whatever his name is."

"Well, for what he's doing, he's just nuts," said Chip.

"I agree with that, too—honestly, dating two women is only going to get you into hot water." said Hank.

"Frankie will get it once they both find out about each other."

"I did that once, when I was around your age, and let me tell you, I got busted so bad, I thought they both were going to butcher my nuts!"

"I could never do that to anyone."

"See, I wasn't so smart. I liked both girls, and invited them to the same place at the same time and, of course, forgot that I did. When they both showed up, I knew I was in so much trouble," said Hank.

"Oh, man. That doesn't sound like a fun time," said Chip.

"When one of them was waiting for me, she got impatient and went looking for me, and saw me talking to the other girl," said Hank.

"Almost like what you see on television," said Chip.

"The funny thing was, before they found out about each other, I had dated them both for about three weeks without either knowing about the other. It was all because I forgot I told them the same damn time," said Hank.

"I'm sorry things didn't work out," said Chip.

"Boy, that's a dream all guys wanted at the time."

"Did you learn your lesson?"

"No. That's why I'm single and have never been married—because I believed the one woman I was actually meant to be with wouldn't take me back after I apologized."

"That truly sucks," said Chip.

"I'm a true ladies' man, but when you're as old as I am and live in a retirement home, you give up your dream of being happy with someone," said Hank. "Well, time for me to see all the ladies in their lovely bathing suits!" He went out the door.

"Now, that's funny," said Chip, thinking about what Hank *said. Well, time for swimming.* Chip got his swimming trunks on and headed to the pool to get ready.

"What's up, my man Miles?" asked Art. "I thought you would be at the pool!"

"You are just the man I'm looking for. I have a question for you, if you don't mind," said Miles.

"Yes, sure. I'll answer anything for you I can."

"When do they get here?" asked Miles.

Art was puzzled when Miles asks that. "Not sure what you're asking, Miles."

Miles got a little closer, turning his head to see if anyone was around to hear. "I am talking about the strippers."

"What strippers?" Art whispered back.

"Well, it's a man's cabin—why wouldn't there be any strippers, sonny? We all need fun occasionally."

Art shook his head in disbelief. "Sorry to burst your bubble, Miles, but there will be no strippers joining us today—or while you're here."

"I better give you these, then, since I won't be needing them," said Miles, opening his bag and throwing his clothes around until he took out a bottle.

"Whoa, Miles! You're making a mess!"

Miles handed the bottle to Art. "Use it yourself."

Art read the bottle and burst out laughing. "I don't need Viagra, but thank you." He gave Miles back the bottle.

"Why not? Are you gay?"

Art burst out laughing. "No, Miles, I am not gay."

"Of course. I was just thinking you look like you really need sex," said Miles.

"Miles, my sex life is not a topic of conversation with you," said Art.

"OK. I just figured since I couldn't use them that I would give them to someone who could have better luck then me."

"You are very generous, but still the answer is no."

"Suit yourself, sonny. But you aren't getting any younger, and these are sure to get you *so* much enjoyment."

"How old do you think I am, Miles?" asked Art.

"In your fifties or something like that," said Miles.

"No way! I'm in my early thirties," said Art.

"Oh wow! You got gray quickly."

"I have a question for you, Miles, if you don't mind," said Art.

"Sure, sonny, what's on your mind?"

"Why aren't you using the Viagra for yourself?"

"I highly doubt the women here would want me, because I tried with a few of them back at Heaven's Ridge—and, nothing. So, that was my cue to stop trying."

"I believe you should never stop trying," said Art.

"I guess you could say I have bad luck. And I'm not that good-looking anymore," said Miles.

"I'm sure there is that one woman who would love to get to know you and see where it goes if you just give it try," said Art.

"Well, sonny, when you get to my age, sometimes, you just want to give up. And that's what I'm doing."

"Well, don't give up! You never know what might happen. You just might hit it big and find that lucky lady."

"You're right. I think I will go out now and see what kind of luck I have," said Miles.

"There you go, Miles! Get them!" said Art. "My name is Art, not sonny, by the way." Art shook his head and laughed, watching Miles.

Chip met Tory at the pool to get things ready for the seniors to swim, since it was going to be so hot out.

"Hi, Tory. Sorry I'm late. I got talking to Frankie," said Chip.

"It's no problem. I came early and cleaned the pool," said Tory. "So, it's all vacuumed, and the PH levels are good. We should be ready to go."

"You did an excellent job, Tory," said Chip.

"Thank you, Chip. At least I'm good for something," said Tory.

"I'm sure there is a lot of things you're good at," said Chip.

"If you asked my mom, she would probably say different," said Tory.

"So, why are you in a chipper mood today?" asked Chip. He wanted to see if Tory would say anything about being with Frankie.

"My parents always said I was a happy baby, but my mother always made it out to be other things," said Tory.

"Well usually you're happy, happy, happy," said Chip.

"I agree with you, but then again, doesn't it make me biased that we're related?"

"Maybe a little bit, but that's OK with me," said Chip.

"Thanks, Chip." Tory punched him in the arm.

"Why did you do that?!"

"We are doing an excellent job of not telling anyone we know each other," said Tory.

"Yeah, it was a clever idea," said Chip.

"I don't think anyone suspects that we are related and are cousins . . . and that we're here to find my mom."

"Do you really think she's here?"

"Yes, I do. I checked with Willa at Heaven's Ridge," said Tory. "Hilda, another aide, convinced your mom to come here at last minute."

"Willa was nice to help us out and find her for me. I hope you know how lucky you are to have a caring girlfriend."

"Yes, Willa is the best. That's why I love her so much."

"I'm curious about something, but I already know the answer," said Chip.

"Sure—you know that you can ask me anything."

"Why don't your parents know about Willa?"

"Well, because I don't think they would accept me as a lesbian," said Tory sadly.

"I'm sorry, Tory. It was a dumb question to ask," said Chip.

"You are the only family I have right now besides Willa, so it's OK to ask," said Tory.

"Will I ever get to meet her sometime?"

"Yes, you will. Besides her, you're the most important person in my life."

"That sweet of you. I'm going to cry," said Chip.

"That's me—sweet as pie. And you're a faker!!" Tory gave Chip a whack on his shoulder.

"How do we know which one she is?" asked Chip.

"We'll figure it out together," said Tory.

"It's been so long since I've seen my mother. I don't know if I will recognize her at all." Chip scratched his head.

"That's one thing I forgot to ask Willa," said Tory.

"It can't be that hard. I'm sure we can figure it out," said Chip.

"True. I mean, there are only nine women here, so it should be easy for us to figure out."

"I just wish I remembered more about her," said Chip.

"Why did you leave your family again? I know you've told me before, but I forget."

"It's OK, I understand," said Chip. "My mom was just very crazy and out of control when my dad passed away. All she wanted was a man to marry so she wouldn't be alone. And she hit on my best friend. I didn't want my father to be replaced by someone else so quickly. My sister was the rock of the family and could deal with it, but I just got tired. So when I got old enough, I emancipated myself. I put myself through school and everything."

"What about your sister?" asked Tory.

"I never turned back, but I did try to stay connected with her. But it was getting too difficult with figuring out when to get a hold of her, so I stopped calling and after high school. I got a job and lived my own life."

"That was very brave of you."

"I just tried to do what was best."

"Well, the seniors will be here soon," said Tory.

"Are we ready?" asked Chip.

"Ready as we'll ever be," said Tory.

Then they heard banging on the gate, and knew exactly what that met. The seniors were finally there to swim. Chip went to the gate and let them in to swim in the pool. Both Tory and Chip went over to the seniors sitting on the bench to get them ready.

"May I help you get your socks and shoes off?" asked Tory.

"Sure. You're such a pretty girl," said Edith.

"Thank you, Edith, that was genuinely nice of you to say," said Tory. "How are you girls doing today?"

"We're fine, because you're sizzling hot, Chip," said Wanda.

"Well, thank you," said Chip, blushing a little.

Tory giggled as she got closer to the pool to feel the water with her foot. "Good afternoon, everyone," she said.

"The perky one is here," said Mona.

"I thought arts and crafts was the perky one," said Agnes.

"I don't know. Everyone's perky around here," said Wanda.

"I don't mean perky like that," said Mona, sticking out her chest.

"Oh, I get it now," said Tallulah.

"Get what?" asked Agnes. "I'm totally lost here."

"Mona is talking about her boobs—which are big and standing at attention," said Wanda.

Tory could feel everyone staring at her. Her face felt red. She didn't know what to say.

"Are you ready to get in the water, ladies?" asked Chip.

"With you? Anytime, honey bunch," said Agnes.

"Well, should we get in the water now?" asked Tory.

"Thank you for the save," said Chip.

"I got your back," said Tory.

"Now, girls, stay calm, I don't want anyone to drown today—or any day—in my pool," said Chip. "Everyone knows how to swim, right?"

"Yes!" they all yelled at once.

"Good. That makes this easy," said Tory.

"So, why don't you put your face in the water and blow bubbles?" asked Chip.

"Exceptionally good, Edith," said Tory.

"Alright. Next, we're going to do the breaststroke," said Chip.

"Did he say *breast*?" asked Tallulah.

"Yeah, that's what I heard, too," said Wanda.

Before Chip could tell Tallulah no, that's not what he had meant, she had already pulled down her bathing suit.

"Whoa, no! Pull it back up, Tallulah—right now!" yelled Tory.

"You're right, Tallulah—I heard the same thing," said Wanda, pulling her bathing suit down and off and throwing it in the water.

"Take it off, girlfriend!" yelled Agnes.

"Wow! This is very refreshing!" said Wanda.

Chip put his hands over his eyes. He kept asking himself if this was really happening.

As the other women laughed, Mona noticed the water was getting yellow. "What's going on?"

"Agnes peed in the pool," said Wanda, starting to laugh again.

"Hey, Agnes, you forgot to wear your Depends," laughed Tallulah.

"Now, you stop it, Wanda. It's not funny," said Agnes.

Edith was trying to be serious, but could not, because she was laughing so hard.

Tory swam over to Tallulah and helped her put her bathing suit back up.

"Come on, Tallulah, it's time to put the girls back in the suit," said Tory.

"It's time for them all to get out of the pool," said Chip.

"You don't want to stay with us?"

"No, not after you peed in the pool and Tallulah got topless!" said Chip.

"No. I think it best you all get out of the water for now," said Tory.

Everyone got out of the water and went to dry off, still laughing about everything that had happened. Wanda didn't want to put her bathing suit back on, because she loved the feeling of being naked, so Tory and wrapped her in a nearby blanket so no body parts were showing.

"Wow. That was interesting," said Tory.

"Yeah—it was almost like seniors gone wild," said Chip.

"You really know how to charm the bathing suits right off them." Tory laughed.

"I really need to watch what I'm saying!" said Chip.

"Yes, you do."

"I know I'll never get that image out of my head now," said Chip.

"Neither will I," said Tory.

"They're just a bunch of senior whack-a-doodles!"

"Now, be nice, Chip—or do you want them to take their clothes again?"

"Sorry, Tory. I'm just in awe of what just happened. And you're right—I don't need to have them take off their clothes again, because one of them could be my mom! And that's totally embarrassing—and still shocking," said Chip.

"Seriously? That shocked you?"

"Yes, it did! Because I didn't expect one word to be the reason they all get naked in the pool!!"

"It certainly didn't shock me," said Tory with a smirk.

"I guess I'll just stay away from the breaststroke," said Chip.

"Since you're in shock, you get to clean the pool, Mr. Breaststroke Man." Tory laughed.

She walked away, turning her head to smile at Chip.

"Boy, she's lucky that she is my cousin," said Chip to himself. He wondered when he should confront her about being with Frankie. Then he thought about it more, and decided he wasn't going to worry about it right then—and maybe he would just not mention it at all. He needed to concentrate on cleaning the pee from the pool and digging out Wanda's bathing suit, which had sunk to the bottom.

"What a wonderful day this has turned out to be," said Chip, shaking his head.

"I'm starving! Swimming makes you so hungry," said Tallulah as she went to the dining hall.

"I agree," said Wanda.

"I don't see how you're hungry when we really didn't get to do much of the swimming part," said Edith.

"Yeah, but getting naked gave me an appetite," said Tallulah.

"Let's just go to dinner," said Agnes.

"Hey, Agnes, are you sure you don't need to go to the bathroom first?" asked Tallulah as they passed the bathhouse.

"No, I am fine. I already went," said Agnes. "But thanks for asking—you never know when I might turn something else yellow!"

Tallulah laughed at Agnes. Then, something caught her eye, and she stopped walking.

"Come on, Tallulah, we're going to be late for dinner," said Mona.

Tallulah kept staring at the empty golf cart outside the bathhouse.

"I'm coming! Keep your clothes on," she said.

They finally made it to the dining hall.

"Smells good! I hope it's worth the wait," said Tallulah.

"Boy, what a day today was," said Agnes.

"I know! I'm so ready to go to bed—but it was so much fun with all the excitement," said Mona.

"Are you kidding me? You're tired?" asked Tallulah.

"Yes, we're tired! What's wrong with that?" asked Agnes.

"It's still early on my watch. We have plenty of time to do more things," said Tallulah.

"Let me tell you something, Tallulah. You're cuckoo sometimes—and this is one of them," said Agnes.

"I'm not cuckoo! I'm just not ready to let this day go in a blink of an eye," said Tallulah.

"I see what you're saying, but why does it have to be today?" asked Edith.

"I was having a good day with the paint fight that Vera started, and taking Frankie's clothes—and of course the pool," said Tallulah.

"Well, true. I agree about taking the clothes. That was wonderful—to see a man's sexy, naked body again. It's been so long for me," said Wanda.

"Yeah, it's been a long time since I've seen one—and especially like that," said Tallulah.

"You girls are being so bad right now," laughed Agnes.

"I love being bad," said Tallulah.

"What exactly do you have planned for us in that evil mind of yours?" asked Agnes. Who regretted even asking her, but knew that when she had a plan, it was always a good one.

"Let's take something for a ride," said Tallulah with a twinkle in her eye.

"*What* exactly are you thinking of taking for a ride?" asked Agnes.

"Well, see that golf cart in front of the bathhouse?" asked Tallulah.

"Yeah, we see it Tallulah. But what are we going to do with it once we get a hold of it?" asked Wanda.

"Let's just take it for a joyride around here and see what else we can find."

The women looked at each other, wondering if they should or not.

"Well, I think I'll just stay on the sidelines this time," said Edith.

"Oh really, Edith? You would be the first person to jump on this idea if we were back at Heaven's Ridge!" said Tallulah.

"I've already had a wild day—why would I want to add to it?"

"That's why you need to make it wilder! One last thing for today," said Tallulah.

"Come on, Edith. It'll be so much fun," said Wanda.

Edith looked at each of their faces. She changed her mind. She was going along with the rest of them.

"That's what I am talking about!" said Wanda, starting to get loud. Everyone was looking at them.

"We're OK. Just so excited to be here! You can get back to your dinner," said Mona.

"People are just so damn nosy," said Agnes.

After dinner, they all saw the golf cart was still there in front of the bathhouse. They looked around to see if anyone was around to catch them. Tallulah got in the driver's side and saw the keys were still in it.

"Let's go cruising, girls!" said Tallulah as she turned the key. The golf cart started right up.

"This is what I call fun!" said Agnes.

Tallulah stepped on the gas a little.

"Are we sure we should be doing this?" asked Wanda.

"Sure, Wanda, why not? They want us to make memories—and we've made plenty of them so far today! Let's add one more to end the night," said Mona.

"Let's go—before we get busted," said Agnes.

"Don't be such a scaredy-cat, Agnes! We won't get busted," said Tallulah, pushing on the gas. The golf cart took off.

Casper came running out right then.

"Hey what are you doing with my golf cart?!"

Oh shit, this isn't good.

"*Woo-hoo*! This is so much fun!" said Tallulah as they took off down the hill.

"Watch out, Tallulah! Don't hit anything!" said Edith.

"Watch out for the big bump at the bottom of the h—" Wanda screamed. But before she could finish her sentence, they hit the bump and went flying, before back on all four tires.

"Where did you get your license from? A Cracker Jack's box?" asked Mona.

They flew passed Siena and Tory, who were sitting at one of the picnic tables at one of the cabins.

"Did you just see that, Siena?" asked Tory.

"I think I did, but I'm not too sure," said Siena.

"Was that Tallulah driving the golf cart?!"

"Oh, shit! We must stop them—before someone gets hurt," said Siena.

They ran after them, catching up to them by the fire pit.

"You're going too fast, Tallulah! Push the break!" yelled Siena.

Tallulah pretended she didn't hear and kept going.

"Watch out for the tree!!" yelled Mona.

"*Ahhh!*" They all yelled at the same time as Tallulah, laughing and enjoying the ride.

Art was down by the creek and saw the seniors go flying by him. He started running after them.

"Move, girls! I got them," said Art to Siena and Tory. They moved out of his way.

Art managed to get close enough, so he grabbed the back fender. He tripped on a rock and began getting dragged by the golf cart.

"Tallulah, stop right now!" yelled Art. "Ouch, ouch!!! Help me!!!"

"Stop, Tallulah!! Right now!!" yelled Siena.

But then, Tallulah realized the gas pedal was stuck, and she couldn't get it unstuck.

"Oh, shit!" said Tallulah.

"Why did you say that, Tallulah?" asked Agnes.

"I can't stop! The damn gas pedal is stuck!" said Tallulah as she went up the hill and around the circle.

"What the hell do you mean, the gas pedal is stuck?!" asked Mona.

"It means I can't stop!!" said Tallulah.

"Oh my God, we're all going to die!!" yelled Agnes.

"Do you know what you're doing, Tallulah?!" asked Mona.

Wanda looked around to see if anyone could help them. When she looked behind her, she saw that they were dragging Art.

"Hey, Tallulah! We need to figure out something fast, because we have a dragger!!" said Wanda.

"What the hell are you talking about, Wanda?" asked Agnes, quickly looking behind her. She saw Art.

"I freaked! Told you this was going to be a bad idea!" said Edith.

"Relax, Edith, we will be OK," said Wanda.

"Oh, shit!! We're going to hit the tree!!" said Agnes, grabbing onto whatever she could find.

Tallulah managed to put the cart on two wheels and miss the tree by an inch, with Art screaming in the back.

Belle heard all thee screaming and came running out of the office to see what was going on. Belle's eyes got big. She just could not believe what she was seeing.

"Oh shit!! This isn't happening," said Belle, dropping her coffee cup. "Harlow, we have a big problem! I need you out here now."

Harlow rushed outside and saw Tallulah and everyone on the golf cart, along with Art being dragged behind it and Tory and Siena running after it.

"What the hell is going on, Belle?!" asked Harlow.

"If I knew, I wouldn't have called you, Harlow," said Belle.

Siena and Tory stopped by Belle and Harlow, trying to catch their breath before talking.

"We saw them coming down the hill and chased them for a while," said Tory, taking another breath.

"Then they went past Art, who decided to chase them, but his shirt got caught when he tripped," said Siena.

"Now they're saying that the gas pedal is stuck," said Tory.

"How do we top this?" asked Belle.

"I don't know, but we need to figure out quick before Art really gets hurt," said Harlow. "Belle, you used to have a golf cart. What did you do when the gas pedal got stuck?"

"What do you mean, what did I do? You were also there when it happened," said Belle.

"What did *we* do?"

"What we did . . . I don't think is safe for a bunch of seniors," said Belle.

"Let me remember what we did," said Harlow.

"Um, we would either hit something or jump out," said Belle. "I don't see any of them attempting to do that."

"I don't see them bailing out, since they're all holding on to each other!!"

"I'm going to be sick!!" yelled Art.

"Oh, poor Art!! I wish we could figure a way to get him loose, then try and stop them," said Harlow.

Harlow and Belle tried to think of something quick, before it became more of a disaster.

"Hold on, Art, we are coming to save you," said Belle.

"OK, but I may have broken something!" yelled Art.

"Do you have a plan, Belle?" asked Harlow.

"We need to get his shirt either off him or looser, so he can just get it off and let go."

"I'll try running next to the golf cart and get on the fender to get his shirt loose and free him."

"I'll figure out a place they can go so we can stop this thing from moving," said Belle.

Harlow started running behind the golf cart and jumped on without losing her balance.

"Hey, girls! I'm here to help you and Art. I'm going to get him first. Just stay calm," said Harlow. She looked at the seniors' faces.

"Yeah, like that's so easy to do right now," said Agnes.

"OK, Art. I'm here to save you. But I do have one question for you," said Harlow.

"Is this really the time to ask questions?" asked Art.

"I just need to know how special your T-shirt is to you," said Harlow.

"I'm not in love with it," said Art.

"I've been dragging him around this whole time?!" asked Tallulah.

"I'm afraid so," said Harlow. "But he'll be OK. Just keep driving. I'm going to lean over the seat. Can one of you seniors hold onto my legs so I can cut Art loose?"

"Yes, I will ,darling," said Mona.

Harlow leaned over the seat as Mona held onto her legs.

"Hey, darling, I'm just wondering if you're aware that you have no underwear on," laughed Mona.

Harlow just shook her head as she cut Art's shirt off.

"I almost got it, Art—and I after I make this last snip, you can let go," said Harlow.

"OK, Harlow, I'm ready," said Art.

"I just about got it," said Harlow as she snipped his shirt.

Art let go and falls to the hard pavement as Harlow held on. Art rolled onto the grass and laid there for a few seconds. Harlow jumped off the golf cart and went to see how he was doing.

"Are you OK?" she asked.

Art tried to speak, but the only words he could get out were "thank you." He sat up and looked at Harlow.

When he could finally talk, he said, "I got all my body parts, so I am good."

"Can you get up?" asked Harlow.

"Yes, I can. Thank you again, Harlow," said Art.

"Let's go—before they hurt someone else," said Harlow, helping Art to his feet.

"Whoa—a little dizzy," said Art.

"Are you going to be OK?" asked Harlow.

"Yes. It just really took the wind right out of me."

"Grab my hand and we will go together," said Harlow. She gave Belle a thumbs up.

"Wow, that was amazing!" yelled Art.

"I have to get back on that golf cart and help them out," said Harlow.

"You go save the seniors—just be careful, Harlow," said Art.

"I wouldn't worry," said Harlow. "OK, girls—it's time to figure out how to stop this thing."

"Good, because I am not having fun anymore! We need to get off this thing," said Wanda.

"How are we going to?" asked Agnes.

Harlow could hear someone yelling. She looked around and saw Belle. "What?!"

"Wait for it to run out of gas to run out!!" said Belle.

Harlow looked at the gas gage and saw it was almost empty. She gave Belle a thumbs up.

"I've got an idea," said Tallulah as she went down the hill.

Tallulah what are you doing?" asked Harlow.

"I know where we can go and stop this thing," said Tallulah.

"No, Tallulah! Let's not do that. We should wait for the gas to run out and it will just quit running," said Harlow.

"No, my idea is so much better," said Tallulah as she started heading for the pool.

"What's at the pool?" asked Agnes.

"Our way off this damn golf cart!" said Tallulah.

"No, I don't think that's a good idea," said Mona.

"We'll be able to get off the golf cart," said Tallulah.

"I like Harlow's way so much better."

"If you remember correctly, you're the one who wanted to steal the damn golf cart! All of this is your fault!!" said Agnes.

Belle ran to the side of the golf cart to let Tallulah know to stay away from the pool. Tallulah didn't listen to her, and decided to go to the pool. They crashed through the gate.

Chip heard a crash, and before he could look, he heard them splash into the pool. Everyone on the golf cart was yelling because it was slowly sinking. The seniors ended up splashing and swimming around. Chip, Tory, Belle, and Siena jumped in the water to save them. Tory went over to Mona and grabbed her.

"That was the greatest ride I've ever taken," said Mona as Tory brought her to the side of the pool.

"When can we do it again?" asked Wanda.

"I must hand it to you, Tallulah—you know how to drive," said Agnes as Chip grabbed her to bring her to the side.

"What strong arms you have, Chip," said Agnes.

He rolled his eyes.

Belle and Siena grabbed Tallulah, Wanda, and Chip went back to get Edith.

"Do you need any help?" asked Belle.

"No Belle, I got it."

Art finally got to the pool, and looked around for Harlow.

He saw her struggling in the water and jumped right in to get her. "I got you, Harlow—just relax." He grabbed her and carried her out of the pool. Belle and Siena passed out towels to everyone so they could dry off while Chip and Tory finished getting everyone out.

Belle looks at the pool quizzically. "Why is the pool turning yellow?"

Everyone looked at Agnes.

"Sorry—it just comes out when I laugh hard. And when I'm nervous," said Agnes, covering her mouth trying not to laugh.

"Is everyone OK?" asked Belle, trying not to get upset.

The seniors shook their heads yes. Art got out of the pool and carried Harlow to where everyone else was sitting.

"Are you OK, Harlow?" asked Belle, wrapping towels around her.

"Yes, I'm fine thanks to Art."

"Well, it was no problem to save a beautiful woman who saved me from what could have been a bad tragedy."

"OK, my next question is, what the hell were you thinking when you decided to take the golf cart?" asked Belle.

"Everyone decided to point at Tallulah. OK, Tallulah—what do you have to say for yourself?" asked Belle.

"You wanted us to make memories, that's why we did it. It was all my idea—but I didn't want anyone to get hurt or even wet," said Tallulah.

"You're damn lucky none of us *did* get hurt," said Wanda.

"I had everything under control until the stupid gas pedal got stuck. I think someone should look at it," said Tallulah.

"Wow, what happened to the gate?" Casper asked as he looked at it.

"It's a long story, and I don't know where to start," said Belle.

Casper walked toward the pool. When he saw the golf cart, his eyes opened wide. He couldn't believe what he was seeing.

"Why is my golf cart in the pool?!"

"I have one question," said Harlow, still trying to dry herself off.

"Oh boy, here we go," said Wanda.

"How did you even get the golf cart?" asked Harlow.

"That's easy—the golf cart was parked in front of the bathhouse with the keys in it," said Tallulah.

"Oh really? The golf cart was by the bathhouse with the keys in it?" asked Belle, looking at Casper.

"Oh yeah. I was fixing the toilet someone had once again clogged up," said Casper.

Everyone looked at Edith.

"It wasn't me again!! Once was enough," said Edith.

"Sorry, Belle. Next time, I'll be more careful, and take the damn keys with me," said Casper.

"I have a question," said Edith, raising her hand.

"Yes, Edith, what is it?" asked Belle.

"Why do you have red lips, Casper?" asked Edith.

Everyone turned their heads and stared at Casper as he tried to wipe the lipstick off.

"No idea what you're talking about," he said.

"Yeah, OK. If you say so, hotcakes," said Tallulah.

Casper gave Tallulah a look, then looked up at Harlow. She just turned her head.

"OK, can we get back to the other big issue?" asked Belle.

"Yes, we can Belle," said Chip, as he wasn't interested in the conversation.

"How are we going to get the golf cart out of the pool?"

Casper scratched his head and tried to figure out what he could do.

"The only thing I can think of is to bring my truck in, put chains on the golf cart, and tow it out," he said. He knelt, still wondering if it was the right thing to do. But he couldn't think of anything else.

"I'll help you get it out," said Art.

Belle went over to him and tapped him on the shoulder. "I think it would be best if you went and let Nurse Juniper look at you first. Then you can help out."

"Yes, ma'am. I will right away—and be back quick."

"As for you five women, fun time is over. You need to go back to your cabins and get those wet clothes off," said Belle.

Wanda, Tallulah, Agnes, Mona, and Edith looked at each other and burst out laughing.

"I thought we could have a wet T-shirt contest first," said Tallulah, winking at the guys.

"No, you're wrong. Fun time is over for today," said Siena.

"I feel like I'm a child again, getting grounded. I got that a lot," said Agnes, laughing.

"I think my parents should have change my name to 'Grounded,' because I was always bad," said Tallulah.

"You aren't the only one who thinks that," said Mona.

"Nothing's going to happen. You're not grounded. All I'm asking is you not to do it again," said Belle.

"Now, wait a minute! All this talk about being grounded is crazy! We're seniors here at this camp—not kids—and we're supposed to have fun! And that's what we did," yelled Edith.

"Edith, please listen to me! None of you are grounded!!" said Belle.

"I haven't had this much fun in one day in my whole life! Thank you Tallulah," said Edith.

"Are you done now, Edith?" asked Belle.

"Yes, sorry. I just wanted to make a point."

"It's OK, Edith, I completely understand. Maybe I shouldn't have gotten so mad at you. I apologize to you all. And one more time: you're not grounded."

"Let's just enjoy the rest of the week," said Harlow, making sure she had Belle's back like she always did.

Belle turned around, and Art was still there. "Art, can you please go see Nurse Juniper for a checkup?"

"Yes, Belle I will go right now. Casper, I will be right back."

"No problem. We'll probably still be here," said Casper as he kept looking at the sunken golf cart and scratching his head.

Harlow touched Casper's shoulder, and he jumped up.

"Do you think you will be able to get the golf cart out of the pool?"

"Probably. But getting it up and running again . . . that's going to be more of an issue."

"Oh, that really sucks," said Harlow.

"The upholstery is ruined, and everything needs to be replaced. Who knows about the engine . . . until I can get it back to the shop." Casper was not looking forward to the project.

"You're incredibly talented. You can fix anything! Or know where to go to get it fixed." Harlow knew she had to give him some words of encouragement, because she knew how he got when he couldn't figure things out.

"I guess we will just have to wait and see after we get it out of the pool," said Casper.

"Well, I have paperwork that needs to be done, and I will probably have to talk Belle off a building after everything that went on this evening, so my hands are going to be full tonight," said Harlow.

"Sure, that's going to be a barrel of fun," said Casper.

"I'll need a list of things that need to be fixed so I can put it in my report for the insurance people," said Harlow.

"Sounds more fun than what I will be dealing with," said Casper

"Well, I'll see you later. I'm here if you need me. Just leaving that out there."

"I appreciate it, Harlow," said Casper, watching her leave.

"Are you alright, Casper?" asked Chip.

"Yeah, I am. Boy, does she still have a nice ass," said Casper, continuing to watch Harlow.

"Would you kill me if I agreed with you?" asked Chip, who was trying to feel Casper out when it came to Harlow.

"No, it's OK with me," said Casper, laughing at Chip, punching him in the arm.

"Then yes, I agree with you about Harlow and her ass," laughed Chip.

"Thanks for helping me get the golf cart out of the pool," said Casper.

"No problem. I'll have to drain the pool and clean it good to get all the pee, gas, and whatever else is in there, to make it safe to swim in." Chip was still blown away those five seniors could have done all this crap today.

"I guess this is what to expect when they have been in a retirement home for so long," said Casper.

"They're one crazy crew."

"I'll go get my truck and chains to hook up the golf cart, and be right back," said Casper.

"OK, no problem. I'll just stay here and drain some of the water."

"Promise I won't be too long. Maybe Art will get back from getting checked out," said Casper, starting to run to his truck.

"Chip started getting everything he would need to get the pool all nice and clean, so it didn't look like a golf cart had been in there. As he went and grabbed everything from the pool shed, he was still thinking about Tory and Frankie. For someone reason, it really is bothering him, and he couldn't figure out why.

If Tory's with Willa, why be with Frankie? He's far from a woman—and if he was one, he'd be an ugly one. Chip chuckled to himself. *Oh well, when she's ready to come forward with the truth, he'll comfort her.*

110 April Carter

Art wondered where Nurse Juniper was.

"Hey Nurse Juniper, are you here?" asked Art.

"I'll be right with you," said Nurse Juniper, coming out of her bedroom.

"Hi, beautiful—I mean, Nurse Juniper," said Art, stuttering.

"Hi, Art. What can I do for you today?" asked Nurse Juniper.

"Well, I'm sure there's plenty that you can do for me, but I'm here because Belle wanted me to have you examine me after the golf cart incident," said Art.

"Wow! What happened to you?" asked Nurse Juniper.

"I'm sure you're not going to believe this, but I got yanked around by seniors driving the golf cart," said Art, trying to be as serious as he could.

"Nurse Juniper looked at Art funny. "You were dragged by a golf cart?" she repeated.

Art looked at Nurse Juniper. "It's a long story . . . in which five seniors were involved. They're all safe now."

"Well, I'm glad that they're safe," said Nurse Juniper.

Art took off what was left of his shirt.

"Well, you have bumps and bruises from when you hit the pavement, but that's nothing to be concerned about. So, everything's OK."

"I have to thank Harlow. She was the one who jumped on the back of the golf cart as it was moving, got me loose, and tried to save the seniors. But they ended up in the pool."

"Oh my! I hope they're all OK!" said Nurse Juniper.

"Yes, everyone is safe and sound," said Art.

"It was a good thing she did, and she did it fast—if your shirt had gotten any tighter around your neck, it could have killed you!"

"Yeah, that really would have sucked!" said Art.

"I don't have any worries, so you're free to do what you want. Just be careful. If your bruises turn an unusual color, please come back."

"I sure will, Nurse Juniper. I hope you have a fantastic evening," said Art as he went out the door.

"You, too, Art," said Nurse Juniper, laughing at him as she watched him.

"He's quite the character, isn't he?" asked Harlow.

"Yes, he is—and he spoke very highly of you," said Nurse Juniper.

"Really? How's that?" asked Harlow.

"You're his hero for saving him," said Nurse Juniper as she walked away.

Harlow stood there for a moment, thinking about what Nurse Juniper had said, then decided to go back to her room and relax.

"I'm back, guys," said Art as he came back into the pool area.

"Well, it's about time!" said Chip. "We were thinking we'd have to do this on our own."

"No, I'm here—with a clean bill of health, thanks to Nurse Juniper."

Casper gave Art a look, but decided to not say anything.

"OK, chains are all hooked up to the golf cart and my truck, so all we should have to do is put it in gear and hopefully, it'll bring the golf cart to the surface," said Casper.

"Let's get this going before it really gets dark out," said Chip.

Casper got in his truck and started pulling the golf cart as Chip and Art tried to push it out of the water left in the pool.

"We almost got it, Casper! Keep going! Just a little bit more!" yelled Chip.

"Yahoo! We got it out!!" Art said as he and Chip high fived.

"That was close—I almost thought we weren't going to get it out," said Casper.

"I know. It wasn't easy to push," said Chip, rubbing his arms.

"Now we just have to roll it onto my truck, and I'll take it to my maintenance shed and see what I can do," said Casper.

A few minutes later, the golf cart was on Casper's truck, and that nightmare was over.

"What a day this has been," said Chip.

"I agree with you there, my brother," said Art.

"You had the worse day, being hooked to a golf cart until Harlow saved you," said Chip.

"I'm very thankful to her. For a little while, I was scared I wasn't going to make it. The way Tallulah drives—that woman shouldn't have a license!" Art laughed.

"Well, thanks again, guys. I need to get this back to the shed before it gets too late," said Casper, who really didn't want to hear about Harlow.

"Yeah, it's been a long day. I'm ready to hit the hay myself," said Chip.

"I'd better relax after the day I had behind the golf cart," said Art.

"I'm glad you're OK," said Chip, shaking Art's hand.

"Me, too," said Casper. "I'll see you later."

He got in the truck and took off, waving his hand out the window.

Art and Chip headed to their cabins, and both hoped it would be a quiet night for them once they got there.

"Is it Friday the thirteenth?" Art asked Chip as they walked back.

"No, it's just another day at Camp Paradise," said Chip.

CHAPTER 9

Next Day Blues

"Boy, what a day yesterday was! My old bones are howling today," said Edith.

"My body feels like I got hit by a truck or something. I can barely move," said Agnes.

As all five of the women sat at breakfast, they were incredibly quiet—which had been unusual for them since they had arrived at camp.

"Hey, girls. How are we doing today?" asked Belle.

"We're all fine," said Edith.

"Never better," said Agnes, perking up so Belle wouldn't be able to tell she felt horrible.

"That's not what you said a few minutes ago," said Tallulah.

"Oh really, Tallulah? What were we saying?" asked Belle.

"Zip it, Tallulah!" said Wanda.

"Um, well . . . I mean . . . they're fine—never better!" said Tallulah.

Edith and Agnes shook their heads, hoping to not get busted.

"Glad you're all good and safe. I'll see you later for the activity." Belle walked away.

"Excellent job, Tallulah! You almost got us busted again," said Agnes.

"I covered quite well, if I say so myself!"

"Yeah, OK. Keep thinking that," said Edith.

"I wonder what kind of things they have in store for us today," said Wanda.

"I'm surprised no perky people have come and told us what's going on," said Mona.

"Yeah, it's a little strange—but they can show up at our cabins at any time."

"Can I have everyone's attention?" asked Belle.

"Oh boy. Here we go now. We're going to hear it," said Wanda.

"I just wanted to let everyone know there will be no swimming today or tomorrow. The pool is under maintenance right now."

Everyone started booing Belle.

"We broke the pool?" asked Mona.

"Oh shit! I wonder if Heaven's Ridge has enough money to pay for our mistakes," said Agnes.

"They can't do that, can they?" asked Tallulah.

"No, that would be ridiculous . . . unless they had good reason," said Edith.

"We'll have a list of activities for you for the day after breakfast, and we'll be coming by all the cabins so you know what's going on," said Belle.

"We better go down to the cabins and wait for what they have planned," said Mona.

"Once again, we must hurry up and wait," said Tallulah.

"See you later, gals. I have to use the bathroom before I go back," said Agnes.

"Don't clog it up!" laughed Mona.

"I don't plan on it. I'll leave that for Edith," laughed Agnes.

"Will you ever let it go?!"

"You already let it go—in the toilet!" laughed Tallulah.

"Ha ha, very funny," said Edith. She got up, deciding it was time to go back to the cabin.

Bessie knocked on cabin one's door and walked right in.

"It's Bessie, with your day's activities," she said.

"Hi, Bessie," said Eloise.

"Hey, Eloise! How are you doing today?"

"I'm fine and dandy in cabin one," said Eloise.

"Well, that's good," said Bessie. I love my job and I love my seniors, who are here for me to take care of," said Eloise.

"Are all the seniors here, by chance, so I can tell them what they'll be doing today?" asked Bessie.

Eloise looked around. They were all in their beds, gabbing at each other.

"Yes, they're all present and accounted for," she said.

"Thank you, Eloise, you're the best," said Bessie. "Hey, how are you all doing today?"

"All good here!" said Agnes.

"Well, I think this place sucks," said Vera.

Everyone turned and look at her.

"Well, sorry you think that, Vera—is there anything I can do to make things better?" asked Bessie.

"Can you get my vibrator back from that perky woman?" she asked.

"Um, yeah . . . wow . . . I'll have to check on that," said Bessie, who couldn't believe what Vera had asked.

"Never mind, jackass. I'll get it myself somehow," said Vera.

"Do you want to know what today's activities are?" asked Bessie.

"Stick it up your ass!" said Vera.

"Point taken."

"She woke up on the wrong side of the bed," said Agnes.

"I can see that," said Bessie.

"So, what do you have planned for us today?" asked Mona.

"Well, thank you, Mona, for asking. That's very thoughtful of you."

"You're welcome. Anything to get this to go a little faster," said Mona.

"Oh, OK, I get it."

"We thought you would," said Wanda. She wanted the conversation to end.

"So, this morning, this cabin will be doing music therapy with Eden. And then, this afternoon, it's going to be art therapy with Iggy," said Bessie.

"Is it just going to be our cabin?" asked Agnes.

"Yes, just for today, though," said Bessie.

"Why?" asked Mona. "I thought we were in trouble!"

"I'm just going by what Belle told me this morning," said Bessie, "which was that each cabin would be doing their own activity instead of mixing and mingling."

"Still sounds like fun," said Mona.

"I'm just going by what Belle asked me to do," said Bessie.

"We know, honey. It's not your fault. We'll just miss Tallulah and Edith," said Agnes.

"I'll see you ladies later. It'll be a wonderful day," said Bessie, going out the door.

"Well, that absolutely bites," said Mona.

"Oh well. Let's just make the most of it, I guess. It's all we can do."

"Your right, Agnes, we should. But it's going to be weird without Tallulah and Edith," said Mona.

"I know I'm right!" laughed Agnes.

"Get off your high horse, Agnes," said Wanda.

"Wow! Tell us how you really feel, Wanda!" said Agnes.

"Sorry! I just can't believe that we can't be with Tallulah and Edith during an activity," said Wanda.

"Your heard Bessie—it's only for today. And we'll see them at lunch and dinner," said Mona.

"I wonder how Tallulah ad Edith are taking the news," said Agnes.

"I guess we'll find out at lunch," said Wanda.

"How's everyone going this morning with you?" asked Eloise.

"Simply lovely," said Wanda.

"If you need anything we're all here until the activity starts," she said.

The four women stared at her as she walked around the cabin.

"Oh, where did Vera go?" she asked.

"We don't have a clue. She left," said Wanda.

"You didn't see anything," said Mona.

"She can't stay in one place anyways," said Eloise, "but I won't go there."

"Sure, no problem, Eloise," said Agnes. She walked out the door and headed up the hill to the bathhouse.

"I wonder what she meant about that?" asked Mona.

"I don't know, and I don't want to know," said Wanda.

"Me neither," said Agnes.

"Let's just go to music therapy. Maybe it'll soothe our souls," said Wanda.

"Yeah, maybe. We'll see how it goes," said Mona.

Agnes, Mona, and Wanda went to music therapy and sang their little old hearts out. They didn't even worry about what Vera was up to. When it was almost lunchtime, they were excited to see Tallulah and Edith in the dining hall.

On their way up the hill, Agnes and Wanda overheard a conversation they maybe shouldn't have listened to with the counselors about who was dating who. They rushed to get to the dining hall to tell the others what they had heard.

"Oh, Tallulah and Edith, I've missed you since breakfast," said Wanda. "It sucked that we couldn't do an activity together, and I was so upset."

"Aww, you're so sweet, Wanda, but I'm not buying it," said Tallulah.

"Why not, Tallulah?"

"I don't know. Something just seems to be funny about it," said Tallulah.

"Oh jeez, Tallulah. I don't know about you sometimes."

"What's wrong?" asked Agnes.

"I was trying to tell Edith and Tallulah that we missed them this morning, but Tallulah doesn't believe me," said Wanda.

"Then let it be. If she's going to be like that and not believe us, then so be it. I don't have time for her childish games," said Agnes.

"Wow—kick me while I'm down!" said Tallulah.

"Well, start believing us when we tell you something, you knucklehead," said Agnes.

"Now I'm a knucklehead!! Oh great, thanks."

"Can someone change the subject?" asked Mona.

"So, Wanda and I overheard a couple of counselors talking about the people who are hooking up here," said Agnes.

"Wow, very juicy," said Tallulah.

"Well, it was exciting . . . but not so exciting I'm peeing my pants," said Wanda.

Everyone just looked at her as she picked up the chicken bone and chowed down on it, not realizing everyone was staring at her.

"I guess our favorite lifeguards are quite the couple," said Agnes.

"I can't wait to go to the pool again when we're allowed, so we can see them in action," said Wanda.

"I highly doubt they'd give us any action. Yesterday, it was all of us giving them the action," said Tallulah.

"Hey, Agnes, was that all the gossip you had for us?" asked Edith.

"Yeah, I guess so. I thought it was great, but I guess no one else did."

"I need to give you some tips, so you know how to eavesdrop better," said Tallulah.

"Oh, really? You think that you can do better than me?" asked Agnes.

"Yes, I do, Agnes."

"OK. We'll see about that . . . and I won't need your help showing me how to do it!"

"Do you want to make a bet?" asked Tallulah.

"No, I don't think so. I know better to make a bet with you."

"I guess you're scared to make it because you would lose," said Tallulah, drinking her milk.

"Let's just see who can get the best gossip and go from there," said Agnes.

"Sounds good to me."

They shook on it.

"Let's go—we still have an entire day left of things to do," said Mona.

"Too bad we won't be able to do it with each other," said Edith.

"I know. But there's always dinnertime. We get to meet at this wonderful table again," said Agnes.

"That is true, my friend, and we will do exactly that," said Mona.

"We will see each other here tonight," said Wanda.

"We should go on another adventure," said Tallulah.

Everyone was quick to yell no.

"Well, fine. I just feel *so* loved," said Tallulah, leaving the dining hall.

"She will never learn," said Agnes.

"Let's get the rest of the day going," said Wanda.

"What about Tallulah?" asked Mona.

"She will be fine. It won't kill her to cool her heals for a little while," said Agnes.

They all decided they would go back to their cabins and see each other later.

CHAPTER 10

Mona's Fried Chicken and More

The pool was finally open after a couple of days, and the seniors were so glad to be back together for their activities.

They were all able to go for a morning swim after breakfast and couldn't wait.

"I can't wait to ask Tory about her and Chip being together," said Agnes.

"Are we sure we should get involved in that?" asked Wanda.

"Sure, why not? It shouldn't be a secret—at least that's what I think," said Agnes.

"If you say so, Agnes. But what if it was you? I highly doubt you would want someone in your business," said Wanda.

"We're always in each other's business, so it doesn't matter to me," said Agnes.

"OK, if you say so. But I'm still not sure about this," said Wanda.

"Relax. We're just going to have a little fun," said Agnes.

"OK, but if it blows up in our faces, don't say I didn't tell you so," said Wanda.

The seniors were excited to be able to get back to the pool, waiting for the gate to open.

"Hey, ladies, are you all excited about going swimming?" asked Hazel.

"Yes, we are, so what is the holdup?" asked Tallulah.

"You're a few minutes early, so that's why the gate is not open," said Fay.

"We are helping out today, so we will see you in there," said Hazel.

"How come you get to go in?" asked Edith.

"Like I said, we are helping, so that's what we are doing," said Fay.

Chip went to the gate to let the seniors in, but before he did, he wanted to make something clear to them.

"Before I open this gate, I want to make sure you understand there will be no funny stuff."

We will be perfect angels," said Tallulah.

"Why do I find that hard to believe?" asked Chip.

"We promise. No funny stuff," said Agnes.

"So let me make it clear again—no peeing in the pool," said Chip.

Everyone started laughing at Agnes.

"Hey! That wasn't funny. And if I remember correctly, I wasn't the only one who peed in the pool."

"One more thing . . . we had to clean the pool and put a new liner in it. So no golf carts in the pool!" said Chip.

"Hey, the pool wasn't the plan, but it was fun taking a dive!" said Tallulah.

"Oh, and lastly, no one gets naked in the pool or they will be asked to get out and not be able to use it again all week," said Chip.

Everyone looked at Tallulah.

"I wasn't the only one getting naked, if I remember correctly," said Tallulah.

"OK, yes, we will give you that one . . . you weren't," said Edith.

"Yes, we promise to be good," they all said at the same time.

"Have a fun time," said Chip as he finally opened the gate.

"Let's get this party started," said Mona as she went through.

Chip gave her a look.

"I'm just kidding, sonny. Keep your shorts on," laughed Mona.

Everyone made it in the pool, and they all stayed together in a corner.

"OK, so there is Tory and Chip . . . so now it's time to expose their relationship."

"This could be fun, or it could be a big disaster," said Wanda.

"Will you relax? Everything will be fine," said Agnes.

"We're just going to have some innocent fun. There's nothing wrong with that," said Edith.

"Thank you, Edith, for believing in me," said Agnes.

"Oh, I never said that. I just want to see things blow up again."

"Jeez, thank you, Edith," said Agnes.

"You're welcome. Anytime, Agnes."

Agnes swam over to Tory to try to talk to her.

"Hey, honey, I wanted to ask you something," said Agnes.

"Sure, Agnes. What can I do for you?' asked Tory.

"I had heard a rumor, and I wanted to know if it was true," said Agnes.

"Sure. Hopefully I can help you," said Tory.

"You know, you're a really pretty girl," said Agnes.

Tory wasn't sure where she was going, but decided to just go with it. "Thank you, I really appreciate that, Agnes."

"I really think that you can pick a better guy then Chip to be with," said Agnes. Tory's eyes got big.

Tory burst out laughing. Everyone looked at them.

"Tory, are you OK?" asked Chip.

"Oh, I have something hilarious to tell you Chip," she said as she swam over to him. "Hey, Agnes, would you like to share what you just told me?"

Agnes swam over slowly, hoping everything would not get put on her.

"So, Agnes was wondering something," said Tory.

"Oh, really? What did you want to know, Agnes?" asked Chip.

"Um, really, it was nothing . . . just something I heard," said Agnes, who felt like she was going to pee in the pool again.

"She told me I could find a better guy than you to be with," said Tory, trying not to laugh again.

"Oh, really? I'm not good enough for Tory? I see."

"I'm thinking I heard the rumor wrong. I'm sorry I took up your time," said Agnes, swimming away.

"Hey, Hazel and Fay, you want to hear something funny?" yelled Chip.

Agnes wanted to sink underwater, but instead just went over where the others were.

"I guess Agnes heard a rumor that Tory and I were together and that she could do better," laughed Chip.

"We know that will never happen," laughed Hazel.

"Why? Is he gay?" asked Tallulah.

Fay laughed so hard, she started snorting like a pig.

"Sorry, but that was so funny," said Fay.

"No, I am not gay, Tallulah," laughed Chip.

"OK, sonny, I believe you," said Tallulah, and she swam away.

"I think it's time to get out of the pool. It's almost lunchtime," said Hazel.

"Yes, time to get all dried off and head to lunch in a little while," said Tory.

Everyone one got out without a problem.

"Let me help you get your shoes on, Mona," said Fay.

"Oh, thank you, darling, you're too kind," said Mona.

"Thank *you*, darling. I try to do my best," said Fay.

"Alright, girls, let's go to lunch. I'm starving from all that swimming I didn't do," said Edith.

"Me too," said Tallulah.

"You're always hungry," said Wanda.

"Yes, I do love my food. You can tell just by looking at my belly," laughed Tallulah.

"At least you don't deny it," said Agnes.

"No, I can't—because you all know me so well!" said Tallulah.

"So, let's get some food," said Wanda.

Agnes and Tallulah let the others go ahead of them while they spent time together at the bottom of the hill. They decided to hide behind a tree so Hazel and Fay wouldn't see them.

"Why are we hiding behind a tree?" asked Tallulah.

"Tory embarrassed me at the pool, so it's time to dig up more dirt," said Agnes.

"Yeah, so? That happens all the time," said Tallulah, who wasn't too enthusiastic.

"Here comes Fay and Hazel," said Agnes.

"So what's the plan?" asked Tallulah.

"All we're going to do is follow them."

"This should be lots of fun."

"You like gossip just as much as I do," said Agnes.

"True, but I would never hide behind a tree to get it," said Tallulah.

They could hear Fay and Hazel talking about something and knew they had to get closer.

"I think one of them is crushing on a guy here," said Hazel.

"There is not a lot of good-looking men around here," said Fay.

"Well, this is exciting!!"

"Will you shut up?! We'll get busted!" said Agnes.

"I think we should keep following them and see what else they have to say. It could be fun!" whispered Wanda from behind Agnes and Tallulah.

"What are you doing here?!" asked Agnes.

"I saw you both behind the tree and wondered what you were up to, and then I just put the pieces together when I saw Hazel and Fay," Wanda.

"I think we should keep going. It gives us something to do—and it's not like we're going to get in trouble for trailing behind them. We're all heading the same way," said Tallulah.

"Yeah, let's get dirt on these people," said Agnes.

Then, before they knew it, Chip was joining Hazel and Fay up the hill.

"Hi Fay, Hazel, and Chip, how are you doing today?" asked Mona.

"We are all doing good, Mona," said Hazel.

"How are you doing today, Mona?" asked Fay.

"I'm doing super-duper," said Mona.

"Good to hear," said Chip.

Then, they all ran in different directions—which confused Mona, who wasn't sure who to follow and which way to go.

"I think I'd rather go back to the cabin and take a nap. This is too exhausting, following them," said Mona.

On her way back to her cabin, she started talking to herself. "This was supposed to be a cabin full of fun, and I'm kicking around stones, talking to myself, and going back to my cabin to take a nap."

"Hi Mona, what is going on in your world today?" asked Iggy, who just happened to walk by.

"I'm doing OK. I'm just wandering around. I'll probably go back to my cabin and take a nap until there's something to do," said Mona, who was quite unhappy.

"Well, we can spend time together if you want to, Mona. I would enjoy your company."

"What would we do?" asked Mona.

"Well, I was just asked by our chef, Frankie, if I would make a dinner with a senior, and I think it's a great idea," said Iggy.

"I'll let you go so you can find who you're looking for," said Mona, starting to walk away.

"I was talking about you, Mona. I would love for us to make dinner together."

"What are we going to make for all these people?" asked Mona.

"Anything you want, girlfriend. It's up to you," said Iggy.

"I'm up for anything, I guess. I have a few ideas."

"Then let's go make some dinner."

They both headed toward the kitchen.

"I do love to cook—even though it's been a long time," said Mona.

"I'm sure once we get going, it will come right back to you."

"I used to love to cook with my last husband. We had a little business that everyone came to in town," said Mona.

"What was your specialty meal?" asked Iggy.

"That's a hard one—because the customers loved everything I made!"

"Did you go to cooking school?"

"No, my mom was a good cook, and she taught me everything I know. And the things I didn't know, I just learned myself," said Mona.

"That is so sweet. I used to do that with my mom and grandmother, too. But then her and my dad got divorced, and that was it," said Iggy sadly.

"If it makes you feel any better, I learned from mom until she died, and I used to cook for my dad all the time until he got remarried, and that was a disaster," said Mona.

"That had to be rough for you, to have a new stepmom and all that," said Iggy.

"It was hard. Especially having a new stepsister at the same time."

"Yikes! That's not easy."

"No, it was not. I ended up leaving when I was about eighteen to go live with my grandmother," said Mona.

"Oh, really? I'm sorry to hear that, Mona. That had to be hard, too," said Iggy.

"It was. But I made it through life fine—minus the husbands . . . besides my last one. He was definitely a keeper," laughed Mona.

Iggy and Mona made it to the dining hall and into the kitchen.

"Alright. Let's decide what to cook," said Iggy.

"To answer your question, my specialty was fried chicken, mashed potatoes with gravy, biscuits, peas, and, for dessert, homemade apple pie," said Mona.

"That sounds so good. I can't wait for you to show me how it's done! Let me go and check the food storage to see if we have enough chicken for everyone."

"Sounds good. I'm so excited to be cooking for everyone!" Mona looked around the kitchen at everything.

There was a loud noise suddenly, and a lot of screaming and yelling going on. Mona wasn't sure what she should do, so just stayed still behind the pots and pans. Iggy came flying out with her eyes covered.

I can't believe what I just saw," said Iggy, all shaken up.

"What happened?" asked Mona, peeking through the pots and pans.

Before Iggy could say anything, Frankie came out with Tory.

"I didn't see anything, so don't worry, I won't tell," said Iggy, eyes wide open.

"We didn't mean for you to see us," said Tory.

"I forgot you were coming. All we were doing was making out," said Frankie.

"I get it. No problem. Let's just leave it alone."

"I just want to make it clear nothing was happening," said Tory.

"Frankie already made it clear. But what I saw was something totally different," said Iggy.

"Well, we were starting to have things happen," said Frankie.

'Please, Frankie, stop talking—it's not helping," said Tory.

"Now, where did Mona go?" asked Iggy.

"Mona's here with you?!" Tory was getting a little freaked out.

"Yes, she was the one I chose to cook dinner with me."

"I'm right here, Iggy," said Mona, coming out from behind the pots and pans. "Don't worry. I didn't see or hear anything Tory, so you don't have to worry about me saying anything."

"I wasn't worried about you, Mona. I'm looking forward to having your dinner tonight," said Tory.

"Well, all I have to say is Frankie, you can do better than Tory. She was nice and sweet and now, well . . . I won't go there. And Iggy, don't be too shocked at what you saw. Frankie doesn't have anything good under those clothes. So can you both please get out of the kitchen so me and Iggy can cook for the seniors?" asked Mona.

Frankie and Tory were speechless, and just left.

"Mona, that was so amazing. I can't believe you said that to them both!" said Iggy.

"Well, I only speak the truth," said Mona. "Are you sure you still want to make dinner with everything going on?"

"Yes, I'm sure," said Iggy.

"We can make a fantastic meal that will make everyone's mouth water!"

"Sounds like we are in for a treat!".

"It will probably be the best treat you've ever tasted," said Mona.

"I cook, too, so I'll be able to help a lot," said Iggy.

"OK, let's get down to business," said Mona.

"I can't wait to get started!"

"If it's OK with you, I'd like to make my famous gumbo. It wouldn't take too much time to make, with everything we have with the rest of the dinner," said Mona.

"Sounds so delicious, Mona. I can't wait to try it."

Mona and Iggy worked as a good team to get everything for the gumbo, the fried chicken, the sides, and the pie ready for everyone. They still had plenty of time, so they also made cornbread from scratch, and sweet potato fries.

"Oh my goodness! Everyone is going to love this!" said Iggy.

"I'd forgotten how it feels to be in the kitchen after twenty years," said Mona, getting a little emotional.

"It all looks wonderful," said Iggy. "And don't worry—I won't tell your secrets about what's in the gumbo or cornbread."

"Thanks, Iggy, for doing this with me. It meant lot to me. It was so much fun!"

"Oh, you're welcome. It was my pleasure, and I enjoyed your company, too," said Iggy.

"There is one thing I could live without," said Mona.

"What's that?" asked Iggy.

"Seeing the love connection between Tory and Frankie."

"I know, me too. I just can't believe I found them in there!"

"Me neither. But I would have took a rubber hose to those two for even thinking of doing that in here, where anyone could walk in on them!"

"Let's set the tables before everyone heads up for dinner," said Iggy.

"Sounds like a clever idea."

It was time for dinner, and everyone had been telling Mona how wonderful the food smelled and that they couldn't wait to try what her and Iggy made.

"Mona, you did a fantastic job! I never tasted gumbo like this before," said Agnes.

"Thank you, Agnes, I appreciate it," said Mona, who could not stop smiling. "Oh, I got gossip for you!!"

"Oh yeah, really?"

"You will never guess who Iggy found making out in the food storage room," said Mona.

"Oh my God! Who could it possibly be?" asked Tallulah, who was with Wanda.

"Frankie and Tory were getting hot and heavy in there!"

"Oh shit, really? They were?" asked Wanda in amazement.

"Yes, I could not believe it myself," said Mona.

Tallulah thought to herself about the other day, when she saw Frankie and Tory heating up the dining room. It was no surprise to her.

"Wow. I can't believe it! I wish I could have seen their faces," said Wanda.

"Me too. But Iggy's expression said it all," said Mona. She was glad she had been hiding behind the pots and pans for a while before they had known she was there.

"There are things going on here we just don't know about, and it's fun to find out!" said Agnes.

"Yes, I agree with you Agnes," said Mona.

"Well, that was a wonderful dinner, Mona. My stomach is full of your fried chicken, so I'm going to get ready for bed. I hope to see you tomorrow," said Tallulah, rubbing her stomach.

"Goodnight," said Edith, heading out the door.

Everyone was so full and tired out, they all went back to their cabins to bed. Mona sat in the dining room for a minute, thinking about the meal she had created and how proud she was.

Frankie came along and started picking things up.

"Do you need any help, Frankie?" asked Mona.

"No, I got it. But thank you for asking. By the way, your dinner was the best I ever had!"

"Thank you, Frankie, I appreciate that," said Mona, heading toward the door.

"Hey, Mona!" called Frankie.

Mona turned around.

"Can I ask you one last thing?"

"Sure, Frankie. What is your question?" asked Mona.

"Do you think maybe you could teach me some things? I would love to make my cooking better—though not as good as yours," said Frankie.

"Sure, anything is possible! I would like that. But only if you do one thing," said Mona.

"What can I do for you?"

"No more spanking the monkey in the kitchen!" laughed Mona.

"I promise I won't. that was embarrassing enough for me to not do that anymore," said Frankie.

"Have good night," said Mona.

"Goodnight, Mona," said Frankie, holding the door open for her.

Mona got back to the cabin and into bed, said her prayers, and went right to sleep before anyone else interrupted her. Another day fine done at camp.

CHAPTER 11

Operation Haze Seniors

Fay, Hazel, and Chip were standing around by the pool, talking before breakfast that morning.

"Why are we here, Chip?" asked Fay. She could be the sweetest person in the world, and would do anything for you, but she could also be brutally honest.

Chip looked at both girls with a big smile.

"What are you up to, Chip?" asked Hazel.

"I have an idea that I wanted to run past the both of you," said Chip.

"Why the both of us?" asked Fay.

"You two are the only ones I can trust, and you both enjoy having fun too," said Chip.

Both Hazel and Fay looked at each other with faces that said, *I don't know what he is talking about.*

"Well, that's true . . . what do you have up your sleeve?" asked Hazel. She wondered what could be on Chip's pig-headed brain.

"Let me just ask you this one question," said Chip.

"OK, go ahead, Chip—I can't wait to hear," said Hazel, getting a little impatient.

"Does anyone want to haze five seniors?" he asked.

The two girls just looked at each other, trying to figure out what Chip was talking about.

"When you talk about 'haze,' you mean, as in, a prank?" asked Fay, confused—which was normal for her.

"Yes, that's exactly right," said Chip.

"Why would we want to do that?" asked Hazel. But then it dawned on her what Agnes had said to Tory and Chip.

"Why would we do this?" asked Fay.

"A couple of them have been listening to mine and Tory's conversations, trying to make them into something they're not—and you both were at the pool when Agnes thought we were dating," said Chip, thinking about what Frankie had told him "So I think we should teach them a lesson or something."

"So, because you and the sexy lifeguard are hot for each other, you want to play this prank on five seniors who just don't know how to mind their own business?" asked Hazel.

"We are not hot for each other! I'm not even interested in Tory," said Chip, trying not to reveal they were cousins.

"Then how come you're blushing?" asked Fay, as both women laughed at him.

"I'm not blushing—it's just hot out this morning," said Chip. "Men don't blush."

"Oh really? OK, no problem. But you're blushing a little bit, Chip," said Hazel.

"You *are* still hot for your partner—and you can't deny it," said Fay, winking at Chip.

"Anyways, we're getting off the subject here. We need to focus—we don't have much time before the seniors go to breakfast and we have to be there," said Chip.

"So, let me get this straight—because they said something to Tory about you two being together, you think we should punish them?" asked Hazel.

"Oh my God, you two need to stop. I don't need that rumor going around here!"

"We're just playing with you, Chip. You need to chill," said Hazel.

Chip kept shaking his head. "You both are so unbelievable."

"I mean, in a way, they have been following us around," said Fay.

"That's true, but also they don't have things to do all the time—maybe stalking us makes them happy," said Hazel.

"Now, you're getting it!" said Chip.

"We're not going to hurt them—and it's simply a haze, that's all?" asked Hazel.

"Yes, that's all. I'm just out for fun revenge—not to hurt them."

They noticed a couple of the seniors going by and looking in through the gate.

"Good morning, beautiful women," said Chip as he waved to them.

"Good morning, sexy—and his bikini babes," said Tallulah.

"Yeah, we like each other so much, we can't stay away from each other," said Chip as Hazel punched him in his side.

The seniors went up the hill, not interested anymore.

"Really? You want to put that in their heads?" asked Hazel.

"It was the only thing that I could think of," said Chip. "We can talk about this later, when no one's around, and you can let me know if you're with me or against me."

Tallulah decided to come back and see what they were up to. She walked up to Chip on the other side of the gate.

"Hi, sexy. You ready to get wet with me sometime?" asked Tallulah.

"You really think this is funny, don't you?" asked Chip.

"Yeah, I do," said Hazel. She blew him a kiss and walked away with Fay, laughing.

Chip saw Hazel and Fay and ran up to them on their way to the dining room to get things set up for lunch. He put his arm around Hazel, but she punched him in the side, wanting nothing to do with him.

"How was swimming, Mr. Romeo?" she asked.

"Well, everyone kept their bathing suits on, and no one peed in the pool this time, so it went rather well," said Chip.

"Well, congratulations—you made it through with no issues." Hazel laughed.

"Oh, aren't we the little smartass?" said Chip.

Fay laughed at the both of them.

"I'd rather be a smartass than a person who makes seniors take off their bathing suits and pee in the pool", said Hazel.

"The bathing suit thing was a misunderstanding! And as for peeing in the pool, I had nothing to do with that—and it's not my fault someone couldn't hold their bladder!"

"OK, you two, can we stop the lovers' quarrel and get things done?" asked Fay, smirking.

"Oh, we are far from being in love!" said Hazel.

"What a way to shoot someone down!" said Chip. "Even if you weren't trying to."

"Are we dating?" asked Hazel.

"No, we are not," said Chip.

"Then, OK, I didn't say anything wrong," said Hazel.

"OK, no problem—conversation is over," said Chip.

"Can we please change the subject?" asked Fay.

"Anyways, the reason I came looking for you is because I have an idea of how we can haze or prank the seniors."

"Hope it didn't take to many brain cells to do it!" said Hazel.

Chip gave her a look and went on: "Do you know that colorful house on Oak Lane they say is haunted? I think it just looks like that because no one has lived there for a while . . . ."

"Are you talking about the pretty purple house on the corner?" asked Hazel.

"Yes, that's the one."

"Isn't it abandoned—and maybe a little haunted?" asked Hazel.

"Yes. That's what I just told you," said Chip.

"Yes, you did, I'm sorry," said Hazel, trying to swallow hard because she had to admit that she was wrong.

"I think if we go through with our plan to haze the seniors, we should use that house," said Chip.

"That's right—*if* we go through with it. Fay and I still need a lot better reasons than because the seniors bug the crap out of us," said Hazel.

"OK, well then, can we talk about it and figure it out?" asked Chip.

"Fine. That sounds good to us," said Fay.

"How about after dinner, when everyone is asleep, we meet down at the firepit?"

Hazel and Fay looked at each other and shrugged.

"Maybe you should haze the seniors by yourself—I'm sure a couple of them have the same IQ as you," said Hazel as her and Fay went inside the dining hall, leaving Chip alone.

"She can be such a bitch sometimes. Why I am so crazy about her?" said Chip to himself.

Edith was behind a tree, listening in. She couldn't wait to see the girls to tell them what she'd heard.

"It's that time again," said Agnes.

"It smells good. Maybe we're in for a treat," said Tallulah.

"Nothing will beat Mona's cooking—that's for sure," said Agnes.

"I agree. It's been so long since I have had a homecooked meal like that," said Tallulah.

"Hey, girls, I got some juicy gossip to tell you," chuckled Edith as she walked over.

"Oh, gossip! I love it!" said Tallulah, getting excited.

Edith looked around to make sure no one would hear them.

"I overheard a conversation . . . well, just Chip."

"Oh, how exciting! Was he talking to himself?" asked Agnes.

"Yes, exactly—he was talking to himself. And he said he was in love with Hazel!"

"Oh, that is very interesting!" said Agnes.

"Yes, it is. I never would have thought he would be a person to talk to himself . . . it's not like he's old, like us," said Tallulah.

"As usual, you're missing the point!" said Agnes.

"OK, what am I missing?" asked Tallulah.

"Let me make it easy for you, Tallulah. Chip likes Hazel," said Edith.

"Oh, really? That's so disappointing. I really wanted him to be with Tory . . . because Hazel is, just, well . . . boring!" said Tallulah.

"Well, either way, we have something on him and Hazel, so it's going to be fun," said Agnes.

"We will have to think of something for them to let them both know they like each other or something like that," said Edith.

"We don't know if he feels the same way, so that might be difficult," said Tallulah.

"Not if we tell each of them at separate times that one likes the other," said Agnes.

"So when should we drop the ball on them?" asked Agnes.

"It's drop the *bomb*, not *ball*—but whatever works for you, Agnes," said Edith.

"Whichever way. Who cares?" said Agnes.

"They'll both be here in the dining hall soon—it might be perfect timing."

"Sure, why not?"

"I'll take Hazel. She seems easy to tell something like this to," said Edith.

"We can drop the bomb on Chip," said Agnes, happy she'd gotten it right this time.

"What do you mean *we*?" asked Tallulah.

"If you want to go with Edith to tell Hazel, go ahead," said Agnes.

"Come on, Tallulah, let's go before Hazel disappears," said Edith, grabbing her arm and dragging her with Edith.

They went into the dining hall and looked around for Hazel.

"There she is over there," said Edith, pointing to the food counter.

"Are we ready to do this?" asked Tallulah.

"I know I am—because this is juicy gossip!" said Edith.

"OK, then let's go—before more people come in for dinner," said Tallulah.

Edith and Tallulah went over to Hazel.

"Wow, look at all this food!" said Tallulah.

"Tallulah, focus on why we're here, not the food," said Edith. "Hazel, I heard a little birdie talking about you!"

"Oh really? And who is this little birdie?" asked Hazel.

"Well, supposedly this birdie likes you a lot. Their words were that they were in love with you," said Edith.

Hazel and Fay looked at each other and started laughing at Edith.

"I really think you got your information mixed up. There's no one interested in me here," said Hazel.

"How do you know, dear?" asked Edith.

"There's no one here I'm interested in, so why would anyone be interested in me?" asked Hazel.

"You are a very pretty girl—any guy would be crazy not to date you," said Edith.

"Tallulah, can you help me here?" asked Edith, turning around to see Tallulah snacking on the food left on the counter.

"Tallulah, what the hell are you doing?" asked Hazel, taking the food away from her. "That's not just for you!"

"Sorry, I was hungry!"

Everyone shook their head. You never knew what Tallulah was up to.

"Hey Edith, did you tell Hazel about Chip being in love with her?" she asked as she licked her fingers.

"Oh, Tallulah, sometimes I don't understand where your brain is," said Edith. "Well, OK, now the cat's out of the bag. That's what I was trying to tell you, with the thing with the birdie . . . which didn't go so well," said Edith.

"Chip is in love with me?" asked Hazel.

"Yes, that's true. I heard him myself. I thought you should know," said Edith.

Hazel stood there and shook her head. Fay wasn't sure what to think, either.

"I have to talk to him," said Hazel.

"No, you can't do that," said Edith.

"Why can't I?"

"He doesn't know I heard him or that I told you, and I just don't think it's a good idea."

"Edith has a point," said Fay.

Hazel was confused. She wasn't sure what to do. "I'll keep it to myself."

"We're sorry for taking up your time, but it was nice chatting with you both. Now, it's our time to split," said Edith.

Hazel and Fay were trying to figure out what had just happened.

"Come on, Tallulah, we have to go now," said Edith, dragging her to their table.

They took a seat and stayed silent.

"Well, I think that went rather well," said Tallulah, taking a dinner roll out of her pocket.

"Were you part of the same conversation I was?" asked Edith.

"Yes, and Hazel took the news rather well, I think," said Tallulah.

"Yeah, especially the part where you totally spilled the beans about Chip having feelings for her!"

"Yes, that was the plan. But I didn't want to just blurt it out!" said Edith.

"At least she knows now, and we don't have to keep it a secret anymore," said Tallulah.

"I guess that's true, but still I don't want it coming back to us," said Edith.

"I don't think it will, because Hazel seems to be a real down-to-earth girl. Chip would be lucky to have her," said Tallulah.

"I hope you're right, Tallulah," said Edith.

"I'm hardly wrong, so we have nothing to worry about," said Tallulah as she snacked on another roll.

"I won't say anything about how often you're right," said Edith.

"Let's just have a great meal with our friends and make it a wonderful day," said Tallulah.

Everyone got to the table and started talking to each other.

"How did your chat go with Chip?'" asked Edith.

"I think I might have confused him a little, but overall, good talk," said Agnes.

"How about you two? Did it go well with Hazel?" asked Agnes.

"Oh, so wonderful. Right, Tallulah?" asked Edith.

"Yeah, it was OK. I was having too much fun eating. I can tell you it's going to be a great meal," said Tallulah.

"Oh, good. So that means that mission is complete. Now, we just watch the fireworks," said Agnes, loving every minute.

"Yeah, I'm sure there will be a lot of fireworks," said Edith.

After a long day, it was time for Hazel, Fay, and Chip to meet down by the firepit.

"I'm really not sure about this," said Hazel.

"You're going to be fine, and I'm going to be there, too, so there's nothing to worry about," said Fay.

"I just don't know if I should trust what Edith and Tallulah told me about Chip," said Hazel.

"I wouldn't worry about that, because if he really had feelings for you, he would have told you, I would think," said Fay.

"I guess you're right. I'm just not going to worry about it, because I'm not ready to date anyways," said Hazel.

"I totally understand," said Fay.

"Understand what?" asked Chip as he caught up to them.

"That today just seemed like a very long day for some reason," said Fay.

"Yeah, that's true, I agree" said Chip.

"Wow, he agreed with us! I am so in shock," said Hazel.

"Oh, stop. Let's get this planning rolling."

The more Hazel thought about it, the more it seemed fun to do this to them. Who knew if they would fall for it.

"So, for what reason besides the seniors being nosy old ladies do you want to do this?" asked Fay.

"OK, so they're nosy. They're getting in our business and spreading rumors that aren't true, and I don't know . . . I just want to do something fun, and thought they'd be a good target."

"It would be kind of fun. I mean, just look at all the crap they've done here in just a couple of days," said Fay, looking at Hazel.

"They had a paint fight, they put a golfcart in the pool, and they even took Frankie's clothes while he was in the shower, " said Chip.

"I don't know, Chip. It sounds like it could be dangerous," said Hazel.

"It won't be dangerous, I swear. No one will be injured," said Chip.

"I still don't know," said Hazel.

"Have I ever put anyone in danger before as long as you have known me?"

"So far, you haven't, but that can change at any moment—you never know."

"We are going to be the ones in charge. We will be able to plan everything out so we know everything going on," said Chip.

"What do you think, Fay? You're a little quiet about this whole thing?" said Hazel.

"Well, they do like to have fun. It could be interesting to do something to them."

"I hate to say it, but you're right, Chip. Just don't let it go to your head," said Hazel.

"Huh? What was that?" asked Chip, being a smartass.

"Yeah, so funny Chip," said Hazel, not really amused.

"If we plan things out safely, then I am in," said Hazel.

"If you promise no injuries, I am, too," said Fay.

"Great. Then let's do this," said Chip.

"This is going to be so much fun," said Hazel.

"Chip, I'm warning you, if one senior gets one little scratch on them, I won't be afraid to hurt you," said Hazel.

"Do you hear us, Chip?" asked Fay.

"Yes, I hear you. So both of you, just relax and stop your squawking."

"You are such an idiot sometimes," said Fay.

"Well, thank you, Fay—coming from you, that's a compliment."

"I didn't mean it as a compliment."

"So, we got the house, we got the seniors. Now we just need the rest of the plan," said Hazel.

"They want to make memories, and that's what they will exactly get," said Fay.

"I'll go on my day off tomorrow to see exactly what shape the house in," said Chip.

"So now, we need them to take the bait," said Fay.

"I don't think it'll be that hard—especially with these women being so nosy and fun-loving," said Fay.

"They are always lurking around listening to us," said Hazel.

"So, if we all talk about the funhouse, then they should get interested in it and want to go and check it out for themselves," said Fay.

"What kind of things should be in the house?" asked Chip.

"Well, you haven't checked it out yet, so I really don't know," said Hazel. "But we've seen the outside, so we can probably try for now just to picture what's in it."

"So, once you get there, we'll have a clear idea of exactly what to do," said Fay.

"Yeah, I see your point. I'll check it out tomorrow and meet you two back here tomorrow night," said Chip.

"I say we turn in for tonight and resume tomorrow," said Hazel, yawning and stretching.

The three of them decided to turn in. There wasn't a lot they could do until tomorrow.

Tomorrow night arrived, and Chip had a lot to tell the girls. He was getting the fire going at the firepit, waiting for them to come. He could hear their laughter, so he knew they were close.

"Well, look who graced me with their presence," laughed Chip.

"I'm guessing that you had a good day off," said Hazel.

"Yes, I did, and I have so much to tell the both of you," said Chip.

They all sat down by the fire.

"So, the house is completely empty besides some old furniture, and you can just go right the door," said Chip.

"It's not locked?" asked Hazel.

"No, it wasn't locked at all," said Chip.

"Wow, that's shocking . . . especially in that neighborhood," said Fay.

"Yeah, I just can't believe that! But that's good—they'll have it easy getting into it," said Hazel.

"So, I believe the house has ten rooms in it. They each have assorted color doors, which looked weird with everything else," said Chip.

"I think ten rooms is good amount in that house," said Hazel.

I would never have guessed there were that many rooms in that place. Outside, it sure doesn't look like it," said Chip.

"Me neither," said Hazel.

"If they don't feel like they can make it up the long staircase, I saw an elevator, and it still works," said Chip.

"Now, that's something you don't see in any house, unless it's a mansion," said Fay.

"That is very true. I mean, I was in shock when I saw it still worked, but I still plan on check it out, so that it's safe."

"How much work does the rest of the house need?" asked Hazel.

"Honestly, not much. It's still in great condition . . . just maybe some dusting and little household chores like that," said Chip.

"That's good, because we got to get this plan in motion before they leave in four days," said Hazel.

"It will definitely be done. And anything else we need to get done will also be finished."

"OK, if you say so, Mr. Fix-It," laughed Hazel.

"You just watch. You'll be amazed by what I can do. So, let's get planning."

"We could do Survivor—the senior version—where we think of all these different things for them to do," said Fay.

"We could make up easy challenges along the way in each of the rooms by their colors," said Chip. "Downstairs, there's a big room where we can jump out and say gotcha!"

"That could be fun! Hopefully they learn their lesson about being nosy," said Hazel.

"Yeah, we can all hope that, but I don't know for sure," said Fay.

"So, while you were checking out the house situation, I was looking for unique names of street signs we can use for each of the challenges," said Hazel.

"This could turn into an interesting challenge," said Chip.

As they went through street names, they produced interesting ideas for things for the seniors to do.

"I really like these names. They're names we've never heard before," said Chip, laughing at a few of them.

"Where did you get this list?" asked Fay.

Hazel told them she had looked them up on Google, and they started laughing.

"It makes it more fun for them and us to make the challenges these names," said Hazel.

"Let's just go through the list and make sure we've gotten it all together, then plan what to do for them," said Fay.

"So, are we ready to go through this list?" asked Hazel.

"Yes, let's do it," said Chip and Fay at the same time.

"OK, so I picked Gasoline Alley, Pudding Ridge Road, Pillow Talk Road, Little Smokey Lane, Alcohol Bloody Mary, Farfrompoopen Road, Hanky-Panky Lane, Stub-Toe-Lane, DUH Drive, and Booger Branch Road," said Hazel.

"I like that Farfrompoopen Road—that's so funny," said Chip.

"I thought of you when I picked it," laughed Hazel.

Why would you think of me for that one?" asked Chip.

"It just sounds something that you would be doing a lot," said Hazel.

"Yeah, I guess I do a lot of pooping," laughed Chip.

"Ew! Gross," said Fay.

"He speaks the truth," said Hazel.

"Unfortunately, I can't deny it. But girls also do the same— I'm just saying," said Chip.

"I think we need to end the conversation, because otherwise this won't get finished," said Hazel.

"Yeah, OK, you're right, as always," said Chip.

"At least he speaks the truth again," laugh Hazel.

"Now we must figure out what we will do for each of them," said Fay.

"We can put in as much detail as we want to," said Chip.

"We all agreed we wanted to do this so they can have fun," said Hazel. She went into her own little world for a minute.

"Come back to earth, Hazel," said Chip.

"Very funny, Chip." she said sarcastically.

She kept thinking about what Edith and Tallulah had told her.

"Where is your mind?" asked Fay.

"Nowhere. I was just thinking about the seniors and these challenges," said Hazel.

"Their first challenge is Gasoline Alley, and it will be in the blue room," said Chip.

"I think we should start off easy and have them try to a build a fire," said Fay.

"Well, I did see a fireplace in the first room. It must have been a master bedroom or something," said Chip.

"That doesn't sound too easy?" asked Hazel.

"It could be, but I can set it up so all they need to do is light it. Hopefully, they won't burn the house down or each other," said Chip.

"That is a horrible thing to think about," said Hazel.

"They might not think it's easy to do. Let's face it—they're a bunch of women."

"Women who have been around a lot longer than us and can do just as much as men."

"There are more women here than men. What does that show, hotshot?" asked Fay.

"OK, you got me there," said Chip.

"Thought so," laughed Hazel.

"Second challenge is Pudding Ridge Road," said Hazel.

"Pudding sounds good right about now," said Chip.

"You sound just like Frankie with his food," said Fay.

"Is all you think about food?" asked Hazel.

"No, I'm not like Frankie, who must always eat every hour of the day," said Chip.

"Are you sure about that?" asked Hazel.

Chip didn't say any more and went on thinking about the next challenge. "That room can be green. What can we do for that besides eating pudding?"

"How about a variety of different puddings we have not heard of before?" asked Fay.

"Everyone loves pudding, but making them weird varieties of pudding is something I am sure they have never done," said Hazel.

"They will never know what's coming to them," said Chip.

Fay took her phone out and looked up different kind of pudding to see what they could use and how to make it.

"OK, here we go. Are you ready for these? They're very interesting," said Fay.

"We have rice pudding, which is original," said Hazel, laughing.

"OK, here we go . . . bread and butter pudding. It sounds like we are in jail," said Fay.

"How would you know about jail?" asked Hazel, giving her a mysterious look.

"I've never been," said Fay. "There is groat pudding.

"Ew, that sounds so nasty and wrong," said Chip.

"It sounds disgusting, like something I wouldn't eat or even touch," said Hazel.

"Wait until you hear this one, Hazel. You're going to love it," said Fay.

"Oh, I can't wait to hear," said Hazel.

"Here you go. Hogs pudding," said Fay.

"If we aren't making it with any pig body parts, I will have no problem," said Hazel.

"Our last one I think is a good one is called jam roly-poly pudding," said Fay.

"That one doesn't seem that bad," said Chip. "Now that I have heard those pudding names, it makes me not want any pudding at all, though."

"I still can't picture you not tasting them all," said Hazel. "Do you think they will try them?"

"I think Tallulah will," said Fay.

"If they're eager to know what's waiting for them at the end, they will," said Chip.

"We do have seniors who love to eat," said Fay.

"I hope they have good tastebuds and empty stomachs," said Hazel.

"I sent you both the ingredients for the puddings so we can start making them," said Fay.

"How are we going to find these things? I'm sure that Frankie doesn't have them in his kitchen," said Hazel.

"Then we will have to improvise the best we can," said Chip.

"That sounds like a lot of fun," said Fay.

"Third challenge is Pillow Talk Road, which sounds so sweet," said Hazel.

"That can be the pink room," said Chip.

"Let them have an old-fashioned pillow fight. I'm sure they had them when they were younger," said Hazel.

"Oh my God, that would be so great. And kind of cute," said Fay.

"Of course, you two would think of something like that," said Chip.

"Did you have a better idea for that room?" asked Hazel.

"No, I don't, OK? I just think it's too girly."

"Oh, Chip, you're such a boy—not yet a man," laughed Fay.

"Would you like to see just how much of a man I am, Fay?" asked Chip, starting to unzip his pants.

"No, I don't want it to come out and bite me!" said Fay.

"Good one, Fay," said Hazel as the girls high-fived.

"Very funny, you two. You don't know what you're missing," said Chip.

"Probably not a whole hell of a lot," said Hazel.

"So, let's get back to where we left off," said Fay. "It's going to be a lot of fun watching them hit each other."

"It would be fun to see that happening. It's not every day you see seniors hitting each other with pillows," laughed Hazel.

"That is so true. And just think of all the feathers that will come out of all the pillows," said Fay.

"I guess it's a great stress reliever," said Chip.

"Speaking of watching, are we going to be able to see what they're doing?" asked Hazel.

"Yes, I do plan on having hidden cameras around the whole house so we can make sure they're OK and haven't killed each other," said Chip.

"In fact, when we are all done going through everything here, I'm going to get the cameras all installed."

"Sounds good to us," said Hazel.

"When will we have to make the pudding?" asked Fay.

"I'm thinking we might have to wait after hours for that, so that we don't get busted."

"True. We can't have this leak to anyone," said Hazel.

"If we're going to get things done right, it might take a couple of days," said Chip.

"Then we can put the plan in motion in a couple days and watch and see if the seniors fall for it or not," said Fay.

"Sounds good. I'd rather things be right than have something go wrong," said Hazel.

"Yes, we know," laughed Chip.

"You honestly think it's funny if one of the seniors gets injured?" asked Hazel.

"No, it wouldn't be funny. I just don't think you should have to preach it every five minutes," said Chip.

"He does have a good point," said Fay.

"We are going to have cameras. We are going through every challenge with a fine-toothed comb so everything will be OK," said Chip.

"Fine, I get what you're saying, and I will stop," said Hazel, shaking her head.

"Can we please go on to the next challenge?" asked Fay.

"Yes, and I think you might like this one, Chip," said Hazel. "Fourth challenge is Little Smokie Lane."

"Leave them candy cigarettes on a table and see who tries to smoke them," laughed Chip.

"I have an impressive idea," said Fay.

"Let them shoot something! Like what they have at the fair every year," said Chip.

"Give them a toy gun and shoot a good target to shoot at," said Hazel.

"I saw a stuffed bear someone must have shot. Maybe that could be their target."

"Why would someone leave a stuffed bear in the house?" asked Hazel.

"Maybe they thought it would scare people away," said Chip.

"I'd rather they didn't shoot themselves or each other, so the bear is a good idea," said Hazel.

"Let them shoot at a moving bear, like what you see at the fairs. I can probably make it so the bear moves. It has a flat bottom, so it shouldn't be too hard," said Chip.

"We can name him," said Hazel.

"No, that's OK. We don't need to go that far," laughed Fay.

"We can use a pellet gun so they won't attempt to hurt each other, though it should go into the bear," said Chip.

"I can just picture how this is going to work," said Hazel.

"Fifth challenge is Alcohol Bloody Mary Road. For that one, the room is orange," said Chip.

"I think they should drink a large cup of V8 juice and we'll make them think it a real blood," said Hazel."

"OK, I am not a fan of tomato juice, so that just sounds so wrong," said Fay.

"We can just make a virgin Bloody Mary, and they'll think they're getting drunk," said Hazel.

"Who wants to have a Bloody Mary?" asked Fay.

"I hate to admit it, but I have had a Bloody Mary before," said Hazel. Fay and Chip laughed at her.

"Really? I am surprised by that," said Fay.

"Yeah. I'm not a big drinker in the first place, I don't really like V8 juice, like I said."

"That sucks," said Chip.

"Why does it suck, Chip?" asked Hazel. "I can't wait to hear this."

"I don't know, so never mind," said Chip.

Hazel and Fay shook their heads but didn't question Chip any more.

"So, what is next on the list?" he asked.

Hazel heard a noise coming from the bushes by the teepee that had been put up near the bridge. "Do you two hear that?" she asked, her eyes wide open.

"Yes, I hear it," said Fay.

"What do you think it is?" asked Hazel as she grabbed on to Fay.

"Really, Hazel, I'm sure it's nothing. Stop grabbing my arm—you're making me lose feeling in it," said Fay, trying to stay calm.

"It's probably just a deer or something," said Chip, who was starting to get nervous himself, but didn't want the girls to know.

Out of nowhere, they saw Casper and Juniper walking together and holding hands.

"Oh my fucking God!" whispered Fay in Hazel's ear.

"I sure can't believe what I'm seeing right now," whispers Hazel.

"I didn't know those two were hanging out with each other," said Chip.

"Really I thought you men talked about girls and things like that," said Hazel.

Casper leaned in close to Juniper and kissed her passionately as the others were hiding behind a tree, watching in amazement.

"That doesn't look like they're just spending time together as friends," said Hazel.

"How long do you think they have been spending time together?" asked Fay.

"I really don't know, but I am guessing a while, the way they're kissing," said Hazel.

"Yeah, that's more like making out if you ask me," said Chip.

"No one asked you, Chip, I believe," said Hazel.

"Oh, boy. I wonder if Harlow knows about them," said Fay.

"I'm guessing no, because she isn't the type to keep something like this in. If and when she finds out, she is going to be upset," said Hazel.

"We don't even know what this is between them," said Fay.

"It's clear that they like each other," said Hazel.

"It's clearly them making out," said Chip.

"You are such a guy, Chip. We all see," said Hazel.

"They're actually only kissing. Not making out. Trust me, I know the difference," said Chip.

"OK, hot stuff, when was the last time you made out—or just kissed someone?" asked Fay.

"Before I came here this summer, if you must even know. But it's not your business," said Chip.

"Oh really?" asked Hazel.

"Do you plan on seeing her when you get back home?" asked Fay.

"Maybe I will. I won't know that answer until I'm home," said Chip.

That didn't settle well with Hazel, because deep down inside, she had feelings for Chip. And she knew that he has feelings for her. But she wasn't sure how to act knowing what she knew thanks to Edith and Tallulah. Chip was ready to blow the secret that he loved Hazel, and that he and Tory were cousins and were looking for Chip's mother.

"Let me ask you this, and whatever you say, I will let it go," said Hazel.

"OK, what is your question, Hazel?" asked Chip.

"Are you a good lover?" asked Hazel.

"Whoa! Where did this come from?" asked Fay, who was stunned Hazel would go there.

"I'm just curious, that's all," said Hazel.

"I'm just not good at making the first move when it comes to women, but when I'm with a woman sexually, they've never had any complaints," said Chip.

"OK, Romeo and Juliet, we need to get off this topic and figure out what are we going to do about what we saw between Casper and Juniper," said Fay.

"I think we should just act like we didn't see anything and let them figure it out for themselves. Then, they will work it out with Harlow," said Hazel.

"True. I'd rather not get involved. We've got other things to focus on. We need to finish our planning," said Chip.

"When Harlow does find out, I don't want any part of it. It won't be fun to watch," said Hazel.

"We have five more to go, so let's get it done," said Fay.

"You're right, Fay. Let's get focused so we can go to bed. I'm getting tired," said Hazel as she yawned.

"Can we go to bed together?" asked Chip.

"Oh, that's a big NO," said Hazel.

"Thanks for shooting me down!" said Chip.

"You're welcome, lover boy," said Hazel.

"OK, the sixth challenge is Farfrompoopen Road," said Fay.

Chip started laughing. "It's just funny to me. Sorry, I can't help it."

"That is a road that you don't hear of every day," said Hazel.

"I've never heard the name before—just like the rest of them," said Fay.

"It's a great time to be in a brown room," said Chip.

"How about deli meats on hard rolls with different kinds of sauce on them?" asked Fay.

"That sounds better then eating pieces of a dead animal," said Hazel.

"OK, so for deli meat, we can do roast beef, ham, bologna, corned beef, turkey, and liverwurst," said Fay.

"You do know liverwurst is not a deli meat, right?" asked Hazel.

"If you can get it in the deli, it's deli meat to me," said Chip.

"You are so unbelievable," said Hazel.

"Yeah, unbelievably handsome," said Chip with a smirk.

"I would not go that far," said Fay.

"Gee, thanks, girls, for ganging up on me," said Chip, shaking his head.

"I just hate to tell you, Hazel, but I agree with him," said Fay.

"About what? That I am handsome?" asked Chip.

"No. Sorry to burst your bubble on that. But if you see liverwurst in a deli, then it's a deli meat." Fay put her head down, knowing Hazel was going to say something.

Camp Funhouse

"OK, well we are all entitled to our opinions," said Hazel.

"OK, so, for sauces I found unique ones," said Fay.

"OK, let's hear them," said Hazel.

"There is monkey gland sauce, mumbo sauce, comeback sauce, banana ketchup, salsa golf, and mojo sauce," said Fay.

"Those are very interesting sauces," said Chip.

"Do we really have to put it on bread? It might be better without," said Hazel. "We can just spread each one on the meat."

"They need a roll to hold onto when eating it," said Fay.

"We can use the bottom roll if they want to pick it up," said Hazel.

"How are we going to make the sauce and pudding all within two days?" asked Fay.

"We can do it. I have faith in the three of us," said Chip.

"That is nice coming from you, Chip," said Hazel.

"I'm just feeling a little overwhelmed," said Fay.

"It will be OK, Fay. And it will be fun for us to do something together," said Hazel.

"That is true. I would love to be in the kitchen making things that are gross but good at the same time," said Fay.

"The seventh challenge is Hanky-Panky Lane. So, that can be in the red room, which has a disco ball already hanging from the ceiling," said Chip.

"We could make it like truth or dare, without the dare," said Hazel.

"How is that interesting, without the dare?" asked Fay.

"There can be dares, but no dirty ones. And get them to dance!" said Hazel.

"Oh, Hazel's got a dirty mind! I love it," said Fay.

"How is that dirty when I said I didn't think we should do dirty dares?" asked Hazel.

"The questions won't be dirty, and it will give them a chance to get to know each other more than they do." said Hazel. "Hey, Fay, do you still have that book in your suitcase?"

"What book?" asked Fay.

"The one that has a pink cover and has over hundred of the most-asked sex questions."

Fay's face got very red. It was hard for her to keep a straight face.

"You have a sex book?" asked Chip, laughing.

"Yes. I think I might have it around somewhere," said Fay.

"Maybe we can use that for the questions," said Hazel. "Then we don't have to look them up."

"Sure, that would make it interesting," said Fay.

"Oh, I'm sure it will be interesting to know about these seniors' pasts—or even their fetishes, if they have any still," said Hazel.

"I'm not sure I want to really go down the sex road with these seniors," said Chip.

"Why is that, Chip?" asked Hazel.

"I already saw two of them naked in the pool. That should explain it all," said Chip.

"Oh, you're big boy. You can take a few seniors talking about sex," said Hazel.

"Don't worry. It'll be OK," said Fay.

"I might have to skip this conversation," said Chip.

"Oh, stop. It won't be that bad," said Hazel.

"We will see about that," said Chip.

"The eighth challenge is Stub Toe Lane," said Fay.

"Sounds like that one should be in the yellow room," said Chip.

"That sounds like a pretty room," said Fay.

"I got this one. And I think you both will be impressed," said Chip.

"OK, Chip, please, impress us," said Hazel.

"There are water tubes with a plastic ball at the bottom, and there's a water tank, or a big bucket of water, and they must go to the tank with a little plastic cup and go to the water tubes, dump the water in them, and keep going back and forth until one of them finishes," said Chip.

"That sounds fun, like something I would like to try sometime," said Fay.

"Yeah, maybe we should try it after this is all done with," said Hazel.

"Of course, the king will beat the both of you," said Chip, flexing his muscles.

Hazel stood up and got in front of Chip. "You really think that you can beat us? I can do circle around you before you even get to the tube!"

"I can beat you with my hands tied behind my back," said Chip.

"I'll be more than happy to except your challenge," said Hazel.

"Challenge accepted. Once all this has finished, and the seniors are back safe, I will beat you," said Chip.

"Keep dreaming, buddy," said Hazel as she nudged him in the shoulder. "The nineth challenge is called DUH Drive."

"I think this time, we should make it trivia questions," said Fay.

"One of us could be the host and come up on a television screen and ask them questions," said Hazel.

"There is one problem with that," said Chip.

"What?"

"If one of us is on the television screen, they'll see who we are and know what we did," said Fay.

"Not if we black ourselves out and do something with our voices," said Hazel.

". . . which we can do. That's not hard to figure out," said Chip.

"Then I see no problem," said Hazel.

"So, you want me to give up my sex questions so you can think of easy trivia questions?" asked Fay.

"You have the book, and I have Google," said Hazel as she held up her phone.

"Well, they were born in the eighteen hundreds, so you might want the answers to be easy," said Chip.

"They are not *that* ancient," said Hazel.

"OK, guys, let's not start again. We only have one more challenge to do, and then we are done for the night," said Fay.

"Yes, you're right, Fay," said Hazel.

"So, the tenth and final challenge is Booger Branch Road," said Fay.

"We have a giant nose, and one person can be the lucky one to pick it through all the boogers and the slime," said Chip.

"Ew, that really sounds disgusting," said Hazel.

"Yes, it is. We can have the slime coming out of the nose," said Chip.

"What are they searching for when picking it?" asked Hazel.

"Hmm, good question," said Chip.

"They all sat there quiet to figure out what the seniors could find in the nose.

"What about gold coins?" asked Fay.

"It does sound like a clever idea," said Hazel.

"Can I pick your nose, Hazel?" asked Fay, attempting to stick her finger up Hazel's nose.

"That is so gross. I'd rather not have your fingers up my nose," said Hazel.

"Sound fun to me," agreed Chip.

"Don't encourage her, Chip," laughed Hazel.

"I can't wait to see how they're going to do all this without killing each other," said Chip. "We are finally finished with everything." He stretched.

"Thank God. I feel like we have been doing this for hours," said Fay.

"It was only three hours," said Hazel.

"It will be fun once they take the bait. Everything else will fall into place," said Chip. "Maybe they will stop listening to other people's conversations, too."

"We will just have to wait and see how all of this goes down," said Hazel. "Now all we must do is put the plan in action in a couple days, and let the fun begin . . . . So, we will just meet up at the bottom of the hill tomorrow to see if we can get them interested."

"Let the adventure begin!" said Fay.

"Yeah, OK, whatever you say. I'm tired, so I'm going to bed," said Hazel. She stood up and stretched, getting ready to leave.

The girls went back to their cabins and got ready to put the plan in action. Chip snuck out of the cabin and headed to the haunted house to start working on the challenges.

"Can I ask you something, Fay?" asked Hazel.

"Of course, you can you know you can," said Fay.

"What do you think of this whole Harlow and Casper thing?" asked Hazel.

"I honestly don't think we should get involved in whatever's going on with those two."

"Harlow and Casper have a past together that will never change, and it wasn't always roses, so seeing different people isn't a terrible thing," said Hazel.

"I don't know . . . maybe you're right," said Hazel.

"Plus, we both know Harlow is so busy screwing guys that she probably doesn't even know who they are," said Fay.

"Screwing, really? That's all you can think of?" asked Hazel.

"OK fine screwing or *bonking* guys," said Fay.

"That sounds much better." Hazel giggled.

"I'm a sucker for romance," said Fay. "You need romance in your life, Hazel."

"No, it's OK. I enjoy being single," said Hazel. She didn't want to tell Fay about her feelings for Chip.

"Listen, Hazel, we are best friends, and I know it has been rough since you lost Milo five years ago. But he would have wanted you to be happy and move on," said Fay.

"Please, don't go any further with that. You know I'm not ready to move on yet."

"You could have fooled me, the way you go after Chip like the tonight," said Fay.

"He was just being his normal self," said Hazel.

"Should we head back now?" asked Hazel.

158 April Carter

"Yes, I'm so tired and my ass hurts from sitting on that rock for so long," said Fay.

"Not my fault you have a boney ass," laughed Hazel.

"Well, I can't help that. I guess I was just blessed to have a boney ass," laughed Fay.

It was one day from the haze of the seniors. And Chip had the majority of everything done. He was lucky that he didn't need to purchase anything, and he found certain items he needed around places like his house. He had everything in place so it would be safe and fun. He installed cameras so that Hazel, Fay, and him could keep close tabs on them. They still had to make all the puddings and sauces for the food challenges.

"Are we sure that we should be doing this to them?" asked Hazel.

"Yes, they will be fine," said Chip.

"How do we know they will even take the bait?" asked Fay.

"Oh, they will, because they're nosy, and they love drama," said Hazel.

"So, are you ready to put this plan in motion?" asked Chip.

"Yes, we are," Fay and Hazel said at the same time.

"Woohoo! Yes, let's do this," said Chip, excited.

"Chip, I do have something on my mind," said Hazel.

"What is it?" asked Chip.

"Do you think we will get in trouble doing this?" asked Hazel.

"Don't worry, everything will be fine," said Chip.

"I really hope you're right," said Hazel.

"If I'm not, I will take responsibility for it," said Chip.

"You would do that so Fay and I wouldn't get in trouble?" asked Hazel.

"Of course I would. I mean, it *was* my idea in the first place," said Chip. "I think we should just think happy thoughts and everything will turn out just the way we talked about."

"Let the games begin," said Fay, laughing.

CHAPTER 12

Hook, Line, and Sinker

Hazel, Chip, and Fay were walking up the hill, talking away, as Tallulah and Agnes walked behind them, acting like the Rockettes and doing the can-can up the hill, being loud.

"I'm surprised I can get my leg up that high! Must be the new hips I got," said Agnes.

"It just shows how flexible you are," said Tallulah.

"I always thought you were the flexible one," said Agnes.

"My husband used to think so when we were in bed," said Tallulah.

"You honestly have no filter for what you say," said Agnes.

"Well, I have always been able to peak my mind," said Tallulah.

Chip almost puked. He turned his head a little to see if they were following them and paying any attention to what they were saying.

"I think we should change one thing," he whispered to the girls..

"What do you want to change? We have everything all set!" said Fay.

"I think we should tell them it's a funhouse instead of a haunted house—they might not buy it," said Chip.

Hazel and Fay looked at each other and thought maybe it might be a good idea. They didn't want the seniors to be too scared, so they nodded.

Chip gave them the signal to start talking about the funhouse.

"Hey, Fay, when is your next day off?" asked Hazel.

"I have Friday off, and I am so excited," said Fay.

"Do you have any plans?" asked Chip.

"Well, I heard from a friend of mine that there is this old house over on Oak Lane that everyone calls the funhouse, and it might be haunted, so we are going to go and take a look and see if it's true or not," said Fay. "You both know how much I love old funhouses."

"You're so weird," said Chip.

Hazel gave him a slap on the back of the head.

"Hey, if she likes funhouses, that's OK. We all have our things we like," said Hazel.

"Hit him harder, Hazel—he might like it!" yelled Tallulah.

Hazel turned around and laughed at Tallulah. Chip just gave her an eye roll look.

"Sorry, I thought that was funny for a hot second," said Hazel.

"It sounds like a lot of fun. I can't wait to go," said Fay.

"Are you off also, Chip?" asked Hazel.

"Yes, I am also off on Friday," he said.

"It seems like you just had a day off," said Hazel.

"Well, I did, but I took this one off because I had something to do," said Chip.

"Then you should come with me and my friend. She won't mind if you come along, and we will have a blast together," said Fay.

"Too bad I must stay here and work. But I hope it's a lot of fun for you." Hazel winked.

"We can have a threesome," laughed Chip.

"Um, no, that's not going to happen," said Fay.

Tallulah giggled a little.

"Is there something funny about that, Tallulah?" asked Chip.

"No, threesomes are fun and there just happens to be two of us here, plus you—that makes three. So let's go have a threesome together," said Tallulah.

"Nope, that's OK. I am perfectly fine not doing that now—or ever—with anyone," mumbled Chip.

"Oh, come on, Chip. Let's make the cabin rumble and bring down the roof," said Tallulah, having a hell of a time.

"Nope. Still good not to have one with anyone," said Chip.

"Sure, you are, Chip," said Tallulah, winking.

"Can we go a little faster?" asked Chip.

The three of them walked a little faster to get away from the seniors.

"That went wrong awfully quickly. But we got our point across," said Chip.

"I hope we got through to them. But I'm not too sure with all that threesome talk," said Hazel.

"Maybe next time, leave the word out of your mouth," said Fay.

"Yes, Fay, you're completely right," said Chip.

"I'm looking forward to this haze even more now," said Fay.

"Hook, line, and sinker—hoping we got our point across," said Hazel.

"Excellent job, everyone. Now, we can enjoy the show," said Chip.

"I feel like we need to tell more people what we are doing so there are no questions when they're gone on this adventure," said Hazel.

"It will be fine, Hazel. Just relax. I think it's best if it's just us or now," said Fay.

"I hope you're right—which sometimes you're not," said Hazel.

Meanwhile, Tallulah and Agnes had heard everything about the funhouse, and couldn't wait to get to the breakfast table to tell the other girls. So they hurried up and bolted ahead of Fay, Chip, and Hazel.

"Hurry up, Tallulah! We must beat them to the dining hall," said Agnes.

"I'm going as fast as my legs will go! I shouldn't have done that can-can thing," said Tallulah. "Agnes you're the flexible one, remember? I'm only flexible in other ways."

"Let's go faster—and let's not put that vision in my head," demanded Agnes.

"Agnes, I am coming. Don't be so damn bossy," said Tallulah.

Chip laughed at them as he watched them run to the dining hall.

"I can get there quicker if I go without you," said Agnes.

"Boy, you're bossy today. I think you woke up on the wrong side of the damn bed," said Tallulah.

"I told you it would work," said Chip.

"Wow. They completely fell for it—I can't believe it!" said Fay.

"I can't believe our plan worked," said Hazel, in shock.

"I told you they were thirsty for gossip," said Chip.

"Get ready for the fun stuff to begin!" said Hazel.

Tallulah and Agnes went to the dining hall. Tallulah held onto the door, huffing and puffing like she was ready to blow someone's house down.

"You girls will never guess what we just heard on our way up here," said Agnes.

Tallulah finally sat down, still breathing heavily.

"What's the matter with her?" asked Wanda.

"I made her do the can-can, then I made her walk fast to get up here to tell you what we'd heard," said Agnes.

"Tallulah, you don't look so good," said Wanda.

"Oh gee, thanks for telling me. I thought I was pretty," said Tallulah.

"Just keep breathing and you'll be fine. It's not like we walked a mile," said Agnes.

"Now I can officially say I don't need to do my morning exercises," said Tallulah, trying to feel her own pulse.

"You do realize if you're moving and talking, you're still kicking, right?" asked Wanda.

"Good point, Wanda," said Agnes.

"You're right for once," said Tallulah.

"Oh, stop your whining," said Agnes.

"Who asked you anyways Agnes?" asked Wanda.

"Oh, pin a rose on your nose," said Agnes.

Everyone laughed at that because it was funny coming from Agnes. She was sometimes quick on her insults—that was for sure.

"OK, we're getting off the subject here," said Tallulah.

"Can you please just be quiet for a minute?" asked Agnes, folding her arms and shaking her head.

"Easy now, Agnes, we are listening to you," said Wanda, giving her the evil eye.

"Should we be talking about this in front of Vera?" asked Mona.

"I don't care what you're talking about. I am just minding my own damn business," said Vera, eating her bacon.

Agnes explained they thought they should go check out the funhouse.

"How are we going to do that?" asked Mona.

"We wait until everyone is sleeping and sneak out of our cabins," said Agnes.

"I don't really like funhouses. They scare me. I keep thinking something is going to pop out at me, and then that's it—I have a heart attack, and life is over," said Tallulah.

"Stop being such a chicken and live a little," said Agnes.

"Have you ever heard 'YOLO'?" asked Wanda.

"Do you mean, *yoyo*?" asked Mona.

"I know what a yoyo is," said Tallulah.

"No, YOLO," said Wanda shaking her head.

"No, I haven't. What does it mean?" asked Tallulah.

"You only live once," said Wanda.

"Which means you need to take chances," said Agnes.

"That's right, Agnes," said Wanda.

"We aren't getting any younger. We need to seize the day and just do it," said Mona.

"That's what I'm talking about, Mona," said Wanda.

"All four of you are really into going to this funhouse thing?" asked Tallulah.

All three of them say yes at the same time.

"Well then, I guess I will go, but if a ghost pops out, I am out of there quicker than anyone!" said Tallulah.

"If that little run up the hill took that much out of you, I don't see you running from any ghost—especially Casper," said Agnes.

"It's not Halloween. There will be no ghost there—especially not Casper," said Agnes.

"Well, if it's haunted, there could be spirits in the funhouse," said Mona.

"You aren't quick at all, Tallulah. You'll most likely break something or someone will eat you," said Wanda.

"Do you really think that will happen?" asked Tallulah

"No, I was just busting on you," laughs Wanda.

It's time to go to art therapy with Iggy," said Mona.

Iggy popped out.

"Are you girls ready for art fun?"

"Yes, we are, Iggy," they said at once.

"You have such a pretty name," said Wanda.

"Aww, thank you, Wanda. That's so nice of you to say," said Iggy.

"You're welcome, darling," said Wanda.

"Hey, Iggy, I got a question for you," said Tallulah.

"OK, Tallulah, what do you have to ask me?"

"Do you believe in ghosts and them living in funhouses?" asked Tallulah.

"Well, I don't really know, because I've never been in a funhouse. I really don't believe in ghosts, so I will have to say no," said Iggy.

"Thank you for your answer. Just something I was wondering about," said Tallulah.

"You're welcome, Tallulah. said Iggy. "Hey, did everyone enjoy the wonderful meal Mona and I made the other night?"

"Oh yes, it was great," said Tallulah.

"I'm glad you liked it, Tallulah," said Mona.

"Well, I will see you in a few minutes." Iggy went to another table.

"It's time to go to art therapy," said Agnes.

Mona was hoping she would enjoy art therapy and that it wouldn't be like arts and crafts had been. They all tried to get up with their aching bones. It's not easy when you're in your seventies or even eighties. But they didn't let anything stop them from having a fun time.

Agnes, Tallulah, Wanda, and Mona went to art therapy. Their project was to make something that makes them happy. Iggy brought out the color pencils and paint, hoping they didn't have a paint fight.

"Pick anything you want and make it beautiful," said Iggy.

"I don't even know how to make my circle look like a sun," said Mona.

"Here. Let's try this, Mona, it might make it better," said Iggy. She gives her an empty coffee cup she could trace to trace her sun. Iggy watched Mona smile as she traced it without any mistakes.

"Thank you very much, Iggy, for helping me," said Mona.

"You're welcome, Mona. It's going to look beautiful," said Iggy. "Well, art therapy is done for the day."

They finished their pictures and gave them to Iggy, then went to get ready for lunch.

"Wow! That went by fast. And I didn't even learn a thing!" said Agnes as she went out the door, shaking her head. Iggy came over to them to see how they felt about the project.

"Did you have fun today?" he asked.

"Yes, it was wonderful, darling," said Wanda.

Iggy went over to Mona to see how her picture came out.

"Wow, Mona, I love what you did! You did a wonderful job with the sun and how it shines on the beautiful blue water," said Iggy.

"Thank you. I just went with what I saw in my head," said Mona.

"Well, that's exactly how to do it," said Iggy.

"You can keep if you would like to," said Mona.

"Well, thank you, Mona, I would love to have it. And I can't wait to look at all the others, too," said Iggy, giving Mona a hug. "Have a wonderful day!"

"Wow! I can't believe it's lunchtime already," said Wanda.

"I'm starving! I hope it's something good," said Edith.

"You never know what we will be having," said Agnes.

"Where have you been, Edith?" asked Wanda.

"In the bathroom again," said Edith.

"Enough said," said Agnes.

Tallulah and Mona came and joined them, and all five of them were once again at the table. They all began to discuss how they were going to get to the funhouse.

"We have one issue to figure it out," whispered Mona.

"What's the problem?" asked Wanda.

"We need to find a way to get there," said Mona.

"We can walk there," said Wanda.

"We want to get there quick—not a year from now!" said Agnes.

"I think I have figured out a way," said Tallulah.

"Oh, this should be good to hear," said Agnes.

"Wow, trust me much?" said Tallulah.

"We could hitchhike," said Wanda.

"I don't think so—unless you want to get kidnapped or killed," said Agnes.

"Plus, who would honestly be willing to pick up five senior women of the side of the road?" asked Tallulah.

"We could walk—it can't be that far," said Mona.

"With our hips and arthritis, I don't think that will work," said Agnes.

"Does anyone really know the area so well that they know where it is?" asked Wanda.

"It's a small town, so it shouldn't be that hard to find," said Agnes.

"Why don't we just take the keys to one of the buses?" asked Tallulah.

Everyone looked at Tallulah with amazement.

"How did you come up with that?" asked Agnes.

"It seemed like a fun idea," said Tallulah.

"How are we going to do that?" asked Wanda.

"Let me oversee this bus situation," said Tallulah, with a crazy grin on her face and a twinkle in her eyes.

"I've seen that twinkle in your eye before, and it didn't turn out good," said Agnes.

"No worries. I'll get them with no problem," said Tallulah.

"What are you going to do?" asked Agnes.

"Tallulah, are you going to flash your breasts like you did at the pool?" asked Mona.

"If I need to, I will," said Tallulah.

"Don't get into trouble, Tallulah," said Wanda.

"Trust me, I won't get in trouble. Have a little faith in me for once."

"We will try," said Mona.

"To be honest, it's a little hard to trust you, but we will try," said Agnes.

"*Should* we trust her?" asked Wanda.

"Not as far as I can throw her," said Vera, sitting at the next table.

"Hey, I know you doubt me, but unless you truly know me, you should trust me, I haven't done one thing to any of you, so there should be no problem," said Tallulah all upset.

"Sorry, Tallulah, you're right—we aren't giving you a fair chance," said Mona.

"Where did you come from, Vera?" asked Wanda.

"Last I saw you was at the table behind us," said Agnes.

"It's none of your flipping business," said Vera.

"Why do I even bother?" asked Agnes.

"That makes no sense, but OK, I got it," said Wanda as she stretched her arms.

"Then it's all set. We'll sneak out tonight after everyone is in bed," said Agnes.

"That gives you time to get the keys, Tallulah," said Wanda.

"Don't worry. I got this," said Tallulah.

"That's what I am afraid of," said Agnes.

"Please have faith in me," said Tallulah.

"Yes, Tallulah, I am trying," said Agnes.

"So, have you thought about what you're going to do to get the keys?" asked Agnes.

"Yes, but I'm not going to share it with you yet. Just know that I will be all ready to go tonight," said Tallulah.

"OK, Tallulah. We will wait for you to give us the word. We will be ready," said Agnes.

"I hope that you can just trust me to not screw this up," said Tallulah.

"Yes, we understand, Tallulah," said Mona.

"You will see what happens next," said Tallulah as she got up from the table and left.

"Where are you going, Tallulah?" asked Bessie as she went out the door.

"I'm on a mission, and can't talk," said Tallulah.

"Well, OK, I won't ask," said Bessie as she watched Tallulah go by.

Tallulah decided to go and think how she can get the keys to the bus without getting busted which doesn't sound hard. So, she went to the hammock.

"Are you OK, Tallulah?" asked Serena.

"Yes, I am. I am just in deep thought right now," said Tallulah.

"Did Frankie burn something again? It does smell kind of funky in there," said Serena.

"I don't think so. Lunch tasted good," said Tallulah, rubbing her belly.

Serena laughed. "You're so funny, Tallulah."

"I'm just going to sit on the hammock and enjoy the lovely weather. We don't have hammocks at Heaven's Ridge," said Tallulah.

"Would you like some help? This hammock can be tricky," said Serena.

"No, I think I can do it myself," said Tallulah.

"OK, but if you need anything, someone's always around. Just yell—and be careful!"

"OK, thank you, Serena, you're a lovely girl," said Tallulah.

Serena left Tallulah at the hammock and went back to the dining hall. Tallulah held down the hammock with one hand and slowly tried to sit down. It flipped her over on the ground.

"Ugh! The ground really hurts!" said Tallulah, shaking her head. She got up and attempted to get on it again. This time, she reached a leg and an arm in to keep it still.

"Come on, hammock, work with me here," said Tallulah. She fell into it on her face and was not able to get herself out. She began swinging with one arm through the hammock, facedown. She put her feet down so she could get loose, and it threw her off again.

"You are a pain in my ass, Mr. Hammock," said Tallulah. Frustrated, Tallulah didn't attempt a third time and just walked away.

Tallulah decided it was time to put her plan in action and get the key. She went inside and saw Belle at her desk.

"Hey, Tallulah, how are you doing today?"

"I'm doing OK. I fell off the hammock a couple times, but I didn't hurt myself—at least, I don't think I did." She adjusted her hips a little. "I was just wondering if Nurse Juniper was busy. I have a personal question to ask her."

"Oh, um, let me check to see if she is in her room or at the nurse's station, I know she hasn't been around too much today," said Belle.

"That seems odd, Belle, don't you think?" asked Harlow as she came down the hallway.

Belle just gave her a look.

"Please just give me a minute to check. This place has been crazy today," said Belle.

"Yes, sure, no problem—take as long as you need to," said Tallulah.

"Well, I must bring these flyers around to the counselors, so I will see you later," said Harlow as she went out the door.

Tallulah peeked around the corner to see if Belle and Harlow were still gone. Tallulah saw the bus key rack in the reception area, but no receptionist at the desk.

"Ha! I think I struck gold," said Tallulah.

Instead of going around to the desk, she leaned over as far as she could. She was having a challenging time grabbing the key, because her boobs were in the way.

"Why did they have to be so big?" said Tallulah as she kept reaching. *BINGO*! She finally got a hold of one, grabbing the closest to her.

"Bus number seven. That sounds lucky enough! And we all need luck."

Tallulah realized she had nowhere to put the key.

"That figures. The one time I wear something without pockets, I need to put something in them," said Tallulah. She decided to stuff it in her bra and move away from the desk before Belle came back and busted her.

"Sorry to keep you waiting. I guess Nurse Juniper must have stepped out," said Belle.

"Oh, that's OK. My hip was just hurting from when I fell out of the hammock, but it's OK. I'm just going to relax in my cabin for a little while." Tallulah slowly headed to the door.

"Are you sure you're OK, Tallulah?" asked Belle.

"Yes, I'm fine. But I am going to rest," said Tallulah.

"You're more than welcome to wait for her here. I'm sure she will be back soon."

"No, it's OK. If it gets worse, I will come back and have her check me out." Tallulah went out the door.

Belle scratched her head, wondering what was going on with the place. "It must be a full moon or something—things are getting screwy today!"

Agnes, Mona, and Wanda waited, wondering why they had to wait by the bathhouse.

"Do you have any idea what we are doing here?" asked Agnes.

"We are waiting for Tallulah, just like our notes said to," said Mona.

"I don't know why we are waiting so long—it's after three," said Wanda.

"All I know is Tallulah asked us to meet here at 3 p.m., and that's what we're doing."

"She's yanking our chain. If it's not true, I'm not going to be happy," said Agnes.

"Will you just chill out, Agnes?" asked Mona.

"Give her a chance to prove herself," said Mona.

"Let's just wait and see what's going on before we do anything," said Wanda.

"I just don't understand why she wanted to meet here, out in the open," said Mona.

"Here she comes! And wow, she's walking fast," said Agnes.

"I never knew she could move that fast!" said Mona.

"Only when there are men or food around," said Agnes with a chuckle.

"She's full of surprises some days, that's for sure. But that's why I like her," said Wanda.

"Don't worry, I'm here, girls," said Tallulah as she got closer. "I have something to show you that will make you so proud."

"I haven't been proud since 1975," said Wanda, rolling her eyes.

"I have one question for you girls," said Tallulah.

"It is a good question, since we waited for you so long?" asked Wanda.

"Who wants to go for a ride with me tonight?" asked Tallulah, trying to get the key out of her bra.

Everyone was wondering what Tallulah was doing and was kind of scared.

"Please don't get naked again, like the pool," said Agnes.

Tallulah twirled the keys around her finger after finally getting them out of her bra.

"Whoa! "Is that what I think it is?" asked Wanda, her eyes popping out of her head.

"Yes, it is. I got the key to one of the buses," said Tallulah, dancing around. "So, how do you like me now?"

"How did you get the key?" asked Agnes.

"I just distracted Belle, which wasn't too hard, and took the keys to the lucky number seven bus!" said Tallulah, twirling the keys, "It was just there waiting for me to take it, so I did."

"They should have been watching the key more carefully," said Agnes.

"Anyone could just take them like I did." Tallulah laughed aloud. "So, who is ready to go to a funhouse tonight and have some fun?"

"Wow! I can't believe we are really going to do this," said Agnes.

"You aren't going to back out, are you, Agnes?" asked Tallulah.

"I mean, this was your idea in the first place," said Mona.

"Yes, I know, Mona, and I will be there with bells on," said Agnes, thinking to herself.

"I know I'm really excited about this. And I also proved you wrong!" said Tallulah.

"Oh really? How so?" asked Agnes.

"I was able to accomplish something without getting caught," said Tallulah, getting in Agnes's face.

"Yes, Tallulah, you did, and I'm sorry if I hurt your feelings," said Agnes.

"It's OK, I forgive you. And I can't wait to do this with you."

"So, what's the plan, girls? I am ready for action and a whole lotta fun," said Tallulah.

"We know you're always up for some action," laughed Agnes.

"We should wait until everyone's asleep and sneak out of our cabins," said Tallulah.

"Do you think it will be that simple to just sneak out?" asked Wanda.

"Honestly, I don't know. I'm hoping so, because I don't have a plan B." Agnes sighed.

"How will we know when it's the right time to sneak out if we are in two different cabins?" asked Mona.

"There are three of you that in the one cabin and Tallulah in the other one," said Agnes, thinking.

"Yes, that's right. I'm all alone—poor me!" said Tallulah. She sighed and shook her head.

"Since our cabins are not far from each other we can have a sort of signal," said Agnes.

"Like a smoke signal or something?" asked Tallulah.

"We are trying not to have someone see us, so that's not a clever idea," said Mona, laughing and shaking her head.

"Why not a flashlight? Someone could flash it quickly when it's time to go," said Mona.

"I have a flashlight in my stuff I can use," said Tallulah.

"I can do the same for our cabin because I have one, too," said Mona.

"OK, good. We got that all settled finally," said Agnes, scratching her head.

"Now, we just wait for it to get dark. Whatever you do, don't fall asleep," said Wanda.

"Then I might want to take a nap, just to be safe," laughed Tallulah.

"Just try not to lose the key between now and then," said Agnes, shaking her head.

"Don't worry, I will keep it in my bra, where it's safe," said Tallulah, grabbing and shaking her boobs.

"That's not reassuring to me, Tallulah," said Wanda.

"It will be safe, I promise. I am the one who got the key in the first place, remember?"

"OK, Tallulah," said Wanda, looking worried.

"We will see you gals at dinner," said Mona.

They all split up and went to different activities so they would not seem suspicious.

Ethel peeked her head out of the bathroom after she saw the girls had left. "We will see what you girls are up to. When I find out, you'll be up a creek without a paddle," she said to herself.

Vera came out of the bathroom lurking around after Ethel had left. She wondered what everyone was up to. Vera decided to follow one of them to see what kind of trouble they were up to.

Chip had also been by the tree when he heard the seniors talking about the haunted house and their plans. He could not wait to tell Hazel and Fay what they were up to.

Chip ran to the dining hall, because he knew Hazel and Fay would be there getting set up for dinnertime.

"Hey, I am glad I found you," said Chip.

"We are always here at this time. It's no secret," said Hazel, a strange look on her face.

"I just overheard the seniors, and they're going to sneak out and go to the haunted house tonight," smirked Chip.

"So, they're really going to do this?" asked Hazel.

"I'm so shocked, and I am not at the same time," said Fay.

"Yes, I heard them myself by the bathroom. They have the key to one of the buses."

"Wonder how they got the key?" asked Fay.

"That is a good question, Fay," said Hazel as she thought about it.

"They were rallying together and making plans by the bathroom?" asked Hazel.

"There is surprisingly quite of bit of action in that bathroom—well outside it, at least."

"Well, we did think they would take the bait," said Fay.

They all agreed.

"Well, I guess we will have to wait and see what happens tonight," said Hazel.

"And explain to everyone here where they are," said Fay.

"We will all go to our beds and act like we are sleeping and listen for when they leave," said Chip.

"Well, you won't, Chip, but Fay and I will," said Hazel.

"Why is that?" asked Chip.

"It's the women leaving—not any of your men," said Hazel, laughing at him.

"Yeah, I guess you're right there," said Chip.

Vera decided to follow Mona. She was the only one who didn't annoy her like the others, and the least cheesy.

Mona decided that she was going to go play games, because she liked to be active when she could. They were playing noodle ball, and Mona decided to play.

"OK, everyone, come and grab a pool noodle," said Serena.

Mona saw Tallulah and wondered why she was there when they were supposed to be doing different things.

"What are you doing here, Tallulah?" asked Mona.

"I didn't want to do anything else, so I came here," said Tallulah.

"What are we supposed to do with these?" asked Mona, hitting Tallulah with the noodle.

"I'll tell you when everyone is ready," said Serena.

"Hurry up and wait," said Tallulah.

"All right, everyone got their pool noodle?" asked Serena.

Everyone shook their head yes.

"The object of the game is to hit the beach ball with your noodle into the goal. The only rule is to not hit each other," said Serena.

"Wow! This looks like a lot of fun," said Clara.

"I agree! I can't wait," said Ethel.

"When I say go, you can start," said Serena.

"Well, I hope so—that's what *go* means," said Vera.

"One, two, three, go!," said Serena, as she got out of the way of the ball.

"Hey Vera, do you want to play on my team?" asked Serena.

"No, I'll just watch. You go and mind your own damn business!"

"OK, but if you change your mind, let me know—we got the winning team!" said Serena.

Jasper hit the ball to Tallulah, who swung the noodle and accidently hit Agnes.

"Sorry, Agnes, I didn't mean to do that," said Tallulah.

"Yeah right, Tallulah," said Agnes.

Clara hit the ball, and it went to Miles.

"Excellent job, Clara," said Serena.

Miles swung and hit Vera.

"Oh no! That isn't good. She is going to kill me!" said Miles.

"Are you OK, Vera?" asked Serena.

"Just shut your damn mouth," said Vera, sitting on the floor.

"I'm really sorry, Vera, please don't hurt me," said Miles.

Vera just stared. Miles started to get scared she was going to hurt him.

"Can I please have the ball?" asked Vera.

"It's all yours, but please don't hit anyone," said Serena, holding her breath. She wanted to close her eyes but was too scared to.

"No promises on hitting someone," said Vera, who had her eye on Miles.

Vera picked up her noodle and puts her hands on it like she was using a hockey stick, lifted it, and hit the beach ball as hard as she could. The ball went up in the air and hit Miles right in the chest. It knocked him down with a clunk.

"Down he goes!" said Wanda.

"Are you OK Miles?" asked Serena.

"Yes, she just knocked the wind out of me," said Miles.

"Vera, that was so wrong of you! I told you to play nice," said Serena.

"Payback is a bitch!" said Vera.

"You need to apologize to Miles," said Serena.

"Nah, I won't say anything, because he did it to me first," said Vera.

Serena helped Miles get up.

"Are you sure you are OK?" asked Serena.

"Let's play ball!" Miles yelled, all fired up.

"I'm out of here!" said Vera.

"That's a great idea," said Wanda.

Vera stuck out her tongue.

"You are such a child, Vera," said Clara.

"I know you are, but what am I?"

"We are all here to have fun," said Agnes.

"That's so funny coming from you," said Vera, giving everyone the finger.

"Don't you think it's a little strange Vera is here?" Mona asked Ethel.

"She doesn't seem like the noodle ball type," said Ethel.

"I don't really pay attention to her. So to me, it's just odd," said Mona.

"I don't know what she likes and dislikes, and I don't care," said Ethel.

"OK, fair enough," said Mona.

Mona yelled to Beau to get the ball, then went back over to Ethel.

"I do have one more question, Ethel," said Mona.

"What could you possibly have to ask me?" asked Ethel, being snotty.

"Are you OK? You seem to be acting a little squirrely towards me and everyone today."

Ethel was getting irritated. She wanted the conversation to end.

"Things are fine, thanks for asking," said Ethel.

"No problem. I hope you have a good day, and sorry I asked," said Mona.

"Don't worry, I know what you're up to," said Ethel, staring at Mona.

"No idea what you're talking about, Ethel," said Mona.

"OK, if you say so," said Ethel.

Mona walked away to get water, watching Ethel.

"Ethel, would you like to start this time?" asked Serena.

"OK, Serena, I will try," said Ethel. She swung the noodle and missed the ball.

"It's OK, Ethel—try again," said Serena.

Ethel tried again and the ball flew over everyone's head.

"Here we go again," said Tallulah, laughing.

"Tallulah, be nice!" said Serena.

"Well, all we do is wait," said Tallulah.

"Hit the ball, Ethel, you can do it," said Serena.

Ethel hit the ball to Wanda.

"Excellent job, Ethel!" said Serena.

Wanda hit the ball, and it went back to Clara. Clara hit the ball to Agnes.

"You got this, Agnes!" cheered Clara.

Agnes hit the ball, and it went to Tallulah. Instead of using the noodle, Tallulah decided to use her feet, kicking it to Blanche. Blanche hit the ball, but the noodle slips out of her hand. She burst out laughing.

"I guess I have sticky fingers," said Blanche.

"That's not all she has," laughed Tallulah.

"Tallulah, you're being dirty- I should wash your mouth out with soap," said Blanche.

"Yummy! Please do," said Tallulah as she licked her lips.

"Hold on a minute! I have an idea," said Serena.

"Oh boy, I can't wait to hear this," said Tallulah.

"Who wants to break into teams and have a little friendly competition?" asked Serena. "Let's pick two captains and go from there."

"Not me! I don't want to be a captain," said Wanda.

"How about Tallulah and Clara?" asked Serena.

"Oh no, I don't think so," said Tallulah.

"Are you afraid you will lose, Tallulah?" asked Clara.

"Oh no, sweetheart—that will never happen," said Tallulah.

"Now, you each must pick four people to be on your team," said Serena.

"Do we have to pick teams?" asked Tallulah.

"Yes, or I'll pick them for you," said Serena.

"No, I will do it," said Tallulah.

"OK, Tallulah, but I have no problem doing it for you," said Serena.

"I pick Agnes," said Tallulah.

"OK, Clara, your turn," said Serena.

"I pick Jasper," said Clara.

"Oh boy, this will be fun," said Jasper.

"Tallulah, your turn," said Serena.

"I guess . . . Blanche," said Tallulah.

Ethel put her head down. She knew she was going to be last, because she always was.

"I pick Miles," said Clara.

"Great! She takes two out of the three men here," said Tallulah.

"Tallulah, be nice now—there are few of you left," said Serena.

"I pick Beau," said Tallulah.

"Thank you for picking me," said Beau.

"Wow, you're a gentleman," said Tallulah.

Mona was upset. She wanted to be on the same team as Beau.

"I pick Wanda," said Clara.

"OK, Ethel, you join Tallulah's team—and Mona, you're on Clara's team," said Serena.

"Let the fun begin," said Tallulah.

The game began. It was close at first, until Team Tallulah got ahead of Team Clara. Both teams tied, then Agnes made the winning goal for Team Tallulah.

Mona could not wait to go to dinner to tell the gals about Ethel and what she had said to her—and to tell everyone what Vera had said she wanted to do to her.

Once everyone got to the table, Mona filled them all in on what she heard.

"So, you will never guess what happened at noodle ball," said Mona.

"What?" asked Agnes.

"Ethel kept saying she knew what we were up to, which I found weird," said Mona.

"I don't honestly think she knows anything. She might just be saying that because she has nothing better to do," said Agnes.

"Yeah, I don't think she does either. But we should be careful tonight," said Mona.

"I don't trust her as far as I can throw her," said Wanda.

"Do you really think you could throw her if you needed to, Wanda?" asked Agnes.

"Maybe if I ate my Wheaties," chuckled Wanda, flexing her flabby arms.

"You probably would have to eat the whole box," said Agnes.

"Ethel does assume a lot—and sometimes just wants to see if we will crack," said Agnes.

"Oh, don't worry. I didn't crack at all. I am a tough nut, with a tough shell," said Mona.

"I'm not going to worry unless we really need to. We need to stay focused," said Wanda.

"Me neither. Just keep your ears open for if she does say or do something," said Mona.

"Yeah, I don't blame you. We all should be on watch just in case—because I'd rather not mess with Vera and Ethel," said Wanda.

"I'm surprised neither of them are here for dinner," said Wanda, pretending to be heartbroken. "Should we let Tallulah know what was going on?"

"Where is Tallulah? It's not like her to miss a meal," said Mona.

"I haven't seen her since noodle ball," said Wanda.

"We need to remember the important thing is that we don't any more suspicion of us," said Agnes.

"Vera knows something, too—and who knows what she will do," said Mona.

"We don't have the time to worry about her, too," said Agnes.

"Let's just go on with tonight's plan, and everything will be hunky dory," said Mona.

"I hope you're right, Mona, because I'm a little scared about this," said Agnes.

"We just have to trust Tallulah's OK and on her way, and that Ethel and Vera don't know anything," said Mona.

"If I didn't think this plan was going to work, then I would have been the first to admit it," said Agnes with a smile.

"I hope you're right, Agnes. You know I believe in you," said Mona.

Tallulah was walking to the dining hall when she heard someone call her name.

"Hey, Tallulah, can I talk to you for a minute?" asked Nurse Juniper.

Tallulah turned around to see who it was.

Oh no, what does she want?

"Hello, Nurse Juniper, it's nice to see you. How are you doing?"

"I'm doing OK. I'm just trucking to dinner," said Nurse Juniper. "I was looking for you because Belle told me that you came in to see me and needed to talk to me."

"Yes, I did. I fell off the hammock a couple times and my hips were hurting a little bit, but I am good now. I rested up before dinnertime," said Tallulah.

"I thought that I saw you at noodle ball," said Nurse Juniper.

"Oh yeah. I did go for a little while . . . then I thought I should rest," said Tallulah.

"Are you sure you're OK? Because we can go to the nurse's station, and I can check you out. It won't take too long," said Nurse Juniper.

"Honestly, I'm fine now I took a little rest. I'm as good as new," said Tallulah.

"I would feel better if you came back to the nurse's station with me."

"Really, Nurse Juniper, I am good. But if I have issues, I will see you," said Tallulah.

"Trust me, it won't take too long. You will be back by the time they serve dinner."

"OK, Nurse Juniper, we can. But honestly, I am fine."

"I just want to see for myself. I would feel bad if I didn't examine you and something was wrong," said Nurse Juniper.

Nurse Juniper checked Tallulah over and saw there was nothing to be worried about. Tallulah just prayed the key didn't come out of her bra.

"You're all set, Tallulah. But if you have any more back pain or hip pain, please see me."

"Promise I will, Nurse Juniper—and thank you very much," said Tallulah.

"You're welcome, and have a good dinner! I heard it might be turkey."

"Oh great! A turkey dinner—and it's not even Thanksgiving," said Tallulah, walking fast to get to the dining hall.

"Oh, by the way, Tallulah, who won noodle ball?" asked Nurse Juniper.

"Not me," said Tallulah, taking off.

"Have a good dinner!" said Nurse Juniper.

"Aren't you coming to dinner, too?" asked Tallulah.

"No, I have paperwork to do, and I'm not really that hungry." Nurse Juniper bit her lip, nervous.

"OK well have a good evening—and make sure you do get something to eat! You're too skinny as it is," said Tallulah.

"I will, Tallulah—and I will see you tomorrow."

I wonder what she is up to, thought Tallulah. *I must eat first, then spy after.*

Tallulah made it to her table and sat down with her favorite crew.

"Where the hell have you been?" asked Agnes, concerned.

"Nurse Juniper wanted to talk to me," said Tallulah.

"About what, Tallulah?" asked Wanda.

"Do you have hemorrhoids?" asked Mona curiously.

"No, I don't have hemorrhoids, you dingbat," said Tallulah, shaking her head.

"They can be a bitch to deal with—I was just concerned," said Mona

"When Nurse Juniper asked, I said I'd hurt my hips when I fell from the hammock," said Tallulah.

"You fell off the hammock?" asked Mona.

"Yes, twice. But I'm OK, so don't worry," said Tallulah.

"Seriously, Tallulah? That's the silliest thing I've heard," said Wanda, laughing.

"Everyone knows how to get on a hammock," laughed Agnes.

"It's true! I wouldn't lie about that happening to me," said Tallulah, almost in tears.

"Oh stop, Tallulah! I was just kidding," said Agnes, starting to laugh.

"Glad you didn't get hurt," said Wanda.

"I just needed a reason to get the key. That was the only way I could think of."

"Well, I just wanted you to know that even though I tease you, you did an excellent job and I'm proud of you for not screwing it up," said Agnes.

"Thank you, Agnes, that means a lot to me," said Tallulah.

"I'm not trying to get all sappy, but I'm glad that we are all here together," said Mona.

"I'll be honest. I wasn't going to come to camp," Tallulah shared, "but Hilda at Heaven's Ridge convinced me to go, so here I am with you gals, and I am just so glad we did all come."

Agnes decided to go back to the cabin to relax before that night's adventure.

"See you girls later," said Agnes. She got up from her chair

"We got this, girl—and we are going to have tons of fun," said Mona with a smile.

Tallulah decided not to go back to her cabin. Instead, she wanted to figure out why Nurse Juniper was so nervous. She went behind the main house and started peeking through windows.

"I really hope that nothing jumps out at me while I'm back here," she said as she peeked through what she thought was Nurse Juniper's bedroom. She could hear voice coming from inside. She looked in the window and couldn't believe what she was saw. *Holy macaroni.*

"I can't believe what I am seeing," she said Tallulah in amazement. "Our Nurse Juniper, who acts so sweet and innocent, is fooling around with Casper, the maintenance guy!"

What a good girl to have gotten a catch like him. I'd better get out of here before someone catches me being a peeping Tallulah. Oh, wait—they're kissing—maybe I can stay for just a few more minutes. Wow, he is an extraordinarily strong man to pick her up like that! Who would have thought Nurse Juniper could be so flexible? Whoa baby—he's big in so many ways!

Tallulah tripped over her feet and before she knew it, she fell in the bushes.

She got right back up after she had counted to ten.

"Did you hear something?" asked Juniper as she and Casper kissed.

"No, I didn't—I was concentrating on your lips," he said, continuing to kiss her.

"You're so sweet, Casper—but maybe we should stop," said Nurse Juniper, looking out the window.

"Why do we need to stop, Juniper?" asked Casper.

"I don't want to, but we need to take it slow. It's all so new to me"

"We are taking it slow, Juniper."

Tallulah couldn't understand how they were taking it slow, with his pants down and her in her bra.

"I just don't want us to get busted by someone here at camp," said Juniper. "Especially when your ex is three doors down from us."

"I don't care what Harlow thinks about us," said Casper, wrapping his arms around her.

"So, if you don't care if she knows or not about us, how come you haven't told her yet?" asked Juniper.

"It's not her business we are together, just like it's not my business if she finds another boy toy to fool around with," said Casper.

"If you say so. But I would feel better if she knew," said Juniper.

Casper looked into her eyes. "I swear everything will be OK. We broke up a while ago, and since then, I moved on with you. I haven't been happier than I am right now."

"You make me happy, too," said Juniper.

"Harlow moved from guy to guy and she couldn't commit to a meaningful relationship. That's why we aren't together," said Casper. He took Juniper's hand "I love you."

She pulled her hand back, shocked.

"Juniper, I have never felt like this with anyone before. You get me. Deep down, we get each other. That's something unique."

Juniper got up close to Casper and grabbed his face. They kissed passionately.

"I love you too, Casper," said Juniper, hugging him tight.

"We need to tell Harlow, so that she finds out by us and no one else," said Juniper. "It just feels like the right thing to do."

"You're right, Juniper. We will tomorrow or next week."

They kissed again.

"We won't be here next week," said Juniper.

"We will have our happy ever after, Juniper, I promise you," Casper whispered in her ear.

"Do you want to go to the next level in our relationship?" Juniper whispered in his ear.

"What is the next level?" asked Casper as he lay her on the bed next to him.

"Let me show you," said Juniper.

Tallulah got an eye full and almost lost her balance.

"I wonder what is going on in this other room?" asked Tallulah, curious. "Oh, my eyes can't believe what they're seeing right now!"

Tallulah's eyes bugged out of her head. *Belle, Little Miss Goodie Two Shoes, is kissing Frankie, our cook! No wonder the food is always on the floor.* She tried to turn her head, but there was a lot of lip action going on in there. *Oh, my they're ripping off each other's clothes! Now, that's my kind of action! I didn't think Belle's breasts would be that small. I could give her some of mine. I figured Frankie wouldn't be that big, and I was right there.*

Tallulah couldn't believe what she is seeing through the different windows. Who would have thought this place would have so much sexual healing going on?

Oh boy, I need to go back to my cabin so I can let what I saw sink in—or cool off—whichever comes first.

As she stepped off the bucket it, she lost her balance and fell off.

Oh, really, this is not my day or night!

Tallulah just sat there.

"What was that noise?" asked Belle.

"I didn't hear anything," said Frankie as he kept kissing Belle.

Tallulah got back to the cabin. She rested on the picnic table before going in.

"Hey Tallulah, how are you doing on this lovely night?" asked Siena.

"I'm good—never better—just looking at the stars," said Tallulah.

"Oh really? Then why is there a leaf in your hair?" asked Siena.

"Oh, I guess it fell from the trees," said Tallulah, hoping Siena would buy it.

"What took you so long to get down here from dinner?" asked Siena.

"Oh, I thought I would try to get on the hammock again and see if I had better luck . . . maybe that's where the leaf came from," said Tallulah.

"Did it work for you?" asked Siena.

"No, I just gave up. And now, I am here and ready to go to bed. It's been a day," said Tallulah, stretching her arms.

"I'm sure you had a long day—I know I have," said Siena.

"Are you OK, sweetheart?" asked Tallulah.

"Yeah, I guess, Tallulah," said Siena.

"You don't seem too sure," said Tallulah.

"When did you know what you wanted to do with your life?" asked Siena.

"Well, I was an only child, and I was quite the handful," laughed Tallulah. "If my parents were still around, they could tell you crazy things about me as a child."

"Oh really? What was the craziest thing you ever did?" asked Siena.

"Oh, my let me think about that," said Tallulah.

"Sorry if I'm putting you on the spot," said Siena.

"No, you're fine, honey. The memory I have isn't so sharp—that's all," said Tallulah.

"I'm sorry, Tallulah, I guess I shouldn't have asked you," said Siena.

"You're a good kid . . . . When I finally got my first job, I never I would have thought I would be a florist for almost thirty years," said Tallulah.

"Wow! Thirty years—that's a longtime to stay faithful to doing one thing," said Siena.

"When you're ready to be in a career, it will come to you. Just don't rush into anything too soon," said Tallulah.

"Thanks, Tallulah. You're really an impressive person," said Siena.

"Well, thank you, Siena! And you're not bad yourself," said Tallulah.

"I'm tired. I think I'm going to hit the hay," said Siena.

"Yes, that sounds like a clever idea. I'm right behind you," said Tallulah.

"Goodnight, Tallulah, and I'll see you tomorrow," said Siena.

"Goodnight, sweetheart," said Tallulah.

Tallulah laid in bed. She was glad it was lights out. She wanted to rest before they left that night.

CHAPTER 13

Crazy Arrival at the Funhouse

The night has finally ended, which the girls thought was never going to happen. To all of them, it was a long couple of hours from dinner until then. All the seniors and counselors were snuggled in their bed for the night. Agnes thought that them going to the funhouse wasn't going to happen because Fay took a while to get to bed. Agnes, Mona, and Wanda slept with their clothes on, so it was less noise and less time to get ready when they got out of bed.

Agnes gave Mona the sign to start turning the flashlight on and off so that Tallulah knew it was time to go.

Tallulah saw the flashlight blink off and on as she laid there, still thinking about seeing Nurse Juniper and Casper kissing and the make out session between Belle and Frankie. Seeing all their naked bodies all in one night is something she thought had been a dream.

Nurse Juniper was a lucky girl to get a hunk like Casper. Wow, who would have thought Belle and Frankie? That's amazing. Too bad Belle doesn't know about him and Tory, but I am sure it will all come out—maybe with a little help by little old me.

Tallulah finally got out of bed and puts her shoes on.

Oh, putting on my shoes used to be so much easier when I was younger Tallulah was thinking to herself. Tallulah stood up and a voice came up behind her very creepy.

Tallulah turned around very slowly and saw it was Edith and she was staring at her.

"What are you doing up so late?" asked Edith as she stares at Tallulah.

"I'm just going to the bathroom, Edith," said Tallulah.

"You don't usually get up in the middle of the night and go to the bathroom," said Edith

"If you say so, Edith, and sorry that you, don't believe me, but I really need to pee like a racehorse," said Tallulah.

"Can I go with you?" asked Edith.

"Why so you can plug it up again?" asked Tallulah.

"I really had to shit that night—that's why the toilet clogged up so badly in the bathroom," said Edith. "So, it's not totally my fault."

"OK, be quiet or you will wake everyone up," said Tallulah, shaking her head.

"Just stating a fact," said Edith.

"Enough said, but you act like I am lying to you, and I'm not, and if I don't go to the bathroom, I'm going to pee and shit all over the floor," said Tallulah.

"I'm not going to stop you from doing your business," said Edith.

"Good. I'm glad to hear that. Now, get back into bed and I will see you in the morning," said Tallulah.

"Good night, Tallulah and don't let the bed bugs bite," said Edith with an evil laugh.

"What are bed bugs?" Tallulah asked herself as she went out the door.

Edith went by Ethel's bed and wondered what she was doing with her flashlight on so late.

"Ethel, are you OK?" asked Edith as Ethel took the sheet off her head.

"Yes, I'm OK. Why do you need to know?" asked Ethel with a weird grin on her face.

"I just wanted to make sure you're OK, that's all," said Edith.

"Alright good night," said Ethel.

"Good night to you too," said Edith.

When Ethel tried to get comfortable and pull the sheet over her head again, the magazine she was reading fell off the bed and onto the floor. Ethel started to panic when Edith bent over to pick up the magazine and turned it over and saw it was *Playboy* magazine.

"Give it back to me, it's not yours," said Ethel as she ripped it out of Edith hands.

"Where did you get this filthy magazine?" asked Edith, even though she was afraid of the answer.

"None of your damn business, Edith," said Ethel.

"OK, calm down Ethel. I won't tell anyone what I saw," said Edith, shaking her head.

"Yeah, right! Everyone always tells on me," said Ethel, getting defensive.

"That you have a copy of Playboy magazine is safe with me," said Edith.

Ethel felt embarrassed about having a sexy magazine.

"Now, I must go to the bathroom before I pee my pants," said Edith, trying not to laugh.

Edith looked behind her to make sure no one was following her as she left the cabin and walked fast to find where Tallulah was going.

In the next cabin, Agnes, Mona, and Wanda were ready.

"Are we ready to go, gals?" whispered Agnes.

"Yes, let's get this party started!" said Mona.

"Woot, woot!" Mona put her arms in the air and starts waving them.

"What is *woot, woot* supposed to mean?" asked Agnes, looking at Mona weird.

"Bessie said it when we were at arts and crafts yesterday. I just thought it was neat to say," said Mona.

"I think you have lost your mind," said Wanda.

"Woot!" said Mona again, chuckling to herself.

"Are you coming, Wanda? We don't have all night," said Agnes. She didn't want to get busted by someone.

"Hold your horses. I'm coming slowly but surely. I am just putting on my support bra," said Wanda, struggling to get it on.

They finally snuck out the door quietly and slowly, so as not to wake anyone. Mona thought it was time to share that they weren't going to be the only ones that's going on this adventure.

"Are you coming, Mona?" asked Agnes. Meanwhile, she was thinking about how she had forgotten to do something.

Mona spoke up: "Yes, but I need to tell you something, Agnes, before we go any further and Tallulah comes," said Mona, scared to tell Agnes.

"Are you going to tell us or just look funny?" asked Agnes.

"We aren't going alone on this adventure," said Mona.

"What do you mean by that, Mona?" asked Agnes.

"Well, I sort of let the cat out of the bag to Beau today when we were spending time together down by the firepit," said Mona.

"You did what?!" screamed Wanda, trying not to get too angry.

"Could you be any louder, Wanda?" asked Agnes, trying to quiet Wanda down.

"I really like him, and he didn't want anything to happen to me, which I thought was sweet, so he wants to go also to protect me," said Mona, shrugging her shoulders.

"Yes, that's extremely sweet, Mona. But does he really have to come with us?" asked Agnes, looking like she was ready to spit nails.

"He is on his way here. Please just let him come. I really like Beau and he won't be in the way," said Mona.

"Yes, I understand you like him, but I thought this was only going to be the five best friends," said Wanda.

"OK, I can understand that. And I get how hard it was to get your heart going for another man," said Agnes.

"Having a man around might not be a bad idea. We don't know what we are in for when we get to the funhouse," said Wanda.

"Now you're OK with him going, after you screamed, Wanda?" asked Agnes.

"I can see where you're both coming from so it's OK with me," said Wanda. "Let's hug we just had a best friend's moment."

"No, that's OK, we all get it, and we are good," said Agnes.

"Are you OK, Agnes? You seem a little off," said Wanda.

"Did you say five best friends?" asked Agnes.

"Yes! You, Tallulah, me, Mona, and Edith," said Wanda.

"Oh, shit we forgot to tell Edith about going tonight!" said Agnes.

"Relax, we can get her in the cabin," said Wanda.

Agnes heard Beau coming—and another voice, too.

"Whose voice could that be Mona?" asked Agnes, shaking her head and mumbling.

"Hi, my beautiful," said Beau, taking Mona's hand and gently kissing it.

"Hey gals, are you ready for a great adventure?" asked Miles.

"Oh, I hope you don't mind I brought Miles along with me," said Beau. He whispered in Mona's ear that Miles had been up, and had followed him there.

"Sure, the more the merrier," said Mona with a huge grin on her face.

"Anything for Mona and her happiness," grinned Agnes.

Beau kissed Mona on the cheek. "You're so beautiful in the moonlight," said Beau, looking into her eyes.

"Here comes Tallulah finally," said Wanda.

Tallulah heard whispers coming from a tree.

"Hey Tallulah, we are right here," said Wanda, waving her arms.

"I can see you and I am coming to you," said Tallulah. She up with them and sat on a stump to relax for a minute.

"What are you doing? We need to go now!" said Agnes.

"Wow. We got men here with us! My wish totally came true!" said Tallulah, ignoring Agnes.

"We sort of added to the five of us, but not by choice," said Wanda.

"I can see that, Wanda, and I am wondering how that happened in the few hours since we had left at dinner," said Tallulah.

"All you must do is ask Mona—it was her idea," said Wanda sarcastically.

"Did you by chance see Edith before you left the cabin?" asked Agnes.

"Yes, I did. She was asking questions, but I didn't answer them," said Tallulah.

"Well, we forgot to tell her we were leaving tonight," said Agnes.

"How did we do that?" asked Tallulah.

"We will answer that later. We need to get going. I don't want us to get busted," said Mona.

"Are we all ready to get this adventure going?" asked Tallulah.

"Yes, let's get on this bus and get cruising," said Mona.

"Do you still have the keys to unlock the bus, Tallulah?" asked Agnes.

"Let me see where I put them," said Tallulah.

"Please tell me you didn't lose them," said Wanda.

"Hold on a minute. I'm still checking," said Tallulah.

"Check your breasts, Tallulah," said Mona.

"Oh yeah. Here. They're in my bra, where I put them. Hold on, I almost got them," said Tallulah as she tries to wrestle them out of her bra.

"Sometime tonight, Tallulah," said Agnes.

"Give me one second, I can feel them," said Tallulah.

"If you don't find them soon, I will reach in and get them myself," said Wanda.

Tallulah finally reached down and got the key out of her bra.

"I thought we were going to get a peepshow for a second there," said Wanda as she laughed.

"Alright, everyone, let's take the bus and get on moving," said Tallulah as she held up the key to bus number seven.

"All aboard!" yelled Tallulah.

"We are going on a bus, not a fucking train," said Wanda.

"Way to spoil my fun, Wanda," said Tallulah.

"Can we just get on the bus?" asked Wanda.

"That's weird," said Tallulah as she opened the already unlocked door.

"What is so weird?" asked Agnes.

"The door to the bus was already unlocked," said Tallulah with a worried look on her face.

"Maybe they forgot to lock it back up," said Mona.

"Let's just get the door open so we can get out of here, Tallulah," demanded Agnes.

"Let's blow this joint," said Mona as she and Beau took their seats together in the back.

"That sounds so sexy to me, Beau," said Mona.

Everyone else got on the bus and took their seats.

"Something smells in here," said Agnes as she plugged her nose.

"Sorry, I couldn't hold it in," said Wanda sarcastically.

"Ugh! Wanda, what am I going to do with you?" asked Agnes, shaking her head.

"Who is going to be the driver of the bus?" asked Agnes looking around at everyone

"That's one thing we didn't work out," said Mona quietly to herself.

"I haven't had my license since 1995," said Wanda.

"I had to many accidents when I had mine, so I just gave up my license," said Agnes.

Before anyone else could answer, they heard a knock on the bus door.

"I told you we would get busted," said Agnes.

"Oh, my we are in trouble now," said Tallulah.

"Everyone, duck down wherever you can find a place," said Wanda.

"How are we going to do that when we are on a bus?" asked Mona.

"Will all of you stop? We will be fine. Just stay quiet," said Agnes. She opened the door slowly and saw it was Edith and Blanche.

"What are you here doing here at this time of night?" asked Agnes.

"We knew you were up to something," said Edith.

"Oh, wow, great detective work, Edith—now go back to the cabin," said Tallulah.

"You took a long time coming back from the bathroom," said Edith angrily.

"What are we going to do now?" asked Wanda.

"Edith, dear, I am so sorry we didn't tell you about the change. We didn't mean it, honestly, so I hope you will forgive me," said Agnes.

"Well, sorry. I am mad. It just wasn't right. But I get it, and I am glad I can go with you guys now," said Edith.

"We have no choice. They must go with us, because if they don't, they will snitch on us, and we certainly don't need that," said Agnes.

"I guess when you're right, you're right, Agnes. Who would have thought there would be eight of us," said Wanda.

"Eight is enough," said Agnes.

"Who else is on this bus?" asked Blanche.

As Edith and Blanche went up the stairs, they noticed Miles and Beau.

"Well, hello, boys! Ready for a ride of your life?" asked Wanda as she winked at both.

"Not to get off subject, but this Miles guy is cute!" said Blanche.

"Hey, Agnes!"

"Yes, Wanda?"

"Do you have that feeling someone is watching us on this bus?"

"Now that I think about it, yes, I do, Wanda," said Agnes.

"Maybe it's the boogey man coming to get us for sneaking out," said Edith in a spooky voice.

"It could be our adrenaline going," said Agnes.

What they didn't know is that there was a ninth person joining them on the bus and this adventure. Vera had known of their plan since she had heard them talking outside of the bathroom.

All of a sudden, she popped up. "BOO!"

She startled everyone on the bus.

"I'll drive the damn bus, you morons," said Vera, taking the key from Tallulah.

"How did you know what was going on, Vera?" asked Wanda.

"Next time, you might want to check the bathroom before opening your mouth," said Vera, sticking her face in Agnes's.

"Did you tell anyone, Vera?" asked Agnes, trying not to show fear.

"No, I didn't. But if you don't let me go, I will go straight to Belle and tell her everything," said Vera.

"She is probably too busy with Frankie. And if it's not Belle, it must be Tory," said Tallulah.

"What are you rambling about, Tallulah?" asked Wanda.

"Nothing, I'm just talking out loud," said Tallulah.

"Let her come. Then we know she won't say anything, and we can just move on and start this adventure," said Beau.

"That's right. Listen to the guy, even though he isn't that bright," said Vera, laughing.

"That wasn't to funny, Vera. We all have feelings," said Mona, sticking up for everyone.

"Of course you will stick up for your boy toy," said Vera.

"OK, fine, you can come, Vera, but try and be nice. We are all here to have fun," said Agnes as she took her seat again.

"I thought you would see it my way. You did almost leave a friend behind," said Vera.

"Can we just go now, before someone else shows up and we get busted?" asked Tallulah.

"We still haven't figured out who is going to drive the bus," said Wanda.

"Were you not listening to that whole conversation?" asked Agnes.

"Yes, why do you ask, Agnes?" asked Wanda.

"Then you would have known Vera is driving the bus," said Agnes.

"I'm driving the damn bus," said Vera.

"Oh boy, we are going to be in deep shit—or probably dead," said Wanda.

"Let's not panic! Maybe she is a good driver," said Agnes, praying to herself.

Vera got in the driver's seat and turned the key.

"Let's blow this place! And you might want to hold on—I'm going to *drive*, and no one can say anything about it," said Vera.

"Um, Vera, when was the last time you drove a vehicle?" asked Mona, scared to know the answer.

"I never had a driver's license, because I never wanted to drive—until now! This is going to be so exciting," said Vera.

"Oh my, we are in so much trouble," said Agnes, who continued to pray they would be safe and get through without any issues.

"Oh God, please be with us and let us be safe," said Blanche, praying.

"OK, I have one question for you morons," said Vera.

"Sure, we will be more than happy to help you in any way we can," said Tallulah, holding on to whatever she could find.

"Can you stop calling us morons?" asked Agnes politely.

"Stop distracting me and just answer my question," said Vera.

"OK, Vera no problem—we will answer anything you have to ask," said Agnes.

"Which one is the gas and which one is the brake?" asked Vera.

"Oh, please tell me she didn't ask that—is she joking?" asked Tallulah, starting to panic.

"Do you want me to drive?" asked Miles.

"No, sit back down, Mr. Viagra," said Vera as she turned the key. The bus started up.

"Ha, ha, Mr. Viagra, that's funny," said Tallulah.

"Not now, Tallulah. We need to figure out how we are not going to die with Vera behind the wheel," said Agnes.

She went up to Vera. "OK, Vera, the gas is on your right and your brake is on your left," said Agnes.

"OK, I got it. You can go and sit your big ass down now with everyone else," said Vera as she put her foot on the gas and the engine started revving up.

"OK, just be careful, and move that lever to the letter D," said Agnes before Vera stepped on the gas again, down to the floor.

Agnes flew into one of the seats as the bus went flying.

"Slow down, Vera!" yelled Wanda as she tried to hold on to whatever she could find.

"Shut up! I got it!" Vera took a wide turn and the tires screeched quickly around the corner.

"Hey, Vera, you forgot to use your signal light!" said Mona, holding onto Beau.

"I don't got time to put the signal light on and steer at the same time!" said Vera.

The tires screeched around another corner.

"I'm guessing she can't do two things at once," said Agnes.

"That's what I was thinking, too," said Wanda.

Everyone was screaming in the back.

"We are going to die!" said Tallulah.

Vera didn't slow down the bus as she side-swiped a car.

"Watch out, Vera! You're going to hit another car!" said Mona, holding on to Beau even tighter.

"Where are the seatbelts in this thing when you need them?" asked Tallulah, panicking.

"Watch that stop sign!" said Agnes as she closed her eyes.

"It didn't say 'stop' to me!" laughed Vera in her evil voice.

"We are all going to die!" said Miles as he tried to find something to hold on too.

"Hold onto me, Miles," said Tallulah as she grabbed him and holds him tight.

"Get a grip, Tallulah! We will be fine," said Miles.

"You just said you thought we were going to die! Make up your damn mind Miles!"

"I feel like I am going to puke," said Edith as she covered her mouth.

"Oh, please don't puke on me," said Blanche, trying to find a bag for Edith.

"This bus doesn't even come with air sick bags either," said Blanche.

"It's not an airplane—there are no air sick bags here," yelled Agnes.

"Hit the brakes, Vera!" said Wanda. But that only made Vera go faster.

"Will someone make her stop before we crash and die?" asked Mona.

"Oh, please tell me that doesn't say that the road is closed for construction!!" said Edith.

Mona spotted the sign ahead and started to panic.

"Don't worry, honey I will protect you," said Beau.

"Your sweet, Beau—even in a state of panic," said Mona.

"Yeah, so sweet. We are in the middle of a crisis here!" said Agnes, shaking her head.

Vera took a wide turn, and before they knew it, they were on two tires. All of a sudden, the bus stopped at a dead halt.

"What just happened?!" asked Tallulah, opening her eyes.

"Vera, are you OK up there?" asked Agnes, trying not to set her off.

"We are here, you idiots," said Vera.

"Did anyone tell her where we were even going?" asked Wanda.

Everyone shook their head no. Vera stood up. "I heard you talking, like I told you before! I knew where the house was, so I knew where exactly I was going."

"We made it, safe and unharmed," said Agnes to herself. As she opened the door to the bus, she noticed there wasn't any road under the tires.

"What's wrong, Agnes?" asked Tallulah, kind of worried what she was going to say.

"I don't think we are on the ground. I believe we might be on a hill or something."

"What do you mean, we are on a hill?" asked Mona.

"We are on top of a pile of dirt from the construction that's going on, and if we move right at all, the bus will slide down the hill," said Agnes, scratching her head.

"What do you mean, we are on a dirt pile?" asked Blanche, stunned.

"OK, I will try to make this easier to understand. Vera parked us on a dirt pile, and if we move right, the bus will fall off it," said Agnes.

"Well, there were no parking spaces open," said Vera.

"Can't believe this is where she decided to park us!" said Edith, trying not to panic.

Vera opened the door.

"It looks safe to get off the bus," she said, going down the steps and looking out.

The bus jolted a little bit, and everyone started screaming.

"Oh, stop your screaming! You're fine," said Vera.

"Then stop moving the bus!" said Agnes.

"Are you coming? Or are you just going to sit there like the bunch of scaredy cats you are?" asked Vera. She got on the pile of dirt and slid down it like a slide.

"Where did she go?!" asked Agnes.

Wanda peeked out.

"I don't see her," said Wanda, "but we got a fun dirt pile to go down."

"We have to slide down a dirt pile?!" asked Blanche.

"Yes, but it's not that bad," said Wanda.

They get off the bus slowly, one at a time, to slide down the dirt pile.

"Wow! This looks like fun," said Wanda. "WOO HOO!"

"Here I go," said Blanche.

Agnes, Beau, Miles, Edith, Tallulah, and Mona, looked at each other, wondering if they should follow or not.

"Let's go, my dear—we can go together," said Beau.

Beau told Mona to sit down, Beau sat down behind her, and wrapped his arms and legs around her. They went down the hill.

Tallulah stood at the top and looked down.

"Come on, Tallulah, don't be such a wuss!" said Vera, coming out from behind the pile.

"Tallulah you're going to be OK! We all did it and know you can, too," said Agnes.

"I'm scared! I don't want to break anything," said Tallulah, breathing heavy.

All of a sudden, Tallulah went screaming and rolling down the dirt pile.

"What the hell happened?!" asked Wanda.

Miles looks at the top of the dirt pile and saw that Vera was up there.

"Vera pushed Tallulah down the dirt pile!" said Miles. "Don't worry, Tallulah I'll catch you!"

He crouched down to stop Tallulah. On the way down, though, she hit a bump and ended up on top of him.

"Thanks for catching me," said Tallulah.

"Miles, are you OK, sweetie?" asked Edith, rubbing his head.

"I'm OK, my dear. I just got the wind knocked out of me."

Edith helped him up. It took him a little while to catch his balance, but eventually, he got it back and was his old self again.

"Vera, really, was that necessary?" asked Agnes.

"Yes, it was—she was never going to go down it unless I helped her, and that's what I did," said Vera, laughing as she slid down the pile to the rest of them.

"Vera, why can't you for one day—or even one hour—just be nice to everyone? Tallulah really could have gotten hurt if Miles hadn't caught her," said Agnes.

"She needed help, and I helped her, end of story," said Vera.

"OK, Vera, if everyone is safe, that's all that matters," said Wanda.

Edith went behind the pile of dirt and puked up everything from the ride and the slide.

"Wow! That ride was the greatest. I can't wait to go again," said Blanche sarcastically.

"It was almost like a rollercoaster ride," said Tallulah, "but I didn't like the dirt hill."

"Are you going to be OK, my darling Edith?" asked Miles again.

"Yes, I will be fine. Thank you for caring, Edith," said Miles.

"It's you I am worried about, because that was so much weight on you," said Edith, stroking Miles's hair.

"I'm OK, my darling, for the last time," said Miles as he kissed her cheek.

"OK, that was exciting—and now, I'm wondering if we should go back to the camp," said Blanche, as she still felt like she was going to puke from the bus ride.

"We didn't come this far to just go back to camp," said Agnes.

"No, we need to stick it out and see what the funhouse is all about," said Wanda.

"Who is ready to go?" asked Agnes.

Everyone held up their hands—even Blanche, who wanted nothing to do with it.

CHAPTER 14

Funhouse Experience and Gasoline Alley

"Look at the funhouse," said Wanda as they all stood in front of it in amazement. Everyone was looking at the purple house, with its crooked shutters and broken windows.

"I never imagined it would be like this," said Tallulah.

"It looks like a rundown house, and it's not beautiful, and sure doesn't look haunted," said Vera.

"Thanks for your opinion we didn't ask for," said Agnes, shaking her head.

"I like the purple. It's my favorite color, and it gives it character," said Edith.

"Have you ever heard the song about the Purple People Eater?" asked Tallulah.

"No, I haven't, Tallulah," said Wanda.

" I will play it for you sometime when we are back at Heaven's Ridge," said Tallulah.

"Do you ever shut up, Tallulah?" asked Vera, getting in her face.

"You aren't a nice woman, no matter how we all try to be nice to you," said Tallulah. She realized what she had said to Vera, but didn't feel bad.

"To each their own," said Vera. She was ready to knock Tallulah out, and Blanche was holding her back.

"Whoa, Blanche, what are you doing?" asked Tallulah.

"Making sure this shithead doesn't hurt you by hitting you," said Blanche.

"Let me go, asshole!" said Vera, trying to break away from Blanche.

"Blanche, just let her go before she gets angry at every one of us," said Edith.

"Will you be nice, Vera, to every one of us?" asked Blanche.

"Fine! I'll be good. But I can't promise I won't hit someone by the end of this adventure," said Vera.

"OK, that's good enough—even better if you don't touch any of us," said Tallulah.

"Should we go in now, or just stay out here and stare at the house?" asked Blanche with a giggle.

"Or we can wait and see if Vera knocks Tallulah out," said Wanda with amusement.

"No, let's not make that an option, Agnes," said Tallulah.

"What are you scared of, Tallulah?" asked Vera, laughing hard.

"No, unbelievably, you don't scare me," said Tallulah, holding back how frightened she really was of Vera. Vera was known as the bully at Heaven's Ridge, and once you got that title, it could never be changed.

"Are we all set to go into the funhouse?" asked Edith.

"I'm a little scared, I'm not going to lie," said Tallulah.

"Me too, even though places like this don't usually scare me," said Mona.

"I got you, Mona. Nothing will happen to my precious darling," said Beau.

"Oh, come on, you're a big bunch of babies. Let's go. It's not even a haunted house—it's a funhouse! So get your asses in there, and let's have fun," said Vera.

They all went through the broken, creaky gate nice and slowly. They could hear an owl in one of the old trees as they head up the sidewalk.

"You would think they could afford someone to mow their lawn," said Wanda.

"No one lives here, so why would they do the lawn?" asked Agnes.

Once they got to the old, creaky stairs, they noticed one of the steps had a hole. They held onto each other to make sure no one got stuck in it. As they anxiously get closer to the door, they felt relieved.

"Are we ready for some fun?" asked Wanda.

Agnes reaches for the doorknob when, all of a sudden, a black cat came flying out through one of the broken windows and hit Edith's leg. She started screaming.

"AAAHHHH!!!"

Wanda lost her balance, and Miles ended up catching her before she fell through a hole in the porch.

"I gotcha! You're going to be OK. It was just a cat," said Miles.

"Great! Now I am going to have bad luck for the rest of my life," said Edith.

"You are going to be OK, Edith, there is no bad luck here," said Agnes.

"It was just a cat—not the devil," said Wanda.

"Oh, thank you for saving me, Miles," said Edith, feeling her heart beating fast.

"You're welcome, sweetheart," said Miles as he kissed her hand.

"Here is another love connection," whispered Tallulah to Blanche.

"I guess I won't be getting lucky anytime soon," said Blanche.

"You want to get lucky with Miles, who carries a bottle of Viagra with him everywhere he goes?" asked Tallulah.

"Yes, that's right, because he pops that pill and his thingy gets harder, and if I am lucky, he might choose me," said Blanche.

"His thingy," laughed Tallulah, wondering if she should go there or not. "Since when does a man have a *thingy* and not a penis?"

"It's the same—I just prefer to call it a thingy," said Blanche.

"Sure, Blanche, if you say so," said Tallulah.

"So, we can go inside now, or stay out here and see what else might come after us," said Mona.

"It's a little chilly out here," said Wanda.

"I'm not chilly—maybe it's just you," said Tallulah.

Vera started laughing behind Wanda.

"What the hell are you laughing at now?" asked Wanda.

"It was me—I was blowing on you. I made you chilly," laughed Vera.

"Gee, thanks for that, Vera," said Wanda, going by her.

"HAHAHA! I got you, Wanda," said Vera.

"Yeah, you got me. That's just so freaking hilarious, Vera," said Wanda, shaking her head.

"She is just trying to get on your nerves," said Agnes.

"Well, it's sort of working," said Wanda.

"Well, don't let her see that, or she will keep going," said Agnes.

Agnes finally turned the knob to the door and opened it carefully. It squeaked open, and they finally made it in the house.

"Wow, look at all the cobwebs—it's disgusting in here," said Edith.

"Where is the house cleaner?" asked Blanche.

"No one lives here, so there is no house cleaner," said Agnes.

"What is that smell?" asked Tallulah as she covered her nose.

"Well, it looks like no one has been here in a while, so it's probably mildew or something," said Agnes.

"Maybe someone died in here—you never know," said Wanda.

"What about these funky lights?" asked Blanche.

"Makes you want to disco dance!" said Tallulah.

Mona and Beau decided to break out doing the robot, and everyone laughed and clapped for them.

"Yeah, I'd rather not dance, because I left my dancing shoes back at Heaven's Ridge," said Blanche.

"Where are my sunglasses when I need them?" asked Edith.

"You don't need your sunglasses at night," said Mona.

"The lights don't look too bright to me," said Agnes.

"I don't know what is new or old anymore, besides me," said Wanda.

"We are in our prime, Wanda—we still got miles left on our tires," said Blanche.

"My tires have a flat in them and could use some air," said Tallulah.

"My miles and the air in my tires ran out when my butt got bigger and added extra baggage," laughed Wanda.

"Oh, Wanda, stop putting yourself down—you're a beautiful lady that will have no problem finding a gentleman caller sometime soon," said Miles.

"I'm flattered by what you said, Miles, but men don't think of me that way," said Wanda.

"That can change, Wanda—just keep your chin up," said Miles.

"So, what about these lights?" asked Agnes so they would get off the topic.

"They are very pretty, and they would look good anywhere in my room," said Wanda.

"Can we move on now?" asked Mona.

"Move on to where, Mona? We are in the funhouse. Let's just explore here and see everything," said Agnes.

They headed to the first double doors they saw. They stood in the long hallway and looked at all the assorted color doors along the way, with names on them. Tallulah opened the doors, careful to make sure another cat didn't fly out.

"Where are the lights in here?" asked Agnes.

"It makes no sense! There was lights on when we came in, and now this room has no light," said Mona.

"Very observant, Mona," said Agnes.

"Whose arm am I touching?" asked Wanda.

"Well, it's me, my darling," said Miles.

Wanda gave him a whack. "Get the hell away from me!"

Miles put his head down and moved next, of all people, to Vera.

"Don't you even dare touch me, or you will lose a hand," said Vera.

"Read you loud and clear, Vera," said Miles as he moved a little more to the right.

"Hey, Tallulah, look what I found," said Blanche.

"What is it?" asked Mona.

"It looks like an old lantern," said Blanche.

"I haven't seen one of these in a long time," said Agnes.

"What is it?" asked Wanda.

"It's an old, antique lantern. I haven't seen one of these since I was a child. My parents used them to light the house," said Agnes.

"How are we supposed to light it?" asked Edith.

Everyone looked around for matches or something to light the lantern with.

"I would be happy to light it," said Vera.

"How are you going to light it, Vera?" asked Wanda.

Vera showed them the lighter she had swiped from Frankie's pocket.

"Where did you get that?" asked Tallulah.

"I took it from Frankie when he was busy," said Vera.

"No thanks, I don't want to blow up today," said Agnes, taking the lighter away.

"Give me the damn lighter back!" said Vera.

"Yeah, no blowing up on my watch," said Edith.

"Listen here, I might be crazy, but I am certainly not stupid," said Vera.

"Are we sure about the not being crazy part?" asked Agnes. "Well, I will be holding onto it and lighting the lantern, Vera."

Agnes carefully lit the lantern, and everyone was surprised by what they saw in the room.

"WHOA! Well, this isn't what I pictured when I stepped in this room," said Beau.

"Why are the walls so purple?" asked Agnes.

"It's the same color as the house—maybe a little lighter. I like it," said Blanche.

"Looks like Barney the purple dinosaur was here," laughed Mona. "Look at the antique furniture in here!"

"Wow, it's so beautiful," said Wanda.

"When I was younger, my grandma had the same type of furniture, and I loved it. It brings back so many memories," said Edith.

"I think we should go and look through the house and see what else is in here," Agnes.

"Yes, that sounds like a good idea. I know that I am curious," said Tallulah.

They all started walking down the hallway and saw a blue door.

"Gasoline Alley," said Tallulah.

"Well, I'm not sure what to think about that," said Wanda.

"I think we should go in and see what it's all about," said Agnes.

Everyone agreed that they should go and check it out. Agnes opened the door, and it was a large room with little furniture in it.

"This is nice and cozy," said Mona.

They looked around and were amazed by everything there. Wanda was looking around and realized that there was something on the fireplace mantle.

"What is that envelope doing on top of the fireplace?" asked Wanda.

Tallulah went up to the fireplace and grabbed the envelope out of Wanda's hand.

"Hey! I was going to read that," said Wanda.

"Well, I got it now," laughed Tallulah.

"Read what the envelope says, Tallulah," said Wanda.

"Welcome to the funhouse adventures. You have found the first envelope for your adventure through the funhouse. You must complete the challenges to go to the next door. Each door down the long hallway is a color picked at random that will lead you to a challenge you must do, specified on the card. Be careful—there are surprises around every corner. Expect the unexpected!"

"What is that supposed to mean?" asked Blanche.

"It sounds like this house has neat things for us to do and see," said Edith.

"What does everyone want to do?" asked Miles.

"We need to go back to camp," said Agnes.

"Really, Agnes? This was your idea—you wanted to come here in the first place," said Mona, her hands on her hips.

"Listen to me, Agnes. you're not flaking on us. You know this was your idea," said Tallulah.

"We are all in this together, and we are going to this as a team," said Blanche.

"One for all, and all for one," said Edith.

"OK, we will do this all together," said Agnes.

"I didn't think you would really chicken out on us anyways—you're too good to do something like that," said Tallulah.

Tallulah read the challenge card to everyone: "Challenge number one says you're to build a fire in the fireplace only using the items provided for you. Once the rope breaks, you will be able to go on to the next challenge. You must participate in at least one challenge. If one person doesn't participate in any of the challenges, they will get a punishment."

"Who knows how to start a fire?" asked Wanda.

"Here is where the men come in, I think," said Tallulah. "Do either one of you know how to build a fire?"

"I was a Boy Scout, and I could probably remember how to do it," said Beau.

"Let me help you, my friend. I was an Eagle Scout in my time," said Miles as he pat Beau on the back.

"What is the difference between the two?" asked Wanda.

"I think maybe they will just show each other up and see who is better with the matches," said Agnes.

"See who is better at what holding their wood," laughed Wanda.

Beau puts the two sticks together and starts rubbing them.

"That is my man," said Mona, cheering him on.

"It's not a contest, Mona," said Edith.

"I know I just wanted to cheer him on, which is not a crime," said Mona.

"Look like it's starting to smoke," said Agnes.

"Keep it going Beau you can do it," said Mona.

"Go, Miles, go!" said Edith.

Mona looked at Edith.

"If you can cheer for Beau, I should be able to cheer for Miles," said Edith.

"Miles, can you hand me more sticks so I can get it going a little more please?" asked Beau.

"Sure, my friend, I'd be happy to do that for you," said Miles.

More smoke started blowing out of the fireplace and, before they knew it, the whole room had filled up. Everyone started coughing and gagging, covering their mouths with whatever they could find. *Poof!* There was fire—and the rope started to burn right through.

"That was good teamwork that we did," said Beau as they shake hands.

"Too bad we couldn't open a window or something to clear out the smoke," said Tallulah.

"It's a good idea, but if we open a window, then someone will know we are here," said Agnes.

"We should put the fire out," said Blanche.

"Then, it may slow down the smoke and not burn us up," said Wanda.

"It's great how the two men are getting along so well," said Mona.

"Why wouldn't they?" asked Tallulah.

"Nothing—never mind, Tallulah—I didn't say anything," said Mona.

"Yes, you did. Now, spill the beans," said Tallulah in a stern voice.

"Mind your own business, Tallulah," said Mona.

"I can't now, because you opened your big mouth, and I am too damn curious," said Tallulah.

"OK, fine. You're not going to leave me alone until I do," said Mona.

"That's right, I won't," said Tallulah.

"Do you remember a couple of months ago when we had that fire drill, and no one could find me or Miles, and supposedly they were all worried about us?" asked Mona.

"Yes, the cute firemen came and I almost fainted so they would give me mouth to mouth," said Tallulah.

"That doesn't surprise me," said Mona.

"Where were you two?" asked Tallulah.

"Nowhere, so mind your own business," said Mona.

"Do you mean you were with him, Mona?!" asked Tallulah.

"OK, fine—in a matter of speaking, yes, we were together in his room," said Mona.

Tallulah was speechless—which wasn't normal for her.

"Let me just say when that Viagra kicked in, it was a magical moment I can't explain," said Mona, grinning from ear to ear.

"Wow, that's amazing, Mona," said Tallulah.

"I got on him and it felt so good, Tallulah," said Mona. Just thinking about it was getting her going again.

"So, the bottle does work!" said Tallulah.

"Yeah, no worries in that department," said Mona.

Tallulah couldn't believe what Mona had told her, and knew that she had to keep her mouth shut—which was extremely hard for her to do.

"Miles was so sweet and gentle, and at first, we were just kissing and holding each other because we were lonely. And then he popped that pill, and we were on top of each other like monkeys," said Mona.

"Wow, that must have been so much fun," said Tallulah.

"We both missed being with someone—and I didn't realize how much until he popped that pill, and we went to town," said Mona.

"I'm sure you did," said Tallulah.

"I can't believe how much I'm telling you, but I had to tell someone," said Mona.

"I'm happy that I am your person to talk to," said Tallulah.

"I can say he is good with his mouth—he went places I didn't even know about, but I wasn't going to stop him, because it was so wonderful," said Mona.

"I do have one question, if that's OK with you," said Tallulah.

"Yes, sure, Tallulah, you can ask anything," said Mona.

"Is he a decent size?" asked Tallulah.

"Hell yes, and very satisfying," said Mona.

"I know how your mind works," said Tallulah.

"Everyone knows me too well," said Mona. "But please, I'm asking you to keep this quiet."

"Don't worry, I got it. I won't," said Tallulah.

"I just want to make something clear. I really like Beau, and I don't need him to know about my little fling with Miles," said Mona.

"I will promise that I will keep my mouth shut and keep it to myself," said Tallulah as she crossed her fingers behind her back. "I do have one more question to ask you, Mona."

"Sure, go ahead, Tallulah," said Mona.

"Beau has been at the retirement home for a while. How come you two never noticed each other until now, at the camp?" asked Tallulah.

"I really don't know. Probably because we were never in the right place at the right time and never got to know each other until we got to camp," said Mona.

"I agree and I totally can see that happening back at the retirement home. You don't get to know everyone like you would like too," said Tallulah.

"We are stuck there for the rest of our lives," said Mona.

"That is why I am glad we are doing this all together," said Tallulah.

"I wanted it to be this way because you, Wanda, and Agnes are all my best friends, and going to summer camp seemed like a great idea, and now we are in a funhouse," said Tallulah.

"Well, you had a great idea, and I am glad you thought about coming to Mystic Summer Camp," said Mona.

"Even with Vera?" asked Tallulah.

"Yes, even with her, Tallulah," said Mona.

"Who knows what will happen to us when we get back to Heaven's Ridge, but I am going to have a damn fun time here and the rest at camp with no worries," said Tallulah.

"I agree with you, Tallulah—let's do exactly that," said Mona.

"For once you agree with me, Mona," said Tallulah. "Anything can happen at any time, so we must watch each other's backs."

"I'm hoping that we all stick together during our time at the funhouse," said Mona.

"Once we return to camp after this, I'm hoping it will have brought us all closer as friends," said Tallulah.

"We'd better get back to the group," said Mona. "So excited!"

"I'm excited to see what coming up next and for the rest of this adventure," said Tallulah.

"The more danger, the better," laughed Vera.

"No, that's OK—there doesn't need to be any danger, just more excitement," said Edith.

"OK, what Vera said is a little scary to me, but I'm looking forward to what comes next," said Agnes.

"Shall we move on to the next challenge?" asked Tallulah.

"Yes, we shall!" yelled everyone.

On to the next challenge . . . .

CHAPTER 15

Pudding Ridge Road

"I was thinking we should just go to the next door, which is green," said Mona.

"Seriously, no one has any opinions?" asked Agnes.

"Do we make it easy and go down the row?" asked Blanche.

"If we jump from color to color, we might get confused," said Edith.

"Some of us don't have a good memory, so I think we need to stay on one side then go to the other," said Agnes.

"Most likely, that's true, since I have no idea what we are talking about right now," said Edith.

"Good point, Edith. But the challenges are on the door, so unless we are not paying attention, I don't see how we will get confused," said Agnes.

"Trust me, one of us will find a way to get confused," said Edith.

"Either way is fine with me, because I'm color-blind and don't know what I am seeing," said Tallulah.

"EENY, MEENY, MINY, MOE, catch a tiger by the toe, if he hollers, I won't let him go," sang Vera. Edith turned her head to listen.

"Has she been sniffing something?" asked Tallulah, trying to be humorous.

"Guess what?" asked Vera in a creepy voice.

"I'm very afraid to ask, so I will leave it to one of you guys," said Wanda.

Tallulah grabbed Agnes's arm.

"Ouch! That hurts, Tallulah," said Agnes.

"You need to ask Vera," whispered Tallulah.

"Why does it have to be me?" asked Agnes.

"You are the one who wanted to come here and invited us all," said Tallulah.

"I didn't invite everyone, Tallulah—she hid on the bus," said Agnes.

"Will you just ask her?" asked Edith.

"Oh my God, not you, too, Edith!" said Agnes.

"OK, I am just going to ask so we can get going," said Wanda.

"Oh, this should be good," said Tallulah.

"Never mind, then—you ask, Tallulah! I don't really care what happened to the damn tiger anyways," said Wanda

"What about the tiger, Vera?" asked Agnes. She stepped backward, with Tallulah still holding on to her arm.

"Will you please let my arm go? I can't feel it when you're squeezing it that hard!"

"I ate the tiger," said Vera as she made a loud roar.

"Um, I think we should get out of here—or just pick a room and hide," said Wanda.

"It was quite tasty in my belly, and now I am full," said Vera strangely, licking her lips. She let out another roar.

"Ew, that's gross," said Wanda, ready to run away and puke at once.

"Don't worry, Wanda—she didn't eat a real tiger," said Tallulah, watching Vera.

"How do we really know she didn't eat one?" asked Edith.

"She is just trying to freak us out," said Agnes.

"First, Tallulah, can you let go of my damn arm again?" asked Agnes, getting annoyed.

"Sorry I didn't mean to hold on so tightly," said Tallulah.

"Do you see a dead tiger in here anywhere?" asked Agnes, looking around.

"No, I don't see one, but that doesn't mean she didn't do something here while we weren't looking," said Tallulah.

"Well, Vera trying to freak us out is sort of working here," said Mona, holding onto Beau.

"Vera sounded like that guy with red hair who has stitches all over his face and bright red hair, who carries a knife and has a very ugly bride," said Tallulah.

"Um, now I am really scared," said Agnes.

"Do you mean Chucky from Nightmare on Elm Street?" asked Edith.

"Chucky isn't from Nightmare on Elm Street," said Wanda.

"No, the other creepy person from Child's Play," said Edith.

"Yes, that's who I am talking about—Chucky is so very scary," said Tallulah.

"He isn't a good guy in general," said Wanda.

"Well, anyone who carries a knife and has red hair is not a good person," said Agnes.

"I used to have red hair!" said Mona.

"OK, but you would never carry a knife with you everywhere you went," said Edith.

"I watched one of his movies once with my grandchildren, and I was more scared than they were," said Wanda, shivering just thinking about it.

"I'm sure you will never see that again," said Tallulah.

"I haven't seen it in a while, since my grandchildren are all grown up, and don't plan to see it, Tallulah," said Wanda.

"I don't think Vera is crazy enough to hold a knife," said Agnes. "We need to get to the next door, or we will never move on to the next adventure."

"OK, this looks like this is the next door we need to go into," said Mona.

"It's a green door—interesting," said Agnes.

"I personally think we should go right and take our chances on what's on the other side," said Mona.

"Then I have a feeling we need to go left, and it's the right way to go," said Edith.

"Of course, you said right is the best way to go Edith you never agreed with me much anyway not then and not now," said Mona.

"I'm so happy you agree with me," said Edith. Mona gave Edith an evil wink.

"Let's just check out what else is down this hallway," said Wanda.

"Why would we want to do that?" asked Agnes.

"It's fun to just explore before we get in another challenge," said Wanda.

"Hold on a second here, we are going to stick to what the note said for us to do, and we are going to stick to the green door, which said Pudding Ridge Road," said Agnes.

"Oh, come on, Agnes, let's just look around then go in," said Wanda.

"OK, fine, we will go, because I can tell I won't win this argument," said Agnes.

They all started to go down the long hallway, hearing the creaking from the floor.

"If you ever wanted to sneak up on someone, you wouldn't be able to do it here," said Tallulah.

"Well, I would hope that no one would do that to a bunch of seniors," said Agnes.

"Yeah, I already had a heart attack with a cat coming at me and I really thought I was a goner," said Blanche.

"OK, enough exploring, let's go back to the pudding room," said Tallulah.

"I agree there is nothing much down here just a bunch of rooms with names on them," said Agnes.

They started getting closer to the Pudding Ridge room and Tallulah started sniffing something in the air.

"What is wrong with you, Tallulah? It's almost like you're one of those dog sniffers," asked Agnes.

"I smell something sweet, like cake batter, pudding, or fluff," said Tallulah ready to lick her fingers and lips.

"Wow, you narrowed it down to only those—I'm impressed, Tallulah," said Wanda.

"The door does say 'pudding,' so that works for me," said Agnes. As Wanda opened the door, Tallulah had her nose ready to sniff whatever was in there.

"Are you a dog sniffing something?" asked Agnes, laughing at Tallulah.

"Maybe she is in heat and needs to get spaded," laughed Wanda.

"What do you smell, Tallulah?" asked Edith.

"It smells like food, which is good, because I am hungry," said Tallulah, rubbing her stomach.

"You're always hungry, just like Frankie, and I'm quite sure you have a food timer in your stomach when it's time to eat," laughed Agnes.

"Come on, let's go in the room and see what's in there waiting for us," said Edith as they all just stood in the doorway.

"I'm going first," said Tallulah as she budged in front of Edith.

"Go ahead, I'm not going to stop you, Tallulah I know how much your food means to you," said Edith.

"Well, thank you, Edith," said Tallulah.

"Well, it's better than losing an arm or a leg—plus I am just too fragile," said Edith.

"Now that's funny Edith," laughed Mona.

"Of course, you would laugh," said Edith.

"It was well worth it," said Mona.

"Hey Tallulah, you were right, it has something to do with pudding," said Wanda as she wandered around the bright neon green room.

"Why would the door be the same color as the walls?" asked Agnes.

"Honestly, who decorated this house? A clown?" asked Agnes.

"At least it's not as dusty as the other room was," said Tallulah.

"You really should have sunglasses if you're going to be in this room," said Beau.

"Oh, I found the challenge envelope," said Mona, going over to the cuckoo clock hanging over the mantle. Mona got the envelope and was waving it around like she won the lottery.

"Can I read it this time?" asked Agnes as she took it out of Mona's hand.

"I guess so since now you have it in your hand," said Mona.

"Sorry I just got a little excited," said Agnes.

"I don't get why you must be so grabby, it's so annoying," said Mona.

"So, are you all ready to hear the next challenge clue or are you going to keep complaining?" asked Agnes.

"OK, let's go read it, Agnes," said Edith.

"Five people must participate in this challenge. In each bowl, there are five distinct kinds of pudding that are all labeled, you must eat all the pudding in the bowl, and if you choose not to finish your pudding of choice, you will be out of the challenge will get a punishment at another challenge just for you," said Agnes.

They all went down the side of the table to see what kinds of pudding there was before they decided who was going to participate in the challenge.

"What do you think Groat Pudding is?" asked Agnes, sticking her nose in it, trying to smell it.

"What does it smell like Agnes?" asked Wanda.

"I'm not sure it has to be a type of rotten food in it's my guess," said Agnes.

"That sounds disgusting," said Wanda after shaking her head.

"I'm not going to touch it or even eat this kind of stuff after smelling that, and I'm not into eating pudding anyways," said Agnes.

"So, you're not going to participate in this challenge?" asked Edith who doesn't look pleased and making a smirk at Agnes the same time.

"I don't have to if I don't want to, and I just said I don't like pudding it's a texture thing," said Agnes as she sat down and crossed her arms.

"Agnes, can you at least go through each pudding with us before we decide who is doing what?" asked Tallulah.

"Fine that sounds fair," said Agnes.

"OK so we saw the groat pudding. Now let's move to the rice pudding, which doesn't look half bad," said Tallulah.

"Bread-and-butter pudding looks like it's more butter than bread—almost more like a soup than a pudding," said Wanda.

"Hogs pudding doesn't sound good—especially when you see parts of a hog in it," said Edith.

"I hear it oinking for you," said Mona.

"Jam-roly-poly pudding sounds best out of all of them," said Tallulah.

"Well, that's definitely a variety of different pudding, and I am still thinking if I want to be a part of it or not," said Blanche.

"Well, hurry up because we want to get this challenge going and on to the next one," said Tallulah.

"So, who are the five that wants to participate in this challenge?" asked Mona.

"I'm kind of curious to try the hogs pudding," said Wanda who had a curious face on her.

"Maybe it will oink away at you," laughed Tallulah.

"Who else is going to try a pudding with Wanda?" asked Agnes.

"Come on, who else wants to do it?" asked Tallulah

"If no one does this, I'm afraid to know what the punishment will be if we don't participate," said Edith.

"I guess I will try the Bread-and-Butter pudding," said Mona.

"We need three more people," said Agnes.

"Are you sure you don't want to do this Agnes?" asked Wanda.

"No, that's OK, I will do the next challenge," said Agnes. Tallulah, Blanche, and Edith all decided to be brave with the pudding and do the challenge.

"I'm going to try bread pudding. It's my favorite," said Tallulah licking her lips.

"Hope you know it's called bread-and-butter pudding Tallulah and Mona is already going to try that one," said Wanda.

"Oh, jeez, OK, I'll do rice pudding, then, if I have too," said Tallulah.

"Blanche will have the groat pudding, and Edith you have the jam-roly-poly," said Wanda.

"That sounds like a yummy one to eat out of all of them," said Edith, ready to eat.

They all stood at the table and looked down at their pudding of choice.

"Yeah, now I am not sure if I want to try the hogs pudding," said Wanda as her stomach started to turn.

"Too late now, you're already there, so may as well try it and make the best out of it," said Agnes.

"Agnes, will you just shut the hell up? You didn't want to do this challenge, so be quiet," said Wanda.

"You have an opinion about all these puddings, Agnes, maybe you need to come here and take my spot," said Tallulah.

"No, that's OK, I will just sit here and be quiet," said Agnes.

"That seems funny, coming from you," said Wanda as she stared at the hogs pudding.

"Maybe it's a good pudding, so just try it, Wanda," said Miles.

"Maybe I will do it for you, Miles," said Wanda as she winked at him.

"Don't be such an oinker, Wanda," said Vera, laughing at what she said.

"Look who thinks they're a comedian now," laughed Tallulah.

"Vera, would you like to take my place?" asked Wanda.

"No, you're a better oinker then I am," laughed Vera.

"Fine I'll eat it, but I don't have to like it," said Wanda.

"That is true, Wanda, and at least you're trying something new," said Agnes.

"Oh, just shut up, Agnes, I've heard enough from the peanut gallery," yelled Wanda.

"Can we just get this over with before I really lose my cool?" asked Wanda.

"Relax, Wanda, they're just getting you all excited for no reason. Just block them out," said Edith.

"How about we all count to three and we try our pudding at the same time?" asked Tallulah.

"That sounds like a clever idea Tallulah I like the way you think sometimes," said Wanda with a giggle and snort.

They all counted together at the same time and picked up their spoons all at once.

"One, two, three let's do this!" they all shouted.

No one did it at first and they all laughed.

"OK we will do it for sure this time," said Edith.

One, two, three and all five joined in eating their pudding together.

Blanche tried her first bite of the groat pudding.

"It's very lumpy and I just ate something that belonged on the floor and surprisingly it has no taste," said Blanche as she makes a funny face.

BELCH!

"Oh, my are you OK Blanche?" asked Miles.

"I thought it was supposed to have raisins in it?" asked Blanche.

"Those sure don't look like raisins to me," said Tallulah as she looked at the pudding that Blanche was tasting.

"What are those little crawling things in it?" asked Blanche.

"Well, by the way they're moving, I would say magots or black bugs Blanche," said Edith.

Blanche put her hand over her mouth as she felt like she was going to puke from them moving in her mouth. She starts heaving and gagging and then running around to see if she could find something to spit them in.

"Seriously? There is no basket in this room for us to spit in," said Blanche as she went around, crazy.

Everyone just stood there and watched her, laughing. Finally, she found a bucket and let everything out that was in her mouth.

BARF!

"I feel bad for the poor soul who goes and cleans the bucket," said Blanche as she held her stomach.

"Blanche, are you OK, dear?" asked Tallulah, concerned, but not wanting to go near her.

"Yes, I am fine, and done eating. I don't care if I get a punishment or not," said Blanche.

"That wouldn't have been one of my favorites either," said Agnes.

"Since when did you ever try groat pudding?" asked Wanda.

"OK, you got me there, but I was just being supportive," said Agnes.

"Oh, I thought you said you don't eat pudding," said Miles suspiciously.

"I don't, Miles, but if I did, it wouldn't be groat or rice pudding—especially if there were bugs in it," said Agnes.

"I thought we were talking about Blanche eating the groat pudding with the bugs, not the rice pudding, and certainly not you," said Edith who had had enough of Agnes then.

"You did say you had a favorite even know you don't eat pudding," said Miles.

"Can we just let it go Miles?" asked Agnes who looked pissed off.

"You're the one who keeps opening your mouth Agnes and you kind of putting your foot in your mouth," said Miles.

"Wow you're all being nasty right now," said Agnes.

"Well, you're not helping the situation," said Edith.

"Sorry I will stop putting my two cents in," said Agnes.

"Yeah right," said Wanda. As she inspected the Hogs Pudding, she noticed things that were not normal for pudding, but gave it a taste anyways.

"The Hogs pudding wasn't too bad if you like a little piece of snout in your pudding," said Wanda as she chomps down on something hard.

"I just got a little snout in my mouth," said Wanda as she shared with everyone.

"Excellent job Wanda you're such a good champion," said Miles.

"Why because I had a pig snout in my mouth?" asked Wanda.

"Just cheering you on my dear I mean nothing by it," said Miles.

"Thanks for cheering for me Miles, I do appreciate it," said Wanda.

"Well, this is a tongue," said Wanda.

"How are you eating all those pig parts with no problem?" asked Mona.

"I just put it out of my mind what I am eating and think of things I would love to eat and replace it with that," said Wanda.

"So, what did you replace everything with?" asked Edith.

"I picked Jellybeans and Milk Duds," said Wanda.

"Interesting way to think about it Wanda I am impressed," said Edith.

"Maybe we all should think that way to get through this challenge," said Tallulah.

"Mine smells funny," said Tallulah as she tried to take a tiny bite of the rice pudding.

BARF!

"I'm guessing Tallulah didn't like that too much," said Agnes as she sits back and laughs.

"That's just disgusting I don't know how they expect people to eat this crap," said Tallulah.

BURB!

"Rice pudding is usually an immensely popular pudding," said Beau, my mom used to make it when I was younger.

"They do it on Survivor," said Edith.

"I've never seen them have Rice Pudding on Survivor," said Wanda.

"Well, they have a lot of rice so I am sure they can make something out of it," said Edith.

"Good for them, but this isn't Survivor," said Tallulah.

"I think the Hogs pudding would be more on Survivor then Rice pudding," said Wanda.

"Oh yeah that's not good at all it's almost like they forgot to add something," said Tallulah.

"Surprised to hear that knowing it's a common pudding that people eat maybe every day," said Agnes.

"When are you going to stop saying things about every pudding if you're not into eating it again it makes no sense?" asked Edith.

"OK sorry for once I will be quiet," said Agnes.

"Well, that's another pudding that's going down the toilet," said Beau.

"So done with eating that," said Tallulah as she put the spoon down, went to the basket and puked everything she had left in her stop.

Now it was Mona's turn to try the bread-and-butter pudding. She picked up her spoon and tried a little bit.

"How is it, Mona?" asked Beau.

"All I taste is butter," said Mona.

"Are you sure Mona?" asked Wanda.

Mona took a little more on her spoon this time and took another bite and swished it in her mouth.

"Yeah, still taste the same all butter no bread," said Mona.

"That's just a crazy kind of pudding and not the kind that came from the floor," said Blanche.

"It wasn't bad tasting it just wasn't good tasting either if that makes sense," said Mona.

"Jam-Roly-Poly is sweet just like me, but not too bad," said Edith.

Mona burst out laughing when Edith made that comment.

"Quiet from the peanut gallery," said Edith.

"Oh, so now we are peanuts," said Tallulah as she just shook her head.

Mona agreed with Tallulah but didn't want to say anything.

"So, what exactly does it taste like?" asked Tallulah.

"Well, I don't want to get you jealous, but it's almost like oatmeal with jelly mixed together," said Edith.

"Well, that sounds interesting and kind of tasty," said Tallulah.

"Do you want to try a little bit Tallulah?" asked Edith.

"No, I still have a little bit of the rice pudding taste left in my mouth," said Tallulah.

"Hey everyone, look I finished my bowl of pudding," said Edith.

"I picked the right kind of pudding to eat I guess," said Edith.

"We are all very proud of you," said Tallulah. Well, thank you very much," said Edith.

On to the next challenge . . . .

CHAPTER 16

Sisterly Love—NOT!

"Alright we are doing well let's keep the momentum going," said Beau.

"Love when you take charge Beau," said Mona as she winked at him.

"Oh, where is that bucket, I must puke again," said Blanche. "I really think you two need to get a room," said Edith.

"Oh, why are you jealous I have someone who loves me, and you don't?" asked Mona.

"Why are you such a bitch Mona?" asked Edith.

"I'm not a bitch, but you're just a stubborn woman and you have always been that way," said Mona.

Mona is such a kind soul and seeing her smile again makes anyone want to smile with her, but if she loses her cool you should watch out because it's not pretty. Edith is hot headed and not afraid to tell people exactly how she feels when it comes to certain things.

"Wow this is almost like we are in a soap opera," said Tallulah.

"I thought you both were such good friends at Heaven's Ridge?" asked Agnes.

"Well, things change and that's all I am saying," said Edith.

"Maybe this adventure will bring you two closers together," said Agnes.

"I'm not putting a guarantee on that," said Edith sadly.

"I'll just hope that we won't hurt each other during all of this," said Mona.

Edith tried to laugh but wasn't working she just wanted to move on.

"No promises there Agnes unfortunately," said Edith as she walks away towards the door.

"Are you and Edith, OK?" asked Blanche.

"Yeah, I am fine, but I can't answer about Edith," said Mona.

"Just making sure it seemed like you both had a little tension between the two of you," said Blanche.

"No worries I'm fine I just not feeling too hot after eating that Bread-and-Butter Pudding," said Mona.

"Yeah, mine was nothing spectacular either," said Blanche.

"I don't know how I could eat something that had creepy crawlers in it," said Mona as she walked back toward Beau when she felt something slimy hit the back of her neck.

Mona turned around quickly and flicked it off her.

"What the hell was that" asked Mona.

"It seems like pudding is on your back," said Tallulah. Mona heard Edith laugh.

"Oh, so you think that's funny putting pudding down my back?" asked Mona.

"Yes, I sure do, Mona," said Edith, snotty.

"Well then let's make it even!" Mona picked up a spoon and scooped up whatever pudding was close to her and threw the pudding across the table and right in Edith's face.

"Bullseye, yells Mona as it got her right in the eyes. Everyone was watching and couldn't believe what they just saw.

"So rude I can't believe you're acting like a child," said Edith as she shakes her head and tries to get the pudding out of her face.

"I'm acting like a child," yells Mona.

"Yeah, you are," said Edith.

"Are you serious?" asked Mona shocked to hear that coming from Edith.

"You're the one who threw the pudding at me first Edith so knock it off," said Mona.

"Why you want more Mona?" asked Edith.

"Oh, don't you dare Edith," said Mona. Squish!

"Oh my god Edith," said Mona who got another spoon full of pudding on her head. That's its Mona goes up to Edith picked up the bowl of groat pudding and dumped the whole thing on Edith's head.

"How do you like me now?" asked Mona.

"What is crawling on my head?" asked Edith as she stays stiff as a board.

"Are you sure you want to know?" asked Tallulah who was enjoying every minute of it.

"Yes, Tallulah I do want to know so please tell me Tallulah," said Edith.

"Well, it seems like Mona dumped the Groat pudding on your head, so you have bugs and magots on you," said Tallulah trying not to laugh. Edith didn't move a muscle with all the magots, and black bugs were crawling all over her.

"Get these damn things off me," yelled Edith.

"How are we going to do that?" asked Tallulah.

"I had to eat them I don't think I am going to touch them sorry Edith," said Blanche.

"Let's see if there is something we can use around here to get them off," said Agnes.

"I can't believe you did this Mona," said Edith.

"Well, if you didn't do it in the first place then we wouldn't have been no problem," said Mona.

"Cool it you two or I will put the hose on you as soon as I can find one," said Agnes.

"A hose might work better getting all these things off Edith," said Tallulah.

Camp Funhouse 231

"Unfortunately, I don't see one around here so that's not an option," said Agnes.

"Well, whoever kept these things around for us probably didn't think there be a pudding fight happening," said Agnes.

"Edith, it looks like we might have to pick everything off you by hand which is going to absolutely gross," said Agnes.

"I don't care what you have to do just get them all off me," yelled Edith.

Agnes and Miles helped get everything off Edith one at a time.

"Here, Edith, I just happen to find something else for you to put on," said Tallulah.

"What the hell is this?" asked Edith.

"I don't know I think it's a gown or something I think I have seen them around Heaven's Ridge if you don't have a night gown or pajamas, they put one of those on you," said Tallulah.

"Where do you suggest I change?" asked Edith.

"Well, you can change here or go outside the door Edith," said Tallulah.

"Just keep me covered," said Edith.

"I think I can manage that," said Tallulah. She held up the Johnny gown so that Edith could change into it after she took off her clothes.

"Are you almost done Edith my arms are getting tired? asked Tallulah and suddenly started itching.

"Yes, just stay still Tallulah," said Edith.

"I'm trying, but something is crawling on me," said Tallulah.

"Tallulah looks down to her arm and saw that a black bug was crawling on her arm. Tallulah tried to move the arm around to make the black bug fall off, but it kept climbing up the arm.

"Stay still, Tallulah, I'm almost done," said Edith.

"I can't Tallulah there is a black bug on me," said Tallulah as she dropped the Johnny gown and went flying across the room trying to get the black bug off her.

"Tallulah you bitch," yelled Edith as she stands there naked.

"Sorry Edith, but the damn bug won't come off," said Tallulah.

"Hold on Tallulah I will help you," said Agnes.

"Agnes removed the black bug from Tallulah's arm and squished it on the floor.

"Thank you, Agnes, for helping it was itching and the crawling on me and it was driving me crazy," said Tallulah.

"OH MY GOD I'M NAKED," yelled Edith who wrapped her arms around herself.

"Oh, shit hold on I'm coming just relax Edith I got the Johnny thingy right here," said Blanche as she wraps it around her.

"Thank you, Blanche, I appreciate you helping me," said Edith.

"I would suggest one thing and that's not to not bend over," said Blanche.

"Why is that?" asked Edith.

"If you bend over everyone will see your ass," said Blanche.

"Oh, this is a nightmare," cried Edith.

"Oh, suck it up buttercup you will survive," said Mona.

"OK we need to get out of this room I think we have caused enough of a mess here and we need to keep moving," said Agnes.

"I agree and I just can't wait to move on," said Tallulah.

"I first want to know what caused that little food fight between you?" asked Blanche.

"You two fight like cats and dogs instead of friends," said Tallulah.

"I never said that we were friends," said Mona "Friends wouldn't throw pudding at each other," said Agnes.

"Wait I thought you both were friends," said Tallulah.

"That is what everyone wanted to think, but we aren't," said Edith.

"What is up with you two?" asked Agnes as she was getting more curious.

"I think we need to just tell them because they're not going to let it go," said Mona.

"I personally think that it's none of their damn business," said Edith.

"If you say so, Edith," said Mona.

"Mona and I didn't just meet at Heaven's Ridge, we have known each other for most our lives, but it's a story for another time and not now," said Edith.

"I'm just trying to forget all these years," said Mona as she walks away.

"Plus, we have the whole house to go through and see what is waiting for us and have fun with all those challenges that's why we are here," said Edith.

"So, let's have fun and let's do this and move on to the next one," said Tallulah to keep things going and keep the peace and before another bug comes and crawls on her.

"Should we just tell them Edith?" asked Mona.

"I don't really care even know I think it's none of their damn business about how we know each other," said Edith getting all upset.

"Well, if no one is going to disclose information I say let's go onward," said Tallulah as she goes to the door.

"All of us here are both your friends so I don't understand why you wouldn't tell us what is going on with you two and obviously there is something going on," said Agnes.

"We have never seen you act like this before with each other especially throwing pudding around," said Wanda.

Mona and Edith looked at each other both giving each other dirty looks. Mona knew that Edith wanted to tell them so that everyone knows their secret they have been hiding since they were sixteen.

"Suit yourself you were always the tattle tale anyways," said Mona as she shakes her head and goes to be with Beau.

Everyone was looking at them strangely and you can see they have questions in their minds before they know what is going on.

"What's going on with the both of you fighting like cats and dogs?" asked Agnes.

"Mona is the dog in fact she is big bulldog," said Edith as she laughs.

"Bulldogs are small you ding bat," said Mona as she laughs back.

"OK fine you're a big Great Dane," said Edith with a laugh.

"Your no pussy cat either you always have your claws out ready to attack especially when things don't go your way," said Mona as she fires back at Edith.

"Whoa alrighty then let's just calm down here a little and go to your corners," said Miles as he gets in between them both as they're trying to hit each other.

"OK you two what gives?" asked Agnes as she is getting tired of the fighting.

Mona and Edith, both gave each other a glaring look at each other before Mona decided to tell them their secret.

"You may as well just tell them Edith because they're just going to try and get it out of us anyways," said Mona looking at Edith.

Everyone moves a little closer to where Edith and Mona were to hear just what they have to say. Mona and Edith look at each other before telling everyone about them.

"Are you two going to tell us or do we have to beat it out of you?" asked Wanda.

"Wanda there will be no beating unless you can do it good and make it look like an accident," laughed Agnes.

"You're a dirty bird Wanda," said Agnes as she chuckled.

"I'm damn proud of it," said Wanda.

"OK listen up everyone Edith and I are related by marriage," said Mona.

"So, we are stepsisters since we were sixteen years old there now you all know," said Edith.

"I'm five months older than her," said Mona with a smile. Sure, they didn't need to know that, but OK, Edith scold at Mona. "Edith, you can just bite me," said Mona.

"Yeah, I can see that you're sisters with an attitude," said Agnes.

"Anyways Edith's mom married my dad a long time ago," said Mona as she looks disgusted every time.

"Basically, Mona's dad couldn't keep his pants on with my mom," said Edith sarcastic.

"Your mom is also guilty of not keeping her clothes on and opening her vagina and letting him be in her," said Mona angrily.

"Wow my virgin ears that I can't wait to hear more," said Wanda.

"Your far from a virgin Wanda,' said Tallulah.

"How would you know anyways Tallulah?" asked Wanda.

"You talk about your daughter and the grandkids all the time," said Tallulah.

"OK well you got me there I guess Tallulah, but you're not the virgin Mary either," said Wanda.

Well, that's something to be proud of," said Tallulah.

"Why haven't we known all of this until now?" asked Agnes with a serious look on her face.

"We haven't spoken in fifty years," said Edith. Mona looked at Edith after saying that to see her reaction.

"Who would have thought that she would follow me to Heaven's Ridge a while after my arrival there?" asked Mona.

"I didn't follow you here I didn't even know this was the place you would be," said Edith. "I lived with my son and his lovely wife for a while, and I kept falling at home in my cute one-bedroom apartment and I lived all alone so when I moved in with him and his wife, he told me it was going to be a temporary visit, and so they didn't feel like they had to always watch me all the time which also means I need a babysitter," said Edith with a tear in her eye.

"That is so sad," said Wanda.

"In other words, we can't keep you forever and we are going to put you in a home, and he thought Heaven's Ridge was a good place to put me because it wasn't a long drive for him to see me," said Edith.

"That's so sad, but I can understand that my daughter couldn't take care of me either and that's why I am at Heaven's Ridge," said Tallulah.

"I can promise you my son didn't know you were there as a resident Mona," said Edith.

"Yeah sure," said Mona.

"You know I wouldn't of came if I knew you were here Mona," said Edith.

"OK, if you haven't seen each other in fifty years then how did you know what each other looked like when you saw each other at Heaven's Ridge?" asked Tallulah.

"Well, maybe fifty years is a stretch maybe it's more like ten years we stopped talking to each other years ago after my stroke," said Edith.

"I came to see you and the nurse told me I wasn't allowed to come in your room," said Mona.

"OK, both of you relax for a minute here," said Agnes with a stern voice.

Everyone was just trying to have all the information sink in.

"So, I am just wondering why you two don't like each other?" asked Tallulah.

"That's going to be a loaded question to answer," said Agnes.

"I'm curious like everyone else is," said Tallulah.

"I always resented Edith for being a part of our family there was no hiding that," said Mona.

"She told me right away when I moved in that she wasn't happy with me being there," said Edith.

"Once she came into our lives my dad gave her more attention and I was feeling left behind in the dust," said Mona.

"It's not my fault Mona, but at least your dad wasn't afraid to have me in the family," said Edith.

"I wasn't afraid when my mom died because we knew it was happening. I was always there for my dad and then you moved in, and I was pushed out of the way by my dad," said Mona.

"Well, it certainly wasn't mine either because we were fine until you moved in, and your mom married my dad," said Mona.

"My dad kicked me out of the house when I was eighteen years old."

"It's not like I had a mom to go to since she passed away when I was younger and no grandparents either I was all alone," said Mona as she is ready to cry.

Beau grabbed Mona's hands to let her know he was there.

"It's not like I was drinking or doing drugs or anything like that," said Mona.

"Plus, you were always out with random boys that both our parents didn't approve of, but that didn't stop you and that broke your dad's heart. He would tell me how much of a good girl you were," said Edith.

"I did it for attention and because I knew you hated me," said Mona.

"To be honest I never hated you like you seem to think, and your dad never hated you either he just couldn't believe how much you changed in those couple of years," said Edith.

"I didn't hate you either I was an only child for a long time and so having a sister and a new stepmom was something new to me and I didn't know how to deal with it, when you did come and moved in it was a big adjustment for both me and my dad," said Mona.

"Well, it was an adjustment to me too," said Edith.

"When you moved in you acted like you owned the whole place like you were little miss high and mighty," said Mona. She had shared that with Edith, and it was something that she held on to for a long time.

"Well, I wish you just came to me and got to know me before running off so you could see that your dad loved us both," said Edith.

"Like I said before my dad was giving you more attention, so I felt like I was an outcast and didn't belong there," said Mona.

"To tell the truth all the time he spent with me he never stopped talking about you after you moved out and he even tried to find you so you could come back to him," said Edith.

"He did really Edith?" asked Mona surprised. Edith put her head down as she spoke.

"Yeah well, I don't believe you so let's just move on," said Mona started to get angry.

"Well, I thought for a minute we were getting somewhere," said Wanda.

"He asked for you when he was in the hospital after his heart attack, but no one could find you we all tried," said Edith.

"Oh, that's so sad," said Tallulah.

"Mona when he passed away you didn't even come to his funeral," said Edith.

"I was there I just hid in the back and when everyone left, I said my goodbyes," said Mona.

"I can't take back all the things that happened between us, but maybe we can let things go, said Edith.

"No, you can't, and either can I, but we can make the best of what time we both have and get to know each other and maybe even like each other," said Edith.

"You are right Edith I just need time to process everything we talked about," said Mona.

"I understand and I hope us doing these challenges together with our friends will bring us a little bit closer and if it doesn't then I'll be waiting for you," said Edith.

"Sorry to cut this reunion short, but we have another door waiting for all of us," said Blanche as she starts walking ahead of everyone else.

"Then let's go and thanks Blanche for letting me and Edith have moment," said Mona.

"Boy, is she stubborn," said Agnes.

"She always has been since I have known her, and she is just like her father was, but underneath he was a kind man and Mona missed it all," said Edith.

"Was this supposed to be a therapy session?" asked Tallulah.

"I'm just letting them have their moment," said Agnes.

"Are we going to do this adventure?" asked Miles

"I don't know, but it's kind of interesting, I think," said Tallulah.

"We have known both of you for a while and we never knew that you were sisters and I think it's great," said Agnes.

"I do agree with you on that Agnes, but it didn't need to come out now," said Blanche

"They could have waited for us to be around the campfire or the dinner table or something," said Agnes with a chuckle.

"Can we get going now we have so much more to see and do and if I don't keep walking, I am just going to fall over and never want to get back up?" asked Wanda.

"I'll catch you my dear you're too beautiful to fall to the ground," said Miles.

"No that's OK I rather just fall on the floor and break a hip," said Wanda as she walked away from Miles.

"What am I doing so wrong that these women are not attractive to me?" whispered Miles to himself.

On to the next challenge…

CHAPTER 17

Vera Bites the Dust

They were all out in the hallway and they noticed there was a punishment waiting for them which they weren't surprised to see.

"We better get it done since we didn't finish all the pudding," said Tallulah "I see London I see France I see Edith's underpants," laughed Wanda.

"Oh, Wanda you're so funny I forgot to laugh," said Edith.

"Edith has a sense of humor," said Mona.

"That's funny coming from you," said Edith.

"Those two are not helping my stomach," said Tallulah.

Mona and Beau were whispering to each other, and it was annoying to the other seniors.

"I know how you feel it's making me sick," said Edith.

"Why did he even have to come with us?" asked Agnes.

"We had no choice remember Agnes, he had already been invited by Mona," said Wanda.

Mona had been behind Wanda and Agnes when they were talking about her and Beau.

"For your information he was worried about not just my safety, but all our safety and he wanted to come with us to make sure we made it out safely so if you have a problem then tough luck," said Mona.

"OK sweetie we totally get it and it's OK with us that he is here," said Agnes.

"I don't get why it bothers you so much that Beau is here?" asked Mona. She was terribly upset that Agnes and Wanda were talking about her and Beau especially after they all found out that Edith as her sister.

"Last I knew it was four of us when we had this idea and it quickly turned to more coming," said Agnes.

"When more seniors showed up all of that wasn't my fault and I shouldn't be the one yelled at for it," said Mona.

"I don't mean any disrespect Mona; I know you have been wanting a man in your life and I will never want to take that from you," said Agnes.

"I'm happy that Beau and Miles are both here," said Tallulah.

"That's because you want a man and because the more, I thought about it the more it's nice to have men around if we ever get in any danger like when Vera was driving," said Agnes.

"Are you and Agnes OK now Mona?" asked Wanda who was just getting herself all in a tizzy.

"Relax Agnes everything will be OK with us," said Mona.

"Agnes decided to open the door and see what this punishment challenge was going to be all about," Blanche.

"Holy shit," said Agnes as she is amazed what is in this room.

"What's wrong Agnes?" asked Tallulah as she came through the door and puts her hand over her mouth.

As the other seniors were going on and on about who did what to who and how. They slowly came into see what the buzz was all about.

"Wow it's a boxing ring," said Wanda.

"Good eye Wanda, you got it right," said Agnes.

"It wasn't hard to figure out captain obvious," said Wanda.

"Who is going to be boxing?" asked Blanche.

"I don't know I haven't found the challenge envelope yet," said Agnes.

"Why would they make this room and door rainbow?" asked Tallulah.

Maybe it will be a punishment where they find out who is the brightest," said Agnes

Miles found the challenge envelope on the mat of the boxing ring.
"OK Miles let's hear who is going to box," said Edith.
Miles slowly opened the envelope and took out the challenge card.
Agnes just knew it was going to be her, so she put her head down to be prepared.
Miles cleared his throat and read the clue.
"Two of you didn't finish all your pudding in the pudding challenge so here is a chance to redeem yourself.
"If one of you chooses not to do this punishment you must choose a person to take your place. If both of you forfeit this punishment you must do the next challenge all by yourself without anyone help.
"The two seniors that have randomly drawn to do this punishment are Blanche and Tallulah," said Miles.
"WHAT!" screamed Tallulah.
"Sorry Tallulah you're one of them," said Agnes.
"Well, I don't want to do it I will be more than happy to do the next challenge alone," said Blanche.
"Well, that just leaves you Tallulah," said Agnes.
"There is no way I am going to do boxing either, so I'll do the next challenge," said Tallulah.
"So, since you both forfeit you must pick someone to take your spot," said Miles.
"Oh this is so unfair," said Tallulah.
"You can change your mind and do it Tallulah," said Miles.
"Oh, jeez no I don't want too," said Tallulah.
"Then you both think about and let us know who you both pick," said Miles.
Blanche and Tallulah look at everyone.
"I'll do it you bunch of pussies," said Vera.

"What did Vera just say," asked Wanda.

"She wants to be one of the ones to do the boxing," said Edith.

"OK so now we have Vera who is going to be the lucky one to be her opponent?" asked Miles.

"Still not me," said Tallulah.

"Me neither," said Blanche.

"I have to vote for Agnes," said Wanda.

"What are you smoking?" asked Agnes.

"Nothing honey, but all you did during the pudding challenge was talk about the pudding and you went on and on about it, so it's your turn to step up and do this," said Wanda.

"I said I would do the next challenge not punishment," said Agnes.

"Yes, you did, and the challenge is right here and now even known they call it a punishment,' said Wanda.

"It's Vera honestly how hard can it be?" asked Tallulah.

"Oh, now you put your two cents in," said Agnes. Agnes can't believe that she must be in a boxing ring with Vera.

"I better get this over with," said Agnes.

Vera saw something in one of the corners and she picked up the pair of pool noodles. She checked them out one at a time. Vera slides her hand in one just to see how it feels. Vera looked around to see if anyone was watching her hit herself in the head with one.

"Let's do this," said Vera said to herself quietly.

"OK so who am I going to hit first?" asked Vera.

"OK I am leaving," said Tallulah. "Me too," said Agnes.

"No, you need to stay and do this," said Edith.

They were on their way out the door when they heard a loud BOOM.

"What was that loud boom?" asked Agnes.

"Is that your stomach growling again Mona?" asked Tallulah.

"I thought it was yours Tallulah," said Mona laughing.

"Maybe it was an earthquake or something," said Blanche as she starts shaking.

"Relax Blanche everything will be OK," said Edith giving her someone reassurance.

Everyone turned to Tallulah because she likes to joke around sometimes.

"It's not me making those noises," said Tallulah.

Wanda looked behind her to see what all the fuss was about, and she couldn't believe what she was watching with her own eyes as they were getting wide.

"Look at Vera over there in the corner with her pool noodle," said Wanda pointing at Vera.

"Look at the way she moves," said Mona in amazement.

"Great now I will have to box," said Agnes.

"Um, Agnes it doesn't look like you're boxing if she has a pool noodle in her hand," said Wanda.

Tallulah starts to whine because she almost had to box Vera. Wanda is still watching Vera and can't believe how good she is.

"You are a wuss Agnes, and I am going to put you down sucker," said Vera.

"We will see about that Vera," said Agnes.

"Wow excellent job on the trash talking," said Tallulah.

"You're not going to haunt me anymore," said Vera moving her legs side to side.

"Who is haunting her?" asked Wanda.

"It must be someone she sees in her mind, and I know she does that from time to time at Heaven's Ridge," said Agnes.

"How is she even doing this because she can't get her arms up that high?" asked Blanche.

"I'm just amazed about what is going on here I don't think I have ever seen her do this," said Edith.

"She must be hallucinating again she does this a lot like I said before," said Agnes.

"I can hear her sometimes from my room, she yells and screams and sometimes they aren't pleasant things she is saying," said Tallulah.

"Agnes you really don't want to do anything while we are all here together?" asked Wanda.

"I'm going to hit the crazy lady with a pool noodle so what?" asked Agnes.

"Oh, my god, I am trying to watch Vera make a fool of herself," said Wanda.

"I didn't want to do one challenge whoopie freaking do, and you're not letting it go Wanda," said Agnes.

"Yes, I am, and I'm excited to see that you're pool noodle fighting against Vera," said Wanda.

"Is anyone listening to me?" screamed Agnes.

"Stop your ruining my fun," shouted Vera.

"See, now Vera is yelling at me," said Agnes just shaking her head.

"Hey Agnes since you can't keep your big mouth shut do you want to come and fight me right now instead of next year?" asked Vera.

This is all you Agnes," said Tallulah.

"I'm ready to take on an opponent," said Vera.

"Oh no Vera I am happy right where I am, but thanks for the offer?" said Agnes. She could not believe that Vera called her out like that, and she knew she had to do it, but was trying to put it off as much as possible.

"Really, Agnes? You're not going to do this either after you already trashed talked Vera?" asked Wanda.

"No, I am going to do it so don't worry Wanda," said Agnes.

"I honestly don't think she can hit that hard, so you won't get hurt in anyway especially because you will be using a pool noodle," said Tallulah.

"Vera talks to things that are not there so this will be cake," said Wanda.

"So, I'm just going to automatically appear in front of her and have her take a whack at me with a pool noodle?" asked Agnes.

246　April Carter

"Listen Agnes as Miles makes his way over, all you need to do is when she comes at you just block her with the noodle and hit her quickly back," said Miles.

"How do you know so much about pool noodle fighting Miles?" asked Agnes.

"I grew up with brothers who love hitting me with things especially pool noodles in the summer in the pool, and I was more of a chess player," said Miles.

"That's so fascinating Miles," said Tallulah with a wink.

"Hey Vera," shouted Agnes.

"What do you want loser?" asked Vera.

"I want you to have a noodle ball match with me," said Agnes as she started having an anxiety act.

"Should we honestly be letting her do this?" asked Mona.

"Well, we did talk Agnes into doing this, so I'm thinking yes," said Wanda with excitement.

"Well, I'm not going to get in the middle of it, I'm crazy, but not that crazy to get in Vera's way," said Edith.

"Do you think Agnes will hurt Vera?" asked Mona.

"I don't think so unless Vera really ticks Agnes off and really beats her with the pool noodle," said Tallulah.

"I have been in Vera's way, and I have gotten hit by her before, and it wasn't a pretty site," said Wanda.

"Agnes knows what she is doing so I am not too worried about her," said Edith.

"Should we start making bets on who is going to win?" asked Mona.

"We could and then if we are wrong no one will know what we would be doing and it would be fun," said Mona.

"My vote of course is for Agnes because I don't see too much of a fight with Vera," said Blanche.

"I don't know Vera can be tough if she really wants to be," said Wanda.

"We just need to sit back and enjoy a good fight," said Beau.

Where is the popcorn when you need it?" asked Tallulah.

"I knew you were still hungry after that pudding," said Wanda.

"Yes, my stomach feels fine now," said Tallulah.

Agnes grabbed the pool noodle and got ready to fight with Vera.

"Miles comes over to Agnes to give her a very quick pool noodle lesson, to make sure you do this right and safe I'm going to give you pool noodle tips I learned from my brothers," said Miles.

"Oh, this should be fun to listen too," said Tallulah.

Do you want to do this with Vera?" asked Agnes.

"No, I do not," said Tallulah. Then shut the hell up," said Agnes.

Wow OK relax girlfriend," said Tallulah.

There are two different places you can hit Vera with the pool noodle, and it won't hurt Vera too much," said Miles.

"That's good because I really don't want to hurt her, but I do want to win," said Agnes.

"There is a whack to her head which you hit straight on and can hit her in the face.

"Ouch that sounds painful," said Agnes.

"A cross hit which is right in the stomach," said Miles.

Well, that sounds better than in the head," said Agnes.

"Basically, just keep hitting her until she is down and cover yourself as much as possible, so she doesn't get you down first," said Miles.

Agnes takes a deep breath and grabs her pool noodle before the match started. Vera just stands there and stares at Agnes.

"Are you ready to rumble Agnes or are you to afraid?" asked Vera.

"Afraid or scared is a better way to say it, but I'm ready to put you down," said Agnes as she gets close to Vera.

"If that's what you call it sure I'm ready to rumble," said Vera.

"I don't think Agnes knows what Vera means by rumble," said Mona.

"I totally agree with you on that Mona, but she will find out fast," said Edith.

"Are you ladies ready to play pool noodle?" asked Miles.

"I'll be ready then I'll ever be," said Agnes.

"Come on bozo let's get this going so I can knock her out with my noodle," said Vera.

"Ready, set, go," said Miles.

At first, they dance around each other waiting to see who throws the first hit. Agnes just looked at Vera with a death stare even if she didn't know she was doing it. Vera threw the first hit and got Agnes in the stomach.

OUCH! "That stung a little Vera," said Agnes as she holds her stomach. Everyone clapped for Agnes.

"Come on Agnes, you can beat her just stay focused," said Miles

"Good thing I didn't eat that pudding it would probably just come back up," said Agnes.

"It's supposed to hurt you moron," said Vera.

"Why can't you be nice Vera?" asked Agnes.

"We are having a pool noodle fight not playing with barbies we don't need to be nice," said Vera.

"Agnes had enough of Vera and her sarcasm and gave her a piece of her own medicine and gave her one good hit in the face.

"Vera had gotten a good hit to the face, and she fell on the ground.

All you could hear was a loud BOOM, when her body hit the bottom of the ring. Agnes was all excited that she got Vera down on the first hit.

"I did it," said Agnes as she raised her pool noodle in the air waving to everyone.

"WOO HOO Agnes," said Tallulah.

Agnes turned around and saw that Vera wasn't moving.

"Should we at least see if she is, OK?" asked Miles.

"Well, I couldn't have hit her that hard with a pool noodle," said Agnes.

Who wants to be the one to see if she is, OK?" asked Wanda.

"I guess I will do it," said Miles even know he wasn't sure why he volunteered himself.

"I'm not going to stop you and she isn't moving so go-ahead Mr. Viagra man," said Wanda chuckling to herself.

Miles goes up to where Vera is laying on the floor and gets in the ring Miles bends over next to her. Vera started to move slowly.

"Are you OK Vera my sweet?" asked Miles.

"I'm not sure you should have called her that," said Wanda with a worried look.

"Vera looked at Miles with a curious look.

"Shut your fucking trap and get out of my face NOW," said Vera angry as she attempts to get up and grabs Miles by the shirt and punches him and he lands in the corner.

All you heard was a loud BOOM as Miles body hit the corner of the ring.

"Well good to know you're OK Vera," said Miles in a shaky voice.

"Now get out of the ring so I can finish with Agnes," said Vera.

"She is fine everyone," said Miles.

"I'm back! Did you miss me?" Vera asked Agnes.

"Not really, but I am glad that I didn't hurt you too much," said Agnes.

"I got another round to go to get you in the face," said Vera as she goes up to Agnes and keeps hitting her with the pool noodle, but Agnes is dunking ever hit she can. BAM! Vera hit Agnes in the face.

"Well Vera one Agnes one I consider it a tie," said Edith as she laughs.

"So, I wonder who is going to win this match," asked Tallulah. Tallulah is just sitting there and loving every moment of it.

"My face is hurting me just watching this, but I am enjoying it so much to stop looking," laughed Mona.

"This is seriously ridiculous to watch her act like an idiot and I am talking about Vera," said Blanche.

"That's not nice to say about Agnes," said Tallulah.

"No, I am talking about Vera," said Blanche.

"I do agree, but Vera doesn't seem to think that, or we would have been done with this by now and Agnes would be with us, and we would be on the next challenge," said Blanche.

"This is a challenge," said Tallulah.

"OK if you say so Tallulah but, it's a punishment because we are only doing this because you and me wouldn't do it and now, I feel bad for Agnes," said Blanche.

"We should just let her go at it so she will feel better, and Agnes will be safe and then we can move on," said Wanda.

"Can all of you shut your mouths? I got this!" said Vera, making another hit at Agnes.

Agnes blocked it. Vera looked surprised that Agnes could block her. Agnes got another good hit in and down went Vera. THUD!

"I don't think this will ever end," said Tallulah.

"What is your problem Tallulah?" asked Mona.

Tallulah just shakes her head and continues to watch Agnes and Vera. Vera stood up with all her energy. She put her hand way back with the pool noodle and made another hit, then another. Vera was getting her hits in on Agnes.

"Come on Agnes, you can do it," said Wanda as she starts cheer for her.

Agnes was getting angry so she would keep hitting Vera wherever she had a place to hit her she was almost like a ninja and kept hitting Vera repeatedly. Vera acted like Agnes was really knocking her out which in a way she was, and Vera went down. Vera stood up again and put both her noodle up and gave one big hit. Agnes tried as hard as she could to cover the hit, but she couldn't do it and went down hard.

"Go Vera! You can do it!" yelled Wanda.

"Why are you cheering Vera on?" asked Tallulah.

"Well, she thinks she can beat Agnes so by cheering for both might get this to end sooner," said Wanda getting into the match.

"Look—Agnes isn't getting up!" yelled Mona.

"Come on Agnes you need to get up don't let Vera win," said Tallulah.

Everyone waited to see if Agnes would get up, but she wasn't. Everyone was in disbelief when they saw what Vera did to Agnes.

"See I told you I could do it," said Vera sarcastically.

"I'm just like John Cena as she parts her arms in the air as much as she can and cheers," said Vera.

"Who is John Cena another resident at Heaven"s Ridge?" asked Tallulah.

"I don't know, but I would like to meet him if he is at Heaven"s Ridge, he sounds cute," said Blanche as she giggles.

"Is he that guy that walks really slow with his walker and his pants always falling off," asked Wanda.

"No that's not the guy's name," said Vera.

"Oh, right that's Oscar," said Edith.

"John Cena is a WWE wrestler you're such a bunch of bozos," said Vera.

"Sorry we didn't know Vera; we don't watch it," said Mona as she sticks out her tongue out at Vera. "I do have one question for you Vera?" asked Mona.

"Yeah, what do you want to know," said Vera.

"What does John Cena have to do with a pool noodle?" said Mona.

"Do you want to hit me with a pool noodle since you have such a smart mouth Mona?" asked Vera as she started walking towards Mona.

"No, I am perfectly fine just eating my words and drinking tea with my words," said Mona with a muffled voice.

"Where did you find the tea?" asked Blanche I could go for tea as she is looking around for tea.

"It's a figure of speech. I don't really have tea," said Mona as she shook her head.

"I knew you wouldn't do it anyways you're a scaredy cat," said Vera as she laughed.

"Anyone else want to go around with me?" asked Vera.

No one answered and just stood there trying to not pay attention to Vera.

Are you all scared?" asked Vera looking at everyone.

Vera could feel that someone was behind her and turned around very slowly.

"Hey Vera takes this," said Agnes as she hits with the pool noodle.

BOOM! "Vera's head hit the floor as Agnes gave her one big hit to the face. "I now can say that it's a successful pool noodle knock out," said Agnes.

"Great job Agnes, I knew you could do it," said Tallulah.

"Yeah, sure you did," said Agnes.

"After what we have witnessed, I'm ready for the next challenge," said Tallulah.

"Time to move on to the next challenge," said Agnes.

"Relax Agnes you just got down hitting a nut job with a pool noodle take it easy for a minute," said Tallulah.

"Should someone check on Vera?" asked Blanche.

"Oh no I already did that," said Miles as he is still a little wary and sore after being in the corner of the ring by Vera.

"You're not a doctor so how did you check her out," asked Wanda.

"Trust me she is running her mouth she is just fine," said Miles.

"I knew all of you were a bunch of fakers and wouldn't do it anyways," said Vera as she gets up and walks away talking to herself.

"See, she is moving and doing OK," said Miles.

"I say we get out of here now," said Beau.

Tallulah shook her head as they started out the door ready for another challenge.

"Are you sure you're OK Agnes?" asked Wanda.

"Yes, that was quite an adrenaline rush for me Wanda," said Agnes.

"Would you do it again?" asked Wanda?

"Well, I wanted to tell you that I enjoyed hitting with the pool noodle even know it was Vera and I am glad that you pushed me to do it," said Agnes.

"You're welcome Agnes" said Wanda as they hug.

"You're all a bunch of phony bolognas," said Vera.

On to the next challenge…

CHAPTER 18

Seniors are MIA

Penny wakes up early like she does every day to go for a jog around the camp. As Penny went back into the cabin, she slowly went past Agnes, Mona, Wanda, and Vera empty beds.

"Where could they all have disappeared too," said Penny as she thought to herself.

"Did I even see them last night Penny kept thinking to herself.

Oh god I can't remember what I did last night.

Penny started to panic a little bit because she didn't know how to deal with the four seniors gone from the cabin. Penny went over to Eloise's bed and woke her up.

"She will know what to do," said Penny to herself. Penny wakes Eloise up.

"What could you possibly want so early in the morning?" asked Eloise.

"Have you seen the seniors last night or this morning?" asked Penny.

"No, I was sleeping now leave me alone so I can go back to sleep," said Eloise as she puts the covers over her head.

"Well, I can't find them anywhere," said Penny as she plays with her ponytail when she gets nervous.

"Where did you exactly look?" asked Eloise as she moved on her back.

"Well to be honest the only one place where they should be right now which is their beds and they're all empty," said Penny as she breathes heavy.

"OK stop breathing like that and calm down everything will be OK," said Eloise as she was about to get her clothes on.

"I'm trying to relax, but it's not easy when I have had panic attacks since," said Penny.

"OK sorry I didn't know," said Eloise. Penny starts getting worried about the seniors. Eloise looks around again to make sure they both didn't miss something.

"Now what are we going to do?" asked Penny.

"Maybe they're in the bathroom or something," said Eloise.

"All at the same time?" asked Penny.

"There is more than one bathroom up there it's not like they're having a foursome," said Eloise before they decided what to do next.

"I don't even want to imagine them doing that," said Penny.

"Let's just go check before we wake up Fay and Tinsley, which we both know isn't pretty when they're both woken up, I don't want them getting upset," said Eloise.

"It's not worth pissing both Tinsley and Fay off," said Penny as she tries to remain calm.

"Let's just go up to the bathhouse and see if they're fooling around up there," said Eloise told Penny.

"Their seniors how can they be fooling around?" asked Penny. They're seniors they can still do things; Eloise tells Penny as she shakes her head.

OHHHH! "I get it now Eloise," said Penny as they go up the hill.

"Wow would have never thought they could still do that at their age," said Eloise.

Penny kept going on about it to Eloise. "Why do you think I mentioned the foursome?" asked Eloise who just shook her head and covered her ears.

"They go up to the bathhouse and check all the stalls.

"Nope this one is empty," said Penny and looks like the bathroom needed to get clean out all over again because it smelled.

YUCK! "This stall is empty too," said Eloise.

"What are we going to do?" asked Penny being serious.

"Wait it sounds like someone is in the last bathroom," said Eloise.

"Do you really think all four of them are using the same bathroom?" asked Penny.

"We already had this conversation especially when one of them is Vera," said Eloise.

"That's true," said Penny. "I don't hear anything now as Eloise knocked on the door to see who was in there.

"I'll be right out," said the voice.

"Why does that voice sound familiar?" asked Eloise.

"I don't know," said Penny as she shrugs her shoulders. They were surprised to see it was Harlow coming out of the bathroom.

"Oh, hi Harlow how are you doing this morning?" asked Penny who was ready to piss her pants.

"Doing OK so far," said Harlow as she is wiping her eyes to wake up and she kept looking behind her.

"What are you girls doing up here so early?" asked Harlow.

"We just went for a jog and then Penny had to use the bathroom," said Eloise as she gives Penny a punch in the arm.

"Ouch," said Penny.

"Oh, I see well, I guess I will see you at breakfast," said Harlow looking at them suspicious.

"Are you OK Harlow you look a little pale?" asked Eloise.

"Yes, I am I just didn't sleep to well, but I will see everyone at breakfast," said Harlow as she went back towards the dining hall.

"Yes, we will be there it's the most important meal of the day," yells Penny.

"That certainly didn't look like a wipe your eyes from sleeping kind of look," said Eloise.

"Then what kind of look was she giving us?" asked Penny.

"It was the just had sex all night kind of look," said Eloise.

"Let's go back to the cabin and see if they're back," said Penny.

"Now you must hold on because I really must go to the bathroom now," said Eloise, but before she went in Art came out of the bathroom where Harlow just did. Penny just stood there with her mouth wide open.

"Hi Art," said Eloise.

"Oh, hi Eloise how are you doing this fine morning?" asked Art.

"I'm fine and dandy here this morning," said Eloise.

"How are you doing Penny?" asked Art. "I'm good also Art thanks for asking," said Penny.

"Hurry up I need to go also," said Eloise still talking to Art.

"Well, I better get ready for breakfast, and I will see you later," said Art.

"Do you think they're dating?" asked Penny.

"Those two I don't know maybe, but it's not my business so I don't care," said Eloise.

"Well, I was just asking since they both came out of the girl's side of the bathrooms," said Penny.

"Good for them. I still don't care," said Eloise.

"Hey Penny," yelled Serena from her cabin. Penny heard her name called, stopped, and looked behind her.

"Why are we stopping?" asked Eloise.

"Serena is calling my name—that's why," said Penny.

"Oh well sorry I didn't hear her I was too busy minding my own business," said Eloise sarcastically.

"Good morning, Serena," said Eloise.

"Yeah, hi Eloise," said Serena.

Eloise wanted to pop her one because of the salty attitude she was giving her.

"Penny I was wondering if you saw Tallulah, Edith, and Blanche around her somewhere?" asked Serena.

Penny and Eloise looked at each other wondering if they should tell Serena that Agnes, Mona, Wanda, and Vera are missing also.

"No, we haven't, but four of our seniors are missing too," said Penny.

"Oh, really?" asked Serena as she looked surprised.

"Where do you think they are?" asked Serena getting concerned.

"That's what we are trying to figure out," said Eloise.

"What do you mean that you're trying to figure it out?" asked Serena.

"We are missing Agnes, Mona, Wanda, and Vera are missing also," said Eloise.

"We looked at the bathrooms, but we ran into Harlow and Art as we were checking and they weren't in there," said Penny.

"Did you let Harlow know what was going on?" asked Serena.

"No, we didn't," said Eloise.

"So, what do we do now?" asked Penny.

"We were just about to wake up Fay, Tinsley, and Tory to tell them what is going on," said Penny.

"I better wake up Hazel, Iggy, Eden, and Siena," said Serena.

"Let's wake them up and meet back here so we can figure out what to do," said Penny.

"Let's meet at one of the cabins so that no one else will get suspicious," said Eloise.

"Sounds like a plan," said Serena. We will meet you at your cabin," said Penny.

"Sounds good," said Serena.

They all went back to their cabins and woke up all the other counselors to let them know what was going on.

Penny and Eloise got back to the cabin and woke up Fay, Tinsley, and Tory.

"What is wrong that you had to wake me up so early?" asked Fay.

"Get up we need to talk to you about something," said Penny.

"OK, no problem it sounds serious," said Fay with her heart beating out her chest because she knew what it was about.

"Hey Tinsley wake up," said Penny as she shook Tinsley.

"OK I'm wake now stop shaking me," said Tinsley.

"Meet us outside we need to talk to you and everyone else about something," said Penny as she goes out the door.

Fay got up and dressed slowly and waited for Eloise, Penny, and Tinsley at the picnic table.

"Didn't mean to wake you up Tinsley," said Eloise.

"What's wrong?" asked Tinsley barely awake.

"This better be important if you got me up this early," said Tory as she was going out the door.

"OK I'm here what is going on that you had to wake us up?" asked Tinsley. "What are you doing here Serena?" asked Tinsley.

Then Tinsley saw that Serena, Eloise, Fay, Penny, Tory Hazel, Iggy, Siena, Betsey, and Eden were all there also. Tinsley started to panic because she thought that someone passed away. Fay and Hazel stayed together so they could figure out how to deal with everything going on.

"I told Chip we needed to tell them what was going on and he didn't listen to me," said Hazel to Fay.

"We need to just not panic, and things will be fine," said Fay reassured Hazel.

"We need to come clean Fay," said Hazel.

"We will Hazel just relax we just need to find the right time to do it, so they won't be upset with us," said Fay.

"Yeah, I would relax if we thought this through enough," said Hazel.

"Hazel just stays quiet," said Fay.

"We have a situation here that we need all your help," said Penny.

"What's going on?" asked Eden.

Penny woke up this morning and she realized that Agnes, Mona, Wanda, and Vera are all missing," said Eloise.

"Tallulah, Edith, and Blanche are also missing," said Serena.

Fay and Hazel just looked at each other and wonder how they're going to manage them knowing why the seniors are missing. Stay calm," said Hazel.

"*I'm* the calm one," said Fay shaking her head at Hazel.

Ace yelled across from his cabin. "Hey, has anyone seen Beau or Miles?"

Everyone looked at Ace as he came over to the picnic table to join the rest of them.

"What's up Ace?" asked Penny.

"I got up early to join Penny for a run, but you were already gone," said Ace.

"Oh, sorry I left early," said Penny.

"As I went by Miles and Beau's beds hadn't been slept in all night," said Ace.

"Has anyone seen them at all since last night?" asked Ace.

"Oh boy," said Hazel to herself as her stomach started to hurt and she felt nauseous.

"You're not the only cabin missing someone seniors," said Eden not looking amused.

"What do you mean?" asked Ace.

"Well, in our cabin we are missing every one of them," said Penny.

"We have three missing in ours," said Serena.

"How is that even possible?" asked Ace?

"Yeah, how is that possible if we were only setting up four seniors?" asked Hazel.

Fay just shrugged her shoulders.

"We have no idea what is going on, but we need to find them and quick," said Penny.

Hazel kept grabbing on to her stomach ready to puke.

"Are you OK, Hazel?" asked Tory

"Yes, I am fine I'm just worried about the missing seniors," said Hazel.

"I'm sure they're OK," said Tory.

"I hope so," said Hazel.

"Do you want me to give you a hug?" asked Tory.

"Nah that's OK I'm not really a hugger," said Hazel.

"Oh, come on a good hug will make you feel better," said Tory as she gives Hazel a hug.

Hazel could smell something familiar on Tory as she was hugging her.

"Do you feel better now Hazel?" asked Tory.

"Sure do," said Hazel. Hazel knew that smell and knew who it belonged too which was Chip. Hazel just sat on the picnic table not letting it bother her that Tory smelled like Chip.

"Should we go to Belle and tell her what is going on?" asked Eloise.

"NO!" shouted Hazel.

"Hazel it will be OK we won't have to worry," said Fay grabs a hold of her and makes her sit down.

"We must do something Fay," thought Hazel.

"What's wrong with you Hazel?" asked Penny.

"Belle has so much going on with taking care of the camp I don't think we should bother her about nine missing seniors," said Hazel.

"Nine seniors are missing, and you don't think that Belle needs to know?" asked Eden.

"If we don't tell her she is going to notice at breakfast time when only four seniors show up," said Serena.

"I think your right Serena we need to let her know," said Iggy.

"We could talk to the four seniors that are here and see if they know something before, we tell Belle," said Iggy.

"Let's go tell her before it gets too late," said Penny.

"We need to look around more and see if we spot them," said Hazel.

"Let's talk to the four seniors first then go look for them," said Serena.

"That sounds like a good idea," said Hazel so they had enough time to talk to Chip about the seniors and not Tory.

So, we can figure how to tell Belle and everyone else what they did.

"I'm not sure Hazel because we have looked in a couple of places and still no sign of them," said Eloise.

Hazel tapped Fay on the shoulder, and they went to talk in one of the cabins where there is privacy.

"We never thought about what would happen after they were gone," said Hazel.

"We need to talk to Chip so that we can figure out how we are going to deal with all the shit that's going on before it hits the fan once Belle knows the seniors are missing," said Fay.

"We'll be right back we are going to check one place," said Hazel.

"Can I go with you?" asked Penny.

"I think you should wait here just in case they come back," suggested Fay.

"We will be right back and hopefully they will be back," said Hazel as they rush down the path.

They go along the back where they know Chip's bed is and try to get his attention.

"Hey Chip, Hey Chip," said Fay.

"Swear he is deaf sometimes," said Hazel as she shakes her head.

He turned his head and saw Fay. He motioned them to meet him in the back of the cabin.

"We have a huge problem that we never thought about when we planned all of this," said Fay as she starts to get frazzled.

"No, we thought about it because I mentioned it, but Chip thought it be no big deal," said Hazel who just stood there with her arms crossed.

"Wow you said all of that in one breath I am impressed," said Chip.

"What did we possible forget?" asked Chip scratching his head

"What we were going to do and, say after the counselors realized that the seniors are missing the next day," said Hazel who was ready to cry and choke Chip at the same time.

"Why do we really have to say anything about it?" asked Chip.

"Seriously Chip that's your answer let everyone go crazy and let them be missing?" asked Hazel.

"No, but if we go along with them then they will never know we had something to do with it," said Chip.

"I kind of like the way you think Chip," said Fay.

"If we confess to what we did we will get in major trouble," said Chip.

"Like I said we never thought about it we just made this plan and let them go off to the haunted house, funhouse sort of thing," said Hazel.

"Don't forget that we can still watch them every step of the way," said Chip.

"Have you been watching them," asked Hazel.

"Yes, I have been, and they're enjoying what the challenges have been so far and a punishment," said Chip.

"Relax Hazel everything will be fine," said Fay.

"That's what I am truly hoping," said Hazel. Hazel still had to panic because of how things had changed in their plan.

"How can we relax when we thought there was only four seniors going and now it's up to nine," cried Hazel.

"How did four go up to nine?" asked Chip.

"We have no clue," said Fay.

"OK now I understand why you're both freaking out," said Chip.

"Didn't you notice when you were watching it that there were a few more familiar faces," said Hazel.

"No, I guess I was just concentrating on everything else going on," said Chip.

"Everything will be OK we can still see them on the video," said Fay as she gave Hazel a hug.

"We better tell the others and then go to Belle just so they know what we did and hopefully not get fired," said Chip.

"That is the smartest thing you have said today, Chip," said Hazel.

"I know you won't let it go until we do the right thing," said Chip.

"Oh, by the way why didn't you just tell me that you and Tory are a thing?" asked Hazel snotty.

"What the hell are you talking about Hazel?" asked Chip.

"You and Tory are dating," said Hazel.

"Oh, really you're Chip?" asked Fay.

"No, I am not dating anyone especially Tory," said Chip.

"Where would you get a dumb idea like that?" asked Chip.

Hazel crossed her arms and looked down at the ground.

"Tory gave me a hug because I was upset about the seniors being missing and she smelled like your cologne," said Hazel.

"Well, I'm not for the last time dating Tory," said Chip ready to lose his cool.

"Whatever Chip let's just go and tell everyone and get this over with," said Hazel as she walks away.

"I guess the seniors were wrong that he liked me," thought Hazel.

"Runaway like you always do when things get tough," said Chip.

"I should go after her," said Fay.

"Yeah, you better," said Chip as he just stands there watching them both walk away.

"She is so fucking stubborn sometimes," said Chip to himself.

"Hazel, can you slow down so I can catch up to you I have short legs remember?" asked Fay.

"What Fay I am OK," said Hazel.

"Oh yeah sure you're I can see that," said Fay.

"I don't get why he can't just be honest," said Hazel.

"Did you ever think that maybe he was honest with you, and you don't want him to be right?" asked Fay.

"How can you say that he is being honest?" asked Hazel.

"Something just tells me that he is," said Fay.

"What if what the seniors said isn't true and he does love Tory?" asked Hazel. "I still think he is being honest," said Fay.

"I don't know, Fay," said Hazel.

"You just don't want to get hurt again, but you feel the same as him so just let it happen and trust him," said Fay.

Maybe your right about the getting hurt thing, but the rest of it I'm not sure of," said Hazel.

"Maybe she just gave him a hug like she did for you," said Fay.

"I'll figure it out later right now we must talk to everyone and let them know what we did and take our punishment," said Hazel.

Chip went right pass Hazel and right to the other cabin where everyone else was.

"Oh no what is he doing?" asked Hazel as they both watched him.

"We got to go Hazel," said Fay.

Hazel took a deep breathe before telling everyone about the plan and she felt even worse than she did before. Chip, Fay, and Hazel met back with all the other counselors waiting to hear what they had to say.

"We have something we need to tell you all," said Hazel who could barely stand up.

Chip, Fay, and I wanted to play a prank on the seniors because of all the trouble they caused so we made them think there was a funhouse they needed to go check it out," said Hazel.

"We honestly didn't think they would take the bait and they did, but at that time there was only Agnes, Tallulah, Mona, and Wanda, the other five weren't apart of it," said Fay.

Chip told them about why they did it in the first place and how he set everything up so they can have fun with the challenges, and they can see everything going on. Fay talked about their whole plan piece by piece.

"I think it was horrible for what you three did and you should be punished for what you did," said Penny.

Eden, Iggy, Serena, Ace, and Art had wished that they could have joined in with the planning and the fun.

"You still can join in," said Chip.

"Chip seriously maybe we should get them," said Hazel looking like she is ready to vomit.

"What would we tell them?" asked Chip.

"Let's try sorry we did this to you please come back to camp with us," said Hazel.

"Will you stop I swear you two are a married couple?" asked Fay.

"They are all fine I have been checking up on them," said Chip shaking his head.

"We need to get them," said Hazel trying to relax but feels like everyone is looking at her.

"And again, say what to them exactly Hazel?" asked Chip.

"Sorry we hazed you, but you need to come back with us now?" said Fay. "I thought you felt the same as me Fay?" asked Hazel.

"Hazel, I did until I looked at Chip's cam, on his phone just a little while ago and they're having fun," said Fay.

"They honestly look like they're enjoying themselves minus crazy Vera is there," said Chip.

"Look Hazel they're all having fun, and they haven't killed each other yet and all nine seniors accounted for, so no one is missing," said Fay.

"Look everyone I'm sorry we didn't tell you or include you we just wanted them to stop listening to everything we were saying and causing havoc here at camp," said Chip.

Everyone went over to Chip's phone and watched what they were doing and were happy to see them having an enjoyable time.

"They do look like they're having an enjoyable time," said Serena as she whacks Chip in the arm.

OUCH! "What the hell was that for?" asked Chip.

"For not including me," said Serena and don't cry over a whack it was a love punch by me.

"Aww look Beau and Mona are holding hands what a sweet couple it makes my heart sing to see them together," said Eden.

"I thought we would have a camp romance and I'm glad it's them," said Iggy.

"How romantic is that?" asked Eden.

"You are just being a bunch of girls," said Ace.

"Yes, and the problem is what exactly Ace?" asked Penny as she gets closer to Ace.

"Nothing, but you don't hear us guys saying any of those things," said Ace.

"Oh, there are guys out there that has a sensitive side," said Serena.

"Exactly because we are guys," said Ace.

"We can dress you like a girl so you can join us," said Penny we all know you giggle Ace.

"I don't giggle," said Ace as he starts to laugh and snort.

"And you know nothing about romance," said Serena laughing.

"All you do is just scratch yourselves whenever possible or on a daily basis," said Fay.

HA! "We can do more than that," said Chip as he puts his two cents in.

Penny puts up her hand in Chip's mouth to shut him up.

"We don't need to know the details," said Penny as she walks away.

"You honestly think that's all we have to think about Penny?" asked Chip.

"Sorry to break your heart, but it's not always about sex," said Art as he shakes his head.

"Could have fooled us," said Eloise after she saw him come out the same side Harlow did.

"Do girls always have their minds in the sexual gutter?" asked Chip as he smirks at all of them.

"No that's mostly a man thing so end of story," said Hazel shaking her head.

"You don't fantasize about anyone Hazel?" asked Chip as he goes eye to eye with her.

She wasn't sure what to say to Chip after that and stays silent for a minute.

"No, I don't Chip," said Hazel trying not to keep the eye contact.

"What kind of things are you thinking about Penny?" asked Ace, as he laughed.

"Noting that you need to know about Ace," said Penny.

"The only thing that was on Penny's mind was Harlow and Art coming out of the bathroom together for a reason it was bothering her, so she just tries to put it out of her mind right now.

"We are getting off the subject here people and my virgin ears don't need to hear this stuff," said Iggy.

"Really you're a virgin still?" asked Ace as he looks at Iggy and how beautiful she is.

"Yes, I am so it doesn't change me and I'm waiting for the right person," said Iggy moving away from Ace.

"Good for you Iggy it's something to be proud of," said Tinsley.

"OK let's get back to the seniors," said Eloise.

"We must tell Belle there is no way to get out of that," said Fay.

"Belle is going to notice most the seniors are not here because it's breakfast time," said Hazel.

"We can't cover for them all it's just not possible," said Hazel as she spoke up so everyone can hear her.

"Your right Hazel I just don't want to see how mad she is going to be when that happens," said Fay.

"I know, but unfortunately, we need to let her know unless someone produces another plan or nine seniors," said Serena.

"I think because it was our plan the three of us should do it because no one had a hand in it happening," said Hazel.

"All of us would like to help and show our support," said Serena.

"Not me, it was their fault this happened in the first time I'm not going to take part in any of it."

"Your right Eloise none of you were a part of it, so that's why we need to take the responsibility and tell Belle ourselves," said Fay.

Hazel and Chip also agree with Fay.

"Then I'm out of here and let me know when they return unharmed or if you're going to have to leave," said Eloise.

"What is wrong with you Eloise?" asked Serena. Serena ran after Eloise to find out what is going on with her.

"Hey Eloise, what's going on you were rough to Chip, Fay, and Hazel?" asked Serena.

"I just don't want to get blame for all this happening, why is that such a problem?" asked Eloise asked she goes up the hill with Serena.

"I know you don't want to get blamed and either do I, but we must be there for the seniors that are still here and the ones who aren't," said Serena.

"I just don't want to be a part of their scheme," said Eloise as she walks away from Serena.

Serena watches Eloise going up the hill and can't believe she is acting like this.

"Don't worry Serena," said Hazel as she puts her arm around Serena.

"Eloise was so happy to be here and now a couple of days later it's like she flipped the switch and doesn't care," said Serena.

"We just need to let her be and she will be fine," said Hazel.

"I guess I just don't want to bail on a friend who might need me," said Serena.

"I know, but when she is ready, she will let you know," said Hazel.

Chip, Hazel, and Fay went to go to see Belle to let her know what they did to the seniors. And hope she doesn't get to mad and fire them.

"Nice knowing you both if she kills us," said Chip.

"Belle is a sweetheart she would never hurt a fly," said Hazel as she opens the door to the office and hears Belle screaming.

"If you can't make it to fix the stove then don't bother coming, I'll find another company willing to fix it," yelled Belle.

"What did you say about Belle being a sweetheart?" asked Chip.

"Well, she can be once in a while," said Fay.

"Then why is Belle yelling as we speak?" asked Chip?

"I'm sure, everything will be fine maybe she is just having a difficult morning," said Hazel.

"I really hope you right about that Hazel," said Chip to her as they're going in the door.

"Hey guys how are you doing this morning?" asked Harlow as they came in the office.

"We are doing OK," said Hazel still wanting to vomit.

"Oh, good so what can I help you with?" asked Harlow.

"We were wondering if Belle was busy?" asked Chip.

"Let me see Belle was on the phone with the stove company and then she stormed off out the door," said Harlow.

"We didn't see her go out this door," said Fay as she takes candy out of the candy dish.

"We are about to tell Belle everything and you're eating candy," said Hazel.

"Well, sorry I'm nervous, and this is what I do and I'm hungry," said Fay.

"Well, as you can see there is more than one door to get in and out of," said Harlow.

"Sorry Harlow we won't disturb you," said Hazel.

"It's OK it has been a long morning for all of us," said Harlow.

"Sorry you have had a shitty morning," said Hazel.

"Let me just call the kitchen and see if she may be there," said Harlow.

"Hey Frankie, is Belle in the kitchen by chance?" Harlow shook her head yes so; they knew she was in the kitchen.

"Oh, she is good can you let Belle know that Chip, Hazel, and Fay are coming to speak to her in a minute?" asked Harlow

I hope she is ready for this," said Chip.

"Thank you, Frankie, I appreciate it," said Harlow as she hangs up the phone. Harlow hung up the phone and turned towards the three of them and let them know that Belle had to go to the kitchen to deal with the stove problem so if you want to go over there that they could go over.

"Oh, by the way what is wrong with the stove?" asked Hazel.

"Frankie almost burned the kitchen down this morning getting breakfast ready and now the stove doesn't work," said Harlow as she was picking things up off the desk.

"Oh, OK no problem we can just wait," said Hazel.

"Are you doing OK Harlow you seem very distracted today?" asked Hazel.

"Yes, I'm good I'm just trying to get things nice and neat here," said Harlow as she keeps cleaning the desk.

"Well, you're doing an excellent job," said Chip.

"Is there anything I can help you with?" asked Harlow still looking distracted.

"No, Harlow we just really need to talk to Belle nothing against you so please don't take that wrong," said Fay who was starting to have a hot flash and ramble on.

"It's OK I totally get it Belle is the camp director and I'm just the camp administrator," said Harlow kind of sad.

"Harlow you're doing an important job making sure everything is running good here, keep up the excellent work that you're doing," said Hazel.

"Thanks Hazel that means a lot coming from you.

"You're welcome anytime Harlow," said Hazel. "No one could ever take your place because you're so intelligent and just like Belle you get the job done," said Fay.

Fay just keeps on sweating as Hazel looks at Fay with a strange look.

"Seriously now you pick this time to sweat like a pig?" asked Hazel shaking her head.

"It's not like I can control when I have them, so it's not my fault, I can't help that I'm having one now it comes anytime," said Fay.

"So glad men can't go through menopause," said Chip sarcastically.

"I'm not even old enough to go through menopause and I think it's time that men to go through it or something to understand what we go through," said Fay.

Ouch! "That was harsh, but also true fact men just don't understand what us women go through on a daily basis," said Harlow.

"Sorry about that Harlow didn't mean for it to come out that way, but I'm just stating something that's true," said Fay as she starts laughing about what she said.

"I think we will go to the kitchen so we can talk to Belle now," said Hazel.

"OK if, you're sure?" asked Harlow.

"Oh, by the way you look like happy today, Harlow," said Fay with a smile.

Oh, thanks," said Harlow with a strange look on her face because before they all thought something was wrong with her.

"You're welcome and have a wonderful day," said Fay.

"I always thought I looked happy Harlow thinks to herself then she remembers what her and Art did in the bathroom this morning and starts giggling to herself.

"We will see you at breakfast in a few minutes," said Harlow.

"Oh yeah, we should be there with are appetites," said Chip.

"Have a good day," said Hazel.

"You too Hazel," said Harlow.

"Are you serious Hazel?" asked Fay jokingly.

"All I said was have a good day," said Hazel, it was the only thing I could think of to say to Harlow," said Hazel.

"Sorry I freaked out a little I thought she was going to catch onto us about what is going on," said Fay.

"Also trying to cover our butts that we saw Casper and Juniper together the other night," said Hazel.

"I told you that I refuse to be the one who breaks her heart," said Fay.

"OK I kind of get why you did it," said Chip.

"Wow you understand me that's the first Chip," giggled Hazel.

"I'm just trying to be a nice guy for once to you," said Chip as he started to get annoyed at Hazel.

"OK you two honestly you should just get a room and do the hokey pokey," laughed Fay.

"No way Jose," said Hazel. Chip shook his head and slammed the door shut.

"What do you have against Chip?" asked Fay.

"Nothing and you and I had this conversation already today and yesterday when I thought he was dating Tory," shouts Hazel.

"Yes, I know, but he has been nothing, but sweet to you and you treat him like he is a bad guy when you know damn well you love him just like he does for you," said Fay as they walk outside.

"Yes, I get it and I know Chip is not a bad guy and there is a chance for us to be together if those rumors are actually true, but I'm just not on the same page as him and I can't guarantee I will be anytime soon," said Hazel.

"Well, you have been on that same page for a while now and both of you have known each other for a long time before this camp at least you could apologize to Chip because you were a little cruel," said Fay.

"He just wants to get to know you on a romantic level and not marry you at least not yet," laughed Fay.

"Why me?" asked Hazel as she was trying not to lose her cool, but gets what Fay is saying.

"He is acting like a child I didn't say anything wrong that I haven't said to him before," said Hazel.

"OK, but he seemed pretty hurt by what you said this time, that's all I'm saying, and men can act like children sometimes and be the sensitive type," said Fay.

"We need to talk to Belle first then I will sit him down and tell him everything," said Hazel.

"I just don't want you to lose Chip as a friend before you get to the next level and because he has been there for you," said Fay.

Please stop being right," said Hazel

Fay just laughed at her.

"Right now, is just not the right time because we must tell Belle about the seniors and the plan, and I'm worried it will go terribly wrong so not I am stressed out," said Hazel.

"Things will be OK, and nothing is going to go wrong, let's find Chip and get this conversation with Belle over with so we can have breakfast hopefully," said Fay.

Fay and Hazel found Chip on the hammock and went over to join him.

"Are we ready to do this?" asked Hazel.

"I guess so," said Chip as he gets off the hammock and gets on his feet.

Chip, Fay, and Hazel found Belle and Frankie making out in the kitchen.

"Oh, shit Belle we are so sorry we didn't mean to intrude," said Hazel embarrassed as she closed her eyes to what she saw.

"We will come back another time," said Fay as her and Chip run into each other trying to get out the door fast.

"No, no, no don't go Frankie was just seeing if I had something in my eye," said Belle nervously.

"Is something wrong you all look worried or something?" asked Belle.

"We were at the time until now I guess you can say that we changed our minds," said Hazel as she is still in disbelief what she just witnessed and uncovered her eyes.

"Well, I guess we will step out for a minute so you can finish whatever it's that you say you're doing," said Fay.

"Honestly, you can stay," said Frankie, as he goes out the door.

Belle finished putting herself back to together.

"OK, now you can tell me why you're worried?" asked Belle looking at the three of them.

"You might want to sit down for this," said Fay.

"Preferably not on the counter where we just saw you," said Chip.

"Oh my God Chip shut up," yelled Hazel who was starting to get embarrassed.

As all four of them sit and explain the whole thing from the beginning of the plan until now, why they made this plan and especially why they did it. To their surprise Belle didn't act to mad about it which surprise them all.

"You're not mad Belle?" asked Chip shocked.

There was one thing that she was mad at and that she wished that she had been a part of the plan just liked the others.

"Well, to me it wasn't the right thing to do because they're our responsibility, but I get why you did it and maybe could of went another unique way with everything," said Belle.

"You did say Chip they're safe, and no one is injured?" asked Belle. "No not unless Vera tries and kills each of them which I don't think is her style," said Chip.

"How did you go from four seniors to nine seniors?" asked Belle.

"Yeah, we don't have an answer for you," said Fay

"We planned on only those four, so we aren't sure what happened there to get five more, said Hazel trying not to panic.

"We didn't think to put a camera on the bus which we probably should of then we would know how they all got on the bus," said Hazel.

"I know how they got on the bus and drove off with it," said Belle.

They all just looked Belle.

"Oh, I know how they got the key to the bus," said Belle.

"How did they do it?" asked Chip.

"Tallulah was in the office asking for Juniper because supposedly she fell off the hammock and wanted Juniper to check her out," said Belle.

"Oh, I see," said Hazel.

"So, by the time I came back from finding Juniper she was impatient and wanted to leave quickly and I let her go," said Belle.

"That sounds like Tallulah," said Hazel.

"I went over to the bus key rack and noticed that lucky number seven had been missing, and I'm guessing that she has taken the key and the bus are both gone, I checked on that this morning," said Belle.

"So, you knew something was already up before we came here?" asked Hazel.

"I thought someone stole it and that it wasn't one of the seniors, but now all I hope is the bus just comes back in one piece or I will take it out of your pay checks," said Belle.

Yes, we completely understand they all said at the same time.

"Wow they didn't waste any time getting to the funhouse," said Chip.

"So, do you have cameras all around the house Chip?" asked Belle.

"Yes, I do and if you want to check it out here you go," said Chip as he handed Belle his phone so she could see for herself.

"Looks like they're all OK," said Belle.

"Yes, they're and hopefully will be back by diner time if they do all the challenges quickly," said Chip.

"I do have one question for you," said Belle.

"Yes, please ask anything," said Hazel.

"How can I be a part of this with you?" asked Belle.

"What exactly do you mean?" asked Hazel. I love pranking people or at least watching them get pranked," said Belle.

"Can I set up the cameras on your computer in the office then you can watch the whole time," asked Chip.

"Then we all can check in on them as much as we want to and keep a good eye on them," said Hazel.

"Yes, you do have my permission to do that and everything you worked on was a great idea," said Belle with a huge smirk on her face.

Wait until you see the finale," said Chip. Why what do you have planned?" asked Belle. When they get closer to the end then I will let you in on it," said Chip.

"Your right Hazel, they do need to be taught a simple lesson about listening to other people's conversations and all the other craziness they have done," said Belle.

"Yes, that's so true," said Fay.

"Are you OK Belle?" asked Hazel as she can tell something is going on with her.

"Yes, I'm fine thanks for asking Hazel," said Belle, I'm just hungry and need something to eat so I am glad that breakfast is coming soon.

"I know I'm sure starving," said Chip as they all look at him.

"How is Frankie cooking of the stove isn't working?" asked Hazel.

"I'm hoping he doesn't burn up a skillet," said Belle.

"I'm sure it will taste great," said Chip.

"Well, I need to go," said Belle, as she breathed in again and walked out of the kitchen.

"I hope you feel better Belle," said Fay.

"Thank everyone and Chip don't forget to install the camera on the computer," said Belle.

"I won't Belle, I'll do it after breakfast if that's OK with you?" asked Chip with a smile.

"That's fine whatever is easy for you," said Belle.

It was time for breakfast and Ethel was very confused with where the other seniors were, but she knows and doesn't want anyone to know.

"I think we will put you here with these handsome men as she pulls out a chair for her.

"That's fine if they don't mind me sitting here with them," said Ethel.

"Let me introduce them to you there is Hank, Jasper, and this cutie fella is Felix," said Serena.

"Oh, don't make me blush sweetheart," said Felix as he gives Serena hug.

"Hey Felix let's not get too fresh there keep your hands above the waist," laughed Serena.

"Hi everyone, how are you doing today?" asked Ethel to get a conversation going.

"Why are you sitting at the same table as us Ethel?" asked Jasper rudely.

"Don't mind Jasper he doesn't like it if someone new comes along in his territory," said Felix.

"You all know me from Heaven's Ridge, but I guess people can forget about knowing me sometimes it's not hard to do," said Ethel.

"Jasper can also be a shy guy and keeps to himself a lot, but if his routine messed up, he gets flustered," said Hank as he tells Ethel so she could relax.

"OK thanks for the tip," said Ethel.

"Your fine sweetheart we all need a beautiful woman at our table occasionally," said Hank as he gives her a wink.

"Are you blind?" asked Ethel.

"No sweetheart I'm only speaking the truth," said Hank.

"Sorry I didn't mean to be rude no one has ever said that to me before," said Ethel.

"By the way I'm Hank and I think I have seen you around Heaven's Ridge before and I am damn proud to now know you," said Hank.

"Why is she still here?" asked Jasper.

"You can leave if it's really bothering you Jasper," said Hank trying not to make Ethel uncomfortable.

"I can go I don't want to be in anyone's way," said Ethel as she puts her head down. "Sorry, that was mean of me to say that to you," apologized Jasper I hope you will please stay and join us.

"I just don't want to be in anyone's way, but it's also a free world too so I can sit where I want too," said Ethel.

"Don't leave on my account, I'm OK with you sitting with us Ethel and don't give me it's a free world crap I don't buy it," said Jasper mumbling to himself.

"I would very much like to get to know you Ethel," said Hank.

"I would really like that," said Ethel finishing her breakfast.

"Does anyone know where the rest of the seniors are today?" asked Felix as he was wiping his mouth with his napkin.

"No, I have no clue all I know is when I woke up, I was the only senior in the cabin," said Ethel even know she did overhear them about their plan, but not going to share that with anyone.

"Maybe they went on a field trip and forgot to tell us I mean that has happened to us before," said Jasper as Ethel tries not to choke on her pancakes.

"Oh, Ethel my dear are you OK?" asked Hank as he comes over to check on her.

"I'm good Hank thank you so much for caring my pancake went down the wrong pipe," said Ethel as she looked at Hank's eyes and they were a blue.

"Aww why wouldn't I sweetheart?" asked Hank.

"You are an angel that spreads her wings beautifully," said Jasper.

"Wow really an angel that's the sweetest thing that anyone has ever said to me," said Ethel starting to blush and could feel her face get red.

Well, I'm glad you liked that," said Jasper.

"Which was a new thing for her because no man had made her feel like that before and she was also hoping that no one could notice. Hank moved over next to her at the table and Ethel's heart was beating fast.

"Ethel I was wondering if you would like to accompany me to music therapy this morning?" asked Hank as he grabbed Ethel's hand.

"I was planning to go there also, so yes; I will go with you Hank," said Ethel with excitement.

"Let's go my dear," said Hank as he took her arm in his and walked away together.

Hazel watched Chip through the doorway of him setting up everything for Belle, she knew that she had to talk to him before things between them got worse than they already were and Hazel new this was the time to do it. Hazel opened the door and Chip didn't even turn around to see who it was.

"Hi Chip, how are you doing so far today?" asked Hazel.

"Doing OK considering I thought we were all going to get the shaft for what we did to the seniors," said Chip still working on the computer.

"I wasn't too worried," said Hazel.

I find that hard to believe," said Chip.

"I know I freaked out when we started this whole idea, but once we started to tell Belle I figured nothing would happen to us that's why I was OK," said Hazel.

"Belle is cool to go along with it," said Chip. "Please you were shitting bricks and that's why you were acting like you were when we told the rest of the group," said Chip. Chip had a weird look on his face when Hazel got closer to him.

"Is there a reason you're trying to get close to me?" asked Chip with a serious look.

"No, I just wanted to see how things were going with the setup," said Hazel thinking this isn't going right.

"They are going well I'm almost done," said Chip.

"Do you want help setting things up?" asked Hazel with a squeaky voice.

"No that's OK I can manage it I mean it's easy to install and like I said I am almost done," said Chip as he turned away from Hazel.

"OK no problem I'll just see how the rest of the seniors are doing," said Hazel as she put her head down and sighed as she goes out the door.

"Chip just shook his head as he watched her go out the door. ERRRR! Hazel drives me crazy sometimes as Chip mumbles to himself.

Belle comes in and hears Chip say something.

"Everything going OK Chip?" asked Belle.

"Everything is good Belle I installed everything so you will see what's going on in each room and you also have sound so you will be able to hear them, but they can't hear you until they go to one room, we have it so they will be answering trivia questions, "said Chip.

"You are very handy man Chip," said Belle as she sat down to look what Chip has done.

"Oh, there they all are, and they look like they're having fun," said Belle as she got all excited about what she is seeing on the screen.

"Yeah, it does," said Chip as he starts cleaning everything up.

"Wow Chip you did an excellent job," said Belle as she keeps watching.

"Thanks Belle that was genuinely nice of you to say," said Chip watching the screen with her.

"So, what was your plan for them next?" asked Belle curious.

"Each room has a different challenge for them to do and complete and if one of them chooses to not do a certain challenge we made a punishment challenge for them in a whole different room," said Chip.

"Wow you really put thought into this," said Belle.

"I went and check out the house and measure it was going to be safe for them and I had a neighbor who had all this equipment, so nothing came out of my pocket," said Chip.

"Well, that was a great idea," said Belle.

"Fay, Hazel, and I made them up and made sure that each challenge was going to be easy for them to finish.

"I agree safety is a good thing," said Belle. We wanted to do something right," said Chip.

"Do we know who used to own the house?" asked Belle.

"No that's something we didn't check on because it has been abandon so long," said Chip.

"I'm getting a feeling someone there knows the house," said Belle.

"Seriously you think that one of the seniors knows the house, Belle?" asked Chip.

"I think by the end of it we will know who it belongs too," said Belle.

Chip sat there puzzled at what Belle had said and was wondering which one of the nine used to live there.

"The only thing I can see that would get in their way of having an enjoyable time is knowing Vera is there with them," said Belle acting just a little worried.

"All I know is we were only targeting Agnes, Mona, Wanda, and Tallulah the other seniors were not involved in the plan whatsoever," said Chip.

"Pillows?" asked Belle confused.

"We figured it be nice to have an old fashion pillow fight," said Chip.

"Sounds like a fun idea," said Belle watching everyone.

"You are incredibly talented Chip you should go to college and see what more you can learn," suggested Belle.

"I thought about it, but something always ended up getting in the way," said Chip just staring at the screen.

"Maybe there is something I can do to help you achieve your goal," said Belle.

" No, I couldn't ask you to do that Belle you have already done so much," said Chip.

"I know, but you have so much potential so just think about it Chip?" asked Belle.

"Yes, Belle I will think about it," said Chip. That's better than nothing," said Belle.

"I have to get going for the next activity and open the pool, but if you need anything just let me know Belle," said Chip.

"Everything looks fine here I'm just going to watch them have their pillow fight for a little while before the next chaotic thing happens," said Belle.

"Well, maybe you will be lucky, and nothing to exciting will happen," said Chip.

"I rather watch the excitement on here then whatever excitement Frankie will have in the kitchen," said Belle

"Yeah, that's true, so I will see you later Belle," said Chip as he breathes knowing things were all good with Belle.

"Have a good day Chip," said Belle.

CHAPTER 19

Pillow Talk Road

"OK, so who is ready for the next challenge?" asked Edith.

No one answered Edith.

"Wow what a tough crowd," said Edith.

"Maybe you just need to take a nap or something," said Tallulah laughing as she said it.

"Who are you talking to Tallulah?" asked Mona looking confused.

"I guess no one because they don't want to listen to me," said Tallulah looking disappointed.

"Most of us are listening to you," Mona.

"I feel like I'm losing my mind," said Tallulah heading towards the door. "You lost it a long time ago Tallulah it's OK," said Wanda.

"Gee thanks for the love," said Tallulah.

"Good everyone is on their feet so let's go everyone," said Wanda as she is trying to take charge.

"We are all coming Wanda take a chill pill or something," said Mona as she goes and opens the door for everyone.

I'm as chilled as a cucumber and that's how I'm going to stay," said Wanda as she walks towards the door.

"Why would you want to be a chilled cucumber anyways, that's weird to me?" asked Tallulah as she goes out the door.

"You honestly never heard that saying before Tallulah?" asked Wanda curiously.

"Sorry I haven't heard it before," said Tallulah.

"You need to honestly get out more Tallulah and get that thing you can hold and look things up," said Wanda. Wanda paused for a moment because she couldn't think what it could the name was, and she was getting mad.

"Whatever it's I'll investigate it," said Tallulah.

"Oh, what is the thing my grandchildren have?" asked Wanda.

"Now I need a thingy you don't even know what it is," said Tallulah shaking her head.

"Oh, crap what is it called?" asked Wanda as she was banging her head against the door trying think of it.

"OK Wanda you need to stop so you don't knock yourself out," said Edith.

"I'm sure if you give it time you will think of it," said Tallulah.

"Lap something," said Wanda.

"Lap dog," said Mona.

"Oh, they're so cute how they just sit on your lap and look at you," said Edith.

"Yes, I agree so precious," said Mona.

"Let's just move on before something else happens and get away from this smell," said Agnes.

"Don't you think we should just make it easy and go to the next door?" asked Agnes.

"That's fine with me if I don't have to walk too far my hips are bothering me anyways," said Edith as she grabs the side of her hips.

"Shakes those hips like you own them baby," said Tallulah.

I'm not your baby and trust me if these were my real hips, I would have no problem shaking them like Elvis," said Wanda. Everyone laughed at Wanda.

"I just want us to try to get everyone to have a little fun around her," said Mona.

"Let's shake what our mama gave us," said Tallulah dancing around the hallway.

"That actually looks like fun what Tallulah is doing," said Mona as she goes to where Tallulah is and starts shaking her hips and her arms.

"Wow you look sexy Mona," said Beau as he screams out to her.

Before they knew it everyone, but Vera was shaking body parts they didn't know they had.

"Wow that was so much fun," said Mona.

"Are we ready now to go through the Pink door?" asked Tallulah.

"Yes, let's do this everyone all spoke up at once and got excited.

"Wow this door is so pretty with the angel wings," said Agnes. "I hope it's not a sign that we are all going to heaven now," said Wanda.

"We have a long life to live before that ever happens," said Agnes. Wow!

"That is a beautiful door," said Tallulah as she reaches out and touches the angel wings and read what it said on the door.

"Angels are your pillows to heaven," said Tallulah.

"Tallulah finally got to open the door and what she saw made her so happy.

"Wow will you look at this room," said Agnes. Everyone comes into the room and see's the pink walls, nice antique couches, and all the pillows all over the place.

"This is nice and looks so comfortable as Tallulah sits on one of the couches," said Tallulah.

"Let's just stay here for the rest of the day or night whatever time it is," said Wanda.

"I would like to, but I don't want to miss all the rest of the challenges that we still have to do," said Agnes.

"Coming from you that's something big," said Wanda.

"Very funny Wanda I just learned my lesson after hitting Vera with a pool noodle, which was an adrenaline rush for me," said Agnes.

"Maybe we should do this challenge before you change your mind," said Tallulah.

"I'm not going to change my mind so don't worry," said Agnes.

"This is genuinely nice room I can tell this is going to be a fun challenge," said Tallulah as she looks around in amazement and picked up one of the pillows to see how soft it was.

"Oh, this pillow feels so nice and soft," said Wanda as she keeps rubbing it on her face.

"We can go in a corner and snuggle in all these pillows, and no one would be able to find us," said Beau as he whispers it in Mona ear.

"Oh, baby that sounds so nice," said Mona as she kissed Beau on the cheek.

"That's my beautiful gal," said Beau as wraps his arms around her.

They sneak off in a corner when no one is looking.

"Where's the envelope with the challenge on it, I don't see anywhere?" asked Agnes.

"Oh, I see where it is," said Blanche as she stumbles over the pillows to get it.

"Please Blanche don't break anything like your hip or rip the pillows," said Tallulah as she starts laughing at Blanche every time she trips over the pillows.

"Thanks for telling me that Tallulah," said Blanche "I tried to tell her to be careful," said Tallulah. Blanche though the only way she was going to get the challenge card trough all these pillows was to do a somersault. So, Blanche took off did a somersault grabbed the challenge card while in the air and landed on both feet with her hands up in the air. Yippy! "Got the challenge envelope everyone," said Blanche.

"Holy cow what the hell was that" said Agnes with a look of amazement and she starts clapping for Blanche.

"Surprised she didn't break her neck doing that," said Edith.

"I think she had told me once that she had been a gymnast when she was younger," said Agnes.

"Oh, how lucky is she and the fact she can still do it at her age," said Tallulah sarcastically.

"She even made it to the Olympics at one time in her life," said Agnes.

"Are you jealous Tallulah?" asked Edith.

"No, I'm not jealous I just don't think it's a big deal," said Tallulah folding her arms.

"That was flat out amazing and to you it's not a big deal," said Agnes as she put her hand on her hips because she couldn't believe what Tallulah just said.

"Well, the landing was a little flat," said Tallulah.

"Oh, really so you think you could do better," asked Blanche. "I probably could do a better landing then you," said Tallulah.

"Oh, we would love to see this Tallulah," said Agnes.

"Yeah, Tallulah show us what you got," said Edith.

Tallulah should have kept her mouth shut because she hasn't done somersaults in a long time.

"Come on Tallulah we are ready to see it," said Wanda.

"I really put my foot in my mouth this time," said Tallulah. "Watch out here I come," said Tallulah. Tallulah gets a running start and jump up flips around three times before landing on her feet.

"Wow you did three flips that's amazing Tallulah," said Blanche.

"Impressive job Tallulah," said Agnes.

As Tallulah just stands there wondering what the hell she just did.

"How did you learn how to do that?" asked Blanche.

"I went to gymnastics camp when I was younger," said Tallulah.

"Wow you got to go to a camp, and I only got a trainer," said Blanche.

"At least you got it, so you worked with someone one on one, and you got to be in the Olympics," said Tallulah.

"You are right Tallulah thanks so much," said Blanche.

"For letting me be competitive for a minute against you," said Blanche.

"Sure, no problem anytime," said Tallulah.

"That was great Blanche," said Edith.

"Thank you it has been a long time since I have done one of those," said Blanche I think that I could have done better with the way I did it, but I landed on my feet so that was a good thing.

"Yes, you definitely did that," said Edith.

"Is everyone ready for the next challenge or are we going to do more somersaults?" asked Blanche.

Everyone screamed YES.

"Just read the stupid envelope," said Vera as she is shaking her head and wanted to move on.

"OK Vera don't be so touchy," said Edith as she falls over a bunch of pillows and lands on her ass.

Everyone chuckles as they watched Edith.

"I'm the touchy one and you tripped over a punch of pillows," said Vera laughing at Edith.

"Everything OK with you Edith?" asked Agnes. "Yes, it's Agnes, so you don't have to worry," said Edith.

"OK I was just wondering that was a heck of a fall," said Agnes.

"Oh, by the way I'm not being touchy, oh just never mind you don't listen to me anyways," said Vera as she shakes her head again.

"You wonder why we don't listen to you," said Miles.

"Please read the challenge envelope before someone else decide to get angry or hurt," said Tallulah as she touched the pillow again and can't get over how soft it is.

"Here is what we will do for this challenge," said Blanche as she starts reading the envelope.

I'm so ready for this," said Edith.

"Everyone must participate in this challenge and the object is to hit someone over the head so your pillow will come apart so don't rip the pillow open or it won't count, and you will be out of the pillow fight challenge and must do another challenge on your own," said Blanche.

"Sounds easy," said Agnes as she gets wacked in the head by Vera.

"Oh, really Vera is that the way you're going to be as Agnes takes the pillow and whacks Vera over the head.

"Wait I didn't know we have started yet," said Wanda.

Tallulah starts laughing as she is watching Agnes and Vera go at it a second time.

"You seriously think you can beat me again old lady," said Agnes to Vera trying to get herself all hyped up.

"Oh, you think that's funny Tallulah," said Blanche as she hits Tallulah in the face.

OUCH! "That hurt Blanche," said Tallulah as she throws a pillow, and it hits Miles.

Everyone grabs a pillow and starts hitting each other and having a fun time. Then the music appeared on this giant tv screen that came down and a video started playing.

"Wow we have music," said Tallulah as pillows are still flying with the feathers from one end of the room to the other.

"This is more fun with music," said Agnes as she watched all the feathers going everywhere.

Then she watched the screen and started dancing to the disco music.

"Look at Agnes everyone," said Blanche as she joins in.

Soon after everyone joined, and still feathers were flying everywhere. Tallulah bends down and pick up a bunch of feathers and just throws them all around like confetti on New Year's.

"Oh, this is so great," said Wanda dancing in circles with her arms up in the air. Almost like she feels free and so happy now that she got to show Miles her moves, but he never moves closer to her as she was dancing.

"Oh well, his loss, because these hips know how to shake," said Wanda. As she continues to dance and wiggle it just a little bit more to "Dancing Queen."

"Now this is what I call fun and I haven't danced like this since my twenty's and back then they called it dirty dancing," said Edith.

Tallulah is still laughing from all the fun and when Agnes gets next to Tallulah, she whacks Agnes on the head.

"You think that's funny Tallulah?" asked Agnes.

"Edith was the one who said it was funny not me," said Tallulah.

"Wanda sneaks up behind Miles and as she hits him in the back of the head," said Wanda. Miles turned around and looked at Wanda.

"I'm sorry Miles I didn't mean to hit you," said Wanda.

"Yeah, right Wanda, I wish I believe you, but I don't," said Miles.

"That's how I show you that I'm interested in getting to know you," said Wanda.

"So, I deserve to get a pillow in the face," said Miles.

"Miles can we please talk about this later and let's have fun together?" asked Wanda.

"I suppose so, but just so you know I like you for you and you don't need to do cheesy things to get my attention," said Miles.

Before you knew it there was feathers flying everywhere because Miles got even and started hitting Wanda and before you know it, they were laughing together.

Agnes noticed that Vera was laying on the floor and not moving starts screaming that something is wrong with Vera.

"Be careful remember what happened last time when she was boxing you," said Edith.

"Let me remind you I won that match fair and square," said Agnes. Agnes gets on her aching knees in Vera's face and ask if she is OK.

"Maybe you shouldn't do that because she will give good left hook," said Wanda.

"Oh yeah you're right Wanda," said Agnes but I know how to block her if she does anything.

"Let me do it Agnes I don't need anything else to happen to you," said Wanda as she moves Agnes out of the way.

Wanda reaches down and starts shaking Vera and asking if she is OK.

"Vera hello are you in there?" asked Wanda.

"Where is she going to go?" asked Agnes as she shakes her head.

"You might not want to shake her so much it's not like she is a rag doll, and you can twirl her around or anything like that even know I am enjoying you doing it to her," said Edith.

"That would be exciting if you could do all that to Vera," said Tallulah. Oh whoops!

"My bad I get going on an idea and I can't stop sometimes," said Edith.

"Is she dead?" asked Agnes.

"I don't think so," said Wanda as she turns around and talk to Agnes.

"Vera opens her eyes wide and tries to stand up as she looks at Wanda get out of her face," said Vera.

"OK, fine I was just trying to help you, but obviously that won't happen again," said Wanda.

Vera stands behind Wanda with a pillow in her hand and before anyone could warn Wanda about Vera and the pillow. Vera had already hit Wanda from behind knocking down to her knees. Vera started laughing evil.

I got you," said Vera.

HAHAHA!

"Wanda are you OK sweetie?" asked Agnes as she is trying not to laugh.

"Yes, but she can stop hitting me anytime it's starting to hurt being on my knees," said Wanda.

Vera, OK you need to stop Wanda has learned her lesson now stop hitting her with the pillow," said Agnes with a stern voice.

"What are you going to do about it?" asked Vera looking serious at Agnes.

Nothing because I already did a pool noodle match with you and won, so why should I do something you lost fair and square too," said Agnes.

Vera just sat on the floor, and said nothing to anyone, and pouted.

"To me it's pointless, and you won't learn your lesson anyways Vera," Agnes.

"Oh yeah is that what you really think Agnes?" asked Vera, as she picked up one of the pillows and hit Agnes and knocked her glasses right off her face.

"OK you two that's enough we are finish with this conversation and throwing the pillows," said Edith.

"Vera, you need to apologize to Agnes," said Tallulah.

"Fine, I'm sorry that you're not smart enough to catch a pillow from me," said Vera.

"I can beat you in anything just like I did with the pool noodle so don't you worry Vera we got plenty of challenges to go and hopefully we can go against each other again," said Agnes.

"I'm ready to rip your face off," said Vera growling.

Agnes just shook her head and walked away talking to herself.

"Did all the pillows get ripped open?" asked Agnes.

"No, not yet and we still have one, two, three, four pillows to throw," said Miles.

"I'm going to check over in the corner," said Tallulah as she goes over to the pillows in the corner.

Tallulah got a shocking surprise when she lifted the pillows and saw Beau and Mona making out.

"Oh, my eyes," said Tallulah covering her eyes with what she saw.

"What the hell is going on Tallulah?" asked Edith.

"I think I'm blind," yells Tallulah.

"What are you two doing under the pillows?" asked Edith.

"We are playing a game called capture the wiener," laughed Beau.

"Oh, how do you play that?" asked Blanche.

"Whoa Beau is on behind you," said Tallulah.

"I don't get why he behind her unless he is oh my God," said Wanda.

"Wanda has the idea," said Mona.

"Honeybun what are you doing under the pillows playing a little catch the feather?" asked Edith as she puts the pillow down on the floor and walked away.

Both Beau and Mona stood up because their moment they were having was over for them because everyone came and joined them, and the magic was gone.

"I wasn't wondering where you two were and I didn't notice you weren't around," said Edith until Tallulah found you.

Are we sure they were just making out?" asked Wanda.

that's what they said, but I don't see how it's just making out if you don't have any clothes on," said Tallulah. "Didn't your husband ever do that when he was about to seal the deal?" asked Tallulah.

"No for me it was one big thrust and then instant fireworks, and all done, and it wasn't even Fourth of July," said Wanda.

"What about you Tallulah?" asked Wanda.

"For me it was a night of pure love and affection and bliss then he died," said Tallulah.

"Oh, that's horrible, but at least he died a happy man," said Wanda.

After a few minutes Mona and Beau came out of hiding under the pillows.

"Listen, guys we are sorry we did our own thing I guess we will be getting another punishment for not helping," said Beau.

"Yeah, you did something alright," said Tallulah winking.

"We just wanted to announce that we are in love with each other," said Mona.

"We are happy for you; everyone said as they clapped and cheered.

"I hate to rain on your parade, but we still have a challenge to get done," said Agnes.

"By all these pillows feathers it looks like they were all done," said Tallulah as she takes a pillow she finds and hides it behind her back and decides to hit Mona.

"Really you just had to do that?" asked Mona?

"Well, it's your turn to let someone hit you with the pillow," said Tallulah.

"I didn't even do anything to you and you're the one who hits me," said Mona.

Another pillow came out of nowhere and hit Agnes.

"It went the wrong way Agnes, I didn't do it on purpose I was aiming at Tallulah," said Mona.

"All you have been doing since we got here is complain, so yes you did do something," said Wanda.

"I haven't complained in a while and not since we have been here and if you remember I knocked out Vera by hitting her with a freaked pool noodle," said Agnes.

Yes, I know you did so just relax Agnes," said Wanda.

"I also got a pillow knocking me off my feet and almost breaking my glasses," said Agnes.

OK I got to so stop yelling at me," said Wanda.

"Do you think I'm still complaining?" asked Agnes who getting really annoyed and her voice was getting louder.

"Sorry I said something Agnes if I had known it was going to get you this mad I wouldn't of did it," said Wanda.

"I'm having the best time here and yes, I may complain, but that's because I am doing things that's out of my comfort zone," said Agnes.

"This has been the best challenge so far," said Wanda.

"This was your idea to come here and do this Agnes and we are here," said Mona with a grin.

"Yes, I agree with that," said Agnes. "We all came here to do this adventure together with you plus the people that got added," said Tallulah.

"Everything is going to be OK the rest of this adventure," said Miles.

"I know, but I want to show you just how sorry I am," said Agnes as she reaches back slowly and grabbed a pillow or two without anyone knowing.

"We totally get it now so let's have fun," said Tallulah.

Well, since you said that Tallulah Agnes decided to heave the pillow across the room, bounced off the back of Beau's head. Beau went down, and Mona went to be by his side.

"Oh, Agnes what did you do to my poor Beau?" asked Mona as she is stung to what she just witness.

"I didn't mean to throw it that hard at Beau and he wasn't even my target," said Agnes.

"Then it wouldn't have hit him," said Mona.

"I wasn't even aiming at him or anyone," said Agnes looking very frighten.

"Beau baby are you OK?" asked Mona.

"Yes, my sweet nothing like a pillow in the back of the head to knock me down," said Beau. Beau got on his feet with Mona's help.

"Sorry I really wasn't aiming at you, and I feel guilty," said Agnes.

"It's OK, but Agnes I do have something for you," said Beau.

"Yes, of course I will take anything as long as we are OK and can look pass everything," said Agnes.

"Then I give you this," said Beau and he showed Agnes the pillow he had the whole time.

"Where did you find the pillow?" asked Wanda as she went closer to Beau.

"Everyone came close as they were all amazed by Beau having another pillow.

OHHHHHH!

"So, who wants to be the lucky person that I hit with the pillow?" asked Beau.

"Hit me I deserve it," said Tallulah.

Everyone was shocked that she came forward.

"Are you sure Tallulah?" asked Agnes.

"Yes, I just want him to hit me so we can go to the next challenge," said Tallulah.

"Well, you heard the lady hit her," said Agnes.

Beau took the pillow and hit Tallulah in the back because he knew it wasn't going to hurt so badly.

"Really that's all you got?" asked Tallulah.

"Yes, Tallulah I really didn't want to hit or anyone hard," said Beau.

"We can move on to the next challenge which I hope will be as fun as this was," said Agnes.

"Sounds good to me," said Tallulah as she walks fast to the door.

"Me too," said Wanda as she cleans up the feathers.

"What are you doing Wanda?" asked Agnes.

"Just cleaning up the mess in here," said Wanda.

"We don't need to Wanda, let's just go on to the next challenge," said Agnes.

"I can't believe I'm saying this, but I can't wait to go to the next challenge," said Wanda.

Well, then let's go my friend as Wanda put's her arm around Agnes.

Yes, my friend I agree," said Agnes.

On to the next challenge…

CHAPTER 20

Little Smokey Lane

Everyone stands outside the black door ready to start the next challenge.

"What is that smell?" asked Tallulah as she plugs her nose.

"Maybe it's the rotten pudding we left down the hall a couple of doors ago," said Agnes.

"It could be a possibility you never know what it could happen here," said Miles.

"Now it's time for us to go through the black door of death," said Edith.

"Why would you think?" asked Agnes.

"Well, isn't it obvious that the last door was pink and angel like and now the door is black," said Edith.

"So, without further ado let's go through the black door and see what happens," said Agnes.

"Wait don't," said Tallulah.

"Oh, why not Tallulah?" asked Agnes.

"Nothing I just wanted to see what all of you would say if I did that," said Tallulah laughing.

"You're such a smart-ass Tallulah," said Wanda.

"Tell me something I don't know, and I rather be a smart-ass then a dumb ass," said Tallulah.

"OK, I would be more than happy to tell you something you don't know and then call you a dumb ass for not knowing," said Wanda.

"OK fine go-ahead Wanda," said Tallulah

"Do you really want to do that?" asked Wanda.

"Yes, I do," said Tallulah. Tallulah wanted to check and see what Wanda was hiding and see if there was something that Tallulah didn't know.

"Waiting for you to tell me Wanda," said Tallulah.

"Maybe I should whisper it to you," said Wanda.

"Already heard all the whispering it's OK you can just share it with me aloud," said Tallulah as she is trying to call Wanda's bluff, but it's not working at all she isn't breaking.

"OK so let me ask you this Tallulah do you have any clue whatsoever on why there is so much whispering going on?" asked Wanda.

"Why are you dragging this on so will you just tell me Wanda?" asked Tallulah who is now starting to get all pissed off.

"OK get ready because I'm going to tell you what it is," said Wanda as she looked Tallulah right in the eyes.

"Let me just ask this one question to you Tallulah?" asked Wanda.

"No let me get in one this one Wanda," said Agnes.

"Do you feel a breeze coming through anywhere?" asked Agnes just waiting for Tallulah to answer.

"No, I don't think so it feels nice in here, so I'm not sure what you're getting at," said Tallulah with a grin on her face.

"OK I'm going to make it simple for you," said Wanda.

"Your pants have been down since the pillow fight," yells Vera out of nowhere.

"What the hell?" asked Tallulah.

Tallulah looked shocked and when she looked down her shorts were around her ankles and all you could see is Tallulah in her depends.

"Why didn't anyone tell me about this?" said Tallulah as she cries.

"Vera just told you about your pants," said Edith as she laughed her ass off.

"This is disgusting why would you all do this to me?" asked Tallulah.

"Oh, relax Tallulah no one did anything to you we just didn't tell you your damn shorts were down that's all," said Mona.

"So, take a chill pill Tallulah," yells Beau in the back of everyone.

"Maybe your pants should be down Beau oh wait they were already," said Tallulah.

"Oh, snap she just got you," said Vera. I have no idea what you're talking about," said Beau.

You think we didn't notice that you and Mona were playing capture the weasel under the feathers," said Tallulah.

"Oh, so now your comedian Vera?" asked Wanda.

"Go pull up your shorts so that we can get going in this room and keep moving," said Wanda enough of this stopping and going let just go.

"Where do you expect me to go it doesn't seem like there is a bathroom close by?" asked Tallulah.

"I'll help you get them up it shouldn't be that hard Tallulah," said Mona who just wants to get this going.

"Thank you, Mona, I appreciate you so much right now," said Tallulah.

"Good now let's go back in the pillow fight room and pull them up," said Mona.

They go back in the room and Mona helps Tallulah get her shorts up.

"Thank you again Mona," said Tallulah.

"No problem anything for a friend even know you made a smart-ass comment to Beau," said Mona.

"Yeah, well it was funny," laughed Tallulah.

"I guess it was a little, but still that moment we spent together was something I won't forget," said Mona.

"Tallulah are you all set now?" asked Wanda.

"Yes, let's do this together as a team," said Tallulah.

"Tallulah is simply happy to be moving on to something different," said Mona.

"I think you would feel better if your pants were up after being down for so long Beau," winked Mona.

Beau brought Mona closer and whisper I had no problem with my pants down when we were under the pillows my dear. Mona face got red after hearing that and whispered back that she loved that he had his pants down. Edith is looking at Mona strangely and wonders what is going on but moves closer towards the door.

"Why are you so red my dear?" asked Edith.

"Nothing Edith I'm just having one of those CRS moments," said Mona shaking her head.

"CRS moments now that's a new one to me, I have never heard of that before, so you're just making it up I'm guessing," said Wanda.

"Of course, you would think that, but I'm not making it up so just stuff it Wanda," said Mona angrily.

"What does it mean if you don't mind me asking you?" asked Wanda being curious.

"Mona takes a deep breath and said *I can't remember shit* is what it means just so everyone knows," said Mona.

Wanda burst out laughing thinking it was the funniest thing that she ever heard in her life.

Everyone turns around and wonders at what she is laughing so hard at.

"I really think that Wanda has lost her marbles," said Agnes.

"Who taught you about CRS Mona?" asked Tallulah.

"My grandmother did before I lost her, she thought every child needs to know at an early age what CRS means because you never know when it might happen," laughed Mona.

"How do you get it?" asked Agnes.

It's not a disease or anything," said Mona.

"Oh, I see, but not really," said Agnes.

"It's just an old saying that my grandmother used to say that's all," said Mona.

"I think that I got it now," said Agnes.

"She had the best sense of humor, and I could see where my mom got it from." said Mona.

"Interesting Mona, by the way what does CRS mean?" asked Edith sarcastically.

"It means can't remember shit, I just told all of you that," laughed Mona.

"Wow maybe I have it," laughed Edith.

"You never know you could," said Mona.

"Come on everyone let's go to the black door and see what kind of things are waiting for us," said Agnes as she opens the door to the room. Everyone goes into the room and covers their nose.

"Yuck it stinks in here," said Tallulah as she is trying not to gag.

"Is Frankie and Fay here?" asked Edith.

"No, I don't see them, so I don't think so," said Miles.

"Why would they even be here with us?" asked Agnes.

"It stinks like cigarette smoke, and you know just how much they love their breaks back at Mystic," said Tallulah.

"Then Fay would come near you, and she would smell of smoke and make you want to puke," said Edith.

YUCK!

"I could smell it to when she got close, so I get what you're talking about," said Agnes.

"Frankie burns everything and smokes, so you never know what smell is coming off his food or his smoking," said Tallulah.

"Focus people we got another challenge to do, and it looks like it might be fun," said Agnes.

"I'm seeing guns so I'm thinking this could be a little dangerous and makes me think of Annie Oakley," said Tallulah.

"I think certain people shouldn't have them in their possession," said Blanche as she nods to the right aiming at Vera.

"Well, let's see what the challenge card said before we determine anything," said Agnes. I like the way you think Agnes," said Tallulah as she follows Agnes around to find the next challenge card.

"This place has made me think like we are in the woods going hunting," said Beau.

"Are you a hunter Beau?" asked Tallulah.

"Yes, I was, and I loved going in the woods with my sons and sit in the deer stand and we talk for hours until we were lucky or not to catch a deer," said Beau.

"That sounds like a nice memory of you and your boys," said Wanda.

"It was just nice to spend quality time with them, now they're married with kids, grandkids, and I have great grandkids," said Beau looking sad.

"So, you will be able to give us a little tutorial about how to shoot if we need too?" asked Agnes.

"I sure can Agnes and it be my pleasure," said Beau bowing to everyone.

"Where is this challenge card Agnes is thinking to herself as everyone goes looking for it in separate areas.

"Here it is," said Mona as she grabs it under the raccoon hat.

Of course, Mona couldn't resist she had to put it on and laughed to herself.

Mona went behind Tallulah and tapped her on the shoulder and when Tallulah turned around, she let out a loud screeching noise and runs behind Miles to protect her.

"Seriously Tallulah you're afraid of a raccoon hat?" asked Agnes?

"No, I just thought it was real for a second when I saw it on your head," said Tallulah.

"Why would I have a raccoon on my head?" asked Mona.

"You are such a wuss Tallulah," said Agnes as she laughs with Mona.

This next challenge everyone must participate.

Take the pellet gun that's left for you and shoot the bear.

Once you shoot the bear and he is down you will need to go and retrieve a flag.

"What if the bear is not a boy?" asked Edith.

"Then if it was a she then she would probably wear a dress and be girly," said Wanda.

"He is wearing a hat, jeans, and a belt," said Agnes so clearly, he is a boy bear.

"I honestly can't believe that we are discussing the sex of a bear that doesn't' really move," said Tallulah.

"Then why is he moving right now?" asked Agnes. Agnes turns around and looks shocked to see this bear was walking around slowly like he is looking for something or someone to eat.

"I have seen this bear before I just can't remember where I did," said Tallulah.

Mona picked up one of the pellet guns and looks down the barrel.

"Show me how to shoot this bad boy Beau?" asked Mona ready for action.

"Oh boy I don't see this as a clever idea," said Agnes.

"Come on Agnes this will be fun for us to get our left-over energy out and use it on a bear," said Wanda.

Beau gives them all a tutorial on how to shoot the pellet gun. Vera is just swinging her gun around everywhere.

"This honestly might be a stupid question that I have but are we shooting at bear or the tree?" asked Wanda who was totally confused.

"Why would you want to shoot at a tree?" asked Tallulah.

"I don't know to spare the bear; I just asked a simple question Tallulah," said Wanda getting mad.

"It was only a simple question, but sure was stupid," said Tallulah. "We are shooting the bear only Wanda no anybody else," said Agnes.

"I do have one question," said Blanche as she raises her hand like she is in school.

"Blanche what is your question?" asked Edith.

"Are we shooting at Smokey?" asked Blanche.

"Who is Smokey?" asked Agnes.

"You know the bear that always steals the picnic baskets from everyone," said Wanda.

Tallulah looks at Wanda funny.

"Smokey doesn't have a picnic basket," said Tallulah.

"Yes, he does I saw him in a movie stealing a picnic basket," said Wanda.

"Wanda, I hate to break it to you that wasn't Smokey the bear it was Yogi Bear," said Tallulah.

"Remember he had a little friend name Boo-Boo," said Agnes.

"Honestly, who names a bear Boo-Boo anyways," said Wanda.

"I do agree it makes no sense to me either and I saw the movie," said Mona who was just trying to get this conversation over with.

"Where I was from, we lived in the country and we saw bears all the time in our yard and we never once named them Smokey or Yogi," said Agnes.

"Well, I'm sure that had to be interesting to see," said Tallulah.

I loved the country it was nice and piece with a lot of wildlife out here," said Agnes

All the sudden there was a loud BANG, everyone covered their ears and duck down and dropped their pellet guns. They were all thinking that someone was shooting at them and didn't know what to do.

"What the hell was that?" asked Agnes as she screamed loudly.

Ah Ha I got the sucker right between the eyes," said Miles.

"What did you do Miles blow up the whole room or something?" asked Agnes trying to figure out if she can hear or not after all that noise.

"OK, the bear is down I shot him square in the eyes, so let's get the flag and get the hell out of here," said Vera.

"That sounds weird coming from you," said Wanda.

"I thought these were only pellet guns?" asked Edith.

"They shouldn't have made that loud of a bang," said Miles.

"How do you know Edith?" asked Tallulah.

"I've seen them before and I know how they sound," said Edith.

"Wow I am impressed with your shooting Miles," said Wanda.

"What a good shot," said Blanche. Vera gets close to Smokey and wonders why he is smoking.

"I thought he liked to prevent fire," said Blanche.

"Never saw anything like that before," said Miles as he just watched was going on.

"Get the flag Agnes and I will figure out why he is smoking," said Miles.

"OK sounds like a plan," said Agnes as they go together and see what is going on. Agnes goes very slowly and removes the flag slowly around the bear's neck.

"Excellent job Agnes?" said Edith clapping.

"Do you see what the problem?" asked Agnes as Miles looks at it.

"Smokey has already been shot twice in two separate places," said Miles.

"Yeah once in between the eyes by me and another shot in his buttocks," said Beau.

"Oh, my poor Smokey," said Edith being dramatic.

"It's not like he really could feel it," said Miles.

"I know, but still, we did try to shoot him down for a flag," said Edith.

"Your cute Edith the way you think about things sometimes," said Miles.

"Thanks Miles I just have a caring nature in me," said Edith trying not blush at Miles.

"Can we keep the flirting down to a minimum and get moving here?" asked Tallulah?

Agnes walks back and notices something is strange with Wanda.

"Are you OK Wanda?" asked Agnes as she got closer.

"No, I'm fine it's just my arthritis kicking in now and bothering me," said Wanda.

"Wanda did you put your Ben-gay on at all?" asked Mona.

"Who is Ben Gay another resident?" asked Tallulah. Agnes just shook her head and didn't answer Tallulah.

"No Tallulah it helps with your aches and the pain you're going to have if you don't get out of my fucking face," said Wanda.

"Touchy, touchy aren't we Wanda," laughs Tallulah.

"To answer your question Mona no, I did 't have a chance to have Nurse Juniper to put it on," said Wanda.

"Oh sorry," said Agnes trying to help her to find somewhere to sit.

"When I went to her office, she was on one of her breaks," said Wanda.

"I'm sure taking a break isn't what she really is doing," said Tallulah whispering to herself.

"What did you say Tallulah?" asked Mona.

"Nothing just thinking to myself that's all," said Tallulah.

"Well, just try not to think too much it might make you go crazy or something," said Edith.

"I'm already crazy and all of you know that so it's not a big secret," said Tallulah.

"So true Tallulah sorry I had to agree with you," said Blanche.

"Don't worry I said I am crazy so at least I admit it," said Tallulah.

"Tallulah my sweet we all love you no matter what," said Miles as he winks at her.

"That is just so encouraging," said Tallulah.

"I've noticed you do a lot of winking at us girls are there just one you want to wink at more than the others?" asked Edith.

"I will let you all know when the time comes," said Miles as he walked away.

"Can someone please answer one thing for me?" asked Blanche.

"We can try Blanche what is bothering you?" asked Mona.

"Has anyone notice that Miles has hit on every single one of us in unusual ways," said Blanche.

That's what we were just talking about," said Edith.

"No, I haven't, but I got busy in different things like eating yucky pudding," kicking Vera's ass, and a pillow fight you know the normal stuff we do," said Agnes laughing.

"Wait a minute you never did eat the pudding and that's how everything started," said Edith.

"I will be more than happy to admit that you have kicked ass in the last couple of challenges, so you won't hear any crap from me the rest of this adventure," said Wanda.

"It takes a lot of guts to kick Vera's ass," said Edith.

"Shut your fucking trap," said Vera as she hears Agnes and Edith talking about her.

"Just giving Agnes a compliment because she was damn good in beating you," said Edith.

"Do you want to have another go around with me in the ring since you have a big mouth and love to talk about people?" asked Vera.

Edith hesitates and thinks about it before answering Vera very carefully.

"Nah, I'm not that dumb Vera sorry to burst your bubble," said Edith as she walks away.

"You are all a bunch of losers," said Vera as she laughs.

"If we are a bunch of losers then why did you even sneak on the bus and come with us Vera?" asked Agnes.

"It's because I am sick and tired of everyone leaving me out of things with everyone and so what I am nosy, so I wanted to see what is going on," said Vera.

"That is the most positive thing you have said to all of us since the day we met you at Heaven's Ridge," said Agnes.

"I wouldn't get used to me being positive because it won't happen every day especially with a bunch of pricks like you," said Vera.

"Well, that didn't take long for her to be mean again," said Tallulah.

"It's about that time again that we go to our next room," said Blanche.

"Right with you there Blanche," said Agnes.

"We had our fun in here, but more fun awaits us in a different room," said Blanche as Agnes and her head towards the door.

"Hey, Tallulah you got your shorts on?" asked Miles as he laughed?

"Oh, shut up Miles," said Tallulah as she pushed him out the door.

"Hey, hey, hey don't push me Tallulah," said Miles.

"You know that you enjoy massages all over your body by someone and you know it," said Tallulah sarcastically.

Mona's eyes just got big because she thought Tallulah was going to spoil the secret that she told her.

"It's time for you to be quiet Tallulah before things accidently slip," said Mona as Tallulah and her go out the door together.

"Tallulah, I trusted you with a secret and you almost let the cat out of the bag," said Mona ready to slap her.

"I told you your secret is safe with me so no worries," said Tallulah.

"I'm trusting you Tallulah," said Mona as she walked away.

"Hey Mona, I wanted to tell you why I said that it's because Miles just really irks me sometimes and things tend to come out of my mouth that are not suppose too but I would never share your secret with anyone," said Tallulah.

"I hope so and I appreciate that Tallulah," said Mona.

As they both go back in and see why everyone hasn't come out yet.

"OK people let's see what awaits us," said Agnes.

"We are all ready to have more challenge fun," said Wanda.

"I thought when we came here this house was going to be big and scary, but so far it hasn't been," said Agnes.

"That's probably why they call it a funhouse," said Edith.

"I agree Agnes things have turned out good so far," said Tallulah.

"Let's keep the fun going in the funhouse," said Wanda.

On to the next challenge...

CHAPTER 21

Bloody Mary Lane

They all go to the next color door that's orange and read the sign for the next challenge they will be doing.

"Bloody Mary Road that doesn't sounds so promising," said Edith.

"It does for me because I am so thirsty," said Mona.

"Maybe we are going to liquor up and have a Bloody Mary or something," said Wanda.

"With the way these challenges are going I don't know what to expect," said Tallulah.

"I know I could go for one of those right now," said Mona.

"Yes, Mona, we get it," said Agnes.

"Why is that you need a drink so badly Mona?" asked Edith

"You all drive me to drink sometimes," laughed Mona.

"Yeah, I can see that happening with everything that has been going on since we got here," said Agnes.

"I have had one before, and I find them disgusting," said Tallulah.

"Really Tallulah I find that hard to believe that there is one alcoholic drink you don't like," said Agnes.

"I used to drink them in my younger years," said Mona as she just turns the doorknob and goes right in the room.

"Wow, she must be thirsty for her to go right in," said Wanda.

"That's my girl," said Beau right behind her.

"Wow would you look at all of this?" asked Mona as she can't believe what she is seeing.

"Looks like we are in brewery or something," said Beau.

"Maybe we will be making our own beer," said Tallulah.

"Oh, so that's what you want?" asked Edith.

"No, but I will go with anything at this time," said Tallulah.

"Oh wow, they are beer steins. I haven't seen these in years when I went to Germany," said Agnes.

"You used to drink beer Agnes?" asked Tallulah.

"No, but my husband and I used to collect them when we traveled and I almost had one that looks identical to this one," said Agnes picking one up and looking at it.

"A lot of memories there for you Agnes asked Tallulah.

"It was the one thing we had in common and loved to do for each other," said Agnes.

"They are neat to look at," said Miles I had a couple myself when I lived in Germany.

"Oh, you have been there too?" asked Agnes.

"Yes for a few years before I came back to the states lovely place," said Miles.

"Yes, I do agree with you on that Miles," said Agnes.

Tallulah went over to Mona and asked her a question.

"Do you think that Agnes and Miles could hook up?" asked Tallulah.

"No, I don't because Agnes doesn't want anyone to replace her husband," said Mona so you still have a chance Tallulah.

"I wasn't thinking about that well OK maybe a little bit," laughed Tallulah.

"Oh, where, oh where is the clue?" asked Vera.

"I found it over on the barrel and here is the clue for this challenge," said Blanche.

"I wonder what we are going to do this time?" asked Wanda.

If you're thirsty for a drink this is the challenge for you at least three of you must participate in this challenge, drink as many Bloody Mary's you can in five minutes. The winner will win a prize at the end of the adventure," said Blanche.

"Well, that doesn't sound too hard to do," said Tallulah.

"OK so who is going to be the three doing this challenge?" asked Tallulah.

Mona quickly put up her hand and she is ready to go.

"Are there two more volunteers that are willing to do this challenge?" asked Tallulah.

"What about you Wanda?" asked Tallulah.

"I would if I liked tomato juice," said Wanda.

"I thought you had a V8 all the time?" asked Agnes.

"Not if I don't need too, but only when Hilda tells me too, I try and get it down," said Wanda.

"I'll do it," said Agnes.

"Good girl that's the spirit Agnes I'm glad you're up for the challenge," said Edith.

"Pretty damn proud of myself that I volunteered," said Agnes.

"OK who wants the last spot?" asked Tallulah.

"Everyone looked at each other before Blanche decided to be the third one.

"We have our three people to participate and there wasn't even any fighting about it," said Tallulah.

"That's a miracle and you didn't even lose your shorts this time Tallulah," said Edith.

"Very funny Edith," laughed Tallulah.

"Yeah, we must be doing something right if we didn't fight," said Mona as she holds her stein in her hand.

"Are you sure you're ready to drink the Bloody Mary Mona?" asked Tallulah.

Before Tallulah could give her, an answer Mona had gulped her first down with in a second. Then Mona let out one hell of a BURP. Mona hands Beau her stein who just happened to be standing next to her.

"Wow that was very impressive sweetie," said Beau as he kisses her.

"It could of use more vodka it's a little flat," said Mona.

Everyone started to laugh when Mona had said that.

"Let's go I have to win this one and I'm ready for another," said Mona.

"If she didn't taste any alcohol then we must be drinking straight tomato juice," said Blanche.

"Either way is fine with me," said Agnes.

"So that met that Agnes and Blanche still had to drink their Bloody Mary and catch up to Mona.

"OK girls grab your steins and drink up," said Mona

So, they did exactly that and drank down their Bloody Mary's, but slowly not in one gulp like Mona. Agnes swished her Bloody Mary in her mouth and then swallowed.

"Yuck it's too warm," said Agnes. Blanche swallowed it right down.

Ding, ding your time is up," said Beau.

"Are you OK Blanche?" asked Agnes. Blanche screamed out BINGO!!

"Well, how about that Blanche has drunk more than Mona," said Edith so happy for her.

"What was the ding about and screaming bingo?" asked Wanda.

She was happy she got the win and other then that I don't know?" asked Tallulah.

"Every time we finish a challenge, I get excited," said Miles.

"I'm sure you do," said Tallulah as she winks at him.

Mona grabbed Tallulah's arm.

"You honestly need to stop grabbing my arm you're starting to leave marks," said Tallulah.

Can you please stop flirting with Miles?" asked Mona?

"Why it's so much fun," said Tallulah.

"Are you jealous or something?" asked Tallulah.

"No, I'm not I just don't want my secret to accidentally come out of your mouth because we have had to many close calls," said Mona.

"I told you that your secret is safe with me so please trust me," said Tallulah.

"Fine OK I will, but I am watching you," said Mona.

Beau comes over to Mona and wraps his arms around her.

"So why are you watching Tallulah?" asked Beau?

"Just making sure her shorts stay on we don't need them to fall off again," laughed Mona.

"Are you sure that Bloody Mary didn't do anything to you?" asked Beau?

"No darling I'm fine to be honest nothing was in it just straight V8 juice no vodka in it," said Mona.

"Well, that's OK I don't want you to be all liquored up anyways I love you just the way you are," said Beau giving Mona a kiss.

"I love you to my darling," said Mona wrapping her arms around him.

"Too bad we can't slip off and be alone again I wouldn't mind being under those pillows with you," said Beau.

"Yeah, that was a lot of fun," said Mona just smiling away.

"Well, another challenge accomplished, and a new challenge awaits us," said Agnes.

"I wonder what is next I enjoy it being a mystery then once you get in the room it's a whole new thing," said Blanche.

"Yeah, sure that's what I was thinking too," said Agnes.

"Everyone ready to go to the next challenge?" asked Tallulah.

"Yes, I am," said Vera and everyone had shocked faces on them because of Vera's enthusiasm about going to another room.

"I'm not going to piss on her cheerios for any reason so if she is happy let's just keep it that way," said Agnes.

"I agree we don't want to set Vera off for any reason," said Wanda.

On to the next challenge . . .

CHAPTER 22

Knockout

Belle tells the truck driver where he can put the balance beam that she rented.

"I think over there by the hammock should be good spot," said Belle.

"Wow what is this going on Belle?" asked Serena as she walked up to the balance beam.

"Isn't this so exciting?" asked Belle.

"What are you doing with all the jousting things and the balance beam Belle?" asked Serena

"I just thought it would bring a little fun to the seniors that are still here, and I also thought if anyone of us have any issues about anything they can do it while jousting," said Belle.

"I just hope it doesn't give them any ideas," said Serena.

"Nah, I'm sure the seniors will enjoy it," said Belle.

"There is a lot of tension here and it will be a clever idea to hash it all out," said Belle.

"This little idea of yours does it have anything to do with Chip and Hazel?" asked Serena.

"Maybe just a little bit I just hate to see a good friendship like theirs go to waste," said Belle.

"By what I have been seeing it may go beyond friendship," said Serena.

"What makes you think that?" asked Belle.

"In my opinion I think they both like each other but are both afraid to tell each other and act one it," said Serena.

"Oh, so you think that's what might be going on, and we will find out tonight if they confess anything," said Belle.

"Yeah, I'm not sure that will happen, but we will see," said Serena.

"Then this is a clever idea maybe then they will admit they like or love each other," said Belle.

"A lot of shit is going to hit the fan tonight," said Serena.

"We need to let the other counselors know that they may or may not be jousting tonight," said Belle.

"I'm excited and it will be so much fun," said Serena.

"Where did the balance beam come from?" asked Frankie.

"I rented it for tonight's activity," said Belle.

"I see and who are you getting to come and do this?" asked Frankie.

"Working on the list as we speak," winked Belle.

"Please tell me I won't be on that list?" asked Frankie.

"I guess you will have to wait and see tough guy and oh by the way I had a great night with you the other night," said Belle as she walks away

Frankie watched Belle walk away to the office.

"I'm so screwed," said Frankie.

Why what did you do now?" asked Serena.

"I don't want to do whatever this balance beam thing is all about," said Frankie.

"Well, maybe you will be one of the lucky ones," said Serena who laughs as she leaves.

"Oh, shit I am so screwed," said Frankie as he keeps telling himself.

It was almost time for the jousting to begin and Belle was getting excited for it.

Everyone was amazed at the balance beams that was in the middle of the basketball court.

"Let's the games begin," said Belle to herself.

"Are you ready for all the gossip and bloodshed to come out Belle?" asked Serena.

"If it will make the drama go away then I'm ready," said Belle.

"Are you going to be a part of any of the teams you have set up for tonight?" asked Serena.

"I'll be watching on the sidelines just like everyone else," said Belle.

"Like I said before Belle get ready for a lot of bloodshed," said Serena.

"Oh, I'm ready bring it on," said Belle.

"Going back to the office to finalize everything quickly and I'll be right back," said Belle.

"Sounds good Belle," said Serena.

Belle was in the office doing paperwork when she heard a knock at the door.

"The door is open," said Belle.

"Hi Belle, can we talk for a minute?" asked Frankie.

"Sure, come on in Frankie," said Belle.

"I know your busy, but I wanted to talk to you about me being a part of tonight," said Frankie.

"Frankie it's only for fun, and I think the other seniors will love it," said Belle.

"I was curious to know who you have as my opponent?" asked Frankie.

"Frankie you're going to be fine I can promise you that so stop worrying and when you see who you will be going against you will see it's no biggie," said Belle.

"If you're sure then I'll just see you later," said Frankie as he heads towards the door.

"Belle gets up from her desk. Hey Frankie," said Belle, and goes up to him.

Yes Belle," said Frankie as he turns around.

"Hey, you're going to be fine I promise," said Belle as they look into each other's eyes.

"I believe you," said Frankie as he gives Belle a kiss.

Tory comes in the door and sees them kissing.

"Hey Tory, how are you today?" asked Belle.

"I will talk to you later," said Frankie as he jets out the door fast.

"Tory are you OK you look like you have seen a ghost or somethings?" asked Belle.

"Yeah, I'm fine Belle I just was curious if I was on your list?" asked Tory.

"Like I have told everyone else you will have to wait and see and trust me you won't be disappointed," said Belle.

"Oh, I see I guess I will just wait and see then," said Tory.

"Are you sure you're OK you look a little flush?" asked Belle.

"Yes, I'm good, and I will see you later," said Tory as she goes out the door.

"Sure, no problem I will see you later Tory," said Belle who is kind of curious why Tory acted like she did.

"Oh well I guess I will just add her to my list, and I know the perfect person for her to go against.

"This is going to be wonderful right Hank?" asked Jasper who was excited about what they were about to see going on, asked Jasper.

"Yeah, I guess if you like hurting people," said Hank.

"It's better than few things we have done here already," said Jasper.

Jasper spots Ethel and Clara and went over to them.

"Would like to sit with him and Hank?" asked Jasper

"Sure if you don't mind us tagging along?" asked Clara.

Ethel was being her quiet self again. Jasper made sure that Ethel sat next to him so he could continue to get to know each other.

"Are you excited about what we will be seeing tonight, Ethel?" asked Jasper.

"No not really, but they told us we should go, and it might be fun to watch so here we are," said Ethel.

"Well, I will try and be good company for you so both and you won't be so bored," said Jasper.

"Just swell," said Hank to himself.

"Is anything wrong Hank?" asked Jasper.

"No everything is just sweet like a smelling daisy?" said Hank.

"OK whatever that's supposed to mean," said Jasper.

"I don't think he likes us sitting here maybe we should go," said Ethel.

"I don't care what he thinks you both are my guests," said Jasper.

Clara and Ethel just look at each other and decided to stay with Jasper.

"If you get scared Ethel, feel free to hang on to me," said Jasper.

"Do you really think it will be that scary?" asked Clara.

"You never know my dear, but you can grab on to my other arm if you need too," said Jasper.

"I will certainly keep that in mind," said Clara giving Jasper a wink.

"Welcome everyone to the first annual Mystic Summer Camp jousting night, boy, do I have a great show for you tonight," said Belle.

"We picked random counselors to come on up and joust each other they just don't know who they're but will soon find out," said Harlow.

"I know it's jousting but trying not to break anything of yours or your opponent," said Belle.

"Most of all have fun," said Harlow as she gets ready to announce the first match.

"I can't believe I might have to joust this is not right and so annoying," said Eloise.

"Do you ever say anything positive?" asked Tinsley. "Yes, when it's the right time to do it," said Eloise.

"Well, you could have fooled me Eloise," said Tinsley.

Eloise just glared at Tinsley and then got up and left. "I called that right," said Tinsley until she see's Eloise talking to Belle, oh this isn't going to be good.

"Hey Belle, is it too late to add my name to the list to joust someone?" asked Eloise.

"No of course not who do you have in mine," asked Belle.

"I want to joust that bitch Tinsley she is always ragging on me for something, and I am so sick of it I want to punch her," said Eloise.

"OK no problem you and Tinsley are on my list, but I am just letting you know that you aren't going to be punching each other," said Belle.

"Good I can't wait to teach her a lesson," said Eloise.

"Alright for our first jousting match of the night I would like Chip and Hazel come on up and get your jousting pole and get on the balance beam," said Belle so excited to get this going.

"Excuse me what was that, Belle?" asked Hazel no believing what she is hearing.

"Chip and you're up here right now and there are no getting out of it and the same goes for you to Chip," said Belle. I don't joust, said Hazel.

"Belle, I don't think it's a clever idea for us to be doing this," said Chip.

"What do you think I am going to cry or break when you hit me?" asked Hazel.

"No, I would never think that of you Hazel, I just don't hit girls," said Chip.

"Hazel takes the jousting pole, and gets on the balance beam, and gets close to Chip. Don't be a wuss and I'm not going to break," said Hazel.

"Yes, I know Hazel, you already told me that," said Chip.

"Then grab your jousting pole and let's do this Chip," said Hazel trying to get Chip going.

"No, I won't do that to you Hazel," said Chip.

"Oh, so now you're going to act all nice and sweet to me because you weren't like that today or yesterday when I wanted to talk to you and you just pushed me away," said Hazel.

"Look I didn't mean too," said Chip.

Hazel looked at Chip before hitting in the chest and Frankie put his arms up against his chest where she hit him.

"Oh, did that hurt Chip?" asked Hazel with a sad voice.

"Not really Hazel," said Chip as he takes a whack at here almost knocking her off the balance beam.

"Well maybe I should do it again," said Hazel, so she hit him again and he almost lost his balance.

"Ugh," said Chip as he bends over grabbing his stomach trying not to fall off the balance beam.

"Come on Chip you know you want to hit me," said Hazel as she is moving closer to him.

Hazel enough of this I don't want to hit you, said Chip.

Tell me why you don't want to hit me Chip, asked Hazel.

Chip just stared at her.

"Come on Chip I'm waiting for the answer," said Hazel.

"You want to know why I don't want to hit you?" asked Chip as he gets in her face.

"Yeah, I do Chip because I need to know," said Hazel.

"Oh boy I'm not sure how she is going to deal with him telling her the truth," said Fay.

"You know what he is talking about?" asked Serena.

"Yeah, and it's a long time coming," said Fay.

Fay caught Serena up to speed about Hazel and her past and everything going on with Chip.

"Chip doesn't know about this guy Milo?" asked Serena.

"No, she won't tell him I'm the only one who knows, but I'm getting a feeling it's going to come out tonight," said Fay.

"Shit, I didn't know Fay," said Serena.

"To make it worst two of the seniors supposedly overheard Chip say that he was in love with Hazel,"

"I thought the reason they were fighting all the time was because they liked each other and that's part of the reason Belle has them jousting so they can confess they love it each other," said Serena putting her head down.

"Belle did this on purpose?" shouted Fay.

"Well yeah sort of, but it wasn't just for them it was also for everyone else that might not be getting along too," said Serena trying to cover her ass.

"I need to talk to Belle about this," said Fay.

"Listen honestly, we didn't know there was more to the story," said Serena.

Fay went over to Belle and told exactly what has been going on with Chip and Hazel.

"Well, I can't stop the match right now when they're in the middle of something," said Belle.

"Yeah, it's going to be something once it all comes out, said Fay just watching them both.

"Hazel, you have the greatest personality, a beautiful heart, you have a smile that just lights up every place you go," said Chip.

"OK thanks for all those generous thoughts about me, but it still doesn't answer my question," said Hazel.

"Shut up Hazel and just let me talk for once I'm pouring out my heart to you," said Chip.

"OK I will shut up Chip," said Hazel right after I do this, she takes the jousting pole and hits Chip in the face and knocks him off the balance beam.

"What the hell was that for Hazel?" shouted Chip.

"You put me on a pedestal and expect me to not react," said Hazel. Chip grabbed Hazel so she couldn't do anything else.

"Now listen to me Hazel, I love you and that's why I have been acting the way I have been because I didn't want to tell you and get have you spooked by what I say," said Chip.

Hazel just looked at Chip like she was speechless.

"Come on Hazel please say something to me?" asked Chip as he reaches for her hand, and she pulls it back towards her.

"I don't know what to say to you Chip," said Hazel as she looks around and everyone is watching them.

"You don't need to say anything just know how I feel, and we can just go on with our lives," said Chip.

Camp Funhouse 321

"I do have one thing to say to you Chip," said Hazel. Hazel thinks about what she is going to say to him and wonder if she should tell Chip that she already knows.

"You're not going to hit me again are you, Hazel?" asked Chip.

"No, I'm not going to hit you, but I could if you like me too because I still have one more hit in me to do to you if I must," said Hazel.

"No please don't hit me just be mine when you're ready I know that you have had a tough time living life," said Chip.

"How do you know about my life and how it has been?" asked Hazel as she looks at Fay. Fay looked up at her and gave her a shrug and mouthing that she had no idea about what he was talking.

"I know what happened to the last guy you were with," said Chip.

"What are you getting at Chip?" asked Hazel.

"I'm talking about Milo," said Chip.

Hazel felt like she was going to break down and cry by what Chip just said to her.

"How could you possibly know anything about Milo?" asked Hazel now getting angry.

"Hazel let's just talk somewhere instead of talking here and everyone watching," said Chip.

Hazel looked at him and ran up to him and just kept hitting him not letting him fight for himself and he ends up on the ground.

"How can you know him and what I went through." said Hazel as she started screaming. Hazel fell to the ground and rolled herself in a ball crying.

"Oh, Belle we should do something," said Serena.

Fay, Belle, and Serena all got in the ring and went to Hazel. Fay grabbed on to her and told her everything was going to be OK.

"I'm sorry I did this to you Hazel I didn't know there was more to the story," said Belle. Hazel just looked at Belle and didn't say anything.

"Let's get out of her sweetie, said Fay helping Hazel on to her feet. They went by Chip, but she didn't look at him.

"Hey Hazel, I'm sorry, but just so you know Milo was my best friend and I loved him too," said Chip.

Hazel stopped and looked at Chip.

"I know that you and I didn't know each other that well, but he talked about you all the time until the day he died, and I vowed to be there for you as much as I could, then when I came here, I swear I didn't know you were here, but the more we spent time together I really began to see what Milo saw in you and I love that about you and deep down inside I fell for you because you were yourself not just because your best friend was my friend was my husband," said Hazel.

Everyone started to have tears in their eyes watching Hazel and Chip.

"I genuinely love you and I am going to leave it like that," said Chip.

Hazel and Fay looked at Chip one last time before leaving the jousting. Chip was nervous by everything that happened, but so glad that he got everything he needed to say to her, and Chip got out of the ring and sat down by Frankie.

"Wow that was intense," said Frankie. "Yeah, it was," said Chip as he was kicking the dirt around with his feet.

"What are you going to do now?" asked Frankie.

"I'm just going to sit here and watch whoever else is going to be jousting tonight," said Chip.

"I met about Hazel?" asked Frankie.

"I really don't know right now," said Chip.

"Do you want my advice?" asked Frankie.

"Not really Frankie because remember I know what you have been up too," said Chip.

"Yeah well, I got myself in a little hot water earlier today," said Frankie.

"What did you burn this time, Frankie?" asked Chip.

"I didn't burn anything, but I think Tory might want to cut off my balls by the end of the night," said Frankie

"That didn't take long," said Chip.

"I sort of got busted by Tory when I got caught kissing Belle," said Frankie not proud of what he did.

"You did what to who?" asked Chip.

"Tory caught me and Belle kissing, but in my defense, Belle came up to me and kissed me not the other way around," said Frankie.

"Oh, shit Frankie why would you let Belle kiss you?" asked Chip.

"I didn't know she was going to do that," said Frankie trying to act all cool and it wasn't his fault.

"Of course, nothing is ever your fault especially when you're making out with Tory and Belle at the same time it's not your fault either," said Chip.

"Do you have a problem with me, Chip?" asked Frankie.

"No Frankie that would make you think that, said Chip sarcastically.

"By the way you're acting like a dink," said Frankie.

As Chip and Frankie stand there and exchange insults to each other Belle came over to talk to them.

"I have a solution for the both of you why don't you take it jousting?" asked Belle.

"I'm up for it if you want to or are you to scared Chip?" asked Frankie laughing at Chip.

"I was just jousting with Hazel," said Chip.

"Yeah, and you made Hazel cry and you didn't even hit her," said Frankie.

"I wouldn't go any further with that and it wasn't my intention to do that to her," said Chip.

"Yeah, right that's what you say, but you did the total opposite," said Frankie.

"Listen Frankie as Chip got in his face what is going on with Hazel and me is none of your damn business so but out," said Chip.

"You should have thought about that before everything came out," said Belle.

"Thanks for being on my side Belle," said Chip.

"Sorry Chip I didn't mean it like that, but I did ask you earlier if anything was going on between you and you said nothing," said Belle.

Chip looks at Frankie before he decides to blow up Frankie game about who he has been kissing and probably much more.

"You know what your famous cook has been doing when he is not cooking Belle?" asked Chip.

"Chip shut your mouth," said Frankie not liking where this is going.

Belle just stands there and looks confused about what is going on and looks at Chip and then at Frankie.

"Chip shut your fucking mouth, or I will do it for you," said Frankie.

"No, Frankie you're going to tell me what Chip is talking about," said Belle getting upset, but she is not sure why.

"Chip is just upset about Hazel, and he has no idea what he is talking about," said Frankie as he stares at Chip.

"I don't have time for this I need to talk to Hazel," said Chip

"No, you need to go and joust it out with me," said Frankie acting like he is a hot shot.

"I want you to look at me Frankie and tell; me what Chip is talking about?" asked Belle.

Chip gave Frankie a look.

"Come on Chip let's joust," said Frankie.

"No, I'm not going to do that," said Chip.

"Stop being such a pussy and let me punch your lights out," said Frankie.

"How dare you talk to me like that especially when I can accidently let a certain thing slip," said Chip.

"Which I hope you do so I know what the hell everyone is talking," said Belle.

"I told you it was nothing Belle," said Frankie.

"You may say nothing, but Chip is saying a lot more than you are," said Belle.

"I think Chip needs to come joust me so I can beat him for everything that has slipped out already," said Frankie.

"Am I going to find out what it's that you both are hiding, or do I need to watch you two joust the crap out of each other first?" asked Belle.

Chip thought about for a second.

"Frankie, do you remember everything you have told me about Tory and Belle," said Chip as he kept going on. Frankie was getting angry, and Belle was getting more curious about what Frankie was hiding not just about her, but also Tory too.

"Fine let's joust it out if it's the only way to shut you up," said Chip.

As they both got ready to joust everyone started to get excited that another jousting challenge was about to begin. Chip and Frankie both get their jousting poles on and were ready to fight. Serena saw what was going on and thought that Hazel should know that Chip was in another jousting match with Frankie, and it wasn't going to be a pretty fight.

The bell rings and both guys are just swinging their poles around.

"You know Frankie, you wanted me to joust and here I am, and you can't even hit me first," said Chip.

"Shut up Chip," said Frankie.

Chip lifted his arms and told Frankie to get him. Frankie came toward him and dodges him and hit him in the face with his jousting pole.

"That's all you got man wow that's wimpy of you," said Chip.

"Oh, really you want more buddy that's no problem," said Frankie as he tries hitting him again and Chip ducks down.

"Ha you missed me Frankie," laughed Chip. Frankie grabbed Chip by the neck and told him that he has him now.

"Frankie, you're hurting him knock it off," said Belle.

"Now why would I do that when he was about to tell you and everyone my secrets?" asked Frankie.

"Frankie I can't breathe let me go you bastard," said Chip trying to get out of his hold as his feet start slipping off the balance beam.

"Do you really think I'm going to let you go when you call me a bastard?" asked Frankie.

"Chip managed to get his leg up and kick Frankie down to the ground as he releases his hands on Chip's throat.

"Are you OK Chip?" asked Tory.

"Yes, I'm fine cousin thanks for asking," said Chip.

"Tory looked surprised that Chip was telling people that she was his cousin but was happy to go along with it. Frankie looked at Chip then looked at Tory and was in disbelief that they were related.

"Do you know what that means Frankie?" asked Chip as he got in his face.

Frankie couldn't look right at Chip as he mumbled the words that he slept with Tory your cousin. Belle almost dropped to the ground when she heard Frankie slept with Tory.

Frankie hit Chip square in the jaw and watched Chip go down.

"Are you OK Chip?" asked Tory as she ran up into the ring to check on him.

"Yeah, I am fine Tory," said Chip.

"Let's get you out of here before Frankie really hurts you," said Tory. Tory helps Chip get up and sits him down on the picnic table.

"Hey, I am still beating the crap out of him," said Frankie.

"That's too damn bad Frankie, I guess you will have to deal with me now," said Tory.

"What the hell are you doing Tory?" asked Frankie.

"Oh, didn't Belle tell you that I'm your next match," said Tory.

"Are you crazy I'm not going to hit you?" asked Frankie.

"Seriously Frankie you think I'm that fragile that I can't manage a little ass kicking?" asked Tory just glaring at Frankie.

"No, I don't think you're fragile if I did do you think I would have leaned you up against the food pantry and screwed you?" asked Frankie.

Camp Funhouse

Belle's heart dropped when she heard Frankie say that and she just wanted to run away and cry. Chip went over to Belle and held her and told her he was sorry what Frankie did to her you. Belle just cried in Chip's arms.

"Listen asshole there is so much we could of did with each other maybe even had a life together, but unfortunately, I can't trust you anymore," said Tory.

"You know that you can trust me Tory stop running away and being a little girl," said Frankie.

"Excuse me what was that you said?" asked Tory.

"You're a little girl who couldn't even tell me that my friend was your cousin," said Frankie.

"Who would have thought that you would confide in someone and tell them all the intimate details of our sex life?" asked Tory.

"Like I said how was I supposed to know I was talking to your cousin?" asked Frankie

"Oh, and I know I'm not the only one you mess around with," said Tory.

"What are you talking about now Tory?" asked Frankie?

"Seriously you have no idea what I'm talking about?" asked Tory.

"I wouldn't be asking if I did," said Frankie.

"It was just today that I saw you kissing Belle in the office," said Tory.

"Oh, that yes, I remember that, but for your information she kissed me first," said Chip, but just so you know I didn't know that Belle was going to kiss me.

Belle raised her head to listen to what Frankie was saying.

"Sorry Frankie, I don't believe you that you didn't know Belle was going to kiss you," said Tory.

"I didn't know I'm being honest, and the kiss met nothing to me at all," said Frankie.

Belle stood up and went towards the balance beam.

"Oh, really it meant nothing at all to you Frankie?" asked Belle.

"It did but being with Tory also meant something to me," said Frankie.

"I don't believe you at all," said Tory. "I feel the same way I don't believe you because when we were in the kitchen it felt like it met something to you," said Belle.

"Then kick the shit out of me I deserve it," said Frankie. Tory went over to Frankie and gave him a whack across the face and then his stomach which that landed him down on the ground.

"Match over I won," said Tory.

"Now it's my turn," said Belle as she grabs the jousting pole and was ready to go. "This is for lying to me as she hits him in the face, this is for making me feel like you loved me, she got him right in the stomach, and this is for all the times you dropped or burned the food," said Belle as she gives him once more hit to Frankie's nuts.

Frankie just laid there and wouldn't look at Belle.

"Oh, by the way you can finish the week here and then find another place to work because it won't be for me anymore," said Belle.

"That was quite impressive how you both ganged up on him like that," said Serena.

"Yeah, it was impressive I agree Serena, but I feel so bad also," said Belle.

"Are you OK Belle?" asked Harlow.

"Never better than I am right now," said Belle.

"I'm so sorry Belle, I know it took a lot for you to give your heart to him," said Harlow.

"Yes, it did, but someday I will find that person, but I'm not in a hurry right now after all of that," said Belle.

"Let's go back to the office and relax Belle," said Harlow as she gives her friend a hug.

"No, I still have matches that need to, finish by other people before it's over with and it can still be a great night for someone else," said Belle.

"Let's go watch the next match together," said Harlow. "Sounds like a clever idea to me," said Belle.

Tory stepped up on the balance beam holding her jousting pole and called for Belle to come up there. Harlow and Belle just look at each other.

"Why do I need to come there?" asked Belle.

"I might be done with Frankie, but I'm not done with you," said Tory.

"I'm not going to fight you if that's what you're thinking," said Belle.

"Why not we had someone in common so we should fight for him," said Tory.

"If you want Frankie go ahead, I no longer want him cooking for me or even himself," said Belle.

"I don't want him either that stopped when I saw you two kissing today," said Tory.

"Then what do you want Tory?" asked Belle as she came up to the balance beam.

"I just wanted to tell you how you're a great employer, but a lousy friend," said Tory.

"Oh, how is that possible Tory?" asked Belle.

"You take away all the men that mean a lot to me," said Tory.

"I kissed Frankie not the whole camp, so you better get your stories right," said Belle.

"Are you sure Belle?" asked Tory.

I have no idea what the hell you're talking about, but it needs to stop now?" said Belle as she pops Tory one in the face with a jousting pole.

"Whoa Belle are you OK?" asked Harlow.

"Yes, but I'll be damn if I am going to let a girl like her talk to me that way," said Belle.

"She had no reason to call you out for something you didn't do," said Harlow.

"After this week she will be gone too and I won't have to see her face," said Belle.

"We do have one issue," said Harlow.

"Which is what?" asked Belle.

"She still is Chip's cousin that you hit," said Harlow.

"He is dealing with Hazel right now so I will talk to him once everything has calm down and I'm sure he will be hopefully understanding," said Belle.

Tory comes up behind Belle, knocks her down, and hits her.

"No one hits me unless I deserve it you got that bitch," said Tory.

"No, you got that wrong you're the one being a bitch all because of a kiss," said Belle.

"I think that both of you need to get over what Frankie did," said Harlow.

Harlow looked over by the dining hall and couldn't believe that Dudley the pizza guy was back at the camp.

"Excuse me for a second Belle I'll be right back," said Harlow running towards Dudley. Dudley gave Harlow a hug when he saw her.

"Wow you're here without pizza this time," said Harlow.

"I had a way to come and see my girl so here I am," said Dudley.

"Where is your truck?" asked Harlow.

"Well, I got fired, but it's OK now I can work at my other job full time," said Dudley.

"What is your other job?" asked Harlow.

"I am a Certified Nurse's Aide at Heaven's Ridge Retirement home," said Dudley.

Harlow was in shock when she heard where he works and wasn't sure what to say.

"I'm so glad you're here everything seems to be a mess tonight," said Harlow.

"I can tell that I came at a bad time I just wanted to see you," said Dudley.

"I'm sorry I really need to take care of this mess before it gets out of hand," said Harlow.

"We can get together this weekend if you like I have it off," said Dudley.

"Yes, that sounds wonderful," said Harlow who was still freaking out.

"I'll give you a call in a couple of days," said Dudley.

"I really can't wait," said Harlow.

Dudley gave her one last kiss and then left.

"Oh, Belle I have something to tell you and I am not sure you're going to like," said Harlow.

"What's wrong now?" asked Belle.

Remember the first night and Frankie got pizza and I was making out with the pizza guy," said Harlow.

"Yes, and can we not talk about Frankie," said Belle.

"OK well that guy Dudley just showed up here and he told him he works at Heaven's Ridge," said Harlow.

"WHAT!!" yelled Belle.

"Calm down he didn't say anything about the seniors I got him out of her quickly," said Harlow.

"This night just keeps getting worse," said Belle.

"Relax Belle everything will be OK," said Harlow.

"What if he was here checking out making sure they are, OK?" asked Belle.

"He didn't ask anything just a date," said Harlow.

"You're going on a date with him?" asked Belle.

"No not really because I'm not interested in him," said Harlow.

"Well, good because we don't need anyone from Heaven's Ridge around here," said Belle.

"Well, I better see what kind of a mess we have outside I'll be back Belle," said Harlow.

Juniper was taking care of Frankie and his wounds.

"Boy you must have really ticked someone off," said Juniper.

"Yeah, I think I made a few enemies tonight," said Frankie.

"It can't truly be that bad?" asked Juniper.

"Where have you been tonight?" asked Frankie.

I didn't want to take any part of the jousting, so I stayed in here and waiting for anyone to come that needed patching up," said Juniper.

"I see that's quite wise it got crazy out there, and I was the one who caused it," said Frankie.

"How did you do that?" asked Juniper.

"I was messing around with two women, and they found out about each other," said Frankie.

"Oh, really that's very interesting," said Juniper as she wraps his ribs tight so he can't breathe.

"I'm guessing that you don't approve of that," said Frankie.

"What would make you think that?" asked Juniper.

"You tied my ribs so tight I can't really breathe," said Frankie.

"Well, I guess you're right then," said Juniper.

There was a knock at the door.

"Oh, know who that can be?" asked Frankie. I will find out when I open the door. Juniper opened the door to see who it is. Frankie could hear a voice but couldn't make out who it was.

"Yes, he is here, and I had to take care of his bruises he got when he got the shit beat out of him by more than once person," said Juniper.

Juniper shut the door and went back to Frankie.

"Who was it?" asked Frankie.

"It was Felix he wanted to make sure that the man with the broken nose was OK.

"Wow he actually cares," said Frankie.

"Only if he knew that you never even broke your nose," said Juniper.

"It's the thought that counts," said Juniper.

"I guess so I never really thought about it," Frankie.

"Well, you're all set I wouldn't try fighting or anything like that for at least a couple of weeks," said Juniper.

"Will you protect me then because it seems everyone is coming to get me?" asked Frankie.

"No, you're on your own with that," said Juniper.

"I am guessing that you're going to take Belle's and Tory's side," said Frankie.

"I wouldn't exactly say that I would just say that what you did was crappy, and no guy should mess around with two women that don't deserve it," said Juniper.

"Yeah, I will have to fix things on my own somehow, but first I need to figure out how too," said Frankie.

"Well, I'm sure there is somewhere to go to think about that, but you can't do it here," said Juniper.

"I see that I am not wanted here so I will go," said Frankie.

"All you need to do is just make things right, but for now you need to go," said Juniper.

You know that you're kind of hot when you get all uptight'" said Frankie.

"OK now you need to go so goodbye Frankie," said Juniper as she opens the door for Frankie.

"Fine thanks for taking care of me and my bruises," said Frankie as he goes out the door.

"Are you ready for your match Harlow?" asked Belle.

"Oh, is it that time right now?" asked Harlow.

"Yes, it is, Harlow," said Belle.

"Why am I doing this again Belle?" asked Harlow.

"You and Casper need to get your anger gone so both of you can move on from each other," said Belle.

It's time for our next match against Casper and Harlow.

"What no way I'm not doing it," said Casper.

"Why not Casper are you scared I might mess your hair up?" asked Harlow.

"No, I am not afraid of that happening at all and you must think your funny if you think you could beat me," said Casper.

"I don't think it's funny because I already know I can beat you," said Harlow.

"Fine I will give in just to show you how wrong you are," said Casper.

"Harlow gets the jousting pole and get on the balance beam and waits for Casper to do the same.

"Come on Casper get me," said Harlow trying to get him going.

When Juniper heard Casper's name, she glued to what was going on out there and was watching what is going on from the door.

"So, what do you want from me," said Casper.

Harlow goes up to Casper and hits him right in the stomach without even flinching.

"I want nothing from you I just want us to get whatever anger we have for each other out and be friends," said Harlow.

"I don't have anger towards you Harlow," said Casper.

"Then how come we had a fight the first day here because I was talking to the pizza guy?" asked Harlow.

"You can't control yourself when it comes to guys and that worries me because I feel like I have to protect you," said Casper.

Harlow hits him in the face this time to make him stop talking.

"That damn bitch thinks she can just go and punch him for no reason," said Juniper.

"Harlow will you stop hitting me with that thing?" asked Casper.

"Yes, I do Casper ever since you left me has been on my mind and because you made me feel like everything was my fault when it's you that ran away," said Harlow starting to cry.

"I left because I felt you didn't love me enough and that I couldn't make you happy anymore," said Casper.

"That's where you're wrong, I was happy with you and I even tried to show you, but you turned me down especially those times I wanted to get sexual with you," said Harlow.

"I guess I didn't see it enough and that's why I left, but there is nothing we can do about it now," said Casper.

"Why is that?" asked Harlow hoping there was still a chance for her. Juniper just watched from the sidelines to see what he is going to say.

Casper struggled how to tell Harlow about him moving on with Juniper.

"Sorry Harlow I moved on and I am with someone else who I do love and shows it back to me," said Casper who put his head down because he felt bad.

"Oh, shit he is really going to tell her about us," said Juniper biting her lip and panicking a little bit. Juniper keeps watching Casper and Harlow as he tells her that he is in love with Juniper.

"Who could that possibly be Casper?" asked Harlow.

Juniper looks right at Casper, and she gave him a nod letting him know it was OK that he told Harlow.

"Answer me Casper there is no reason you can't be honest with me," said Harlow.

"I'm in love with Juniper," yelled out Casper.

Everyone looked surprised when he said it. Harlow just stood there and stared at Casper.

"Well, OK I'm not sure what to say," said Harlow.

"Sorry Harlow, but I had to move on," said Casper.

"Yeah, sure I get it and now I must do the same," said Harlow as she gives a look to Art.

"I'm truly sorry Harlow," said Casper as he wasn't sure what else he could say to make this better for her.

"I just got one last thing to say to you have a nice life asshole," said Harlow as she punched him hard in the stomach and then walked away. Harlow got down from the balance beam and stared right at Casper as she went running away.

"Good luck he is your problem not mine anymore," said Harlow as she went passed Juniper.

"He was much happier with me, anyway," said Juniper.

"Oh, really bitch you really want to go there?" asked Harlow.

"I already did," said Juniper.

"You better close your trap, or I can do it for you," said Harlow.

Belle overheard Harlow and couldn't believe how she was talking to Juniper.

"You need to tell Juniper your sorry," said Belle.

"Why should I she took Casper from me," said Harlow trying to hit Juniper, but Belle stood in the way.

He was never your sweetie he left you a long time ago, said Belle.

Casper hasn't been yours for a couple of years now so it's time to let go," said Belle.

"Fine, whatever I'm gone, and I hope you're all happy," said Harlow as she runs towards the hill.

Casper tries to run after her, but Belle stops him.

"Give her sometimes she will be OK," said Belle.

Juniper just looked at him and he went over to her and gave her a hug. It wasn't long when Harlow was gone and came back but didn't say anything to anyone.

Everyone ignored her so that there was no more trouble at least that's what they were hoping.

"Can we get back to me and how hurt I am?" asked Harlow.

"Grow up Harlow I'm sure it isn't the first time a guy has dumped you before you're being so dramatic," said Juniper.

"You bitch why would you even say that to me?" asked Harlow as she kept going after Juniper.

"Harlow go and cool off somewhere," said Belle.

"Fine Belle you don't need to be such a bitch either," said Harlow as she goes stomping off and Art right behind her.

Art followed Harlow to wherever she was heading because he didn't want her to be alone like she was before.

"Hey how are you doing?" asked Art.

"I'm OK I guess you don't need to stay with me if you don't want too," said Harlow.

"Trust me here is nowhere I rather be then with you sweetheart," said Art.

"Then I would love your company," said Harlow.

"You saved my life Harlow when, I was stuck to the golfcart by my t shirt, so I am returning the favor," said Art.

"Well, I didn't want anything more to happen to you more than the bruises you got, and I was so worried about you," said Harlow.

"How about the fun we had in the bathroom," said Art trying to make her smile.

"That was fun and they first time I did something in the bathroom," said Harlow.

Dudley what about we did in your vehicle was fun for the both of us, said Harlow.

"Harlow, I don't know what you want or even if you want me, but I do think you're attractive, funny, and a great personality and if it's time you need, I will give it to you," said Art.

"Appreciate it Art and thank you," said Harlow.

Belle ran past them and stopped to see if everything is OK.

"How are you both doing?" asked Belle

We are both going to be OK as Harlow puts her head or Art's shoulder. I'm glad to see a smile on your face and I honestly didn't think you were going to walk down the hill because you're not a fan of the dark," said Belle. They all just laughed.

"Can you believe tonight and what Harlow said to me?" asked Casper.

"Sorry but, Belle was right you did embarrass her in front of everyone and didn't think of her feelings," said Juniper.

"Oh, so you're going to take Belle?" asked Casper.

"Casper think about it you spilled the beans and you told everyone that was watching that match that you loved someone else, and you were over Harlow so it's not me agreeing with Belle, said Juniper.

"Shit, your right your right Juniper," said Casper as he puts his head down.

"Sorry Juniper maybe next time I should just be honest before opening your mouth and say the wrong," said Juniper.

"I have to admit you're right and I am a jerk," said Casper.

"You followed your heart so that's not a wrong thing be happy you deserve it, and we deserve it together," said Juniper.

"I agree let's be happy together," said Casper as they kiss.

"Can you do something for me?" asked Juniper.

"Yes, I will do anything for you my love," said Casper.

"I think it's only right that you apologize to Harlow so that you two can be friends and not enemies," said Juniper.

Casper thought about for a minute and see's Juniper point and agreed to apologize to Harlow.

"This will be our last match of the night I do hope you enjoyed it and I hope you have a good night after," said Belle.

"Let's see more jousting," yelled Jasper who as really getting into it. "Will you shut up?" asked Hank.

"OK everyone let's calm down and watch the last match," said Serena.

"Next, we have Tinsley and Eloise," said Belle.

"Excuse me what in the hell is going on here?" asked Eloise.

"We are going to joust bitch so get ready to get the hell knocked out hard by my stick," said Tinsley.

"OK well that's crazy even for you to think I will do that with you of all people," said Eloise.

"I want to play a friendly game of jousting and maybe beat the crap out of you because of how annoying you're and how you just don't care what goes on with anything," said Tinsley.

"Still not doing it and I never said I didn't care," said Eloise.

"I don't care I will whack you off this balance beam you if you don't want to get this match going makes no difference to me," said Tinsley.

"You won't do it because you will break a nail or something and cry all the way home," said Eloise.

"That just shows how you don't know me bitch," said Tinsley.

"Tinsley takes her jousting pole and hands the other one to Eloise.

"If you won't do it up here, we can do it any place just tell me where and when," said Tinsley already to go.

"Fine we can do this, but don't tell me I didn't warn you," said Eloise.

"Are you ready to rumble Eloise?" asked Tinsley as she gave Eloise the evil eyes.

"Is that honestly supposed to scare me because I don't know what it's supposed to mean?" asked Eloise.

"No, I'm just showing you how serious I am about beating the crap out of you," said Tinsley as she gives Eloise a hit and she goes down fast.

"That's all you got is pushing me down bitch?" asked Eloise as she gets up and punches Tinsley in the face with the jousting pole.

"Wow you have guts to hit me in the face I guess I should return the favor as Tinsley's attempts to hit Eloise," said Tinsley,

"You're not so quick like you like people think you are," said Eloise just walking away.

"Really that's all you got one hit and you're done," said Tinsley as she goes after Eloise and rips her shirt.

"I thought you got the point that I'm done and now you're making mad," said Eloise.

"I just wanted you to see that you need to care whether it's with all the counselors or even the seniors," said Tinsley.

"Why would I be concerned about the seniors when it was Fay, Hazel, and Chips fault in the first place," said Eloise.

"We all need you just not the attitude you give us daily and the seniors that are still here care and need you," said Tinsley.

"You are right, said Eloise.

"What is your problem with me anyways?" asked Tinsley.

"You act like you're better than all of us," said Eloise.

"No, I don't I'm a very caring person and if you got to know me you would know I am not that kind of girl," said Tinsley.

"I still find you annoying, but OK I get it so sorry for everything except hitting you that felt good," said Eloise.

"Let's just finish the week out and just be happy with each other then we won't have to see each other again," said Tinsley.

"I'll try, but I can't promise that I won't want to hit you again and oh by the way I was the one who put the gum in your hair the first night we were here," said Eloise.

"Why would you do that to me?" asked Tinsley.

"It's simple I wanted too," laughed Eloise.

"Never mind it's not worth it I'm just going to walk away," said Tinsley.

"That's right bitch walks away," said Eloise to herself.

Belle got on the balance beam and made her little speech that she usually does.

"Thank you for everyone that came tonight sorry everything got all crazy and out of order and I wanted this to be fun for all of you, so congratulations to all the ones who participated and won, and I'll see you tomorrow for more Mystic Camp fun," said Belle.

"Are you OK as Casper takes Juniper in his arms and kisses her on the cheek?" asked Casper.

"Yes, I am, and I can totally manage Harlow and her temper tantrum," said Juniper chuckling.

"Yeah, you can manage anything and thank you for setting me straight and I did exactly what you asked, said Casper.

Juniper just looked at him for a second until it dawned on her what she asked him to do.

"I'm glad you apologize now maybe we can move on from all of this Harlow drama," said Juniper.

"I hope so and I think it's a clever idea that we go back to my room and relax," said Casper.

"That sounds like good idea and the best idea I have heard all day," said Juniper.

Everyone was back to their cabins or rooms and nursing all their bruises and hurt feelings. It was a night to get everything out in the open and that was one thing that Belle wanted especially for Chip and Hazel. Belle just didn't think it would be her heart that was broke again this time by Frankie of all people. Tomorrow will be another day and hopefully everything that happened can be fixed and not broken and everyone can move on, and everything can get back to normal even know no one knows what is normal anymore.

CHAPTER 23

Farfrompoopen Road

The seniors go to the next door which is brown with meat hanging from the door.

"That is so gross," said Edith trying not to puke.

"Why would someone think to do that?" asked Tallulah.

"I don't think we should go in this room it seems to me that maybe someone is playing a sick joke with us," said Wanda.

"We will be fine don't worry about its Wanda," said Agnes.

"If you think it's safe then fine I will," said Wanda.

"You are worried for no reason," said Edith.

"Why do you say that?' asked Wanda.

Edith went up to the meat hanging on the door and touched one.

"Ewe that's so gross," said Wanda.

"Wanda it's a dog toy," said Edith as she squeezes the toy, and it starts squeaking.

"Oh, OK now I feel better about going in the room," laughed Wanda. Tallulah started laughing.

"What are you laughing about Tallulah?" asked Agnes. All of you actually thought it as real meat and it's a dog's chew toy," laughed Tallulah.

"Oh, Tallulah shut up," said Agnes. "Oh boy someone has their cranky pants on," said Tallulah.

"At least I know how to keep mine up," laughed Agnes.

Tallulah just put her head down and shut up.

"OK let's go through the door," said Edith as she opened the door and there was a strange odor coming from the room.

"Did someone fart or something it stinks in here?" asked Wanda as she plugged her nose.

"Everyone turned and looked at Tallulah and she just shook her head no. "Why is it always me?" asked Tallulah.

"You are the one that's always doing something," said Agnes.

I'm a good girl," said Tallulah.

"Yeah, sure you're we just haven't seen it yet," said Wanda.

"Well gee thanks for having faith in me everyone but remember who got the key so we can be here," said Tallulah as she looks and sees what is on the table.

As everyone stepped closer to the table, they could see a white tablecloth on the table like it was going to be a fancy meal.

"I hope whatever is under these tops is something good," said Edith.

Tallulah got closer and realize there was only five place settings with five plates.

"I guess the rest of us are going to starve because there are no plates for all of us," said Wanda.

"That's OK with me after the whole pudding challenge, I rather not try what might or might be under those tops," said Blanche.

"I have a bad feeling about this, and it's never good when there is automatically a puke bucket at every setting," said Edith.

"Well, at least they have one this time because the pudding challenge didn't have any of this," said Blanche.

"That's true and it would have been nice to have something to put all those gross things that Mona put on me somewhere else then putting them all over the floor," said Edith.

"Listen I'm going to say this so everyone can hear me," said Mona.

"I'm sorry that all happened, and I am truly apologizing to you Edith," said Mona.

"Yeah, I feel the love," said Edith.

"Oh, will you stop being, so pig headed no offense to what is under these tops," said Agnes.

"Can we just get this over with and then we can be each other's therapy session," said Tallulah.

Everyone agreed to just let it go for now.

Beau had noticed the challenge card sitting in the middle of the table against the flowers that look like they have seen better days. Beau reached for the card and volunteered himself to read what the challenge was going to be. Be our guest Beau," said Edith.

"It's time to eat and you all must be hungry, but only five people must participate in this challenge, each place setting has a plate of a deli meat and a sauce on top of it, you must eat the whole thing and if you fail at this challenge a punishment will be ready for you.

"So, who here is hungry enough to eat what has served to you on this challenge?" asked Beau.

"Let's just see what we are in for before deciding who is doing it," said Agnes.

"That sounds like a clever idea," said Mona.

Everyone went around the table and looked at the different cards that were set out in front of the plates.

"Roast beef with Monkeygland sauce sounds like the Groat pudding we did in the other challenge," said Tallulah. I agree to that,' said Edith.

It sounds like this one is not for me," said Wanda.

"It sounds interesting so that might be the one for me, but I am still not sure," said Mona.

"You said almost the same thing when you tried the pudding that you didn't like," said Edith.

"That is true also, but you never know what can be," said Mona.

"Let's just go to the next one," said Miles.

"Ham with mumbo sauce," said Mona.

"It sounds fruity and spicy all mixed together," said Edith.

"Maybe it could be almost like a sweet and sour sauce or something," said Agnes.

"Don't you usually put that on chicken or something?" asked Tallulah.

It doesn't sound half bad to me so I might take this one if no one else wants it," said Wanda as she sits down in front of it.

"Well, OK I hope you enjoy it Wanda," said Blanche.

"This next plate I just don't understand I guess it's not sinking into my brain," said Beau.

"What is that darling?" asked Mona.

"This one said Bologna with Comeback sauce," said Beau.

"Yes, it does darling," said Mona trying to understand what he is talking about.

"Where are we coming back from?" asked Beau.

"I agree it's a tricky thing to understand, but maybe it means we are coming back to the best challenge that's yet to come," said Mona who is just trying to make Beau feel better.

"I guess sweetie, but you never know they could be tricking us somehow," said Beau.

"I'm sure no one is trying to do that it's just something they want us to try and eat," said Mona.

"YUCK!!"

"What's wrong Vera?" asked Tallulah.

"I don't like bologna," said Vera.

"Well, you don't have to eat it if you don't want to there are two more that we still have to go too," said Tallulah.

"Yes, I know smartass," said Vera as she walks away.

I was only trying to help," said Tallulah.

"We know that Vera is just being Vera I guess if that makes sense," said Agnes.

"Are we almost done going through these?" asked Edith.

"We have two more than its decision time," said Agnes.

"Oh, great I can't wait not really," said Edith.

"This one doesn't sound half," said Miles to himself.

"How about corned beef and banana ketchup?" asked Blanche.

"It sounds good, and I love ketchup," said Miles.

"Even though it's banana ketchup?" asked Blanche.

"It can't be too different then the regular kind of ketchup," said Miles.

"If you want this one then you can have it Miles," said Agnes.

"Sure, why not," said Miles acting all excited to try the Corned beef with the Banana ketchup.

"I've never seen someone so excited to try something it's so weird," said Tallulah.

"Whatever floats his boat," said Edith.

I agree with you sister," said Tallulah.

"We aren't sister," said Edith.

"No, it's just an expression, but we are good friends so we could be sisters and I know that Mona is your sister," said Tallulah.

"That is so sweet that you think of me that way and yes Mona is my sister I am not claiming that she is," said Edith.

"Well, I do, but we need to focus on the challenge now," said Tallulah trying to get off the subject.

"Yes, your right you're so smart Tallulah,' said Edith.

"Don't let that get out then everyone will want to be me," laughed Tallulah.

"OK I won't it will be our secret," said Edith.

"Are you two with done your pow wow?" asked Agnes.

"Yes, we are," said Tallulah.

"So, what is the last one?" asked Tallulah.

"Turkey with Salsa Golf this one seems to be calling my name and I'm going to try it," said Beau.

"Why is that darling?" asked Mona.

"It has my two favorite things Salsa and golf," laughed Beau.

Wanda was listening to Mona and Beau conversations to see what they were talking about.

"I don't think there is going to be a golf ball on the turkey," said Wanda.

"You never know that's why I will be surprised when I try it," said Beau.

I bet you will be buddy," said Edith.

"Leave him alone Edith I think it's cute that he is so happy about this," said Mona.

"I'm sure he is happy after everything you have done for him and with him," said Edith as she walks away.

"I don't get why she needs to be such a bitch after all of these years," said Mona.

"I don't know sweetie, but someday she will come around," said Beau.

"I hope so because I actually miss her as my sister even when it was my choice to leave when I was younger," said Mona.

"Once we get back to camp, we can all sit down and talk," said Beau.

"OK who wants which one of the three plates left?" asked Tallulah.

"I'll do that Bologna and Comeback sauce," said Agnes.

"Congratulations Agnes," said Edith.

"Why is that?" asked Agnes.

"This is your first food challenge you have done," said Edith.

"There has only been one before this one and I told you I don't eat Pudding," said Agnes.

"Yes, I know Agnes sorry I was cheering for you I didn't know it was a crime," said Edith.

"Well, it didn't seem like it," said Agnes.

"OK you two knock it off we still have two more plates to go," said Tallulah.

"How about you Tallulah?" asked Wanda.

"Nah not this time around I am still burping up the Pudding," said Tallulah.

"Doesn't surprise me that you're not," said Wanda.

Tallulah leans across the table facing Wanda.

"Shut it Wanda," said Tallulah. Do you want to make me bitch?" asked Wanda.

"OK you two knock it off we are here to have fun and get this challenge started and done with," said Mona.

"Have fun knocking her out," said Tallulah.

"We already had a noodle match we don't need to do it all over again," said Agnes.

Wanda got tired of Tallulah's mouth and stood up from her chair and walked right in front of Tallulah.

"Hit me," said Wanda trying to get Tallulah going.

"Tallulah lifted her fist as high as it could go but couldn't do it.

"I knew you wouldn't do it because you're kind and you wouldn't hurt a fly," said Wanda.

"That was so sweet of you to say, but you forgot one thing Wanda," said Tallulah.

"Oh boy this isn't going to be good I can tell," said Agnes.

"What's that Tallulah as Wanda gets right in her face?" asked Wanda.

WHACK! Tallulah hits Wanda in the face. Wanda landed by the table which was able to catch her fall.

"Not again sometimes I feel like I'm with a bunch of children," said Agnes.

"Come on you two enough of that we need to get this challenge going," said Edith.

"You saw it she started it," said Wanda.

"Yeah, she did, but you egged her on Wanda," said Agnes.

"Yeah, OK it's always me," said Wanda.

"It's the both of you not just you," said Edith.

"Now both of you sit and let's do this," said Agnes.

"I'm not in this challenge," said Tallulah.

"Then back away so we can get this down," said Agnes.

"Fine I will," said Tallulah as she left with her hands folded.

"Why every challenge is there drama?" asked Agnes.

"We all want attention and that's the only way to do it I guess," said Beau.

"I actually think that you're right Beau," said Agnes.

Everyone that's participating sits in their spots table and ready to begin the challenge.

"I think that we should take our tops off together and just dig in," said Agnes.

"I really don't think taking our tops off is a clever idea Wanda," said Wanda.

"I'm talking about the tops on the plates Wanda," said Agnes.

"Oh, sorry I thought you met our tops," said Wanda embarrassed.

"I really don't think it will be as bad as the pudding challenge," said Miles.

"You could be right Miles I guess the only way we will know is to try it," said Wanda.

"Should we count to three again?" asked Agnes.

"Nah that wasn't so effective before," said Wanda.

"Can we just get this done and over with?" asked Vera.

"So much for patients I guess, but then again it's Vera so that just sums it up," said Agnes.

"We are talking about Vera and I'm sure she doesn't have any patients," said Tallulah.

"That's kind of what I just said a second ago," said Agnes.

"Watch your mouth," said Vera.

"What are you going to do to me Vera?" asked Tallulah.

"Please don't provoke her," said Agnes.

"You will see if you don't shut the hell up," said Vera.

"You're crazy," laughed Tallulah.

"Stop calling me crazy," said Vera.

"Tallulah stop or this challenge will never start or finished, and Vera is willing to do this challenge," said Agnes.

"Oh, alright I will stop," said Tallulah.

"OK now that everything is all settled now are we all ready to chow down?" asked Agnes.

Everyone answered, but one person. Agnes looked over at Beau and saw he had already started eating what was on his plate.

"Why didn't you wait for us?" asked Agnes.

"I was hungry and if I had to wait for all you to stop bitching and moaning then I would be waiting a long time," said Beau.

"OK I understand and get it so let's chow down," said Agnes.

Everyone took off the top and looked what they were going to be eating.

"Doesn't look half bad I will have to say that," said Wanda.

"Looks normal and tasty to me," said Agnes as she looks at hers.

"So, who wants to take the first bite?" asked Agnes.

"I guess since I already did, I'll tell you what it tastes like to me," said Beaus.

"OK that sounds fair," Wanda.

"The turkey tastes like it real like Thanksgiving and there as definitely salsa, but no golf ball like I was hoping, but it was if there had been a golf ball there it has a very unfamiliar taste," said Beau.

"Can I try a little bit?" asked Mona.

"Sure, my love," said Beaus as he takes a little and feeds it to her.

Mona starts chewing it with a weird look on her face.

"Not too bad there is a taste that I can't identify with the salsa, but it's good," said Mona.

Wanda tasted her Ham and Mumbo sauce and as she took a bite, she swished it around in her mouth and looked around and took another bite.

"So, what do you think Wanda?" asked Edith.

"It's not bad either it's a little spicey with just a kick of sour taste in it," said Wanda.

"That is a good mixture," said Edith.

"So, to me it's BBQ sauce with a little kick of something that I just can't describe," said Wanda.

"Well so far everything has been good so that means that the rest of us will be even better," said Agnes.

"Then why don't you try yours Agnes?" asked Wanda.

"Someone else can go next if they want, I'm in no hurry to try mine," said Agnes.

As Vera sits next to Agnes, she started to get nervous.

"You have a choice either you can eat it, or I'll make you wear it," said Vera.

"That's not nice Vera to say that to me," said Agnes.

"Well stop being such a chicken and eat it," said Vera as she gets closer to Agnes.

"Alright I'll just back off Vera," said Agnes. Agnes took a bite and thought it tasted just like the sauce they used on McDonalds Big Mac.

"It probably shouldn't be on bologna maybe roast beef or something, but it's good and now makes me want Big Mac and I haven't had one in years," said Agnes.

"For me it has to be close to thirty years since I have had anything from Mc Donald's," said Wanda.

"Yeah, it has been a while for me also," said Agnes.

"Anyways let's just keep moving on," said Mona.

I can't wait to dip into that ketchup," said Miles as he just puts the whole Corned beef and Banana ketchup in his mouth.

"Did he just inhaled that?" asked Tallulah.

"Yes, he sure did," said Agnes.

"Miles did you swallow all of it or is it still in your mouth?" asked Tallulah.

"Can't you see his mouth is full and he isn't able to answer you," said Edith.

"Well, you never know he could of swallow it whole," said Tallulah.

"Yes, girls I am fine, and it was delicious, and I wish I could have another one," said Miles.

"You can have mine," said Vera.

"No dear that's OK I want you to have it for yourself," said Miles.

Vera was about to throw it at him when she realized if she did then they would have to do an extra challenge and didn't want to do that because she already volunteered once, and it didn't need to have to do a challenge by herself.

"So, what exactly did it taste like?" asked Wanda.

"To tell you the truth I don't really know I ate it quickly I don't remember tasting it," said Miles.

Just going to guess it was great since you did that and you wanted another one," said Wanda.

"I've never seen anyone eat that fast," said Tallulah very impressive.

"OK Vera it's your turn to try your Roast beef with Monkey Gland sauce," said Agnes.

"Here you can taste it for me Agnes I insist," said Vera.

"No that's OK I had my own to try Vera, but thank you for asking," said Agnes.

"Thanks for having my back idiot," said Vera.

"Now Vera stops acting like a child and just eat it so we can get out of here," said Agnes.

"Fine be that way," said Vere as she took the whole thing in her mouth and didn't do anything after that.

"Swallow it Vera," said Agnes watching Vera's eyes get big.

"Is she choking?" asked Tallulah.

"No, she is just holding it in her mouth and not swallowing," said Agnes.

"This is not a joke Vera just swallow the damn meat," said Wanda.

Finally, Vera swallowed everything, but then started to act strange more than usual. Vera got out of her chair and started jumping like a monkey.

"Seriously why now does she have to do this when we are all done with this challenge?" asked Agnes.

"OK I have had enough I say we just forget that she is acting like a damn monkey and go," said Wanda.

"Yeah, I agree because I want to get out of her and onto something else," said Tallulah.

"OK Vera you can keep acting like a monkey or you can stop so we can move on," said Agnes.

It didn't work at all Vera as she was still jumping around until she suddenly just stopped and stood there.

"What is she doing?" asked Tallulah.

"I really don't have the faintness idea," said Agnes.

"Well, are we going or just stand here like morons?" asked Vera.

"So now we can move on to the next challenge," said Miles.

"Good because now this room is making my skin crawl for whatever reason," said Agnes.

Well, I have to say that food challenge went better than the last one," said Wanda.

"Yeah, it was rather good stuff this time around," said Miles.

"I'm just hoping that there are no more food challenges, and it will be smooth sailing from here," said Agnes.

"How many more do you real think we will have to do?" asked Tallulah.

"Not sure but let's just get it done so we can get to the end of this and hopefully go back to camp," said Edith.

"Someone must be worried about us by now," said Agnes.

"Yeah, I was thinking the same thing," said Tallulah.

Everyone waited by the door and were ready to head out.

On to the next challenge...

CHAPTER 24

Hanky-Panky Lane: The Truth Must Come Out

"This is a nice red door," said Tallulah.

"Hanky-Panky Lane," said Agnes as she read the sign on the door.

"Oh boy there better be none of that in here," said Wanda.

"Why not?" asked Mona as she laughs.

"You and lover boy over there already went under the pillows," said Wanda.

"Let's just go in and see what it's all about," said Tallulah as she let herself in. Everyone went into the room and couldn't believe everything that was in there which were two love seats with red and pink pillows and a mirror on the ceiling. Agnes looked up at the mirror and she couldn't believe what she looked like.

"Wow," said Agnes.

"This room is so beautiful I just can't get over it," said Tallulah.

Wanda also looks up to the mirror and saw herself.

"Do I really look that fat?" asked Wanda who kept posing in the mirror.

"No Wanda the mirror adds ten pounds so your good," said Agnes.

"Oh, OK that's good I was starting to worry if I was that fat," said Wanda.

"Yes, Wanda you still have your girlish figure unlike the rest of us," said Tallulah.

"Girlish figure I haven't had one of those in years all I have now is a large rump," said Mona.

"Well, you look beautiful to me my darling," said Beau.

"It looks like I got mine back," said Wanda as she sucks in her stomach and lets it all out.

"Has anyone seen our next challenge card?" asked Edith.

Everyone looks all around to find it and it was a tough time find it. Agnes finds it in between the couch cushions and realizes on the stand that there are glasses on wine.

"Hey everyone, who wants wine," said Agnes.

"Did Agnes just say wine?" asked Tallulah as she is looking all over for the glass of wine.

"It's right here Tallulah," said Agnes as she points it out to her.

"Oh boy it's real wine," said Tallulah just chugging it down.

"Was it good Tallulah," laughed Mona.

"Oh yes it was as," said Tallulah as she let out a burb.

"That was attractive Tallulah," said Miles.

"I never claimed to be a good-mannered woman their Miles," said Tallulah.

"I can see that," said Miles as he just shakes his head.

"Leave her alone Miles this is the one thing so far that makes her happy so let her have the wine," said Agnes.

"No problem there," said Miles as he walked away.

"Hey, I found the clue," said Tallulah as she moves the glasses of wine over a little to get the clue on the table."

"I actually found it in between the couch cushions, but I forgot about once I saw the wine," said Agnes.

"Give it to me," snapped Edith as she rips it out of Tallulah's hand. "Wow can you be anymore rude?" asked Tallulah.

"Whatever Tallulah go and drink another glass?" said Edith.

"Oh boy this isn't going to be a fun challenge I can tell," said Agnes.

"OK what does the clue say Edith?" asked Wanda.

"Get ready for the truth to come out, you must answer the question aloud and answer all the questions that are in the bowl. All questions must answer if you refuse to read a question of give an answer than you must do a punishment by yourself.

"This is going to be a fun challenge I can tell," said Blanche.

"Well, I have nothing to hide so I am not worried," said Wanda.

"Get ready for the skeletons to come out of the closet," said Agnes.

"What skeletons?" asked Tallulah.

"Don't worry Tallulah there aren't really skeletons in the closet in fact I don't even see a closet, so we are all good," said Agnes. Agnes looks down on the floor and see's Vera laying on the floor making snow angels in the mirror.

Mona stopped and wondered what Agnes was looking at until she saw Vera and then it came clear that.

"Vera have you lost your mind?" asked Wanda.

"Whatever makes Vera happy let her do it," said Agnes.

"Yeah, I agree with you Agnes," said Mona still watching her.

Everyone sat on the couches and got ready for this challenge to begin.

"So, who wants to go first?" asked Wanda. Everyone just looked at each other and no one said anything.

"I'll start then we can just pass it down to everyone," said Agnes. She picked out the first question and opened it. As she looked at it, she started laughing.

"What does it say?" asked Edith.

"Oh, this is so funny," said Agnes.

"Then read us the question," said Wanda.

"My question is if I have every gone skinny dipping before," laughed Agnes.

"Oh, nice question," said Tallulah.

"Would you like to answer it then?" asked Agnes.

"No that's your question," said Tallulah.

"OK so to answer the question no, I haven't, and I don't plan on it," said Agnes.

"It's not that bad I have done it before just having the water touch my naked body made it feels good," said Wanda.

"For some reason that doesn't surprise me," said Mona.

"I'm surprised Tallulah hasn't said if she has or not," said Blanche.

"No, I have not," said Tallulah.

"There is your answer Blanche," said Agnes.

"Wanda your turn to pick a question," said Agnes.

"Oh, goody I hope mine is a juicy one," said Wanda.

Agnes just handed Wanda the bowl so she can pick a question. Wanda unfolded the paper and was excited to see what her question was going to be.

"Go ahead and read it," said Edith.

"Was I a virgin before you got married to your husband.

"Yes, I sure was because in my family you don't have sex until you're married," said Wanda.

"It was like that in my house to my mom was extremely strict with us on that," said Agnes.

"I was married to many times to stay a virgin for them all," said Tallulah.

"How many times have you been married?" asked Mona.

"I was married I think three or four times that last husband died quickly after we were married and every one of them it just seems our marriage was a blur because one minute they're there and one minute they're dead," said Tallulah.

"I'm sorry to hear that Tallulah," said Edith.

"My real love died and left me, and I didn't want to be alone, so I kept getting married," said Tallulah.

"Being alone is not easy I felt the same way when my husband died, but I never wanted anyone else," said Agnes.

"Losing a loved one is never easy," said Tallulah.

"We are all here for you Tallulah when you need us," said Edith.

"I have amazing friends," said Tallulah.

"That was a sincere thing for you to say," said Agnes.

Wanda passed the bowl to Mona next, and she picked one out.

"Hope it's a juicy one," said Wanda.

Mona was scared what the question might be, but she took one from the bowl.

"Come on read it Mona," said Agnes.

Mona took a deep breathe then looked at the question she picked.

"What is the most bizarre nickname that you have ever had?" asked Mona

"That is good question," said Beau.

"Why is that?" asked Mona.

"Well, I never knew you backed then so I thought it was something I could get to know you better I didn't mean anything by it," said Beau.

"I guess back in high school they used to call me hot buns," said Mona.

"Why is that?" asked Agnes.

"I guess back in high school I had a nice set of buns," said Mona.

"Well, I think you still do have great buns," said Beau as he tries to pinch Mona's ass, but she stopped him.

"I used to be called hot lips when I was younger because I was such a good kisser," said Wanda.

"Can I try those lips out?" asked Miles.

"No, we can't Miles," said Wanda.

"Ouch that must have hurt being shot down again," laughed Tallulah. BURB!

"Well excuse you Tallulah," laughed Edith.

"Anyone else have any bizarre names?" asked Agnes.

"People call me crazy," said Tallulah and I don't know why.

"Probably because you're crazy, but I love you a bunch," said Agnes.

"Yeah, sure I feel the love," said Tallulah.

"Now it's your turn sweetie pie," said Mona to Beau.

"What is your biggest regret.

"That is a tough one," said Beau.

"My biggest regret was drinking all that wine," said Tallulah as she laid on the floor near Vera.

"I told you not to drink them all," said Agnes.

"Yeah, yeah, yeah," said Tallulah.

"I guess you can say my biggest regret is not finding Mona sooner in life and seeing what kind of future we could have had before coming to Heaven's Ridge," said Beau.

"Oh, Beau you're the sweetest man in the world, and I would have loved to spend the rest of my life with you," said Mona.

I know that we all live at Heaven's Ridge, but that shouldn't stop you from bring together after we leave camp, said Wanda.

I agree with Wanda, you found each other instantly when we came to camp don't let going back to Heaven's Ridge change what you have, said Agnes.

"I love you Beau and that isn't going to change whether we are in this funhouse, or camp, and or even Heaven's Ridge I am yours forever," said Mona putting her head on his shoulder.

"I would like that to very much so," said Beau as he gives Mona a kiss.

"Aww that's so sweet," said Tallulah as she waves her legs in the air.

"What are you doing Tallulah?" asked Agnes.

"Just exercising my legs," said Tallulah.

"Are you feeling OK Tallulah?" asked Edith.

"Yeah, I feel find Vera found a snack or something and shared it with me and I feel great," said Tallulah.

Everyone watch Vera and she was standing on her head.

"Should we be concerned?" asked Mona.

"Nah they aren't killing each other so their fine to me," said Agnes.

"Should we go on to the next person or keep watching them?" asked Wanda.

"Let's keep going because Tallulah and Vera are just out of their minds," said Agnes.

"It's your turn Edith," said Agnes.

Edith digs down deep for the right question.

"I got it," said Edith.

"OK so now what does it say?" asked Agnes.

"Have you ever cheated on anyone in your life.

"No, I haven't that was easy," said Edith.

"Really you never cheated on a boyfriend or husband before?" asked Wanda.

"No, I don't believe in cheating it's bad," said Edith.

"Well, that was simple," said Blanche.

"Now it's your turn big boy," said Wanda, as she winks at Miles.

"Oh, goody my turn," said Miles. He was happy with whatever he pulled out of the bowl.

"What was the greatest day of your life. Miles sat there and thought it about it for a little while because it was a tough for him to think of just one just thing.

"Well, when I was a teenager, I had always wanted to run a successful business just like my dad and so, I put myself through college for business and saved any money that I earned for it, and I went for a loan at a bank and then within a year I was a proud owner of a huge night club," said Miles.

"Wow that's interesting Miles," said Agnes.

"What was the name of your night club?" asked Tallulah.

"My night club was called Shake It, Don't Break It," said Miles.

"That is a very interesting name for a night club," said Agnes.

"I think I have been there before," said Tallulah.

"Have you Tallulah or is the snack Vera gave you still making you loopy?" asked Agnes.

"No, I really think I have been there, and my first husband and I went there to go dancing back in the seventies," said Tallulah.

"Sure, you have been," said Miles.

"Let me see if I can remember it had a disco ball, and it had wallpaper with crazy wild colors and a painting of a one-hundred-dollar bill one of the walls," said Tallulah.

"Yes, Tallulah that's correct," said Miles.

"Sounds like it was a happening place to be," said Agnes.

"It was and thank you very much Agnes," said Miles. I'm just wondering something?" asked Tallulah.

"Oh boy I don't think this is going to be good," said Edith.

"Sure, Tallulah ask me anything my sweet," said Miles.

"Why are you such a horny toad, but actually I mean why did bring a bottle of Viagra to camp?" asked Tallulah.

"That isn't as bad as I thought she would say," said Edith.

"I like to please the women without getting attached to them," said Miles.

"Oh, I see," said Tallulah as she just ignores Miles.

"Blanche, you're next so pick a question any question," said Miles.

"I think I will take this one," said Blanche. Blanche picked up the paper and looked at the question before reading it.

"So, what does it say?" asked Agnes.

"It asks if I'm afraid of getting old," said Blanche.

"When I was fifty, I had my first heart attack and at that time I wasn't scared, but I wanted to live a long healthy life, so I vowed to myself to do things that made me happy and keep myself healthy as well," said Blanche as tears come down her face.

"I'm sorry to hear that happened to you," said Edith.

"My next heart attack was ten years later and this time I was under a lot of stress when things with my family were happening, and I had to have surgery which scared the living hell out of me, and I thought I was going to die and so yeah, I am in my seventies now almost eighty and I am scared that every time I fall asleep, I won't be here anymore, and I won't be with you and that's why I hopped on the bus to come here," said Blanche.

"You wanted to remember what we are doing so that the memory of all of us together doesn't fade away," said Wanda.

"Yeah, I guess you can say that, but I want you all to know that even with all the fighting and bickering I love all of you and I always will no matter even if I wake up or not," said Blanche.

Miles put his arm around Blanche to comfort her as everyone came up to her to give her hugs showing that they're here for her.

Hey Tallulah, it's your turn as Blanche hands her a question for her to answer.

"Do you want me to read the question for you?" asked Agnes.

"Yeah, sure go ahead," said Tallulah acting like she doesn't care.

"Here is your question what's the one thing in your life that you would change?" asked Agnes.

"I would have made sure that my first husband didn't die like he did, and we would have had a happy long life together with our kids," said Tallulah.

"I'm sorry Tallulah about all of that, but at least you have a lot of memories," said Edith.

"The one thing I wish is that my son would come back in my life I miss Chip so much," said Tallulah.

"Did she just say Chip?" asked Agnes. "I heard it too," said Edith.

"It can't be the same Chip we know from camp because she would have said something," said Agnes.

"What if it is?" asked Edith.

"Hey Tallulah, how old was your son when you last saw him?" asked Agnes.

"He was a teenager, but that was almost fifteen years ago," said Tallulah.

"The age matches Chip," said Edith.

"Whoa this is crazy," said Agnes.

"What is going on?" asked Wanda.

"We think that Tallulah's son is Chip from camp," said Edith.

"Holy shit! "You're kidding?" asked Wanda.

"No, we aren't and now we have to bring them together somehow," said Agnes.

"How can we do that when we are here now?" asked Wanda.

"We need to get these challenges done quickly so we can get back to camp," said Agnes.

"Don't you think the other ones are going to notice why we are speeding through the challenges?" asked Edith.

"Do you have a better plan?" asked Agnes.

"Let's just keep going we must be almost to the end of this," said Edith.

"Edith is right because I don't want to ruin this adventure for anyone because it wouldn't be fair," said Agnes.

"When we finished, we will high tail it the hell out of here and bring them together," said Wanda.

Agnes, Edith, and Wanda all agree to keep going so they can continue to make memories with everyone because Blanche got them thinking it might be the only adventure, they go on together.

Hey Vera, I got a question for you as Wanda leans over her to tell her the question.

"Are you jealous of anyone in the room?" asked Wanda.

Vera didn't respond at first.

"Get out of my face," said Vera.

"Oh boy this isn't going to be easy," said Wanda.

"Vera just answers the damn question so that we can move on," said Agnes.

"Fine no I'm not jealous of any of your ugly people," said Vera.

"What are these?" asked Wanda.

"They look like mushrooms or something," said Mona.

"I bet you that's why Tallulah and Vera are acting squirrelly," said Wanda.

"Ew, gross," said Agnes.

"They are both coming back to earth so they should be OK on the next challenge," said Wanda.

"I hope so because I'm not carrying them out of here," said Agnes.

"There is still one more question for all of us to answer," said Wanda.

"Why is there another question?" asked Agnes

"I don't know I didn't put it in there," said Wanda.

"OK ask the question so we can get out of here," said Agnes.

"Go around the room and say one positive thing about someone," said Wanda.

Tallulah you go first," said Agnes. Why me?" asked Tallulah.

"You usually have a lot to say," said Agnes. I feel that we have come closer than we were at Heaven's Ridge, and I appreciate your friendship even if you're a little crazy," said Tallulah.

"Aw that was so sweet of you," said Agnes.

"Edith we never did have the best relationship when we became sisters and even know there are times, I still hate your guts I am glad that we have done this adventure together and I hope we can work on our relationship and be sisters again," said Mona.

"Mona, I think that we have done a lot growing up and growing old I have always waited for this day that we can make amends and be sisters again," said Edith.

Yippy the sisters are back together," said Tallulah.

"Miles you bring a lot of amusement on this trip, and I am glad I am getting to know you and you're hot and to everyone else I love you like sisters and I am glad you're a part of my family," said Wanda.

"I don't have a positive thing to say about just one person here, but I do have something to say to everyone that's here, and I am glad that we are getting to know each other and that this adventure has brought us closer together and I'm damn happy that I met Mona," said Beau.

I'm glad that I met you to Beau," said Mona.

"I came on this camping experience to get a woman in the sack, but instead I made eight new friends that I can't wait to hang out with," said Miles.

"I am glad you came with us even know you hit on all of us here," said Wanda

"Agnes you're one tough cookie, but I love you more than anything besides men," said Tallulah laughing on the floor.

"That was very touching Tallulah I am glad you put a lot of effort into it," said Agnes

"Beau thanks for being here and taking care of Mona and making her happy and I hope that you have a long happy life together and to everyone else I hope that with all that we have been through that we can come closer as friends," said Blanche

"Vera you're a mean woman, and I can't think of one positive thing to say except this I am glad to see that your humor is coming out more and seeing you have a fun time makes me happy," said Edith.

"You are all a bunch of assholes, but if I can tolerate you know I can when we are back to camp and back at Heaven's Ridge," said Vera.

"You are a good person Vera when you aren't trying to hit all of us," said Agnes.

"For Blanche I will just speak for Vera if you don't mind, but you're a very spiritual person and I have enjoyed this adventure with you and I hope to know more about you as time goes on," said Wanda.

"Well, that was the last question," said Mona.

"Well should we proceed to our next challenge?" asked Agnes.

"I think we should I can't wait to see what is next on our challenge journey," said Wanda.

"Come on Tallulah and Vera get off the floor now we must walk to the next door," said Agnes.

They both get up and move in slow motion.

"Eventually they will catch up to us I think," said Edith.

"We will let them go through the door first," said Agnes as she kept pushing them out the door.

On to the next challenge…

CHAPTER 25

Making Amends

Frankie walked back to the camp and stood there and looked around. It was early so no one was awake yet. He decided to go in the kitchen and make breakfast for everyone and it was the least he could do since he acted the way he did, but he did realize that he had things he needed to work out in his head, and in his life. There was still that one person he couldn't get out of his head and planned to make things right with her just as soon as he could.

Frankie made bacon, eggs, sausage, toasts, and fruit, orange juice and cranberry juice. Frankie heard Belle's voice on the loudspeaker that breakfast would be soon. So, he knew that she would be in to make something which Frankie wasn't sure what since she can't really cook. Frankie saw Belle coming and decided to hide in the kitchen by the food storage. Belle opened the door to the kitchen and went in and looked around looking a little confused because of all the food that was waiting on the counter.

"Who did all of this?" asked Belle to herself as she looked around.

"Hello, is anyone in here?" asked Belle because she had a feeling that she wasn't alone.

Frankie came out from the food storage.

"I'm in here Belle," said Frankie as he startled Belle. Belle just stood there not knowing what to say.

"I made breakfast for everyone it was the least I could do after acting like an ass the other night," said Frankie.

Belle still stayed there silent just looking at him thinking whether she should slap him or just hug him for helping.

"I'm guessing are shocked to see me since you haven't said anything since you came through the door," said Frankie.

"I'm not sure what to say right now," said Belle.

"Oh, good you didn't lose your voice like I thought," said Frankie trying to make Belle laugh, but it wasn't working, and he knew that, but he wanted to at least try.

Belle walked up to him and slapped him across the face not once, but twice.

"I was waiting for that even know I was hoping for a warmer welcome," said Frankie.

"Yeah, well you should have known that wasn't going to happen," said Belle.

"Well, I could at least hope Belle," said Frankie trying to get closer to her.

"I would stay right there I wouldn't want you to get to close to the knives that are out," said Belle.

"Yeah, your probably right about that," said Frankie as he stepped away from Belle.

"What are you doing here Frankie?" asked Belle.

"I was thinking about you and here and the other night," said Frankie looking down on the floor.

"Yeah well, I rather forget about that night and yesterday almost got worse than the night before, but we all managed to get through it," said Belle.

"Why what happened?" asked Frankie.

"Nothing Frankie everything is fine now," said Belle giving him the evil eye.

"OK sorry I care, and I am still here for everyone," said Frankie.

"If you cared you wouldn't have made me and Tory feel you wanted to be with us or played us," said Belle get piss off.

"That's why I wanted to make breakfast so people can see I am not just some heartless jerk, said Frankie.

"I'm sure that's why you did it, said Belle. "You don't need to believe, but it's the truth," said Frankie.

"Yeah, I am sort of having a tough time believing you right now," said Belle.

"Fine you don't have to believe me, but I am sorry for hurting you and just so you know my feelings for you were real," said Frankie.

"Then why did you need another girl by your side especially Tory," said Belle.

"I wish I had an answer for you, but I don't, and I know it was wrong and I'm just so sorry," said Frankie starting to tear up.

"I just don't know any more what I want or even what's going on one day to the next," said Belle.

"I really wish you would tell me what's going on so I can try and help you," said Frankie.

"No, it's OK I am a big girl I can handle it myself," said Belle as she walks by Frankie.

"I'm trying to change Belle, I need you to see that," said Frankie.

"I don't think today is that day and I must go now and let everyone that breakfast is ready," said Belle.

"By the way you're welcome for breakfast, at least I can do something right," said Frankie as he went out the door and slammed it.

Belle just stood there not trying to cry, but it was so hard not to.

Belle runs into the office and starts to cry.

"Hey Belle, what's, wrong?" asked Harlow as she wrapped her arms around Belle.

Belle just couldn't say anything because she was crying so much.

"Come on Belle tell me what is wrong," said Harlow.

Finally, Belle calmed down enough to tell Harlow that Frankie made breakfast.

"Frankie is here are you sure?" asked Harlow.

"Yes, he was making breakfast for everyone when I went in the kitchen, he popped out on me," said Belle.

"What the hell Belle he doesn't belong here," said Harlow.

"Well, I didn't fire him, so I guess he does have a right to be here," said Belle.

"True, but where has he been hiding in his cabin for a day?" asked Harlow.

"He was trying to make amends with everyone including me because the light came on in his head," said Belle.

"You didn't give in to any of his influences?" asked Harlow.

"No, I didn't, but he did try, and he did apologize for everything, that went on with us, and Tory," said Belle.

"Do you honestly believe that in only one day everything is fine and let it go?" asked Harlow.

"I want to forgive him, but I can't right now, and he knows that, and he promise he isn't going to push anything," said Belle.

"Yeah, because nothing is never going to happen with the both of you again," said Harlow.

"Oh, really and why do you say that?" asked Belle.

"Like you said before you're not interested in him and if he screwed you over once he will screw you over again," said Harlow.

"You know me to well," said Belle.

"You and I both know it's for the best you don't give into Frankie's temptations," said Harlow.

"Don't worry I will never give in to him again I can tell you that," said Belle as Belle left the kitchen.

"We will see," said Harlow to herself

"Well, breakfast went good," said Harlow.

"Yes, I'm glad it did, and I am super excited that the seniors will be home today," said Belle.

"Yeah, that will be great I can't wait to hear everything they have done," said Harlow.

"I think Frankie's idea about all of us being there is a good idea also," said Belle.

"Um, Belle are you OK?" asked Harlow.

"Yes, I am why do you ask that?" asked Belle.

"Well, because it was Chip's idea and not Frankie's," said Harlow.

"Oh, shit I'm sorry I did," said Belle.

"Don't worry everything will be fine at least I hope so," said Harlow.

"Yes, I know it will be as long as I get my names straight," said Belle.

"I'm sure you will be able to do that once o relax for a little bit," said Harlow.

Frankie decided since things didn't go well with Belle that maybe he should try to talk to Tory, so he headed down to her cabin to see her. He went the back way so that no one saw him. Frankie waited until Tory was alone before knocking at the door. Tory came to the door and Frankie was standing right in front of it. Tory froze and didn't say anything at first.

"Hey Tory," said Frankie.

Tory still stood there in silence just looking at Frankie.

"Another one who is going to be silent on me," said Frankie.

"Well, you're a real asshole to just showing up here," said Tory.

"That is so much better and thank you for saying that I do appreciate it," said Frankie.

"Seriously you're thanking me for calling you an asshole," said Tory.

"Yes, I am because I was and then I left the one thing that was important to me," said Frankie.

"OK now you're just making no sense," said Tory.

"If I were so important to you then I wouldn't of saw you kissing Belle and everything else that happened that night wouldn't have happened," said Tory.

"Yes, you're right," said Frankie.

"Did you just agree with me?" asked Tory.

"Yes, that's right I agreed with you," said Frankie.

"It might not happen again I am thinking," said Tory.

"Listen I just came by because I wanted to say I am sorry for the other night it wasn't right for what I said or did and I hope that you will forgive me someday," said Frankie.

"Yeah, you were brutal with me, but I had every right to get upset especially when I saw you kissing Belle," said Tory.

"Like I said before your right I was wrong to do that especially with the way I feel or felt for you," said Frankie.

"I can't trust you anymore Frankie as much as I want too," said Tory.

"I know and I should be mad at you for lying to me, but I'm not," said Frankie trying to grab Tory's hand.

"How did I lie to you as Tory takes, her hand back?" asked Tory.

"I didn't know you and Chip were cousins," said Tory.

"OK I'm going to explain everything to you, but it's really not going to matter now," said Tory.

"What do you mean doesn't it matter now?" asked Frankie.

"I just don't know what is going on with you or anyone right now," said Tory.

"What can I do to change your mind?" asked Frankie.

"I wanted to be with you, because everything that my heart felt I met to you," said Tory.

"I could tell that you were not doing it for attention," said Frankie.

"As for me and Chip being cousins, I really don't know why we were keeping it a secret I guess it's because we wanted people to know us as individuals and not as related or something stupid," said Tory.

"I get it, but you do realize the people here wouldn't have treated you any different because you were here working and were related to each other," said Frankie.

"Well, I know that now, but also Chip is also here for another reason that I can't tell right now so we just didn't want to make it more awkward than it's now," said Tory.

"What reason would Chip really want to be here?" asked Frankie.

"When it's time for everyone to know then he will tell everyone, but I'm not saying anything," said Tory.

"Plus, don't you know that Belle and Harlow are like best friends from high school so it wouldn't of matter," said Frankie.

"Wow I didn't know that about the two of them, but I rather not talk about Belle I'm still salty from you kissing her," said Tory.

"Let's get it straight she kissed me first not the other way around," said Frankie getting a little annoyed.

"OK I will stop, but I can't just go back to you right away," said Tory.

"I will wait for you if I have too because you mean so much to me," said Frankie.

"All I ask is that you just give me time and let things work out on their own," said Tory.

"I can deal with that if I don't lose you Tory, I love you and that won't change," said Frankie.

"I should go I have to get to breakfast I don't want to be too late and have everyone suspicious where I am," said Tory.

"Yeah, I must go and see someone else and make things better with them also," said Frankie.

"Who if you don't mind me asking you that?" asked Tory.

"Your cousin Chip I put him in a position I shouldn't of, and he almost wanted to punch me so I might give him the opportunity," said Frankie.

"I don't think it's the right time he still working things out with Hazel," said Tory.

"Oh, I'm glad to hear that their relationship as friends will finally be moving forward," said Frankie.

"Well, I better go now," said Tory trying to get by Frankie.

"Sure, no problem, but there is just one more thing before you go," said Frankie as he grabs Tory and kisses her passionately. Tory tries to get away, but she just can't help herself on how she feels for Frankie.

"I have to go Frankie to breakfast," said Tory as she gets by him and walks away.

"I guess I will see you later Tory," said Frankie.

"If you're lucky," said Tory as she winks.

Frankie went down to the men's cabin to see if Chip was in the cabin. He didn't see him in their so he thought of other places that Chip could be. Frankie went to the pool, and he wasn't there so he decided to try Hazel's cabin. He saw them walking towards the dining hall and decided to wait until after to talk to him. For now, he was just going to wait it out somewhere so no one could find him even know Tory will say something to someone about seeing him. Frankie just sits by the firepit and thinks about everything that has been going on.

"Well, well, well, I never thought that I would see your face here again," said the voice that was coming from behind Frankie.

Frankie turned around slowly not knowing who was behind him. When Frankie realized that it was Chip, he relaxed and felt relieved. As for Chip he wasn't so welcoming and decided to give Frankie a punch in the face as pay back for everything that happened the other night.

"I'm guessing you missed me, right buddy?" asked Frankie.

"It's not like you left and went anywhere," said Chip.

"You woke up on the wrong side of the bed," said Frankie.

"Nope always the right side of the bed," said Chip.

"If you say so," laughed Frankie.

"What the hell are you even doing here Frankie?" asked Chip?

"I thought about everything that went on and I wanted to make amends with everyone and clear my head and what my heart wanted," said Frankie.

"I'm trying to follow what you said, but for some reason I just can't," said Chip.

"Listen Chip I'm sorry for everything I put you through especially being in the middle of Belle and Tory and if I had known you two were cousins, I wouldn't have said anything to you," said Frankie. "I find that hard to believe Frankie," said Chip.

"I just wish you were honest with me about the both of you being related," said Frankie.

"Sorry man, but I just didn't want anyone think we are here with some sort of motives because we are cousins," said Chip.

"You weren't ever kissing cousins, were you?" asked Frankie as he laughed about it.

"What the hell man you're one sick puppy," said Chip.

"It was only a question man sorry I didn't mean to make you sick by saying it," said Frankie.

"I'm not so don't worry about me, and I will never be like that with Tory because I think after everything, she has been through that she needs to be happy and that's all I want," said Chip.

"Well then let me ask you this," said Frankie.

"Oh boy I can't wait to hear what you have to ask?" asked Chip.

"I believe in my heart that I love Tory and I was wondering if you would be against me asking to out and maybe dating her?" asked Frankie.

"Are you kidding me after what happened with you, Belle, and Tory?" asked Chip.

"Yes, I know, and it was all a mistake, but I swear Tory is the only one I want, I promise that I'm being honest," said Frankie.

"What about Belle?" asked Chip.

"I'm not interested in her at all Tory is the one who has my heart not Belle I swear," said Frankie.

"Before you do anything you better really think about what you're doing because I don't want to see nether one of them upset because you were stupid again," said Chip.

"Yes, I will do just that if it means you will believe in me," said Frankie.

"All I want is all the mistakes fixed and everyone happy," said Chip.

"I will show you that your opinion of me is so wrong," said Frankie.

"Well, I must see Hazel before the activity starts and hopefully, I will see you later," said Chip as he walks away.

"I'll show everyone that I am not going to screw up again," said Frankie as he decides to see if Tory is around again. Then he decided he needs to produce a plan to impress Tory so she would know that he is for real then an idea clicks, and he has an idea and goes to make it so it will work out.

"Hey Chip, where have you been?" asked Hazel.

"I just saw a familiar face and had to set somethings straight," said Chip.

Hazel looked puzzled and wasn't sure if she should ask or not.

"Frankie came to see me," said Chip.

"What the hell is he doing?" asked Hazel.

"I guess in one day he realizes how much he wants to be with Tory," said Chip.

"How is that even possible after all the damage he caused?" asked Hazel.

"I really don't know darling," said Chip as he grabs Hazel hand and holds it.

"I wonder how Belle and Tory are taking all of this?" asked Hazel.

"I don't know maybe we should just check on Belle and then go to see Tory," said Chip.

"Sure, let's go before the activity starts," said Hazel as the go hand in hand to the office to talk to Belle.

"Hey Belle, we just wanted to stop by and see how you were doing?" asked Hazel.

"I'm doing good since the last two days have been nerve racking and crazy," said Belle.

"I know Frankie is here I saw him this morning he stopped by and talked to me," said Chip.

"Oh, that situation well nothing has changed with me, and I put my foot down and told Frankie exactly how I felt," said Belle.

"Well, that's not what I expected, but good for you Belle to stand your ground," said Hazel.

"There is no way Frankie is going to wiggle himself back into my life not after everything that happened," said Belle.

"Good for you I am proud of you," said Chip.

"Does Tory know he is looking for her?" asked Belle.

"Yes, Tory does know because I'm assuming after seeing you and that didn't go so well, he went right to her?" said Chip.

"I wonder how she took everything?" asked Belle.

"I know she came to breakfast, but she was very quiet," said Hazel.

"I'm going to be meeting her at the pool soon so I am sure she will say something," said Chip.

"Oh, by the way I have been meaning to ask you why didn't you and Tory share that you were cousins?" asked Belle.

"I honestly don't have a reason we just wanted people to know us as people and not related I know it was stupid not to say anything, but it's just felt weird telling someone I guess," said Chip just frazzled at what he told Belle.

"It's OK Chip it doesn't matter either way and I have nothing against Tory even after everything that has happened," said Belle.

"Well, the way I see it if you have nothing against her then you need to tell her, so she knows," said Hazel.

"Yes, I know I don't know if she will even talk to me," said Belle.

"Tory doesn't stay mad often, so I think you have a good chance to make things better," said Chip.

"Hopefully, I won't run into Frankie because I am not ready for round two with him," said Belle.

"I don't know where he could of went after I left him," said Chip.

"That's OK Chip I don't really want to know where he is anyways," said Belle as the phone rang.

"Well, we better be getting going to the activity and we will talk to you later Belle," said Hazel.

"If I see Frankie, I will make sure he goes the other way," said Chip.

"Oh, Chip is everything all set for later back at the funhouse?" asked Belle.

"Yes, I snuck in, and they didn't even hear me," said Chip.

"Well, some of them can't really hear that good anyways," laughed Hazel.

Yeah, that's true," said Chip.

"I can't wait to see their faces when they see us, said Belle.

"Oh, there is something I do need to talk to you about, but it can wait until later if you like," said Chip.

Hazel just looked blankly at Chip not knowing what he is talking about.

"I promise I will tell you everything when I get back," said Chip as he kisses Hazel on the cheek and goes out the door.

Chip stopped by Tory's cabin to see how things were going with her and to talk to her about what is on his mind. Chip knocked at the door and Tinsley opened the flap of the door.

"Hey Tinsley, is Tory here?" asked Chip.

"I thought you were seeing Hazel?" asked Tinsley.

"I am guessing no one told you that Tory and I are cousins," said Chip.

"Kissing cousins?" asked Tinsley.

"Oh no definitely not that," said Chip.

"Oh, it must have been a rumor then," said Tinsley.

"What was?" asked Chip.

"Someone had said you were hot for Tory, but obviously that wasn't true if you're with Hazel," said Tinsley.

"I was never hot for Tory we just kept that were we cousins quiet for whatever stupid reason," said Chip.

"I know all of this I was just busting your balls Chip that's all," laughed Tinsley.

"That was a good one you almost had me believe you," said Chip.

"I'll get Tory for you," said Tinsley.

"Thanks Tinsley," said Chip.

Tinsley went up to Tory and told her that her boy toy was outside waiting for her. So, she got her hair up and make up on so she could look good for Frankie. When she went out the door Tory was a little confused because it was Chip and not Frankie.

"So good at joking round its funny," said Tinsley.

"Just remember karma can be a bitch sometime," said Tory.

"Bring it on," laughed Tinsley.

Chip and Tory just laugh at her as they walk away.

"Wow you look all nice and pretty I'm guessing that you were not expecting me to show up," said Chip.

Not really, but I love your company also," said Tory.

"Well don't stop me from your plans with your boy toy and we can talk tomorrow," said Chip.

Are you sure?" asked Tory.

"Yes, you go and meet Frankie and just be careful and don't forget we are all going to the funhouse," said Chip.

"I'll be there I have to go and meet Frankie by the firepit so I will see you later," said Tory.

"Frankie saw Tory in the cabin and motioned to her to meet at the door hoping that no one else see him there because he doesn't want any trouble or to not see anyone.

"Hey your back," said Tory.

"I said I be back and here I am, and I was wondering if you would take a little walk with me so that we can talk?" asked Frankie.

"Yeah, sure just meet me down by the river in about fifteen minutes I must do a couple of things first before I can go," said Tory.

"Sure, I will wait for you if you want and I will see you later," said Frankie.

"Looking forward to it and maybe things will turn out good again with us," said Tory.

Frankie wanted to kiss her but wasn't sure if it were the right time so he just left so she could do what she needed to do.

Tory dressed fancy and even put a little make up on just to impress Frankie a little bit even know Tory wasn't sure what he needed to talk to her about and she wasn't sure if she honestly wanted him back. Tory headed to the river when she heard someone calling her name and she stopped walking and turned around to see who it was.

"Oh, shit what does she want?" asked Tory as she saw Siena coming behind her.

"Hey Siena, what's going on?" asked Tory?

"Where are you going all sexy?" asked Siena.

"Nowhere just walking around until it's time to go to the funhouse," said Tory hoping Siena will turn around and go away.

"Can I join you I wouldn't mind seeing what else is here?" asked Siena.

"Um, sure you can we just have to watch out for the skunks there has been a lot of them around because I saw one the other night and I had to run so I didn't get sprayed," said Tory hoping that would scare Siena into not going.

"I wouldn't want to get sprayed by a skunk I know my cat did once and that was such a smelly situation for us and the poor cat who had to get tomato juice all over him," said Siena.

"Oh, poor cat," said Tory hoping that memory will change Siena's mind.

They hear something coming out of the woods and Siena took off like a rocket.

"Are you OK Siena," yelled Tory.

"Yeah, I just changed my mind I just hope you will be OK without me," said Siena.

"Oh, don't worry I will be careful," said Tory laughing her ass off especially when she knew it was Frankie making all the noise.

"You are very clever Frankie," said Tory laughing.

"Who me nah I just know how to scare the shit out of people," laughed Frankie.

"Thanks for getting her away I was afraid she would never leave," said Tory.

"It was no problem now it's just you and me," said Frankie as he put his arm around Tory.

Tory got a nervous feeling when Frankie did that with his arm, and she wasn't sure what she is supposed to do so the only thing she could think of is just go with it.

They finally got to the river and sat on the small dock that was there to look out at the water and the soon to be night sky.

"It's nice out this evening," said Tory.

"Yeah, remember the last time we were down here together?" asked Frankie.

"Yeah, we almost frighten the fish when we decided to go skinny dipping and we made love under the stars," said Tory.

"That was such a fun night for us because we were all alone and it as so quiet," said Frankie.

"If I remember it was a first for the both of us and I mean the skinny dipping," said Tory.

"Yeah, it was and now here we are, and everything seems like it changed for us," said Frankie.

"So, did you ever plan to make things more real with us," asked Frankie.

"See, that's where things changed for me and were different when I was with you everything was good almost too good and I felt like you were the one and only person I could commit too," said Tory.

"Really," said Frankie just looking at Tory.

"Everything with you felt right and made sense and I knew what I wanted, and I planned on telling you the day of the jousting match, but then I saw you and Belle kissing and all those feelings went away just like that," said Tory.

"I want to make one thing clear she kissed me first and I had no idea she was going to do that," said Frankie.

"I know that now, but I felt like my heart got ripped right out of my chest it hurt so badly," said Tory.

"Then everything with everyone blew up that night," said Frankie.

"That's right it did and from there I didn't know what to do," said Tory.

"You're an amazing person Tory and I am so sorry for everything I said and everything I did that night I was the biggest asshole, and I shouldn't have been, and I hope that one day you could forgive me, and we could rekindle what we had," said Frankie.

"I don't totally forgive you yet, but that's slowly going away, and I would also like to see where we can go from here, but I want one thing in return?" asked Tory.

"Sure, anything for you Tory," said Frankie getting all excited.

"I want us to wait until this camp session is over and we can have a normal relationship with no Belle or anyone else from here and that includes my cousin," said Tory.

Frankie sat there in silence thinking about what Tory just said before answering her.

"OK I will agree to it because I love you so much and I don't want to be apart from you, but you need to do something for me," said Frankie.

"I will do anything you want," said Tory.

"If you get scared or something seems off or thinking about running away you come to me, and we talk about it?" asked Frankie.

"Yes, if you do the same with me," asked Tory.

"Yes, babe I will," said Frankie as he got closer to kiss Tory.

"Oh, and by the way as Tory looks at Frankie, I love you too," said Tory as she kisses him again.

They both sat there holding each other and watched the fish swim around and talked about things and then Frankie walked Tory back to her cabin.

I wish that you could go with us," said Tory.

"Where are you going?" asked Frankie.

"We are going to the funhouse where the other seniors are and we are going to surprise them," said Tory.

"I don't see why I can't go I really would like too," said Frankie.

"I want you there also, but I don't want us being together to ruffle any feathers," said Tory.

"We will keep our hands to ourselves and behave," said Frankie.

"Then let's do it," said Tory.

"So, we will meet back at my cabin in a couple of hours because I still have to go back to the pool," said Tory.

"Do you want me to come with you?" asked Frankie.

"I'll be fine sweetie and it won't be too long then we will be together again," said Tory.

"OK if you say so I hope that time goes by quickly," said Frankie.

"Me to so try and stay out of trouble," said Tory as she gives him a kiss on the cheek.

"Thank you for that I really appreciate it," said Frankie.

Chip looked all over for Tory until he spotted her at the pool.

There you're I have been looking for you," said Chip. "I thought we agreed to meet by the pool," said Tory.

"Maybe we did I don't know I'm just got so much on my mind, and I feel like my head is going to explode," said Chip.

"So, what's on your mind?" asked Tory who was wondering if there were problems in paradise already.

"Nothing I just keep thinking about my mother and if she is here or at the funhouse or maybe she didn't even come," said Chip getting all frustrated.

"You need to relax and not think about it all the time," said Tory.

"I can't help it I just want to know who she is since I can't remember," said Chip.

"Remember you left her for a reason," said Tory.

"I know and now so many years later I just can't wait to find her because I can't remember her," said Chip.

"Have you even talked to Hazel about all of this?" asked Tory.

"No, I haven't yet, but I guess I better or she will probably give me an ass whipping," said Chip.

"Well, that isn't bad since we all know you love getting your ass whipped," laughed Tory.

"Things will be OK Chip and we will figure out who your mom is," said Tory.

"Now I'll go tell Hazel what is going on, so she won't kill me," said Chip.

I'll be around if you need to talk," said Tory.

Chip went over to Hazel's cabin and knocked on the door. Iggy opened the flap and peeked out to see it was Chip.

"Oh, Hi Chip how are things going with you?" asked Iggy.

"They are good can I see Hazel please?" asked Chip.

"Sure, no problem I'll get her," said Iggy.

"Are you OK Iggy?" asked Chip.

"Yeah, I'm fine I just wish a guy would come to the door sometime and ask for me for something like date," said Iggy looking all sad and depressed.

"Oh, cheer up Iggy your prince charming is out there somewhere looking for you," said Chip.

"If you think so," said Iggy as she went to get Hazel.

"What is going on with these girls today Chip asked himself.

"Do you really want me to answer that?" asked Hazel.

"No, I'm afraid to even know the answer right now," said Chip.

"Don't worry Iggy will be OK," said Hazel.

Do you want to go for a little stroll with me?" asked Chip.

"I sure would love that," said Hazel.

Chip took her hand in his and they walked up to the hammock and laid together for a while just talking.

"So, what is bothering you today?" asked Hazel.

"How can you tell something is bothering me?" asked Chip.

"You just have a certain attitude when something is on your mind and you told me in the office when we were Belle that you would tell me later," said Hazel.

"That's true I did and also hopefully, it's not a bad attitude," said Chip.

"No, I just can tell when something is on your mind that's all," said Hazel.

"Still thinking about my mother and meeting her again," said Chip.

"Really I wasn't sure you were looking for her after all the things you told me I got the impression that you didn't want to know her," said Hazel.

"Well, I do and that's what me and Tory have been doing," said Chip.

"You and Tory are looking for her," said Hazel who was a little confused.

"Yes, I was the one who left and now I am the one who wants to be a part of her life again," said Chip.

"Has anything new surfaced about her?" asked Hazel cuddling up to Chip.

"We think she is here at camp," said Chip.

What is making you so sure she is here?" asked Hazel.

"Well Tory had a girlfriend at Heaven's Ridge and supposedly she came here for camp, but I don't know if she is actually here or at the funhouse," said Chip.

"So that's why you wanted to come here so bad?" asked Hazel.

"No that's not the reason," said Chip.

No not yet and that's why it's driving me so crazy, said Chip.

Everything will be OK, said Hazel. Yeah, Tory told me the same thing, but I am not sure I believe her right now, said Chip.

"I know what you're going to say, but I'm just going to put this out there," said Hazel.

"You can say whatever you need to I trust you," said Chip looking into her eyes.

"I've been thinking a lot about what you said, and there is one person we can go to that could help you out with finding your mother," said Hazel.

"Who could that be?" asked Chip.

"I think we should talk to Belle about all of this I think she could help us in a big way and plus she knows the Director at Heaven's Ridge," said Hazel.

"How do you know that?" asked Chip.

"I overheard Harlow and Belle talking about it," said Hazel.

Chip laid there for a long while before saying anything to Hazel.

"I'm guessing with the silence that you didn't like my idea," said Hazel as she tries to get out of the hammock.

"No wait and Chip grabs her before she out of the hammock.

"It's not you sweetie so please don't leave me here right now and you're right that I maybe Belle could help me," said Chip.

"To me it's just another person who knows, said Chip.

"That person has connections to so many things that would help any of us out, said Hazel.

Yes, I agree that's why we can do it together tomorrow, said Chip.

"Yes, we both will go there I would never want you to do this alone," said Hazel.

"Glad you're always by my side except when we are sleeping, said," Chip.

"We might have to talk about the sleeping arrangements once camp is over at the end of the week," said Hazel.

"I would like that very much, said Chip as he kisses Hazel warm lips.

Chip and Hazel went right to Belle's office to talk to her before the day had begun and they had to get ready for the surprise for the seniors.

"Are you ready to do this," asked Chip.

Chip hesitated for a minute then shook his head yes.

"Let's do this," said Hazel as they go in the office together. Belle just happened to be sitting at her desk.

"Hey you two," said Belle.

"Hi Belle, how are you today?" asked Hazel.

"Good so far, but it's still early day," said Belle.

"That is true,' said Chip.

"So, what can I do for the you two?" asked Belle

"We were just wondering if we could talk to you about something," said Chip.

"Is anything wrong?" asked Belle.

Oh no nothing like that, said Hazel.

"Oh, before I forget I just peeked on the seniors and Tallulah and Vera were high," said Belle.

"I don't remember us saying we were going to get them high, so I have no idea," said Chip.

"It's OK it was just the funniest thing to watch, and I enjoyed watching them race against each other that was great too," said Belle.

Good we are glad it's all coming together," said Hazel.

"Sorry anyways what is going on with you two?" asked Belle?

"Remember when I had told you about how I left my mother because she was well crazy," said Chip.

Yes, I do Chip," said Belle looking all concerned.

"I just want to come clean on the real reason me and Tory didn't tell you we were cousins the truth is because we knew that my mother was going to be here and we didn't want everything to be weird here if that makes any sense," said Chip.

"I honestly think it wouldn't have been weird and you two should have been honest with me and everyone here," said Belle.

"Yes, I know and once again I am sorry for not telling you and we both feel bad," said Chip.

"Well, Tory is not number on my friends list right now, but you did what you had to do," said Belle.

"I think Tory feels bad, but she is just not the type to come forward and say sorry until she is ready," said Chip.

"So how did you find out that your mom was going to be here?" asked Belle.

"When Tory was with Willa her girlfriend who also works at Heaven's Ridge," said Chip.

"How did Willa know that your mother was at Heaven's Ridge?" asked Belle.

"That I really can't tell you because I don't know how that happened," said Chip as he is thinking this was a bad idea.

"Did you call any other facilities looking for her?" asked Belle.

"I couldn't give Tory my mother's first name or anything like that and that's all I know because I obviously have a different last name then her because I changed it," said Chip.

"What makes you think she is in a retirement home?" asked Belle.

"I don't know I'm just taking chances here," said Chip.

"I get what you're saying Chip and I'll see what I can do to help you," said Belle.

"Thank you, Belle, I would appreciate it so much," said Chip.

"I do want to know one thing if that's OK with you?" asked Belle.

"Yes, sure anything," said Chip.

"Why do you want to find your mother now?" asked Belle.

"I grew up most of my young life not wanting to be around her because of reasons like being crazy, but now that I am getting older and now in a committed relationship with someone, I can see my whole life with and I want to be able to share that with my mother and plus who knows how much longer my mother might have to live," said Chip looking back at Hazel.

Hazel gives Chip a wink like she is all in with him and the relationship.

"So, Willa for sure said she is here, but never giving you a name?" asked Belle.

"Yes, that's right, and I have no idea why she didn't," said Chip.

"Well, I can take a guess why she didn't because it's the same policy that every business has and it's HIPPA," said Belle.

"I have heard of it," said Hazel. "How come I have never heard of it?" asked Chip.

"We didn't really go through that when we were training you so that's my fault," said Belle.

"It just means that you can't give out a senior or anyone's information to someone that's not a family member or don't have permission to know things," said Hazel.

"Oh, so I get it now even know I am whoever she is son I can't know anything about her until we accidently run into each other," said Chip.

"Let me call Heaven's Ridge and talk to Aspen who is the Director of Nursing and somewhat of a friend and see what I can do for you, but no promises," said Belle.

"Thank you again Belle," said Chip as he keeps shaking her hand.

"Give the lady back her hand Chip," said Hazel laughing at him.

"When I find something out, I will let you know so don't worry I got this," said Belle.

"Yes, thank you again," said Chip.

"You don't have to thank me until we find her for you so go and get things ready so we can leave soon to the funhouse to bring our seniors home," said Belle.

"Yes, we will Belle," said Chip as Hazel is trying to drag him out of Belle's office.

"So, do you feel better now that we talked to Belle?" asked Hazel.

"Yes, I do, and I guess if I really thought about, I would have really wondered why Willa never gave Tory her name," said Chip.

"Yeah, it's a little weird that she never did either, but it's in Belle's hands now, so we just must wait," said Hazel. "Your right and thanks so much for sticking by me on all of this," said Chip kissing Hazel. "You're welcome and I wouldn't want to be doing anything else, but be with you," said Hazel.

"Now let's get things ready," said Chip. Belle sat there for a while thinking about what she had to do for Chip but didn't know how to deal with Aspen after all these years.

"What's up?" asked Harlow.

"Nothing much I'm just sitting here waiting to make a phone call," said Belle flipping her pen around on the desk.

"Why are you waiting if you're the one making it?" asked Harlow.

"It's long story, but I am going to have to call Aspen and I am not looking forward to it right now or anytime," said Belle.

"With what you told me about your past with her it wasn't your fault that you were not ready to go down that road with her," said Harlow.

"Ready like I always was with her, but I couldn't go through with it because then it would never stop," said Belle.

"What would never stop?" asked Harlow.

"Us being together and then another broken heart comes along because one of us can't handle the relationship," said Belle.

"Oh, I see that part you didn't tell me about," said Harlow not knowing what to say next.

"If it's business, you're calling about then just keep it that way and don't let her change the subject," said Harlow.

"That might work, but you know me I find some way to just screw it up," said Belle slamming the pen on the desk.

"I wouldn't go that far, but you know what you need to do and just don't fall for any of her crap she does to make you like her again," said Harlow.

"I'm not even close to be going down that road again with her," said Belle.

"You really need to join one of Eden's yoga thingy's it's sure to make you feel better," said Harlow.

"Yeah, maybe before I make a call that I might regret," said Belle.

"Good Eden has a yoga class starting now," said Harlow.

"Great and you can join me since you look like you're doing nothing," said Belle.

"Sure, why not I could use a time to relax, and it was my idea," said Harlow.

"Sounds good so why don't we get ready to go off to yoga we go," said Belle.

"Yes, Let's do it," said Harlow.

Belle and Harlow were off to join a couple of seniors and Eden to do yoga. Eden sat in front of them with her legs crossed and started the class off with breathing techniques which was making Belle feel much better. After all the breathing exercises they got into stretching and breathing at the same time.

"Harlow you were right this is helping," said Belle as she is bending her body in all diverse ways.

"Glad it's helping you Belle it's quite easy to clear your mind from everything that has been going on," said Harlow almost ready to fall over.

After the class was over Belle went over and talk to Eden.

"Great class I learned so much from it," said Belle.

"So glad that you enjoyed it and yes it free's your mind from everything," said Eden.

"I enjoyed it also," said Harlow just jumping around.

"I don't know what got into her," said Belle.

"Maybe she finally found her energy it can take a little bit," said Eden.

"Thank you again Eden and I look forward to coming to another class here or wherever you have them when you're not at camp," said Belle.

"I will give you all the information you need when you're ready," said Eden.

"Sounds good and have a wonderful day and we will see you soon at the funhouse," said Belle.

"So, is it that time to make that phone call?" asked Harlow.

Belle sat at her desk and could feel all the stress come back to her.

"Yeah, I know I have too," said Belle.

"Well, you don't have to, but you did promise Chip," said Harlow.

"Yes, I know Harlow and I will call Aspen soon," said Belle. I'm just thinking how I'm going to approach her still," said Belle. I just need to confront a problem head-on and just call her as Belle continues to talk to herself. Belle picks up the phone and starts dialing Aspen's number, but then hangs up the phone.

"Well, I'm guessing you didn't want to them," joke Art.

"Yeah, I guess you can say that in a way," said Belle.

"What's up Art?" asked Belle.

"Nothing I was just wondering if Harlow was around?" asked Art.

Oh, did I hear my name?" asked Harlow.

There she is Art," said Belle. Harlow comes out of her office to see Art.

"Hey sweetie," said Harlow.

I was just wondering if you're not too busy if you wanted to go hiking with me and Jasper?" asked Art.

"You got Jasper to go hiking with you?" asked Belle.

"Yeah, he was all for it when I asked," said Art.

"That's very impressive Art," said Belle.

"Well, thank you Belle it wasn't too hard he used to go camping in the Adirondacks when he lived there," said Art.

"Yeah sure unless you need me here Belle?" asked Harlow.

"No go ahead and have fun, be careful, and be back in time to go to the funhouse," said Belle.

"OK mommy I will," said Harlow sarcastically as she goes out the door.

"Mommy I don't think so," said Belle to herself.

"Harlow peeked in one more time oh and one more thing don't forget to make that call," said Harlow.

"Yes, Harlow I will so go away and have fun, but too much fun," laughed Belle.

"We already went there in the bathhouse," laughed Harlow.

"Too much info Harlow," said Belle.

"Bye Belle, I will miss you," yelled Harlow.

"There are times I just don't know about that girl and why I am friends with her," laughed Belle to herself.

"OK it's time to make this call and not put it off any longer," said Belle as she looks around and see is if anyone by chance needs her, but no one is around which is just my luck as Belle continues to talk to herself.

Belle finally picks up the phone and calls Aspen.

"Hello this is Aspen how may I help you?" asked Aspen as she files her fingernails.

"Hello Aspen, it's Belle do you have time so we can we talk?" asked Belle.

"Yes, Belle I can talk now," said Aspen.

"Oh, good I was afraid I caught you at a tough time," said Belle sweating buckets for whatever reason.

"Are the residents, OK?" asked Aspen.

"Yes, they're all fine," said Belle.

"OK well that's good," said Aspen.

"Well, I do have to talk to you about something," said Belle.

"Sure, I am here to listen," said Aspen.

"One of my employees is searching for his mother they have lost contact with when he was younger and since then would like to be reacquainted with her," said Belle hoping she didn't go in circles.

"OK so what can I help you with?" asked Aspen.

"Do you have a resident who is missing her son and would like the same thing to happen like my employee does?" asked Belle.

Aspen sat there for a while and thought about it.

"You do know this information is against all HIPPA?" asked Aspen.

"Yes, I know I just thought maybe you could look pass it and help a mother and son get back together," said Belle. Belle honestly felt like she may pass out from talking to Aspen she just can't believe all the feelings she brings back to her.

"I guess we could do that I just need to figure out who it is, and I can let you know," said Aspen.

"Sure, that sounds good to me, and I will let him know what is going on also," said Belle.

"I just need to talk to the staff and see what they say because they usually know more than me sometimes," said Aspen.

"Sounds like a clever idea," said Belle.

"I'll call you back just as soon as I find out maybe we can have dinner or something," said Aspen.

"It could be a possibility we will have to wait and see," said Belle.

"Well, I am glad it wasn't a no," laughed Aspen.

"Well, like you said just call me back and we will go from there," said Belle.

"Sounds good and have a good day Belle," said Aspen.

"You are too Aspen," said Belle as she hangs up the phone.

Belle got off the phone and up from her desk and went to find Chip to let him know she made the phone call. Belle decided to go to the pool first to see if Chip was there and that he was.

"Hey Chip and Tory," said Belle.

"Hey Belle, is everything OK?" asked Chip.

"Yes, "I just wanted to let you know I did call Aspen and that she is going to investigate whether your mom is there and who she is so when I find out I will let you know," said Belle.

"Thank you, Belle, for everything," said Chip.

"I just want the both of you know that you don't need to keep secrets and if you think you need to then you can come to me where it will be between us," said Belle as she walked away.

"Do you think she is mad because we weren't honest with her?" asked Tory.

"No, I don't think Belle is like that it's more of a trust thing with her she puts so much in for us, and she wants that in return," said Chip.

"Maybe, but you never know with her maybe I broke her trust with the whole Frankie thing," said Tory.

"Yeah, I know I get it," said Chip.

When Belle got back to the office the phone was ringing and she was hoping it was good news.

"Hello this is Belle how may I help you?" asked Belle pushing papers out of the way.

"Hello Belle, it's Aspen calling you back," said Aspen. Belle knew that voice from anywhere.

"So, did you find out any information?" asked Belle.

"I talked to all my aides and nurses and a couple of them have heard one resident wishing she could see her son again," said Aspen.

"Well, that's great news I'm so glad to hear that," said Belle.

"Are you able to tell me who this resident is?" asked Belle getting nervous that Aspen won't tell her.

"I will tell you, but you need to do something for me in return," said Aspen.

Belle knew that was coming because she knows how Aspen is so she was ready to do whatever she wants so that she can tell Chip what he wants to know.

"That's fine I have no problem with that," said Belle.

" I figured you wouldn't that's why I am willing to tell you who it is," said Aspen.

Belle was getting excited to find out which one of the seniors it was that was Chip's mother.

"So, it seems that Tallulah McWhorter is your employees' mother because she tells the story a lot about how he left her and so on," said Aspen.

Belle almost dropped the phone when she heard Tallulah's name and she was thinking about how Chip is going to take the news.

"Wow that's impressive to hear and I can't wait to let him the employee know who it is," said Belle

"Yeah, so getting back to what I would like in return," said Aspen.

Typical Aspen getting right to the point for everything no fun in the middle unless it's on her terms.

"Yes, what can I do for you?" asked Belle.

I was thinking we could have dinner together and make it a night to remember," said Aspen.

Belle wasn't sure what to say to what Aspen asked her.

"Dinner is good, but that's all because I don't want to feel rushed again like last time if something is going to happen between us it needs to be on our own terms," said Belle.

"OK I will take it just because we do have fun together," said Aspen.

"I do agree with us having fun if it doesn't go too far this time," said Belle.

"How about Saturday night?" asked Aspen.

"Sure, that would be fine because all the seniors will be back at Heaven's Ridge by then," said Belle.

"Oh, that's right it's going to be hard for you to see me knowing the residents are going to be home?" asked Aspen.

"No, it won't be, so you don't have to worry," said Belle just wanting to get off the phone now since the conversation wasn't going in the right direction.

"I will call you later and we can make plans if that's OK with you?" asked Aspen.

"Yes, that sounds good I'll be waiting for your phone call," said Belle.

"I'll talk to you later," said Aspen as she hangs up the phone.

"Bye to you to Aspen," said Belle as she hangs up the phone.

Belle just couldn't wait to tell Chip about who his mother is and knew he was going to flip when he found out. She went by the pool again and Tory told Belle that he was with Hazel. So, Belle decided to go to her cabin to see if they were there and luckily, they were.

"Oh, good you both are here I have great news for you Chip," said Belle.

"Did you find out who my mother was?" asked Chip.

"Yes, I did you might want to sit down before I tell you because this is going to shock you," said Belle.

"Please tell me it's not Vera?" asked Hazel.

"No, it's not Vera," said Belle.

" Oh, thank God on that one," said Hazel.

"Are you ready to find out who your mother is?" asked Chip. "You bet I am Belle I have been waiting a long time to know who it is," said Chip.

Chip took Hazel's hand and held it tight because he started to get nervous.

"Who is it Belle we can't wait any longer?" asked Hazel getting excited.

"Alright so Aspen questioned all her employees and a couple of them had said that this person has been talking about her son," said Belle.

"Will you just tell me who it is," said Chip getting impatient.

Belle braced herself before telling Chip.

"Your mother is Tallulah," said Belle.

Chip burst out laughing because he thought that Belle was playing a joke on him.

"I'm not kidding Chip it's true Tallulah is your mother," said Belle.

Chip sat there in silence and shock, and he didn't know what to say.

"Are we sure?" asked Hazel who couldn't believe it either.

"Yes, I'm sure that Tallulah is your mother," said Belle.

"Oh my god the woman who got naked in the pool is my mother," said Chip who almost puked.

Yeah, that would be her," said Belle.

"I honestly don't know what to think about this right now," said Chip.

"Yeah, I totally understand I get it and I am also very shocked by it too, but Chip at least now you know who it's so you can decide if you want to have a relationship with her or not," said Belle.

"Tallulah isn't that bad I mean yeah, she stole a golf cart, took off her clothes in the pool, and took Frankie's clothes, but I can tell you the times I got to know her which wasn't too long she was sweet," said Hazel.

"Holy shit we sent her and the others to a funhouse what kind of son am I?" asked Chip.

"We all know that they're safe because I check the television a lot to see what they're up too," said Belle.

"Everything will be OK Chip we are all here for you and will be once she is back also," said Hazel as she holds on to Chip tighter.

"Tallulah will be OK, and you will too," said Belle.

"Sorry I am freaking out I just am shocked and can't believe Tallulah is my mother," said Chip.

"I must get going it's almost time to head to the funhouse so we can bring your moth end the rest of the seniors back to camp," said Belle.

I appreciate it Belle I really do, and we will be right behind you to the funhouse," said Chip.

"I know you do and once you stop overthinking about it you will see that things will be fine," said Belle.

"Your right Belle," said Chip.

I hope that we didn't get you in too much trouble with Aspen?" asked Hazel.

"No, I just have dinner with her that's all," said Belle.

"Well, that doesn't seem to be that bad," said Hazel.

"No, it's not at all I suppose it could be worse," said Belle as she went out the door.

"Well, we better be going," said Hazel.

"See you soon, Belle," said Chip. Chip and Hazel just sat in the cabin for a while until Chip wanted to talk.

"Are you OK now?" asked Hazel.

"I will be OK once I know that her and the other seniors are back safe, so we better go," said Chip.

"Soon we will be there to get them, and you heard Belle they're doing OK and whatever challenge they have is bringing them closer to being better friends," said Hazel as she wraps her arms around Chip.

"I still can't believe it's Tallulah am I being punked or something?" asked Chip. Hazel just laughs at Chip as he rambles on about Tallulah.

"No that's what we sort of did to them," said Hazel.

"Oh, crap what were we thinking?" panics Chip.

"Shut up and listen to me everything will be OK so what if it's Tallulah at least it's not Vera then you would be in deep shit," laughed Hazel.

"Yes, you're right about that," said Chip.

"So, let's get going before Belle has our head," said Hazel.

"I think I'm ready," said Chip. "I love you," said Hazel.

"Well, I love you too," said Hazel.

CHAPTER 26

Stub-Toe-Lane

Agnes looked at the yellow door and read the sign. "Let me see here what this sign says," said Agnes as she read Stub-Toe-Lane.

"Interesting I wonder what this room is going to be all about," said Wanda.

"Well, we need to go inside to see instead of staying out here," said Agnes.

Tallulah and Vera come out of the Hanky-Panky room skipping together like they were little school children.

"I never thought I would see the day that both of them are spending time together," said Wanda.

"Yeah, that's very weird to me," said Agnes.

"Let's get this challenge going," said Edith as she pudges in front of Agnes and Wanda.

"Yes, I do agree with you Edith, but remember we can't rush to much or someone will know that we are up to something," said Agnes.

"I highly doubt she will even know we are doing these fast if she is hanging out with Vera," said Edith.

"I think you're right she is not herself and this is the time to get these challenges over so we can tell her about Chip," said Agnes.

"We need to tell Tallulah now, so she knows," said Edith.

"No, I think we need to wait until we are back to camp because I am afraid of what she will do before we get back there," said Agnes. Agnes opens the door so that everyone can come in and look around.

"Wow it looks like an obstacle course," said Blanche who was getting excited for it.

"This looks like a lot of fun and something we will enjoy," said Wanda.

"This is so cool," said Mona as she comes in and looks around.

"Maybe we can go skinny dipping," whispered Beau in Mona's ear.

"Maybe sometimes we can make that dream come true just not here with everyone around," said Mona.

"Of course, not my darling," said Beau.

"We don't want to scare them like we did with the pillows," laughed Mona.

"I understand my darling and your right," said Beau.

"I can see the challenge card," said Edith as she goes over and gets it in one of the stations that are set up.

"At least it was easy to find this time," said Blanche.

"Oh yes let's get right into this challenge," said Agnes.

"Since when are you in a hurry to get done with a challenge?" asked Tallulah.

"I just want to keep my old bones moving," said Agnes.

"Sounds good to me to," said Beau as he keeps thinking about skinny dipping with Mona.

"OK Edith read the challenge," said Wanda.

"Five people must people in this challenge and you must take your cup go to the water pail grab as much water as you can in your cup go back to your station and dump it in your tube and the first person who gets their ball to come out of their tube first wins," said Edith.

"Well, that sounds easy enough," said Blanche.

"Who are going to be the five people?" asked Edith.

Vera put her hand up fast and everyone just stared at her.

"OK Vera is one now we need four more," said Edith.

"I'll do it with her," said Mona.

"Three more to go," said Edith.

"If Vera is doing it then I will too," said Tallulah.

"Since when did they become besties?" asked Agnes.

"OK that a girl Tallulah, now I need two more," said Edith.

"I will," said Agnes.

"How about one of the men?" asked Edith.

"Why do they need to join us I am sure an all-female competition would be a lot of fun?" asked Agnes.

"OK then who is going to be the last female?" asked Edith.

"I'll do it," said Wanda.

Alright everyone gets ready at your stations and let's have fun and don't stub your toe," said Edith.

"Alright is everyone ready to rock this challenge?" asked Edith.

"Everyone," screamed yes and were ready to go.

"This is going to be a good challenge to watch," said Miles.

"On your mark get set GO," yelled Edith.

"Everyone is starting off strong and Agnes is in the lead," said Edith.

"Come on Mona baby you can do it," screamed Beau.

"Vera is a little behind, but catching up fast," said Edith.

"Tallulah is spinning around like a ballet dancer for whatever reason," said Blanche who can't control her laughter loses all her water in her cup and must go back and get more.

"Come on Agnes, you can do it," yelled Edith.

Vera is crawling on the floor to get to her tube.

"What does Vera think she is doing?" asked Blanche.

"With Vera you never know," said Miles.

"Mona's tube is almost full, and she is almost on her way to finishing first.

"You only have a little left to do Mona darling," said Beau.

Blanche, Miles, Beau, and Edith all cheer on Mona as she goes to the water one last time to fill in her tube.

"MONA WINS," yelled Edith at the top of her lungs.

Beau runs up to her and grabs her in his arms.

"You did it my darling," said Beau. "Excellent job Mona I'm so happy for you," said Agnes.

Yahoo! You deserved to win Mona," said Tallulah.

"Thank you everyone I have never won anything in my life," said Mona.

"That was so exciting, and I'm so glad that you won Mona," said Agnes.

"It's time that we go to the next challenge since we are on such a roll," said Wanda. You're right as everyone got ready to go out the door together.

Tallulah wait until everyone was out the door and then you heard her scream.

Everyone turned around and saw that Tallulah was all wet.

"What happened to you Tallulah?" asked Wanda. Did you piss your shorts?" asked Wanda.

"Vera why would you do that to me?" asked Tallulah.

"You looked like you needed to get cooled off, so I poured water over your head," laughed Vera.

"Well, now that's kind of funny Tallulah," laughed Agnes.

"Now I'm all wet and there is no way for me to dry off," said Tallulah.

"Tallulah you're going to be fine this isn't the end of the world," said Agnes.

"Yes, it is," cried Tallulah.

Hey Tallulah watch this," said Wanda as she picked up some water and poured it on Agnes head.

"Now that's funny," laughed Wanda.

Before everyone knew it, they were all throwing water at each other. Tallulah and Wanda were slipping all over the floor and they couldn't stop laughing.

"When you lost your shorts that was the end of the world now a little water on you isn't anything it's fun, said Edith.

"Yeah, listen to Edith she knows what she is talking about for once," said Agnes.

As they were all soaked and wet, they thought that was the best time they have had since they got to the funhouse.

"I really should get you all back, but I won't because I'm the better person," said Vera.

"I won't either because I'm the better person," said Tallulah.

"I'm proud of you," said Agnes.

"Yeah, your just so wonderful," said Vera as she goes out the door and waits by the next one, they're going too.

"She is just going to be so much fun this next challenge," said Wanda.

"I don't even care right now I just want to keep moving on even in my wet clothes," said Agnes.

"Yes, let's do that and see what is waiting for us," said Wanda.

"That challenge went way to fast, and we even had a water fight we are getting so good at these challenges," said Wanda as they head out the door.

On to the next challenge . . .

CHAPTER 27

DUH Drive

"I can't believe we are on our way to almost the last challenge," said Wanda.

"Here we are to the second to last door, said Tallulah.

"Well, let's go through this DUH Drive and we can get closer to DUH end of this," laughed Agnes.

"It's pronounced DUH not D U H," said Wanda.

"Can you make words out of those letters?" asked Tallulah.

"No, I can't, and I don't want to," said Agnes. "I can think of something," said Miles.

"Oh, really you can?" asked Edith.

"I can make a whole sentence if you want me too?" asked Miles.

"Oh, whatever I don't care let's just go in," said Agnes.

"It's a pretty Turquoise," said Wanda.

OK enough about the door let's hear it," said Agnes.

"I'm Done Under Her," laughed Miles.

"I had a feel it was going to be something perverted, but I wanted to hear it," said Agnes.

"Oh, my that was so funny," said Tallulah I'll have to remember that one.

"We all know she won't," whispered Agnes.

"Miles you have such a dirty bird, but I love it," said Tallulah as she opens the door.

They walked in and were not impressed with the room.

"There is only a couch a chair and a television," said Agnes. It's not creative in here," said Wanda.

Everyone sat on the couch while Tallulah, got the clue that was on television screen. Miles got up and tried flipping the channels.

"Have you ever heard of a television that doesn't have cable," said Miles.

"So, what are we doing now?" asked Agnes.

Tallulah started reading the card. Everyone must participate and answer questions on the television screen you will have five seconds to answer each question before the answers pops up on the television screen and the person with the most points will win the game. You must click the button on the remote to go through each question one at a time.

"We need to put our thinking caps on," said Agnes.

"Where are they?" asked Tallulah.

We are talking about our brains," said Agnes which you're lacking.

"You are so cruel Agnes, and I never did anything to you," said Tallulah as she moves somewhere else and sits with Wanda.

"OK sounds easy so who has the remote?" asked Edith.

"Here it's on the stand," said Tallulah as she picks it up from the table and starts clicking it.

"Answer all questions right to finish this challenge," said Tallulah reading the television.

"Question number one," said Agnes.

"Is cereal a soup? Well, that's easy it's not a cereal," said Wanda.

"Who would ever think that soup is a cereal that's dumb and disgusting?" asked Tallulah.

"Yeah, I agree Tallulah," said Agnes.

"On to question number two," said Tallulah. Is a hot dog a sandwich?

"Well, that's also a no," said Edith. "It's on a bun not bread," said Wanda.

"Who knows maybe there is someone out there that thinks it can be on bread," said Edith.

"When we didn't have hot dog rolls to put our hot dogs on, we used bread," said Mona.

See, there is our someone," said Edith.

"Next question three," said Edith. How long does it take to boil an egg?

"It takes five minutes," said Wanda.

"No that's too short of time," said Edith.

" It's around ten to twelve minutes," said Mona.

"Well done Mona you got the answer correct," said Edith.

"Of course, I did because I own my own business and I used to make a lot of egg salad and deviled eggs," said Mona.

"On to question four," said Beau. What was the first state to be in the thirteen colonies?

"What is a colony?" asked Tallulah.

"Oh boy this not good," said Agnes. "Isn't Rose," said Edith.

"No that's a Golden Girl you ding bat," said Agnes.

"It is Delaware," said Miles.

"Yes, you got it right Miles, said Blanche.

"Question five," said Wanda. Name three primary colors?

"Pink, Purple, and Blue," said Tallulah.

"No that's not right," said Agnes.

"Your right those are my favorite colors," laughed Tallulah.

"What does primary even mean?" asked Blanche.

"It's all the dark colors," said Wanda.

"How about blue, yellow, and red," said Beau.

"Good one Beau," said Miles.

"I still remember somethings from art class," said Beau.

"Let's move on to question six," said Blanche.

"This time it's a picture," said Edith.

"What is that?" asked Tallulah.

Spell the word orange

"Is this a trick question?" asked Wanda.

"I don't know if it's or not," said Agnes.

"Do they want the color or the fruit?" asked Edith.

"Both the color and fruit spelled the same honey," said Agnes.

"So, it's O R A N G E, right?" asked Mona.

"Looks good to me considering the answer is right on the television screen," laughed Agnes.

"Oh yeah, I didn't see that there," said Mona.

"It's OK Mona it could have been a trick question," said Beau.

"Yeah, we got another question right," said Miles.

"On to question number seven," said Mona. What year did the movie titanic come out?

"Didn't it sink?" asked Agnes.

"Yes, it did," said Wanda.

"So how could they make a movie about it if it's still in the ocean?" asked Wanda.

"You can remake what happens in a movie and not use the original boat," said Tallulah.

"Oh, that's interesting," said Edith.

"So quick we need to figure out a year," said Agnes.

"How about 1997," said Edith.

"Why that year?" asked Agnes.

"I don't know it just sounded good to me," said Edith.

"Wow good guess you were right Edith," said Tallulah.

"Of course, I am because I am that good," said Edith.

"Yes, you're Edith," said Agnes.

Are you good in the sack too?" asked Miles.

"Wouldn't you like to know?" asked Edith as she winks at him.

"Yes, I sure would like to know," said Miles.

Edith just shook her head and kept her mouth shut.

"Question number eight," said Miles.

"Who sang the song "My Way?"

"Oh, what's that guy's name," said Tallulah.

"That's what we need to figure out," said Wanda.

"No, I know who it is, and I just can't think of it," said Tallulah.

"Well, we must hurry up," said Edith.

"Oh, I got it," said Tallulah as she gets excited and stands up.

"Hurry up Tallulah," yelled Agnes.

"Old Blue Eyes Frank Sinatra," said Tallulah.

WOO HOO! We got it right excellent job Tallulah," said Wanda.

"Shut up everyone and let's get to question number ten," said Vera.

"We are only on question nine," said Tallulah.

"Oh, dammit I'm so bored," said Vera.

Question nine," said Wanda. How many weeks are in a year?

"There is seven days in a week, so I don't know," said Blanche.

"I know the answer," said Miles.

"OK then let's hear it Miles," said Agnes.

"The answer is fifty-two," said Miles.

"Excellent job Miles, you got it right," said Wanda.

"I do still remember somethings that I learned in school," said Miles.

OK last question magic number ten," said Wanda. What is the largest bone in the human body?

"My legs are longer than any part of me," said Wanda.

"They are looking for a bone," said Agnes.

"My head is big," laughed Edith.

"We know, but that isn't a bone," laughed Agnes.

"It's your damn femur," said Vera out of nowhere. "Oh, I never thought of that," said Wanda.

"Do we really think she is right?" asked Edith.

"Let's just see if she is," said Agnes. "

As they wait for the answer, they became quiet.

Camp Funhouse 409

"By golly look at that Vera was right after all," said Wanda.

"See, I told you I knew what I was talking about," said Vera.

"You're right Vera we should have believed you," said Agnes.

"Wow I can't believe this was our second to last change and now we get to go back to camp soon," said Mona.

"Then there was a voice on the television that told everyone that they aren't done with the challenges yet and that another door awaits them.

"We knew this wasn't going to be the last one," said Tallulah.

"What else could we possible have to do?" asked Agnes.

"Well, maybe we will find out who planned all of these challenges," said Wanda.

"True so let's get moving and see what is next," said Edith.

"I hope whatever is waiting for us I hope all of you know that I have enjoyed doing all of this with you," said Edith.

"Me too, Edith and it feels so bittersweet that it's ending right now or after this last challenge," said Mona.

"Come on let's go people," said Vera as she kicked everyone out the door.

On to the next challenge . . .

CHAPTER 28

Booger Branch Lane

"Wow we are finally on to door number ten and it's such a pretty purple door," said Agnes.

"This is so exciting I can't wait to get to the end," said Wanda.

"Why don't you like being with us Wanda?" asked Tallulah.

"No, I didn't say that I just met it nice to go back to camp and see the rest of the people we haven't see in a couple of days," said Wanda.

"Yeah, I guess, but I do like spending time with all of you also," said Tallulah.

"Well, that's sweet of you to say Tallulah," said Agnes.

"Well, it's how I feel because you just never know what is going to happen with us someday down the long road," said Tallulah.

" That's a valid reason also," said Edith.

"Let's see what is waiting for us next," said Blanche as she opens the door and goes in and when they got inside, they got a shocking surprise.

"Why is there a big nose in the middle of the floor?" asked Agnes.

"How are we supposed to know what is in it?" asked Edith.

"Well, I know that I can be a smart ass so I'm thinking maybe snot is in it," said Agnes.

"It's oozing slime out its nose that's gross and definitely not snot," said Tallulah.

"I thought maybe it would turn you on," said Agnes laughing.

"That's not the way to turn me on," said Tallulah.

"We don't want to know how to turn you on," said Miles.

"I find that so surprising since you have been making comments since the day we came here and now you have nothing to say," said Tallulah.

"You do nothing for me unfortunately Tallulah," said Miles.

"You turn me on big boy," laughed Tallulah.

"Glad you can joke about it," said Miles.

"At least I was serious about you turning me on," said Tallulah.

"I'm flattered, but still, us together no sorry I don't see it," said Miles.

"I see that I am not loved," said Tallulah. You're better off without him," said Blanche.

"So, who is going to get the challenge card from the booger nose?" asked Wanda.

"Not me I'm not touching it," said Edith.

"Must I do everything here," said Blanche.

"What the hell does that mean?" asked Agnes.

"It just seems like I'm always finding the challenge cards," said Blanche.

"It's not like it's not hard to find it's hanging from the nose," said Agnes.

"Do you want to read the clue or are you to tired doing that to?" asked Tallulah.

"Oh, just shut up Tallulah I got it," said Blanche.

"One person must climb up and reach in the giant snotty nose as far as they can to retrieve your very last clue," said Blanche.

"Ewe that's so disgusting," said Tallulah trying to hold down anything that was in her stomach as she watched the snot just come out and go everywhere.

"I can tell you right now you can count me out I'm not doing it," said Agnes.

Tallulah saw a bucket of water and decided to dump it on Agnes head.

Splash!

"Why in the hell am I always the target and I am still wet from before?" asked Agnes.

"I just thought you needed to cool off a little bit more," laughed Tallulah.

"Before Tallulah could say another word Vera got behind her and dumped the other water bucket on her head.

"Now that's funny and what you did to Agnes was not," said Vera walking away.

"Thanks for sticking up for me Vera, I appreciate it,' said Agnes.

"Payback is a bitch and no problem it's the least I could do since you beat the shit out of me with a pool noodle," laughed Vera.

"This challenge looks fun," said Wanda.

"That doesn't surprise me that you love the challenge and Agnes is backing out," said Tallulah

"What is that supposed to mean?" asked Agnes getting mad.

"You haven't pulled your weight during this adventure," said Tallulah.

"Were you with us in most of the challenges because I have especially when I pool noodled Vera to the ground," said Agnes.

"You are still a little high from that mushroom you ate back at hanky-panky, aren't you?" asked Wanda.

"Your right we are going to be over with this adventure soon, and you want to sit out," said Tallulah.

"Will you two stops bickering and Tallulah leave Agnes alone she has done challenges with us so just stop," said Wanda.

"Let's just get this challenge done so we can do our last one or whatever they have ready for us," said Agnes.

"Fine if that's the way you want it then we will just do it," said Tallulah who has no idea what she is saying.

"Listen up everyone I have decided that I'm going to be the one to pick the nose," said Mona. Everyone just looked at her as if she as not serious about it.

"Are you sure you want to do it?" asked Edith.

"I'll pick the nose I'm the one with the nose picker finger," said Mona as she bends her index finger

"Mona has a nose picker finger?" asked Edith.

"Everyone has a nose picker finger you never know when you might need it to pick your nose," said Wanda.

"That's gross and I don't do that," said Tallulah.

"Everyone picks there nose occasionally it's a natural thing," said Tallulah.

As Mona gets ready to do the challenge Wanda is still wondering which finger picks the nose good.

"Is anyone going to help me?" asked Mona again.

"Not me I don't want to ruin my manicure," said Tallulah.

"That doesn't surprise me," said Agnes.

"Then why don't you do it?" asked Tallulah.

"My back aches still from getting hit with the pool noodle," said Vera, YA, YA, YA sure it does," said Tallulah.

"Oh my God get the hell out of my way I will help her out," said Vera. WHOA! Vera takes it easy as she picks up Mona and shoves her in the nose, as Mona yells.

Mona's her legs are hanging out of the nose as she keeps reaching to find the envelope that they need.

"Are you OK my dear?" asked Wanda.

"Yuck someone really needs to blow their nose more often it's so sticky and yucky," laughed Mona.

"Oh, don't worry she sounds fine," said Beau.

"Do you see the envelope?" asked Tallulah.

"Pull me out right now?" asked Mona.

Everyone grabbed her legs ad yanked her out of the nose and she landed right on Beau.

"My Mona is fine," said Beau as he grabbed her in his arms.

"Thanks for catching Beau," said Mona.

"It's not like I had a choice, but I'm always happy to help you my dear," said Beau.

"Did you get the envelope?" asked Tallulah.

"Yes, I got it Tallulah," said Mona.

Mona pulled the envelope out with the green slime dripping from it.

"Excellent job Mona," said Agnes.

"Anything to get moving on and do it for the team because no matter what anyone thinks we have been a team the whole time we have been here and no one should say anything else about anyone here," said Mona putting her foot down for all the crap that happened and have said since they started this adventure.

"Well, said my Mona," said Beau as he kisses Mona.

"So, what does the challenge card say?" asked Agnes.

Mona opened the envelope and started reading the card: "Dear Seniors, Congratulations for winning all your challenges. We hope that you have learned a lot about yourself and the others who are around you. Please go down the staircase and go to the banquet room there will be your final prize waiting for you. You're all well deserving for what you all conquered while in the funhouse. Thank you and come again! From the Challenge Gods."

"Well, should we go?" asked Agnes.

"Yes, I'm ready," said Tallulah.

"You look puzzled Wanda," said Mona.

Well, I don't understand one thing in on the envelope," said Wanda.

Which part?" asked Agnes.

"Well, I find it a little weird that they called us seniors," said Wanda.

What is weird about that?" asked Tallulah.

"I think you're overthinking this and I think we just need to go and see what our prize is that's waiting for us," said Agnes.

"I guess you're right," said Wanda.

"Let's go finish this adventure up," said Agnes as she held the door open for everyone.

CHAPTER 29

You Are on Candid Camera

"I just can't believe how fun they're having together," said Belle as Serena and her sit there and watch everything that has been going on for the last few minutes.

"I think they will be done soon so we should make sure everything is ready to go," said Belle.

"Now they're running a race that's so freaking great, I'm loving all of this," said Serena.

"I am also enjoying this, but now I have to find my list that I made," said Belle as she stretches and realizing that they have been watching the seniors for way to long.

"At least you know they aren't getting into trouble," said Serena.

"That would be the first," said Belle.

Chip came through the door to check and see how everything is going and if everything is going on schedule.

"Oh, we spoke to soon," laughed Belle.

"What does that mean?" asked Chip.

"Nothing just an inside joke," said Serena.

"Oh, I see how it is," laughed Chip.

"We are happy to see you here Chip," said Belle.

"I just stopped by to see how long we had until we had to leave, I need to make a stop along the way?" asked Chip.

"You planned the activities, so you tell me Chip?" asked Belle.

"Well, it looks like we have about an hour or little less depending how fast they go," said Chip.

"Well, we better get things backed and moving," said Belle.

"I'm so excited about all of this," said Serena.

"I do have to tell you that you're incredibly talented Chip," said Belle.

"Thanks Belle, but I had some help with Fay and Hazel," said Chip.

"I'm still impressed with your abilities," said Chip.

"It's no big deal, I just learn how to do things with help learning from people and I wanted to make it fun for the seniors," said Chip.

"Yeah, it's interesting for them, and it will be interesting as we let them tell us everything they did," said Serena.

Belle was telling Chip about everything that she has seen so far, and Chip could not believe what she was telling him. At least they're all getting along now said Serena.

"Hope you know Belle we did are still sorry to you and to you also Serena and to all the other staff members for not including you in all of this," said Chip.

"It's OK Chip we are all here now putting in our input, so we are all working together to make it fun, said Belle.

"I sometimes wish I went to college and got the opportunity to gain experience with all this stuff and even more with what there is to offer," said Serena.

"What's stopping you from going to college Serena?" asked Belle who was curious why Serena wasn't making plans for her future.

"It's extremely complicated in my life and with my family," said Serena.

"Your still young and there is so much out there for you to learn and waiting for you," said Belle.

"Same goes to you also Chip I know you were thinking about college but changed your mind at the last minute," said Serena.

"Who did you hear that from?" asked Chip.

"Tory and I were talking one day, and your name came up and at that time I figure out you were cousins," said Serena.

"So, you before the jousting match that we were cousins?" asked Chip.

"Yes, that's right," laughed Serena.

"I'm glad everyone knows now and there are no secrets," said Chip.

Even know there was the secret about Tallulah being his mother, but he wasn't ready to tell everyone yet.

"What if someone could help the both of you so that you can pursue your dreams and make things happen in your life so you can be happier?" asked Belle.

"Belle you would do that for us?" asked Serena.

"I wasn't necessarily thinking me, but then again you never know what might happen and only time can tell," said Belle, thinking about what exactly she could do for them and if you wait and see what happens and all the dreams that do come true while we are here.

"I couldn't ask you to help me and do that Belle and you know that' said Chip as his fingers start to twitch.

"Both of you relax and enjoy this week with the seniors that are still here that's all I am asking you both to do," said Belle

"By the way things look two of our seniors already had too much fun," said Belle.

"Yeah, who would have thought this would go from a nice adventure to seniors eating mushrooms," said Serena.

"What mushrooms I didn't do that, and I wouldn't?" asked Chip who was getting worried he was going to get blame for something he didn't do.

"Nice save Chip," said Serena.

"Relax Chip it's OK Vera and Tallulah are the happiest they have ever been," said Belle.

"I just swear we had nothing to do with it I promise you that," said Chip.

Chip kept thinking about who would have put those mushrooms there for the seniors to get a hold of.

"Sorry Belle I shouldn't have said that to you I just wanted to be honest," said Chip.

"I'm shocked that Beau and Mona got that close that fast," said Serena who was trying to change the subject.

"I'm not when we were at the campfire, they couldn't stop looking at each other," said Belle.

"When you're in love you just let things happen, I guess," said Serena.

"Speaking of love, I need to go and get something I will see you at the funhouse in a little while," said Chip.

"We will see you soon Chip," said Belle.

"Boy he is acting strange," said Serena.

"He is a man so it's a normal thing," laughed Belle.

Well, getting back to Mona and Beau I just hope nothing stops them from having a fun time together," said Belle because they sure do deserve it even know Vera is there, but she looks like she is having a fun time also.

"I think when they find out everything, they won't listen to anyone's conversations again," said Serena.

"Well, it's almost that time we should get everything in the buses and head out," said Belle.

"I'll go and get Ethel and Clara," said Serena.

"I'll grab the keys and have everyone meet us out front," said Belle.

"This is going to be so much fun I can't wait to see their faces," said Serena.

"They are going to be so surprised," said Belle.

"I will see you in a few," said Serena as she goes out the door.

Belle turns on the loudspeaker and made an announcement letting everyone know to get to the buses so that everyone can load in it. "Our Seniors Are Coming Home!

CHAPTER 30

Surprise!!

Everyone gets on the one of the buses and are ready to go. Hazel and Fay wanted to make sure that Belle didn't need anything else before they got on the bus.

"I should be all set I got my list and art helped me back the bus so all we need to do is just get on," said Belle.

"Well, OK I guess we will get on the bus," said Hazel.

As Hazel and Fay were coming out of the office Chip had stopped by.

"Is everything OK?" asked Hazel.

"Yes, I just wanted to ask Belle one quick question," said Chip as he gives Hazel a kiss.

"Are you riding on the bus with us?" asked Fay.

"Yes, I will be right there," said Chip.

Hazel seemed a little suspicious but headed to the bus so they could talk.

"Are you coming Chip?" asked Hazel.

"I'll be right behind you I need to talk to Belle about something relax everything is fine," yelled Chip.

I can wait for you if you like?" asked Hazel.

"Go ahead I'll be right there," said Chip why is she making it so difficult as Chip talks to himself.

"So, what is going Chip?" asked Belle

I was wondering if I can add something to our plan at the funhouse?" asked Chip.

"Depends on what it is," said Belle.

Well, before we tell my mother about me being her son, I want to ask Hazel to marry me," said Chip.

"Oh, Chip that's great I am so excited," said Belle as she jumps out of her chair.

"If you need me for anything I'm here, but you do what you need to do," said Belle.

"That is why I had to cut out ahead of time so I could go and pick up the ring and I was going to go right to the funhouse, but I thought I should ask you if it was OK," said Chip.

"Wondering what you were up to, but I knew eventually I would see or hear what it was all about," said Belle.

"I've been waiting for this day all my life and I'm excited to share it with everyone," said Chip.

"I'm so happy for you and I can't wait to see Hazel's face when you propose to her," said Belle.

"Even my mother who doesn't know I'm her son yet, but I feel this is the right things to do," said Chip.

"I think it's great that you and she will come together tomorrow," said Belle.

"I don't want to wait, but I need to do this and thanks for everything you did to help me," said Chip.

"It was no problem, and I am so glad I will be a part of your proposal and bringing you and your mom together all at once," said Belle as she thinks about the dinner she must go to on Saturday and then the light went on in her head.

Instead of having dinner along with Aspen on Saturday we can make Friday their last day at the camp and beach and BBQ Day so that Heaven's Ridge people can join everyone here.

"Oh my God I am such a fucking genius Belle said to herself.

"The buses parked down the street a little so that no one would see them.

"It was time for the shocking surprise, and everyone was so excited about seeing the seniors. Even all the five seniors were excited to go on a trip even if they had no idea where they were going.

"Alright everyone gets off buses," said Belle.

"There is the other bus," said Hazel.

"Why is it on top of a sand pile?" asked Ethel.

"I'm not sure Ethel, but I'm sure there is a good reason for it," said Hazel.

"OK so how do we get to that room without them knowing about it?" asked Belle.

"Chip thought about it for a minute then told Belle there was another way to get in through the back and there is another staircase we can use," said Chip.

"Alright sounds good let's get everyone, and everything unloaded from the bus.

"Oh, this is going to be so much fun," said Tinsley who gets excited about everything even if she was clueless about what is going on. They all go to the back of the house and open the door quietly, so no one hears them coming in.

"OK Chip where is the door?" asked Belle.

"When we go up the stairs it's on the first floor and it's a banquet room," said Chip.

Everyone went up the stairs quietly as every step was creaking. Eloise and Ace helped the other seniors up the stairs because the steps were steep.

"We got you don't have to worry we got you," said Eloise.

I'm starting to break a sweat," said Jasper.

"I feel the same way," said Ethel as Jasper grabs her hand to help her up the stairs.

"That's why we are going slowly and everyone else is ahead of us," said Ace.

They finally made it to the top and just in time to see how everything was coming along. Belle put up a curtain so that the seniors didn't see who was behind it until they pulled it down. Hazel and Fay put the puzzle pieces all mixed up so the seniors can put it together. Art and Casper brought in a big box that was going to filled with lots of confetti and balloons so when one of the keys opens it then it all will come out. Frankie made goodies for all of them to have when they were all together.

"Looks great Frankie you out did yourself again," said Belle.

"You're not mad that I am here?" asked Frankie.

"It wouldn't be a party without you here," said Belle.

"I had a little help from Tory," said Frankie.

"You both did great," said Belle.

"Thanks Belle and thank you for being so understanding with Chip and I and me and Frankie being together," said Tory.

"I'm happy for the both of you," said Belle as she walked away.

Belle went off to find Chip to see how he was handling proposing to Hazel.

"How are things going with you?" asked Chip. I'm a little nervous, but I'm doing great, and it's exactly way I want," said Chip. "So happy for you two you have come a long way in just a week, and I wish you happiness," said Chip.

"I owe you everything if it weren't for you and that corny jousting match, we wouldn't be together," said Chip.

"I guess it was a little corny, but at least no one really got hurt or people's feelings," said Belle.

"Yeah, but everything seems to be right back where it was," said Chip.

"I think you two really did it all by yourselves you just needed a little push and a hit with a jousting pole," laughed Belle.

"Now I just hope she said yes," said Chip. I'm sure, she will so no worries there," said Belle.

"Thanks for your confidence in me Belle," said Chip.

"No problem and thank you for letting me be the first to know what you were doing," said Belle.

"Your welcome Belle," said Chip.

"Hey Belle, the seniors are over with their next challenges, so they're on their way here," said Harlow as she shows Belle the screen on the tablet.

"Oh, great OK everyone let's get in our places they will be in here soon," said Belle.

Everyone got in their spots and were ready to surprise them.

Everyone could hear them coming and stayed quiet.

"I thought you said we were over with all the challenges Agnes?" asked Wanda.

"I thought we were, but it looks like we aren't and that's what the damn card said," said Agnes.

"Puzzle Time," said Edith, as she reads the door.

"Well let's get in there and see what it's all about," said Wanda.

"I don't know anything about doing a damn puzzle," said Blanche.

"They open the door and see the curtain and the table with the puzzle.

"Here is the clue," said Tallulah as she goes right to it.

"Congratulations you have made it to the end of the Funhouse all you have to do now put this puzzle together and you can go to your prize that's waiting for you," said Agnes.

"Oh, this is so exciting," said Edith dancing around.

Fay is on the other side of the curtain trying not to laugh.

"Did you hear something?" asked Tallulah.

"No, you must be hearing things or its your stomach talking to you," said Agnes.

"Yeah, sure I'm hearing things," said Tallulah.

"So, who knows how to put a puzzle together?" asked Agnes.

"Not me I like word searches," said Mona.

"Not me either and I'm not going to go in the slime," said Wanda.

"That was the last challenge we did," said Agnes.

Everyone just stared at Vera as she is just looking the other way.

"Do I look like I do stupid puzzles?" asked Vera.

"Vera has a good point there," said Blanche.

"I only do word searches," said Tallulah.

"Do you know who loves puzzle and could solve this quickly?" asked Edith.

"No who," said Agnes.

"Only if Ethel were here, she could put the puzzle together, but I am glad she isn't she has caused so much trouble for us at Heaven's Ridge," said Wanda.

"That's true she could, but she is not here so we have to do it on our own," said Edith.

"It will be OK," said as she started to cry.

"I don't even know why she came with us to Mystic Senior Camp in the first place," said Agnes.

"OK let us get back to the puzzle and not keep bashing Ethel who can't defend herself now we can do this just like all the other challenges we have been doing," said Blanche.

"It's called teamwork," said Tallulah.

"Oh man just don't screw this up," said Vera.

Everyone starts talking at the same time on which piece goes in what spot.

"That's not right it needs to go on the top," said Wanda.

"Why wouldn't it go there?" asked Agnes.

"That's not right it needs to go on the top like I said before and this piece matches the bottom," said Wanda.

"Just try it and shut the hell up," said Vera.

"For someone who isn't really helping has a lot to say," said Agnes.

"I agree with Wanda," said Mona. I had enough of your shit Vera and if you can't say anything nice don't say anything at all," said Agnes.

"Never mind what I have to say doesn't matter obviously," said Mona.

"I heard you Mona," said Wanda.

"Fine suit yourself I quit with all this crap and all of you I'm leaving," said Vera.

"Knock off your shit Vera like Agnes said we are in this together," said Wanda.

"Almost like the three amigos," said Blanche.

"Amigo's?" asked Tallulah.

"OK fine here is one you can understand musketeers," said Blanche.

"Three musketeers," said Wanda.

"You counted wrong because there is nine of us here," said Tallulah.

"OK sorry I counted wrong the nine musketeers I'm not perfect," said Wanda.

"No one gets what Wanda is talking about she isn't making any sense?" asked Agnes.

"No, but I get what she is saying it's almost like we are doing teamwork," said Tallulah.

As they all worked together to get the puzzle together, they realized that working to together actually works and finally solved the puzzle.

"H.O.L.Y, said Tallulah.

"Yeah, she can spell," said Agnes.

"Very funny Agnes," said Tallulah.

"What is that supposed to mean?" asked Agnes.

"Maybe we are all going to hell," said Tallulah.

"Holy is not hell, is it?" asked Blanche.

"Hey, don't go there," said Agnes.

On the other side of the curtain everyone is laughing at the conversations the seniors are having.

"Do you have any idea what it means Miles, since you're good with letters?" asked Tallulah.

"No, this time I don't have a clue what it means," said Miles.

"I'm missing my bed," said Mona.

"You already had hanky-panky under the pillows," said Agnes.

"What else do you want?" asked Blanche.

"Mona and I can find a place for round two if you like," said Beau.

" Oh, please don't go there my virgin ears," said Blanche.

"Your far from being virgin and I think we already went through this before," said Tallulah.

"I think we better jump out quick before they really go at it," said Belle.

"Yeah, I agree as much as it's fun to listen to them," said Hazel.

"On the count of three we will jump out," said Chip. One, two, three," said Belle.

Everyone jumped out and threw confetti at the seniors as the curtain came down. Everyone from the camp yelled surprise to the seniors.

"How the hell did you get here?" asked Tallulah.

"Surprise to all of you," said Belle.

"Oh my God I can't believe you're all here," said Wanda. Still in shock the seniors were getting hugs from everyone.

"How did you know where we were or that we were here?" asked Agnes. Chip, Hazel, and Fay came forward to tell them how they know and told them the whole story. Surprisingly, the seniors were not mad, but happy because it brought all of them closer as friends.

"Oh, even with Vera?" asked Serena.

"Yes, even with dear old grouchy Vera," said Agnes.

"That is amazing to hear," said Belle.

"We are sorry that we were invading on your privacy," said Agnes.

"You guys did a wonderful job setting up everything," said Edith.

"Well, that was all Chip," said Hazel so proud of him.

"We were curious what H.O.L.Y stands for?" asked Tallulah.

"Oh, Chip why don't you answer that question for Tallulah?" asked Belle as she gives him a wink.

"I would love to answer that question," said Chip.

"Sonny why are you sweating so much it's not that hot in here?" asked Wanda.

"It is just warm in here," said Chip.

"See you didn't believe me when I said that many rooms ago," said Tallulah. Chip couldn't believe how much he was like his mother, but he couldn't let that distract him from what he was about to do.

"So, what does H.O.L.Y stand for, or do we have to wait for another hot flash to happen?" asked Edith as she is laughing.

"The word H.O.L.Y means "High in Loving You and from the day I met Hazel we got to know each other more than we did when we were kids I fell in love with her," said Chip as he faces Hazel.

"Oh, he is going to pop the question," said Mona.

"Oh, this is so sweet I think I am going to cry," said Tallulah ho was technically watching her baby boy Chip goes closer to Hazel and grabs her hand.

"I know we had our difficulties this week, but there is no one in this world that I rather be with then you I love you Hazel," said Chip.

"Oh, here he goes," said Harlow grabbing onto Art's hand trying not to cry.

"I would love it if you would be my wife and spend the rest of your life with me?" asked Chip as he slipped the ring on Hazel's finger.

"Well sweetie what is your answer going to be to him?" asked Miles?

"I would love to be your wife, so my answer is yes," said Hazel as she looked at Chip.

"I love you so much," said Chip as they kiss, and everyone is cheering and clapping.

"There is no one I would rather be with than you, and I love you so much," said Hazel.

"I remember that feeling just getting in engaged and how happy I was," said Mona.

"You can always have that feeling again," said Beau.

"How darling I don't think married life in a retirement home is exactly a high of life," said Mona.

"No, but I don't care where we are I am happy anywhere with you," said Beau giving Mona a kiss.

"Are you as happy as we are about Hazel and Chip?" screamed Wanda.

"Yes, we are, and we wish we could do that also," said Beau.

"Why can't you" asked Tallulah?

"It's not that we can't do it because we know we can it's just how we will be spending the rest of our life together," said Mona.

"Who the hell cares where you live if you both are happy and can be together forever," said Tallulah.

"You know Tallulah you're a very smart woman and don't let anyone else tell you something different," said Beau.

"I never do listen so that won't be a problem," laughed Tallulah.

"When we get back to Heaven's Ridge and we can plan something together," said Mona.

"That is my girl," said Beau as he kisses her.

All the food and drinks are gone, and it was time to return to camp for the next couple of days.

"Well, everyone it's time to get on the bus and head back to camp for the last couple of days, and I want to say congratulations to Chip and Hazel," said Belle.

"Thank you, Belle," yelled Hazel. Casper got the bus off the sand pile careful and didn't even leave a mark as the others got on the other buses.

"Do you want me to drive?" asked Vera.

"No, it's OK Vera I got this," said Belle.

"Yeah, that's what I thought," said Vera as she laughs down to her seat.

"So excited to go back to camp,' said Tallulah just thinking about other good things that may happen while she is still at camp.

"Still so much more to do and to see and I am looking forward to it," said Agnes.

This adventure is far from over yet so stay tuned for more.

CHAPTER 31

Chip and Tallulah's Reunion

"So, how do you think Tallulah is going to take that Chip is her son?" asked Harlow.

"I honestly don't know how it's going to go," said Belle.

"If they both have been looking for each other then I don't see it being a problem because they both want to be reunited," said Harlow.

"Yeah, I know you're right, but first I'm just going to get Tallulah here and talk to her before the big reveal and just see where here head is at," said Belle.

"You are so good with people I wish I were like that sometimes, but I am usually too busy chasing guys, but that's about to change," said Harlow.

"Yeah, but you don't have to do that anymore because you have found your guy," said Belle.

"Yeah, Art is my guy and I think always I'll be, said Harlow.

"You think that you two will be together for a long time?" asked Belle.

"I think so because he doesn't treat me like other guys did before and that's one thing that I have always wanted, but too scared to take that leap," said Harlow.

"And Art is that big leap?" asked Belle.

"Yes, I do believe he is," said Harlow.

"He is a keeper I really like him to, and I see how much he makes you happy and that's just wonderful Harlow you deserve it," said Belle.

"Thanks Belle and someday you will find your Mr. Wonderful, or should I say Ms. Wonderful," laughed Harlow.

"There won't be either I'm giving up on both so end of story," said Belle.

"I guess we will have to wait until Saturday to find out," said Harlow.

"No, we won't because I canceled with Aspen," said Belle.

"Why would you do that?" asked Harlow.

"I was only doing as a favor for finding out who Chips mother was, and I have another idea in the works," said Belle. "What is that plan?" asked Harlow.

Well, we are inviting Heaven's Ridge employees here for a beach day and BBQ," said Belle.

"That could be fun," said Harlow.

"It will be an important thing to do before we send the seniors back to Heaven's Ridge," said Belle.

"I have an idea and I want you to listen before you say anything," said Harlow.

Belle just gives Harlow a look.

"Just listen first and then judge me after," said Harlow.

"I won't judge you I just can't guarantee that I will do whatever you have up your sleeve," said Belle.

"Do you know how you always wish you could help people make their dreams come true?" asked Harlow.

"Yes, I do and that's what I did for Tallulah and Chip," said Belle.

"Yes, so why don't you asked Aspen if he could get these counselors a job at Heaven's Ridge?" asked Harlow.

"I can make sure they get the schooling they need that's no problem and I have already been in contact with the dean, and he was happy to help," said Belle.

"It's not a horrible idea and I do like to help people with you by getting them the right classes they need," said Harlow as she sits there and ponders the idea.

"It might work, but we will have to be sweet to Aspen so it can happen," Belle.

"What do you think Belle?" asked Harlow.

"OK I will talk to Aspen, but I'm not making any promises," said Belle.

"I know, but it's worth the chance to just ask Aspen," said Harlow.

"I'll call her later today to see if they all will be willing to come for the BBQ after everything with Tallulah and Chip happens," said Belle.

"We should be like Charlie's Angels or something the way we make things happen," said Harlow.

Belle just sat there and laughed at Harlow.

Chip came to the office to meet Tallulah after all these years, and you can see the excitement on his face.

"Are you ready to meet your mother?" asked Belle.

"Yes, I am, but I will be honest I am shitting bricks nervous," said Chip.

"Well since you put it that way, I don't blame you I'm nervous for the both of you," said Belle.

"Thank you so much for everything," said Chip.

I will have one of the girls get her and bring her here and then I will talk to her and see were her heads at and then you can come out and hopefully instant love," said Belle.

"I really hope so," said Chip.

"Do you want Hazel here with you?" asked Belle.

"No, I told her to wait and then she can come after," said Chip.

"OK, but anytime you want her here to let me know and I will get her," said Belle.

"Thank you, Belle, for everything you have done for me and everyone else at this camp," said Chip.

"You're welcome it was no problem," said Belle.

There was a knock at the door.

"I wonder who that could be," said Chip.

"No idea," said Belle as she tells them to come in.

"Hello Hazel, what are you doing here?" asked Chip.

"I know that you told me to wait, but I just wanted to wish you good luck," said Hazel as she puts her arms around Chip and gave him a kiss on the cheek.

"Thank you for coming I'm so nervous," said Chip.

"Suck it up you will be fine this is what you have been waiting for all these years," said Hazel.

"I know I have I just can't believe that this day has finally come," said Chip as he holds on to Hazel for a little bit longer.

"Sorry to break this up, but it about that time," said Belle.

"I won't be too far away if you need me," said Hazel.

"Thank you, babe," said Chip.

"For what?" asked Hazel.

"For loving me," said Chip.

"Your welcome sweetie and I love you," said Hazel.

"I love you too baby," said Chip as Hazel goes out the door.

"Are you ready?" asked Belle.

"Yes, I am let's do this," said Chip.

"Great I will tell Harlow to get Tallulah and you go relax in my office until she gets here," said Belle.

"Harlow it's time to get Tallulah if you're not busy?" asked Belle.

"No not at all I will be more than happy to get Tallulah for you," said Harlow.

"Thank you Harlow I appreciate you," yells Belle as Harlow goes out the door.

Harlow head down to Tallulah's cabin and knocks on the door.

"Hello Eloise, is Tallulah free to come with me for a little while?" asked Harlow?

"Yeah, sure come on in and I will get her for you," said Harlow. Eloise went to Tallulah bed and told her that Harlow would like to talk to her.

"What did I do now I just got back I haven't had time to do anything," said Tallulah.

"Hey Tallulah, it's OK you're not in trouble Belle has something she needs to talk to you about that's all," said Harlow.

"Oh, alright it's not like I'm busy anyways," said Tallulah.

"That's a girl," said Penny. As Harlow and Tallulah head back to the office they started talking.

"So how does it feel to be back to camp?" asked Tallulah.

"I am glad that we all came here and got to go on our adventure because it brought us so much closer and the ones, I wasn't close to before has gotten closer too if that makes any sense because I know that I am rambling," said Tallulah.

"Oh, that's great to hear Tallulah," said Harlow. I'm going to cherish what memories we made together just like Belle said the first day," said Tallulah.

"Yeah, Belle is big on that and that's why she wanted everyone to do it and I am so glad that you took it to heart and made your memories," said Harlow.

"Belle is very smart for doing this camp for us seniors it was such a clever idea," said Tallulah.

"Well, here we are," said Harlow as she opens the door.

"Belle we are here," said Harlow.

"Oh, great I will be right out as Belle calls from one of the rooms.

"I feel like I am in the principal's office," said Tallulah

"You aren't in any trouble," said Harlow.

"Belle just wants to talk to you it's no big deal," said Harlow.

"OK if you say so," said Tallulah as she thinks of when she stole the keys.

"Welcome to my office Tallulah I'm so glad that you're here," said Belle.

"Oh really," said Tallulah still wondering what she is doing there.

I recently heard that you have a son and that you would love to find him," said Belle.

"Yes, I would very much so," said Tallulah.

"So, let me ask you this what if I told you I found him for you and that he was looking for you also," said Belle.

Tallulah was so excited she jumped up from the chair and almost on the desk that Belle was at.

"Easy Tallulah calm down and please sit down and relax," said Belle.

"Where is my son?" asked Tallulah.

"Well, it's quite a coincidence that he is working here at camp," said Belle.

"My son has been here all along and never said anything to me?" asked Tallulah as she was about to cry.

"Yes, but you must remember that he didn't remember who you were either," said Belle. "He came to this camp because he knew and had a feeling that you were going to be here," said Belle. "He wasn't sure at first, but then I made a phone call and made sure it was a sure thing," said Belle.

"Oh boy I hope it wasn't anyone I got naked in front of," laughed Tallulah.

"Belle didn't know where to go with that one, so she just let it go.

"So, your son is here and wants to meet you right now Tallulah," said Belle.

"Oh yes can I meet him please?" begged Tallulah.

"Yes, I will get him right now and bring him out here," said Belle.

Tallulah brushed her fingers through her hair and pulled down her shirt a little more, so no skin was showing, but her arms. Belle goes in her office and checks on Chip.

"Are you ready to meet her because she is so excited to meet you?" asked Belle.

Chip took a deep breathe before answering Belle.

"Yes, I am I think I am just so nervous," said Chip.

"It is totally OK for you to be that nervous, but I will be there, and I think once you see Tallulah you will be fine," said Belle.

"Maybe I should have had Hazel stay with me," said Chip.

"I can still go and get her if you want me too," said Belle.

"No, it's OK I know she will just tell me to suck it up buttercup anyway," said Chip.

" Let's go meet your mother," said Belle as she puts her arm around him to let him know she is here for him.

Belle ad Chip came down the hallway as Tallulah stood up because she could hear them coming.

"OK Tallulah her is your son Chip," said Belle as her and Chip walk closer to the desk where Tallulah was standing.

"Oh, my baby boy I have missed you so much," said Tallulah as she leaves lipstick all over his face from kissing him.

"Hi Tallulah," said Chip as that was the only thing, he could think of to say.

"Don't hi Tallulah me you call me mom," said Tallulah as she whacks him on the back of the head.

"Hey that's not cool mom," said Chip.

"OK I'm sorry about that, but I have missed you so much all these years without any word," said Tallulah.

"I have missed you to, and I wanted to say that I'm sorry I left you all those years and I'm not going to leave you ever again," said Chip.

"You are the one that's getting married," said Tallulah as she was getting all weepy.

"Yes, Hazel and I are getting married sometime hopefully soon," said Chip.

"My boy is getting married," said Tallulah as she does a little happy dance for him.

"OK Tallulah we see you're happy just please be careful," said Belle.

Tallulah's face got red quickly when she realized that she got naked in front of her son.

"What is wrong?" asked Chip as he looked at Belle not knowing what was wrong.

"Oh, you know," said Tallulah as she realized what she did at the pool that day.

"No, I don't so please tell me?" asked Chip.

"The pool me getting naked," said Tallulah as she put her head down.

"Don't worry about it I have and now we can start over as mother and son," said Chip.

"I would really like that," said Tallulah.

"Me too mom," said Chip.

"Oh, he called me mom," said Tallulah as she starts to cry.

"Oh, please don't cry I thought that would make you happy," said Chip.

"They are happy tears because my son is back in my life and never going to leave again," said Tallulah.

"Yes, I am, and I'm not going anywhere," said Chip.

"Oh, you're so handsome." said Tallulah

"Oh, you know who else is at the camp?" asked Chip.

"No who?" asked Tallulah.

"Tory your niece," said Chip.

"Do I know her?" asked Tallulah.

"No not really, but she is also eager to meet you," said Chip.

"Sounds good to me," said Tallulah.

"I'm so glad today has finally come," said Chip.

"What happens when I go back to Heaven's Ridge?" asked Tallulah.

"Then Hazel and I will have to visit you and maybe have you help plan our wedding," said Chip.

"Oh yes, I would love to help the both of you," said Tallulah.

"Are you ready to go back to your cabin now," asked Belle.

"Do we have to go?" asked Tallulah.

"Well, I do have to go back to the pool so everyone can go swimming later," said Chip.

"Will Tory and Hazel be there?" asked Tallulah.

"I can ask them to be there if you like?" asked Chip.

"Yeah, I would like that, and I promise I won't get naked again in the pool," said Tallulah.

"I'll see you later," said Chip.

"Do you promise you will?" asked Tallulah holding on to his hand.

"Yes, I do mom," said Chip as he tries to get his hand out of the hold, she has on him.

"Come on Tallulah I will bring you back and I am so happy that you both got reunited with each other," said Harlow.

"OK I'm ready to go back to the cabin," said Tallulah.

"I'll see you later," said Chip.

"Just think Tallulah pretty soon it will be lunch time and I am sure you're hungry," said Harlow as they go out the door.

Harlow walks with Tallulah and she is so excited about telling everyone she has a son.

This is so exciting, said Tallulah.

I am very happy for you, said Harlow.

Well, here you're safe back at your cabin, said Harlow.

Oh, thanks again for everything, said Tallulah as she hurry's back inside to tell everyone about Chip being her son.

Harlow stood outside and could hear Tallulah screaming that she met her son.

Why is Tallulah so happy, asked Iggy? Tallulah just reunited wither son, said Harlow.

Oh, really who is her son, asked Iggy?

You won't believe me if I told you, said Harlow. I might you never know, said Iggy.

Chip is her son, said Harlow.

Oh, really wow that's amazing, said Iggy.

Yeah, it was a great reunion between the two of them, said Harlow as she walked back to the office.

OK relax Tallulah and sit down before you break a hip or something, said Edith. Now tell us what is going on slowly, say Blanche.

You know how I talked about my son and how he left me so many years ago, asked Tallulah?

Yes, I do remember you tell us at the funhouse, said Edith.

Well, I know who is now and we got to see each other for the first time, said Tallulah.

That's so wonderful Tallulah you must be over the moon excited?" asked Serena.

Yes, I am I really am, said Tallulah.

So, are you going to tell us who is your son?" asked Edith. Well, you will never believe who it is, said Tallulah.

Come on Tallulah we are all dying to know, said Siena.

My son's name is Chip, said Tallulah.

Chip the guy whose clothes we stole?" asked Edith.

Yeah, that's the one isn't sweetheart, asked Tallulah as she looks at Hazel.

Yes, that's right Tallulah it is, said Hazel as she gives Tallulah a wink.

Tallulah walks over to Hazel and gives he a big bear hug.

So happy you're marrying my son and I can't wait for all of us to get together and start the planning, said Tallulah.

Oh, my me neither it will be so much fun, I am so glad you will be a part of it, said Hazel.

Can I go to the other cabin and let them know about my son?" asked Tallulah.

Sure, why not it's not like you're going to take off to another funhouse, laughed Eden.

"Yeah, you're funny," said Tallulah as she went out the door.

"Should we follow her?" asked Siena.

"No, I am sure she is just going to the other cabin," said Serena.

"Knock, knock is anyone home?" asked Tallulah.

"Oh boy, what does she want?" asked Agnes.

"Come in, Tallulah," said Eloise.

"How are you doing?" asked Tallulah.

"Fine and dandy," said Eloise.

"I just wanted to tell the girls the great news if that's OK," asked Tallulah.

"Yes, it's OK with me?" said Eloise.

Tallulah went in the cabin and right over to where the girls were.

You will never guess what happened to me this morning?" asked Tallulah.

We have no clue, said Agnes.

Did you set someone on fire?" asked Wanda.

No and that's not even funny, said Tallulah.

Just a question, said Wanda as she sits down on her bed.

So, are you going to tell us, or do we have to guess?" asked Mona.

Boy you're a cheery bunch today, said Tallulah.

So, Tallulah what is the big news?" asked Agnes.

I met my son, said Tallulah.

How did you meet him?" asked Wanda?

He works here and I didn't even know about it, said Tallulah.

Oh, my really, said Agnes.

So, are you going to tell us who it is?" asked Mona?

My son's name is Chip, said Tallulah beaming from ear to ear.

Wow holy shit that's great, said Wanda.

Thank you Wanda I am so happy now that I have him back in my life, said Tallulah.

That's a reason to be happy, said Agnes.

That's really awesome, said Penny who overheard what Tallulah was talking about.

So glad you finally found Chip, said Fay.

Thank you everyone I am happy you're back in my life, said Tallulah.

Well, I promised my cabin I would not stay to long, said Tallulah.

We will see you at the Hawaiian night later Tallulah, said Agnes.

Tallulah turned around and looked at everyone around her.

Hope you all know even know I just said, but I am happy to have all of you all in my life to and you will remain there forever, and it brought all us seniors together, said Tallulah.

That was sweet, said Fay trying not to tear up.

I can't believe that tomorrow is the last day here, said Tallulah.

Yeah, I know I feel like we just got here, said Wanda.

So don't I, said Agnes.

Well catch you later, said Tallulah as she leaves the cabin and heads back to hers.

It's sad, that by this time tomorrow we will be back at Heaven's Ridge, said Agnes.

Yeah true, but I am looking forward to going back, said Mona. Not me I am going to miss you all, said Wanda.

You're going back with us, said Agnes.

Oh yeah that's right, said Wanda.

Well, let us get ready for tonight, said Mona.

I'm sure it will be a blast and our last thing we will be here, said Wanda.

Let us just make the best of it and enjoy our last night here, said Agnes.

CHAPTER 32

The Beach and BBQs

Belle was getting everything organized before the employees from Heaven's Ridge showed up. Casper came and to let her know everything was all set up for the beach BBQ.

"I put all the picnic table there and put up the volleyball net and a tent are up where the food is going to go so it's out of the sun," said Casper.

"Thank you so much for doing this in such short notice," said Belle.

"It was no problem because everything is all set for the Hawaiian party," said Casper.

"Oh, crap I forgot about that it's tomorrow," said Belle.

"Everything will be fine Belle we got everything under control," said Casper.

"I'll go and do it right now and I think I will volunteer Art to help me get the rest of what we need," said Casper.

"Any reason why?" asked Belle.

"No, we just have become buddies, so I like having his help," said Casper.

"Oh, I see," said Belle.

"It doesn't have anything to do with him and Harlow together," said Casper.

"I didn't say a thing," said Belle.

"No, but I did know where you were heading," said Casper.

"I'm glad Harlow is moving on," said Casper.

"Did I hear my name?" asked Harlow who came down the hallway.

"Casper is just getting everything ready for when we all go to the beach today.

"Oh, good it seems like it will be a lot of fun," said Harlow.

"Oh, before you go Casper cane you bring the golfcarts out from with the trailers hooked to them?" asked Belle.

"No problem, Belle," said Casper.

"I just thought that would be easier to transport everyone," said Belle.

"I think that's a great idea it beats walking in this heat," said Harlow.

"Yes, it sounds like a good idea we just might have to take a couple of trips out and back, but it will be good," said Casper.

"Thank you, Casper, for everything," said Belle as Casper goes out the door.

"Can all staff please meet in the dining hall," said Harlow on the loudspeaker.

"That was great Harlow thank you so much for doing that for me," said Belle.

"Your welcome Belle anything for my bestie," said Harlow. I love when you're chipper like this it has been so long Harlow," said Belle.

"Well, Art and I talked everything out and he was the only one who was by my side with the thing with Casper and I saved his life so that brought us closer together," said Harlow.

"He is a nice man, and I could see how he really likes you and you need happiness in your life I just hope I didn't overstep when I asked Casper to do all of things," said Belle.

"So don't you deserve happiness Belle and no I am glad that Casper is here helping you," said Harlow.

"No, I told you before I am happy being alone and that's what I will be doing for a long time I shouldn't have gotten together with Frankie and now I regret it, but he is happy with Tory so that's good," said Belle.

Camp Funhouse 443

"I know Belle and I'm sorry all of that came out, I guess we both learned a lesson from everything that was going on," said Harlow.

"Yeah, a jousting match wasn't the best idea, but it sorts of worked in other ways because we found out a lot, we didn't know about who works here," said Belle.

"Let's get going to the dining hall and let everyone know what is going on," said Harlow.

"Oh boy more excitement I can't wait for this," said Belle.

Everyone came into the dining hall wondering what is going. Belle and Harlow came in and went to stand in front of all the employees.

"Tory looked at Belle, so she knew everything was going to be OK.

"Frankie was standing off make sur everything was OK because he had no idea what this meeting was for.

"We are going to have a great day today.

"If some of you didn't hear we will be having a beach day and BBQ with the Heaven's Ridge people as a surprise to the seniors," said Belle.

"So, we need your help getting all the seniors to the beach before the employees come today," said Harlow.

"You do realize that the seniors are leaving tomorrow so they will see them anyways," said Eloise.

"Why can't you just have fun for one day I just don't get you," said Tinsley who wanted another crack at Eloise.

"Just asking a question that's all," said Eloise starting to get upset by the way Tinsley and it was bugging her.

"Yes, you're right Eloise, but we just thought it be a fun day for everyone," said Belle.

"What if we don't want to go to the beach?" asked Eloise.

"Well, this time you have no choice because I want all hands-on deck," said Belle.

Eloise just shook her head.

"OK so we need all the counselors to help load the seniors on golf carts in one hour," said Harlow.

"Can the activities people help with the games?" asked Belle.

Iggy, Eden, and Serena all said yes. They went to load the trailer with beach games that everyone would enjoy. By the end of the meeting more people decided to get involved and help Belle out and she was so glad they were by her side and was ready to help the seniors get to the beach. Well, I still want no part of this part, but whatever it doesn't matter," said Eloise.

"Do I need to beat the shit out of you this time?" asked Tinsley as she gets in Eloise's face.

"Fine I'll do whatever you want now just get out of my face Tinsley," said Eloise.

"I thought you would see it my way," said Tinsley.

"Yeah, OK Tinsley keep telling yourself that," said Eloise as she goes out the door.

"Well, that didn't go as bad as I thought it would," said Belle as she talks to Hazel, Chip, Fay, and Harlow.

"Yeah, I honestly thought it was going to go a to worse with Eloise," said Harlow.

"Yeah, what the hell has been going on with her?" asked Hazel.

"I honestly wish I knew," said Belle.

"So, what can we do to help?" asked Hazel.

"Can you go check with Frankie and see what he has planned for the BBQ?" asked Belle.

"Sure, that will be no problem," said Hazel as she went into the kitchen to find Frankie.

"I better go and just see how Ethel, Clara, Blanche, Edith, and Tallulah are doing," said Serena.

"Well make sure they have lots of sunscreen on," said Belle.

"I shouldn't be gone to long," said Serena as she goes out the door.

"Serena is such a caring person," said Belle.

"Yeah, she is a great person," said Chip.

"I hope after here she can find a job that she is going to love," said Belle.

"I hope we all find that," said Chip.

"I think we need to go get everything we need or at least see if we forgot anything," said Belle.

"Hey Frankie, are you in here?" asked Hazel was looking around.

Hazel went in the back to the food storage, and he wasn't in there. Hazel found a big box on the counter, and she decided to look in it. It had all the food we would have for the BBQ and there was a note left in the box. Hazel read the note and felt heartbroken, but knew she had to bring it to Belle. Hazel ran back to the office and told Belle about the food and gave her the note.

"Belle, I'm sorry for everything I did to you and to Tory even know we have made amends I'm not sure I belong with her. I will be happy knowing that I won't be a pain in the ass anymore. Keep smiling and always remember you will have a place in my heart. Love, Frankie. P.S. I hope you enjoy all the BBQ stuff it was the least I could do for you.

"Damn it Frankie why did you pick now to leave?" asked Belle to herself.

"I'm sorry Belle, but why would he do this to us again?" asked Hazel.

"Don't worry we got this remember," said Belle.

"Still, it was pretty shitty of him to just up and leave and I hope that Tory is OK," said Chip.

"You can go check on her if you want to," said Belle.

"Nah if she needs me, she will find me getting things ready is more important," said Chip.

"Thank you Chip I appreciate so let's get moving," said Belle.

"It was finally quitting time at Heaven's Ridge, and it was one of their busier days.

"I'm so glad the day is over with I felt like it was never going to end," said Hilda as she rubs them.

"Hey Dudley, are you almost ready to go?" asked Willa.

"Yeah, I'm coming I just have one more book to finish," said Dudley.

"So, you two are really going to this BBQ?" asked Hilda?

"Yes, and Delia is going also?" said Willa.

"Everyone here was invited so why not go?" asked Delia. "Do you have room for one more?" asked Hilda.

"Sure, why not I'm sure they're going to be OK with it, said Willa and if they aren't then to damn bad is what I say. Get my stuff and I will meet you our front Willa," said Hilda so happy she can go.

"Sounds good we will be leaving in ten minutes if Dudley ever gets done doing his books," said Willa.

"Not my fault we have to answer all these stupid questions that makes no sense," said Dudley.

"I'll be in my car waiting for you, but you don't come soon I'm leaving without you," said Willa.

"You're such a team player Willa," laughed Dudley.

"I do believe her when she said she will drive away," said Florence.

"Oh, shit I guess your right I better go," said Dudley good I'm done anyways.

"You don't need to rush because we are all going on one of the buses so we can go together," said Aspen.

"Have a fun time," said Florence.

"Everyone is coming so there is no excuses why you can't go with us," said Aspen.

Let's go to a BBQ," said Willa as they start heading to Mystic.

Belle started to get nervous when she realizes that it was almost time for the people from Heaven's Ridge to come.

"Oh, I hope this works out today," said Belle to herself.

"Are you almost ready Belle they will be here soon?" asked Harlow.

"Yes, I am I just was thinking how I hope today goes OK," said Belle.

"I know you get tired of hearing it, but just think positive," said Harlow.

"Who is working on the BBQ?" asked Belle.

"Chip has volunteered to make the hamburgers, hot dogs, and chicken at the beach," said Harlow.

"I didn't know he was so nifty with food," said Belle.

"Me either, said Harlow.

"I'm sure the food will be good," said Belle.

"With everything going on I don't remember if I said sorry about Frankie and him leaving," said Harlow.

"I'll be OK Harlow it only stings a little bit; said Belle and I'm not even worried about him right now I just must make sure everything goes smoothly today. We will all be her to back you up so don't worry," said Harlow.

"Well, it's almost time so let's get this done and over with," said Belle.

"All the seniors got on the golf cart and were ready to go to the beach.

"Can I drive?" asked Tallulah as she laughed.

"No Tallulah I think I got it this time," said Art.

"Why can't she drive is it because you don't want to be dragged behind it again?" asked Wanda.

"No, I'm still recovering from the last time," said Art.

"I'm sure you're sonny," laughed Tallulah.

"Alright we are ready to go to the beach," yelled Serena who went with the first group of seniors and counselors.

Hazel went with the last group that were ready to head to the beach.

"Wow it's a bumpy ready," said Ethel.

Well, if you need to then you can grab onto me," said Jasper.

"Thank you, Jasper that was very nice of you," said Ethel.

"Wow it's so beautiful out here and such a nice sunny day," said Tallulah.

"Yes, I agree it's nice out," said Agnes.

"Well, here we are," said Serena.

"Wow look at the water it's so blue," said Edith. "It's beautiful here and I can't wait to get out and explore," said Tallulah.

"Haven't you explored enough at the funhouse?" asked Agnes.

"No, I haven't, and I just like looking around that's all," said Tallulah.

"Don't go too far because we have company coming," said Hazel.

Who is coming?" asked Wanda.

"You will see when they get here," said Hazel.

"Now let's get the trailers unloaded and everything set," said Serena. Everyone got everything set up in fun time.

Then Art went back with one of the golf carts and Hazel took the other one back to get the Heaven's Ridge employees.

"Hi everyone and welcome to Mystic Senior Camp, I'm Belle the Camp Director.

"I'm Willa, Dudley, Hilda, Delia and the rest of the crew is getting off the bus," said Aspen.

"Nice to meet you all and glad you could come this afternoon for our BBQ and Beach Day.

"Let's go into my office and you can meet my Camp Administrator Harlow and another staff member," said Belle.

"We are not trying to not to be rude, but we are really interested in seeing our residents if that's OK with you," said Delia.

"I completely understand, and you will see all of them soon at the beach, I just want you to show you how this camp runs," said Belle.

"So, in this building we have my office, and Harlow's office, and the nurse who you will also meet at the beach," said Belle.

Harlow came out of her room and shook all their hands and explained how she is the Camp Administrator there and all the seniors are a joy to have here.

"Don't you mean residents?" asked Hilda.

"Well, OK residents that works to," said Harlow.

"Let's go to the dining hall where we have our meals a few activities like playing games," said Belle.

"That's sounds like they have a lot of fun in here," said Hilda.

Belle continued to walk into the kitchen.

"The kitchen is right over here where we make amazing meals," said Harlow.

"Iggy one of our activities girls cooked a fantastic meal with Mona," said Belle.

"Everyone was raving about it for a while," said Harlow.

"I didn't know she could cook," said Delia.

"Mona actually owned a restaurant with her last husband, and I can tell you she didn't lose her touch at all," said Belle.

"Oh, I love food," said Hilda.

"Hi Chip, how are things going in the kitchen?" asked Belle.

"Things are going great in here I'm just getting all food for the BBQ it's going to be a great feast for everyone," said Chip.

I would like you to meet the Heaven's Ridge group," said Belle.

Oh, by the way this is Chip he is one of counselors, lifeguards and he cooks for us occasionally," said Belle.

"I am a man with many talents," said Chip.

"I like a man like that," said Delia as she winks at him.

"He just recently got engaged to someone," said Belle.

"That's a shame," said Delia.

"Well, I hope you brought your appetite," said Chip.

"I always have an appetite for food," said Hilda.

"I have an appetite for whatever you're cooking," said Delia.

"It's time to go see the rest of the camp and let Frankie I mean Chip get back to making the BBQ spectacular," said Belle.

"It will be spectacular because I can make fireworks with you," said Delia.

"OK Delia, you need to cool off a little let's go outside and breathe in that air," said Hilda.

"They both went outside for a little air as the others kept talking to Chip and Belle.

"Well, we better get going on our tour and meet the others outside," said Belle.

I will see you when we leave to the beach and have a fun time," said Chip.

"Shall we go on with our tour?" asked Belle.

"Is this tour over yet we want to see our residents right now?" asked Hilda.

"That's the plan after our tour," said Belle.

Here is our bathhouse that has a guy and girls' side," said Belle.

"There isn't a lot of showers in there," said Aspen.

"No, but it works well for everyone," said Belle.

"Ewe that's gross," said Willa.

Well, let's go down the hill and check out the pool and their cabins," said Belle.

"Wow that's a nice pool," said Florence.

"Yes, it is, and the residents love it," said Belle.

"This is better than our pool," said Hilda.

"Over here we have one of the girls' cabins," said Belle.

"They sleep on cots?" asked Aspen.

"Yes, they do, but no one has complained about sleeping on them," said Belle.

"I find that hard to believe because Agnes doesn't like beds like that," said Clark.

Belle looked at her watch and saw it was time to go to the beach.

Chip was helping Hazel get things loaded on the golf cart when they came up the hill.

"Well, hello again sailor you want to go out for a drink sometime?" asked Delia.

"No, Chip doesn't because his girlfriend that he plans on marrying, which is me, would get be piss off at him if he did," said Hazel looking at Delia giving her the evil eye.

"Thanks for that sweetheart," said Chip as he winked at Hazel.

"No problem honey buns and don't call me sweetheart," laughed Hazel.

They all got on board of the golf cart and headed to the beach. Chip decided to drive this time. Delia sat next to him beating Hazel who said in the trailer with everyone else. Delia leaned forward so Chip could see her breasts. Chips eyes got wide when Delia leaned forward, and he almost went off the road.

"Everything OK up there, Chip?" asked Hazel.

"Yes, I am fine I just had something in my eyes," said Chip as he looks at Delia.

They finally got to the beach and all the seniors were so shocked and excited to see everyone. Everyone got off the golf cart and started waving to the seniors. Hazel went to the front of the golfcart.

"So, what was the real reason you went off the road?" asked Hazel.

"Well to be honest because I know that you aren't going to like it, but it was because Delia was trying to show me her breasts," said Chip. Hazel punched him in the side.

"I didn't look as much as she wanted me too and I acted like it distracted me," said Chip.

"Hey Jasper, would you like to come with me and Hank and fly the remote-control planes?" asked Chip.

"I used to do it when I was a kid so sure why not," said Jasper.

"Hey Hank look up in the air," said Siena as she looks up, in the sky. Hank looks up and see is the planes up in the sky side by side and he couldn't believe it. Once Chip and Japer got closer, he continued to watch the planes until they came down.

"Do you want to try and fly it," asked Chip.

"Oh, hell yes, I would," said Hank all excited.

Chip hands him the remote and explains certain things to him so he knows how to work it.

"There you go you got it Hank," said Chip.

"Wonderful job Hank," said Belle. Jasper and Hank stand next to each other and fly together at the same distance.

"Wow isn't this amazing Jasper?" asked Hank.

"Yes, it is, and I am glad we are flying together," said Jasper.

"Oh, me to brother," said Hank.

While Hank and Jasper were flying their planes everyone else broke up in teams and played a friendly game of volleyball.

Clara decided that she wanted the teams to be the girls against the guys.

"Sounds fair to me," said Hazel as she sticks her tongue at Chip.

"Oh, really you're going to start the trash talking?" laughed Chip.

"Yeah, you got that right," said Hazel.

"Oh, Chip you know that there is no chance that you boys are going to win against us," said Fay.

"Oh, that's what you think I see how it's going to be," said Chip.

"Girls are better than boys," said Harlow.

"Oh, you think so honey," said Art running over to give her one last kiss that she will never forget.

"I can definitely deal with that," said Harlow

"Now what were you saying about us guys?" asked Art.

"Yeah, I don't remember saying anything," said Harlow as she stands there in her own world.

"Snap out of it we have a game to win," said Tinsley as she moves in front of Harlow.

"Well excuse me for being in the way and in love," said Harlow as she goes back in front of Tinsley.

"Oh, bitch don't get in my way," said Tinsley.

"What is your problem Tinsley with me?" asked Harlow.

"Hey, you to stop and let's get this game going,' said Belle.

"Sorry Belle," said Tinsley as she tries to get in front of Harlow again.

"Tinsley do you want to be in the front?" asked Harlow.

"If you don't mind since I'm more athletic then you," said Tinsley.

"Oh, you think so Tinsley," said Harlow.

"I do know and that's why I'm going to be upfront," said Tinsley.

"Then go ahead, but I guarantee I will be more athletic than you," said Harlow.

"Are you two done bickering?" asked Serena.

"Yes, we are," said Tinsley.

"Good let gets going with this game then," said Serena.

The game finally started, and it ended up being a little rocky because Harlow and Tinsley kept trying to beat each other for the ball. At one time everyone on the team just stood there until they were all done trying to beat each other. By then Clara didn't want to participate anymore and was ready to quit.

"Hey Clara, don't quit we are sorry that we hurt your feelings," said Tinsley. "We will play like everyone else," said Harlow really feeling bad about hurting Clara's feelings.

They all put their feelings aside and ended up having a tie game. Fay was the last one to serve so everything rested in her hands. She bumped the ball, and it went high in the air and all the guys were scrambling to see which way the ball was going to go. "I got it," said Art as he trips, and it bounces off his head and hits the ground and Edith managed to steal it and bounce it back to the girl's side. Art just laid there and couldn't believe what just happened as the girl's cheer in victory. Harlow went over to Art and kissed him on the cheek.

"It was a good try honey, but I told you we were going to win," said Harlow as Art grabs her and puts her on the ground with him. Harlow starts laugh and then kisses Art. Harlow gets back up and walks away.

"Hey sweetheart where are you going?" asked Art.

"You snooze you lose sweetie," said Harlow.

"Good game everyone," said Belle.

"We know the men are the real winners since you cheated," said Ace.

"We didn't cheat," said Tory.

"You had Edith as a decoy and snag the ball," said Chip.

"No one said we couldn't, so we won fair and square," said Tallulah laughing.

Everyone settles back at the table to get a snack or a drink.

"That was so much," said Hazel.

"You are a good volleyball player Hazel," said Agnes.

"I almost went pro when I was in college," said Hazel.

"What stopped you from doing it?" asked Serena.

"Tore something in my knee and after having surgery on it the doctor said going pro wasn't a clever idea because my knee could get hurt again and it could get worse, so I quit and never went back," said Hazel.

"Sorry to hear that you would have been a badass player," said Siena.

"Thanks that means a lot to me," said Hazel.

Chip came up behind her and wrapped his arms around her.

Chip reached over for a cookie and felt something hit his back. He looked behind him and saw that Felix had hit him with the nerf gun.

"Did you just hit me?" asked Chip.

"Yes, I did buddy," said Felix.

"Do you want to rumble?" asked Chip.

"Yes, I do," said Felix.

Ace snuck behind them both and started shooting at them.

"Here is your gun Felix let's get Ace," said Chip.

"I'm ready to go," said Felix getting so excited about it.

Before you know it all three of them are hunting each other down.

"Looks like everyone is having a fun time today," said Belle.

"Yeah, this was such a clever idea to do this," said Ethel.

"Let's watch everyone with the nerf guns," said Belle.

"Sounds good to me," said Ethel

"Are you ready to show everyone what we can do with our guns?" asked Belle.

"Yes, but I don't see our guns," said Ethel.

Belle went under the table into a box and brought out to super soakers.

"We don't have nerf guns, but we do have these," said Belle as she shows Ethel the guns.

"Wow looks at them this is going to be so much fun," said Delia.

"Yes, it will be so let's get them," said Belle. Belle, Ethel, and Delia set out to get everyone that they can before they run out of water in their guns.

"Get Ace," yelled Belle. Ethel runs after Ace trying to get him wet and succeed with no problems.

"That water is cold," said Ace as it drips down his back. HA!

"I got you Ace," said Ethel as she walks fast to get away from him.

"Excellent job Ethel," said Hilda who joined in.

Belle looked around to see who her target could be and decides to get one of the seniors, so she heads toward Felix and gets him in the chest. Felix really got into character and acted like Belle really shot him.

"Are you OK over there Felix?" asked Belle.

"Yeah, that was a lot of fun," said Felix.

"I'm glad to hear that darling," said Belle s she shot him again.

Serena was sitting on the picnic table enjoying the sun.

"Hey Serena, what's up?" asked Hazel.

"Nothing I'm just chilling a little bit," said Serena.

"Yeah, I hear you it just has been a crazy week that I will never forget," said Hazel.

"We lose seniors, and you gain a husband to be its just crazy," said Serena.

"I know, but I'm very happy," said Hazel.

"Fay is almost done setting up the picnic tables for everyone to eat," said Belle.

"Well, it's almost time for the BBQ Chip is almost done cooking," said Harlow.

Aspen saw Tallulah siting at one of the picnic tables and went over to talk to her.

"How are you doing?" asked Aspen.

"I'm doing good and so happy right now," said Tallulah.

"What is making you so happy?" asked Aspen.

"I had a fun time this week at camp and the funhouse, and I found my son who I am never going to let go of," said Tallulah.

"Well, that's amazing Aspen. "Yeah, I know I am just so happy," said Tallulah.

"So what funhouse are you talking about?" asked Aspen who was eager to know what was going on here.

"Mona, Beau, Wanda, Edith, Agnes, Blanche, Miles, Vera, and I all went on an adventure," said Tallulah.

"I'll be right back," said Aspen as she heads towards Belle.

"I have a question for you," said Aspen.

"Sure, what's going on you look a little frazzled," said Belle.

"Well, I was just talking to Tallulah, and she mentioned that certain residents went on an adventure together," said Aspen.

Belle wasn't sure what to say, but she knew that she couldn't lie to Aspen after telling her about Tallulah being Chip's mother.

"I think you need to sit down," said Belle as she was thinking how to tell Aspen what was going on.

Yes, they did go on an adventure, but the important thing is that they all made it back safely," said Belle hoping that worked a little bit.

"Whose idea was it to go to this funhouse?" asked Aspen.

"I honestly don't know if it was just one person or a bunch of them," said Belle.

"How do you not know their plan?" ask Aspen as her voice was getting higher.

Chip and Hazel went over to help Belle.

"Listen Aspen and anyone else that wants to know," Hazel. Delia, Hilda, and Aspen were all listening.

"We were the ones we set them up all because they were always listening to what we were talking about and we wanted to only teach Mona, Wanda, Agnes, and Tallulah a lesson," said Hazel.

"Don't blamed them for what we did," said Agnes.

"They had known idea that we were going to take the keys and go to this funhouse," said Wanda.

"We knew exactly what they were up to because Chip put a camera a in there so we can watch them so we knew every step they were taking," Belle.

"So, they did all of this on their own?" asked Aspen.

"Yes, they did, and we are so proud of them," said Hazel looking at the seniors.

"I'm not happy about what happened here, but as long as they made it safe that's all I care about," said Aspen.

"Who does that sound like?" asked Hazel as she whispers to Chip.

The seniors were so happy to her that aspen wasn't mad for what they did.

"Let's get something to eat I am starving," said Jasper.

"Just remember to save some food for the rest of us," said Dudley.

Jasper turned around and just laughed at him. Everyone was settling down to eat and enjoying everyone's company. It was nice to hear the laughter of the seniors that you haven't heard since they got here.

Belle went over to Serena who looked white as a ghost.

Are you OK Serena you don't look so well?" said Belle.

"No, it's nothing like that I just haven't seen this person in a long time," said Serena.

"Who is she if you don't mind me asking?" asked Belle.

"She is my sister Felicity who I haven't seen in years," said Serena.

"I didn't know you had a sister,' said Belle.

"Yeah, but that's a story for another time," said Serena.

"I totally understand and I'm here if you need me," said Belle.

"Thanks Belle, I might take you up on that offer if things don't go well," said Serena.

As Felicity came closer Serena started to get nervous.

"Wow Felicity you're here in front of me," said Serena.

"Yes, I am Serena and how have you been doing?" asked Felicity.

"Not bad and where have you been all these years?" asked Serena not knowing what else to say.

"I'm a single mom and I have three kids and I work as a nurse at Heaven's Ridge," said Felicity looking nervous.

"How do you two know each other if you don't mind me asking?" asked Aspen.

"We are sisters," said Serena.

"Wow more sisters this is so amazing," said Dudley.

"Will you shut up," said Delia as she hits him on the back of the head.

"Well, sit down and join us," said Belle trying to be friendly. Belle asked questions so that she could get to know Serena's sister Felicity.

"It has been a while since we have seen each other," said Serena.

"Our mom had passed away when we were young, and our father couldn't take care of us, so I took over since I was the oldest and raise Serena and our brothers," said Felicity.

"I didn't want to be burden once I was a little older, so I left when I was sixteen and went to school and worked at the same time," said Serena.

"That must have been hard for you?" asked Belle.

"Yes, it was, but I got through it," said Serena.

"So, you both lost touched after it happened or something?" asked Harlow.

"I told her if she was going to leave to not come back just like a parent might say to their kid if they were to do that," said Felicity.

"So, you haven't talked to each other since?" asked Belle.

Serena and Felicity looked at each other and told Belle and Harlow that it was true.

"Well, maybe since you're both here then you can talk and maybe get the sisterly love that you both had for each other back," said Belle.

Mona and Edith heard their story and decided to share their story also.

"After this trip to the funhouse I finally have my sister back and I'm so glad," said Mona.

"I think with everything it will take time to make things better, but I would be willing to make it work because I have missed my sister," said Serena.

I feel the same way I would love for her to hear everything I went through with my marriage and your three nephews that I want to meet their aunt Serena," said Felicity.

"That's awesome for you two and I hope you can get that relationship back that you had when you were kids because you don't want to miss out on each other's life because you might get old like us and regret somethings like we did," said Edith.

"I think same should go for Willa and Juniper because they're sisters also and also took a hard road," said Serena.

"How do you know that?" asked Belle.

"They were ready to punch each other before I stopped them before they drowned themselves," said Serena.

"Where are they now well believe it or not these two lovely ladies talked to them and got them to be sisters again," said Serena.

"You two did that for them?" asked Belle who gave a smile to Mona and Edith.

"Maybe everyone should go into the funhouse then you will come out a whole different person," said Edith.

Belle got on the picnic table so that she could give her speech and so everyone can hear her.

"Hello everyone and I hope that you got all the food that you wanted, and you leave here with full stomachs and happy hearts," said Belle.

Harlow got on the picnic table to and helped Belle.

"I also want to thank the Heaven's Ridge crew for coming and joining us for the BBQ and I hope that all of you enjoyed yourselves," said Harlow.

"Have a great night and see you tomorrow," said Belle.

"So be safe going home and we will see you all tomorrow when the residents go home." said Harlow trying not to cry.

CHAPTER 33

Goodbye Mystic Senior Camp, Hello Heaven's Ridge

"Is everyone all ready for the first annual Hawaiian night at Mystic Senior Camp?" yelled Belle.

Everyone started cheering once the music came on.

"This is so much fun and sad at ted same time," said Wanda.

"Hey, look at this I just got lei," laughed Tallulah.

"That isn't what I thought you were going to say, and I am glad I was wrong," said Wanda.

"I'm trying to be good," said Tallulah.

"That will never happen," said Agnes.

"Thanks for having faith in me," said Tallulah.

"Well, I tried to have faith in you, but sometimes it doesn't work that way," said Agnes.

"I have faith in you because when Mona and I went through everything you brought us together," said Edith"

"Thank you Edith I appreciate your friendship and I am here for everyone if you just give me a chance," said Tallulah.

"Can I have everyone's attention," said Belle.

"Oh boy here we go again with the long speech," said Edith.

"I just wanted to thank all the counselors and everyone who really busted their butt to make this week special for the seniors that were here, and I am so happy that all our seniors are here under one roof," said Belle.

"Do you think Belle is going to cry at the end of her speech?" asked Wanda.

"Nah I think she will be OK," said Agnes.

"I want to congratulate Chip and Hazel on their engagement," said Belle.

"That is my boy," yelled Tallulah.

"Yes, if anyone didn't know we have a mother and son reunited for the first time in years and I am so happy for them," said Belle.

Chip was feeling all embarrassed when Belle mentioned that.

"Oh, don't get so embarrassed now you have a whole lifetime with your mother," whispered Hazel.

"Oh boy, but I can't complain I am happy right now and couldn't asked for anything else," said Chip.

"I'm so glad to hear that," said Hazel hold on to Chip tight.

"Have a good night here and we will truly be sad to see all of you go, but hopefully all of you will be back next summer," said Belle. Everyone clapped at Belle's speech.

"Can I have all the seniors together so that we can take a group photo?" asked Serena.

"Oh, this is so great," said Iggy.

"I'm going to miss you Serena you're so sweet, and I will always remember you," said Ethel.

"I'm glad that we had a chance to get to know each other and I have an idea why don't we take a picture just you and me so we both have something to hold on too," said Serena.

"I would like that Serena," said Ethel as they both get into the picture and make a memory.

"Thanks for taking the picture of us I will always remember you," said Ethel as she started to cry.

"It will be OK, and we will see each other again soon we got more sandcastles to make," said Serena.

"Yes, we do," said Ethel.

"Just keep smiling like you do, and everything will be OK," said Serena.

Everyone continues to dance the night away and make memories that hopefully they will remember for a long time.

Belle saw Tory by the appetizer table and went over and talked to her. "I know I never got to talk to you at the beach," said Belle.

"It's OK I know that it was pretty hectic with everyone around," said Tory.

"I'm sorry that Frankie left once again you did an outstanding job tonight, said Belle. Thank you Belle I tried my best as always, said Frankie. Have an opportunity for the both of you and if you're interested in," said Belle.

"Well, I kind of had a feeling he wasn't going to stay in one spot once he told me he wanted a commitment with me," said Tory.

"I have talked to Aspen back at Heaven's Ridge and she has agreed to give everyone at the camp if they want it a job.

"She would love it if you would be an aide at Heaven's Ridge and the local college is willing to pay for you to go to school to be an aide all expenses paid thanks to Harlow and you can work at the same time and learn from it hands on unlike others who don't get that opportunity," said Belle.

"How does Harlow tie into our schooling?" asked Tory.

"She is the English professor there and can pull a lot of strings," said Belle.

"Wow oh my god I never thought I would be able to go to college in my life," said Tory getting excited.

I'm guessing you except the job offers?" asked Belle. Tory said yes on the spot.

"I thought you would say that, and I am so proud of you," said Belle.

"That was nice of Aspen to do that for all of us here," said Tory."
"Yes, it was," said Belle.

"Did everyone else except the job offer?" asked Tory.

"I haven't made the announcement yet, but I wanted to do yours personally," said Belle.

"Thank you very much," said Tory who was starting to cry.

Tallulah, Wanda, Mona, and Agnes sat at their table one last time before the party was over.

"Well girls it has been fun, and I can't wait to see what awaits us when we get back to Heaven's Ridge," said Agnes.

"We are all closer as friends so at least we got each other when we are there," said Wanda.

"That is true our bond is so much stronger than before," said Mona.

"Let's make a toast to Mystic and to the funhouse and may another adventure await us somewhere," said Agnes.

"If there is another adventure I can't wait to go," said Wanda.

"Just say when and where and I will be there for it," said Tallulah.

"Tallulah I just wanted to say how much I respect you and you're a great person inside and out and I'm so glad that we got to know more of each other," said Edith.

"Me too girlfriend you're the best on top of me," laughed Tallulah.

"I would want it any other way," said Edith laughing with her.

"You two are going to make me cry if you don't cut it out," said Agnes.

"I also wanted to say to you Mona I know that we had our difficulties, but I am so glad that we reconnected here, and I finally feel like I got my sister back," said Edith.

"Right back at you sister," said Mona as they grab each other's hands and hold them.

"To you Vera wherever you're lurking around you're a great competitor and I would go against you any time," said Agnes.

Vera popped out from under the tablecloth and gave Agnes a thumbs up and she went right back under.

"Well, at least she agrees and gave me the right finger this time," laughed Agnes.

"I can't believe that today is the last day," said Agnes just a little sad.

"Yeah, I know it feels like we just got here," said Mona.

"Well in a way we did because we were gone so long but it was well worth it making memories and getting closer to everyone," said Agnes.

"Yes, I agree with you Agnes," said Wanda as they pack their stuff up.

"I wish that we could stay a little longer just so we got the feel for the camp," said Mona.

"I understand that, but maybe next summer we will be able to come back just like Belle said yesterday," said Agnes.

"I hope so because I would come back no problem there," said Wanda.

"Me too because thanks to this camp I found Beau," said Mona.

"Are you already to go girls the bus will be here soon?" asked Eden.

Yeah, we are all packed as all the girls grabbed their bags and looked around one last time.

As they walked out, they see Tallulah and the other seniors coming out of their cabins.

"I want to stay," cried Tallulah.

"It will be OK Tallulah we are all together and that's what matters," said Agnes.

"Let's see if the bus is here," said Blanche.

"Can everyone stand in a line?" asked Belle

"Oh boy what is she up to now?" asked Wanda.

"Who knows, but we better do it," said Agnes.

"Can I have all the staff right here behind the seniors," asked Belle.

"Alrighty everything is all set Belle," said Harlow.

"Thank you, Harlow," said Belle.

"I thought before your bus comes that we take a group photo so that everyone here will remember their experience," said Belle

"Didn't we do that last night?" asked Wanda. "Yes, but that was only all the seniors," said Serena.

"That sounds like a great idea," said Tallulah.

"I will be sending you each your own photo so you can remember your time here," said Belle.

Agnes could hear someone sobbing and looked around to see who it was.

"Wanda why are you crying?" asked Agnes.

"I don't know I'm just so happy, I guess.

"Well, get a grip of yourself," said Agnes.

"I'm trying I just can't believe we're going home," said Wanda.

"I know, but we got this," said Agnes.

"So, everyone stands up as straight as you can and smile," said Belle as she snaps a few pictures.

"Oh, that was great," said Harlow.

"Yes, it was for sure," said Belle.

"So, are you going to tell everyone the great news?" asked Harlow.

"Yes, just as soon as the bus gets here," said Belle.

"Why is that?" asked Harlow.

"You will see," said Belle as the bus pulls up.

All the employees including Aspen got off the bus. The seniors were starting to get excited about seeing them.

"Thank you for coming," said Belle.

"You're welcome," said Delia.

Tory looked at Willa and gave her a smile.

"Aspen and Belle stood in front of everyone.

I know that today is a sad day for you and a joyful day for us," said Aspen.

"We have produced an idea so everyone will have a job until camp next year," said Belle.

Everyone looked confused on what is going on.

"I would like to hire all the Mystic camp employees and make them apart of Heaven's Ridge," said Aspen.

Everyone starting cheering.

"Belle has also arranged with Harlow schooling for all of you in being an aide or for nursing already paid in full," said Aspen.

"What?" asked Serena.

"You will also get full benefits for working at Heavens Ridge," said Belle.

"Wow that's amazing," said Serena.

All of you are welcome back next year to work and that includes Heavens Ridge," said Belle.

Clark looked excited to be a counselor for someone.

"So, anyone who I interested in working at Heaven's Ridge please see me and I will sign you up," said Aspen.

Chip and Hazel looked at each other and knew they wanted to do it and didn't hesitate to talk to Aspen.

"We both would be interested in working at Heaven's Ridge," said Chip.

"If I'm not wrong you're also Tallulah son?" asked Aspen. "Yes, I am," said Chip.

"Welcome to Heaven's Ridge I will be more than happy to have both of you on board," said Aspen.

"Are you going to work at Heaven's Ridge Eloise?" asked Penny.

"Probably not," said Eloise.

"Why not it sounds like a wonderful place to work and free schooling you can't do any better than that," said Penny.

"I don't know it sounds too good to be true," said Eloise.

"Then if you think about it, we can see each other all the time," said Penny trying to make everything look better.

"I'll think about it OK," said Eloise walking away from Penny.

"Well, it looks like everyone said yes to the job offering except Eloise, Casper, and Juniper," said Aspen.

"I'll talk to them and see where their head is and I will let you know," said Belle.

Belle had caught up with the three that didn't say whether they would work at Heaven's Ridge

"Can I talk to you three?" asked Belle.

They all just looked at each other like they were in trouble or something.

"Did we do something wrong Belle?" asked Casper.

"No, I just was curious why you didn't want to work at Heaven's Ridge," said Belle.

"I just don't see myself being an aide or nurse you know I like to use my hands and get them dirty," said Casper.

"You sure do," laughed Juniper.

"Well, I wasn't thinking that position was for you anyways Casper and I was hoping that Aspen would of just came up to you to told you the position she wanted you for," said Belle.

"What did she want to tell me?" asked Casper with a strange look on his face.

"They do need help in their maintenance department," said Belle.

"Doing what?" asked Casper who still wasn't sure what it was all about.

"You would be the Director of Maintenance and Housekeeping so you would oversee everything like keeping the buses going, you would have a cleaning crew and you would oversee the people who do the laundry," said Belle.

"Wow that's huge," said Juniper.

"You have said that before," grinned Casper.

Juniper just gives him a look.

"You will be on salary to so you can run them anyway you want," said Belle.

"Wow that's amazing," said Casper still in shock.

"So, what do you think?" asked Belle.

"Well, hell yeah, I will take it," said Casper.

"So, what about you Juniper are you interested in being a nurse there?" asked Belle.

"I'm not sure because that means I will be working with Willa and I am just not sure I want to do that," said Juniper.

"I get it, but at least it's a guaranteed education and job for as long as you want it to be," said Belle.

"I do have my RN, but I guess I could go further with my education and another excellent job," said Juniper.

"What if we want to come back next year for the camp, "I can't do both can I?" asked Juniper.

"Well, when that time comes then you, me, and Aspen will sit down and discuss it because I'm sure you're not the only one who wants to come back," said Belle.

"I didn't think I was going to be the only one to come back," laughed Juniper.

"So, what do you think sweetie?" asked Casper.

"Well, you will be there so that's one good thing I'm just not sure that place can take me and my sister," laughed Juniper

"Just don't blow the roof off completely," joked Belle.

"Yeah, I know, but I guess I will try it," said Juniper.

Casper got so excited he picked Juniper up and hugged her.

"OK Eloise it's down to you and what you want to do?" asked Belle.
"I don't want to be an aide," said Eloise.

"OK then what do you want to do?" asked Belle.

Always wanted to be a nurse," said Eloise.

"Well, then your wish will come true," said Belle.

"Really it's that easy?" asked Eloise.

"Yes, it is, and Harlow and Aspen will get you started with everything you need to know," said Belle.

"Wow you two are amazing and I really appreciate it," said Eloise thanks I will tell Harlow you said that it will make her head even bigger, laughed Belle.

It was time for the seniors to leave and it was bittersweet to see them go, but they will be back again someday. There was a lot of hugs and a lot of tears and that was just the counselors the seniors were even worse. As I watch all of them get on the bus, I do wonder how many I will see again next year or the year after that. I wonder if they enjoyed themselves at camp or in the funhouse, I wonder if they will remember how close of a group they are. Those are things I'll just have to wait and see as time goes by. All that was left were the memories that we shared and the happiness that everyone gave to the seniors and a vibrator which I still don't understand and why it was brought here and playboy magazine I also don't understand why it's here, but if it made those seniors happy then so be it.

"It's never goodbye its always I will see you later or until we meet again. Until we meet again at the next adventure . . . ."

CHAPTER 34

One Year Later

Today is an incredibly sad for me and all of Heaven's Ridge. I woke up this morning and as I always do, I gave my Mona a kiss on her cheek before getting out of bed. She was ice cold to the touch and my first instant was to run and get Delia who as on this morning. Delia and Felicity declared her gone to heaven. My sweet Mona is gone, and I will never be able to get her back and be able to tell her just how much I loved her. So, this ends our adventure together, but you will always be my Mona forever. Until we meet again my love.

-Beau-

I can't believe that Mona is gone she was so full of life, and she was always there for you no matter if she knew you or not. I can't imagine not seeing Mona here every day it's just so sad and heartbreaking, but I will always remember Mona, and she will be forever in my heart. You will never be gone I will see you in Hazel's and Chip's baby girl who also shares your name Mona Lisa McNorton. She is extraordinarily strong and great lungs like you when you and Beau were in the pillows, but I won't go there.

-Tallulah-

I didn't even know that she was sick it happened so fast. I feel so bad because I lost my sister, and I didn't get enough time with her to reconnect. I don't know what I will ever do without her. Yeah, we had a love hate relationship at the beginning, but we made amends and we would spend a lot of time together talking about the good old days. Oh, who am I going to do that with now? Who is going to be the one to sit at the bar with me and listening to old country music while having a drink? She was my angel and I hope that she is looking down on me and sees just how sorry I am for everything. I love you sisters always.

-Edith-

Well, I must be honest I didn't really know Mona until we were at the funhouse together. Even after we got back here, we just say a simple hi to each other passing by. It's sad to know that someone you spent a week with has gone and I wish I could have to know her more. I'll miss you Mona just keeps watching us.

-Blanche-

So heartbroken I feel like a piece of me has went with Mona She was my best friend and someone I could count on. Now I might have to rely on Tallulah which isn't going to be easy. So sorry your journey had to end so quickly especially with Beau. I will be there to watch over him and make him happy when he is sad and don't worry, I won't sleep with him. Take care up there and know you will always be my best friend and I love you, Mona.

-Agnes-

Well, girlfriend if you were in such a hurry to get into heaven you could have told me I would have put a movie about it on and we could have watched it together. What am I going to do now that you're gone? You were the bright light in everyone's hearts and now there is a silence and darkness in the building. Keep us in your thoughts up in heaven and I will always be thinking about you. Keep shining your star bright so we know where you are.

-Wanda-

So long sorry I didn't know you, but I know you're a nice person and I hope to see you sometime soon if I ever make it up there, I'm thinking heaven is not ready to take on me. Just make room for me if I'm the next to go.

-Vera-

You made Beau a happy man and I will make sure he stays positive and happy. He is safe with me, and I will even share my bottle of Viagra if he ever needs it. Sorry we didn't really get to know each other, but just by what Beau told me about you I know that you're someone special.

-Miles-

About the Author

April Carter is the Resident Counsel President of the nursing home where she lives, which has given her first-hand insight into the lives of seniors in residential care. She helps plan activities and manage personalities-and sometimes, she writes it all down! April always loved English classes in school, and she never gave up on her dream of writing a book. She loves horseback riding, taking pictures, spending time with family and friends, boat rides, antique cars, hot air balloons, karaoke and reading books.

April lives in Fort Edward, New York, not far from her hometown of Fort Ann. She lived there for most of her life, close to her family.

In Loving Memory
of
Ella Huntington (aka Mona)
1928–2021

Printed in April 2023
by Rotomail Italia S.p.A., Vignate (MI) - Italy